"You must be Lord Robert Jamison," she said, stopping several feet away from him. "I recognize you from the sketch Elizabeth gave me."

"I am indeed he. And you must be Mrs. Brown."

"Yes." Not even a ghost of a smile touched her lips. He racked his brain for something to say, but she surprised him into further silence by stepping closer to him. So close that her scent drifted over him, a tantalizing combination of sea air and—he inhaled deeply—some sort of flower. Before he could identify the delicate, elusive fragrance, she rested her gloved hand on his sleeve and rose up on her toes, leaning toward him.

Egad, she meant to kiss him! Was this how things were done in America? He didn't want to hurt Mrs. Brown's feelings by rebuffing her very un-British greeting.

Lowering his head, he brushed his lips over her mouth. And everything in him stilled. For the space of several heartbeats, he couldn't move. Couldn't breathe. Couldn't do anything save stare down into her shocked eyes while two impossible words pounded through his brain.

At last.

Whirlwind Affair

Jacquie D'Alessandro

A Dell Book

Published by
Dell Publishing
a division of
Random House, Inc.
New York, New York

ISBN: 0-440-23713-0

Printed in the United States of America

Published simultaneously in Canada

November 2002

10 9 8 7 6 5 4 3 2

OPM

This book is dedicated with my love
and admiration to Jeannie Pierannunzi for
showing me what courage and strength
and facing down fears is all about.
And for reminding me that every day is a gift
to be cherished. Jeannie, it is an honor
to be your friend.

And, as always, to my wonderful,
supportive husband Joe—
the man of my whirlwind dreams;
and my incredible, makes-me-so-proud son,
Christopher, aka Whirlwind Junior.

Acknowledgments

I would like to take this opportunity to thank the following people for their invaluable help and support:

My editor, Liz Scheier, for her kindness, cheerleading, and wonderful ideas.

My agent, Damaris Rowland, for her faith and wisdom.

My critique partners, Donna Fejes, Susan Goggins, and Carina Rock, for all the good times.

My mom and dad, Kay and Jim Johnson, for a lifetime of love and support.

My in-laws, Lea and Art D'Alessandro, for the priceless gift of their son.

My sister, Kathy Guse, whom I am very proud of.

Martha Kirkland, my best research source, for being so generous with her time and knowledge.

Denise Forbes, Pat Pruitt, Nancy Krava, and Julie Teasley, for the great book signings.

Kathy Baker, bookseller extraordinaire, for her kindness and support.

Michelle, Steve, and Lindsay Grossman, for all the laughs and fun and for being such great peeps.

And a cyber hug to Connie Brockway, Marsha Canham, Virginia Henley, Jill Gregory, Sandy Hingston, Julia London, Kathleen Givens, Sherri Browning, and Julie Ortolon. You Looney Loopies are the best!

A very special thank you to Wendy Etherington and Jennie Grizzle. Thanks also to the members of Georgia Romance Writers.

And finally, thank you to all the wonderful readers who have taken the time to write or email me. I love hearing from you!

Whirlwind Affair

Chapter 1

A shiver snaked down Alberta Brown's spine, and she gripped the *Seaward Lady*'s wood railing. Hoping she appeared outwardly calm, she quickly scanned her surroundings.

Crewmen shouted to one another, laughing as they tossed thick ropes and adjusted sails in preparation for the ship's imminent arrival in London. Voices from the bustling English port drifted over the tangy sea-scented air, blending into an indistinguishable hum. Passengers stood in clusters around the ship's rail, chatting in excited tones, grinning, waving to people on the docks. Everyone appeared perfectly normal and eager at the prospect of stepping on dry land after nearly three months at sea on the voyage from America. No one's gaze appeared fixed upon her.

Still, she could not dismiss the eerie sensation of menace. The weight of someone's stare surrounded her like a shroud. Her heart thumped in slow, hard beats, and she forced herself to draw a deep, calming breath and return her attention to the nearby active port. *I am perfectly safe. No one is trying to hurt me.*

She prayed to God it was true.

Yet she couldn't banish the sick feeling that it was not. She glanced downward at the froth tossed upon the hull as the ship cut through the gentle waves, and her stomach turned over. Dear God, less than three hours ago she'd fallen into that indigo water. . . .

A shudder passed through her, and she squeezed her eyes shut. The shock of being shoved from behind, falling . . . falling, desperately clawing the air, frightened cries ripped from her throat, cut off when chilly water closed over her head. She would be forever grateful to the trio of barking dogs who'd alerted a quick-witted crewman to the accident. Yet in spite of his fast thinking and her swimming ability, she'd nearly drowned.

The accident. Yes, that's what everyone was calling it. An improperly secured winch had swung around, catching her between the shoulders, propelling her over the side. Captain Whitstead had reprimanded the entire crew.

But was it really an accident? Or had someone purposely unfastened the winch and pushed it toward her?

Another tremor edged through her, and she sternly told herself it was merely due to the fact that her hair remained damp under her bonnet. Yet she could not ignore the fact that her near-tragic tumble into the sea was not the first strange incident to befall her on this voyage. First had been the inexplicable disappearance of her silver wedding band. Had she lost it—or had it been stolen? While the piece held no great monetary value, she sorely missed the sentimental token, as it was a physical reminder of what she'd had . . . and what she'd lost.

Then there was that headlong flight down the stairs, which thankfully had not resulted in any broken bones, although the painful bruises marking her skin had taken weeks to fade. She'd felt a shove . . . common sense told her it was merely an accidental jostle, yet she couldn't dismiss the feeling that she'd been pushed. And what of the mysterious stomach malady she'd suffered last week? No one else had been ill. Could someone have tampered with her food?

But why? Why would someone wish her harm? She'd asked herself that question dozens of times, yet could not arrive at a definite answer. She *wanted* to believe she was perfectly safe, but an inner voice warned her that the possibility she wasn't was all too real. Had some threat from the past followed her to England?

She glanced around again, but noted nothing amiss. Her unease abated a bit and she gave herself a mental shake. The ship would dock in less than an hour. She'd simply melt into the crowd and disappear into the anonymity offered by a large city. No one knew her here. No one knew . . .

Her gaze lowered, riveting on her black mourning gown, the stark bombazine rippled by the brisk breeze. An image of David's warm smile flashed through her mind, and she squeezed her eyes shut in a vain attempt to ward off the on-slaught of pain that thoughts of her late husband still brought, even now, three years after his sudden death. Dear God, would the ache squeezing her heart ever cease? Would she ever truly feel whole again?

Her fingers involuntarily drifted over the material of her gown, while in her mind's eye she pictured the small item hid-den beneath the voluminous folds, sewn into the hem of her petticoat. To keep it safe. And always close to her. Especially after the unexplained disappearance of her wedding band. *This is the last leg of my journey, David. After I right this last wrong, I'll be free.*

"Alberta! There you are. The boys and I have been searching for you everywhere!"

Allie turned toward the familiar, imperious voice, grate-ful for the interruption of her disturbing thoughts. Baroness Gaddlestone approached Allie with a vigor that belied her plump figure and sixty-three years. Of course, part of the reason for the baroness's brisk pace was the three energetic Maltese straining at the ends of their leads. "The boys," as the baroness referred to her furry brood, dragged their mistress along as if they were mighty oxen and she were a produce-laden cart.

Pushing her worries firmly aside, Allie crouched down to receive the enthusiastic yip-filled greeting the small balls of fluff bestowed upon her.

"Edward, behave yourself," the baroness scolded as the smallest of the trio dampened Allie's face with joyful kisses. "Tedmund! Frederick! Cease at once!"

The boys blithely ignored their mistress, as was often the case when they were excited, but Allie enjoyed the dogs' noisy confusion. Indeed, she owed them a debt she could never repay. Their insistent barking had alerted the crewman when she'd fallen overboard. She therefore quite willingly overlooked their individual bad habits and focused on their undeniable charm. What did it matter that Edward was fond of marking every bit of wood and rope within his reach as his own? Of course, on a ship, this kept the small dog quite busy, and he fell into his doggie bed each night completely exhausted.

And how could she fault Frederick's predilection for nipping ankles when he'd all but dragged her rescuing crewman to the rail while his brothers barked themselves hoarse? Her gaze found Tedmund, who had wandered several yards away to engage in his favorite activity, this time with a discarded pile of rags. Oh dear. She had tried on numerous occasions to explain to Tedmund that it was not polite to try and make puppies with anything other than a female dog—and then, only in private—but Tedmund remained unrepentant.

After discreetly removing Tedmund from the pile of rags, Allie doled out equal parts of affection for all three dogs, then stood and gazed down at their prancing antics. "Sit," she commanded.

Three canine bottoms instantly settled on the deck.

"You simply *must* explain to me how you do that, my dear," the baroness said, her voice tinged with exasperation. "I've been unable to calm them since I told them we were arriving home this morning. You *know* how anxious they are to run in the park." She beamed a smile at her babies. "Don't worry, darlings. Mama promises to bring you for a nice, long walk this afternoon." The boys' tails swished across the deck like a trio of mops at the happy news.

Warmth stole through Allie. She genuinely liked the

baroness, whose bright green eyes and rounded elfin features reminded Allie of a grandmotherly sprite. She was grateful to the woman for hiring her as her traveling companion. Without the baroness, she wouldn't have been able to afford the passage to England. And there was no denying that the baroness's lively, talkative nature and her energetic pets had relieved some of the loneliness Allie had lived with for so long.

"You were looking for me, Lady Gaddlestone?"

"Indeed, my dear. I wanted a private moment to thank you for your excellent companionship on this voyage. My previous companion who accompanied me *to* America proved *most* unsatisfactory." She leaned closer to Allie and confided, "Several times I detected the odor of *brandy* on her breath. Most shocking. But worst of all, she had *no* patience with the boys. Edward, Tedmund, and Frederick could not abide her at all. Oh, that Mrs. Atkins was simply horrid, wasn't she, boys?" The baroness wrinkled her nose and shivered, and the boys narrowed their black eyes and growled their agreement. Allie could almost hear them saying, "Yes, Mama, she was horrid, and if she ever dares come back we'll bite her ankles, chew her shoes, and piddle on her bedclothes . . . again."

"But *you*, my dear," the baroness continued, smiling warmly at Allie, "you are what I call a 'dog person.' Not everyone is, you know."

"I enjoyed your company as well, Lady Gaddlestone." She looked down and winked at the trio of mischief-makers. "You and the boys."

"Yes, well, I hope you enjoy your visit to my country." Her gaze flicked over Allie's black mourning gown. Sympathy softened the woman's features, and reaching out, she clasped Allie's hands. "Clearly you adored your David, but three years is long enough to mourn, my dear. I understand perfectly that it's difficult to move on. Heavens, I never thought I'd recover when Gaddlestone passed on. But time does heal those wounds."

Allie pressed her lips together to keep them from trembling. "Some wounds can never truly heal," she said quietly.

"I understand how you feel, my dear. But you're still young. Don't close your mind to the possibility of finding happiness again. The Season is well under way. A mere word from your friend, the duchess of Bradford, could offer you entrée into any soiree you wished to attend. 'Twould do you good to socialize a bit." Her gaze turned speculative. "I recall you saying that the duchess's brother-in-law will meet you at the dock?"

"Yes."

"Very handsome young man," the baroness mused. "Known him since he was a boy. Always high-spirited, and quite the charmer. Of course there was that trouble several years ago; some transgression or another . . ." A frown creased her brow. "I cannot recall the details. I was traveling in the north at the time, and my mind isn't what it used to be. Most vexing." Her expression cleared. "Oh, but you know how these gossipy things flare up, then fizzle out once the next enticing *on dit* comes along. I remember most clearly that Lord Robert's incident occurred just before Lord Feedly's only daughter eloped with one of their *footmen!* Oh, such a scandal! *That* news usurped all else at the time, and reached me, even all the way up in Newcastle. And I do recall that Lord Robert's misconduct did *not* concern a young lady, so you've nothing to worry about. Lord Robert has always been a perfect gentleman." She waved her hand in a dismissive gesture. "Naturally, young men are prone to find themselves knee-deep in at least *one* mishap, and this happened a long time ago. I'm certain he'll prove an entertaining escort during your journey to Bradford Hall."

The baroness gave Allie's hands a final squeeze, then released them. "Come along, boys," she said. " 'Tis time for your morning snack before we disembark." As the boys pulled her away, she called to Allie, "I'm sure we'll see you on the pier, my dear."

Alone again, Allie reached into the deep pocket of her skirt, withdrawing the last letter she'd received from Elizabeth, who was now the duchess of Bradford. The brief missive had arrived two weeks before Allie sailed to England.

Unfolding the thick vellum, she reread the words, although she knew them by heart.

Dear Allie,

I cannot tell you how excited I am at the prospect of your visit. I am so eager for you to meet my wonderful family, most especially my husband and darling son. Unfortunately I will not be able to meet you in London as I'd planned—but for a very happy reason. At the same time your ship is scheduled to arrive, Austin and I shall be awaiting the imminent birth of our second child! Indeed, by the time you arrive at Bradford Hall, I may already be a mother again. Please do not worry that your visit will be inconvenient. I recovered from James's birth with what Austin calls "alarming speed," and as you know, I am most robust. And do not worry about your journey to Bradford Hall. The estate is only several hours from London, and I have already extracted a promise from Austin's brother Robert that he will meet your ship and escort you here. I've enclosed a sketch of Lord Robert, and I shall give him one of you so that you can easily find each other at the pier.

I am counting the days until we see each other again, Allie. I've missed you so!

Wishing you a safe journey, your friend,

Elizabeth

Allie stared at those last two words that always brought an ache to her heart. Your friend. *Yes, Elizabeth, you have always been my friend. If only I had appreciated and understood that more. . . . I bless your forgiving nature.*

Drawing a deep breath, she slowly slid the letter behind the second sheet of vellum and stared at the sketch of Elizabeth's brother-in-law. Elizabeth's considerable talent with charcoals had only grown over the years, and the image all but leaped from the page.

It would be easy to pick this man out of a crowd. She

perused his features and her stomach knotted. He reminded her of David in so many ways . . . his crooked smile, his laughing eyes, the boyish charm so evident in his expression. Except Lord Robert Jamison was even more handsome than David, something she would not have thought possible.

She recalled Lady Gaddlestone's words regarding Lord Robert. *There was that trouble several years ago; some transgression or another.* What had he done? The instant the question popped into her mind, she shoved it aside. It did not matter. His past was of no concern to her. Nor did it matter what he looked like. He sparked no interest in her other than the fact that she wanted him to get her away from the docks and the menace she'd felt, as quickly as possible. Still, guilt pricked her at the thought of his wasted trip to fetch her.

How would he react when she told him she had no intention of traveling to Bradford Hall with him?

Robert Jamison stood on the pier watching the *Seaward Lady's* crew secure the majestic vessel to the berth. He dragged a deep breath into his lungs, and a smile eased across his face. Damn but he loved the docks. Loved the sight of crewmembers working in perfect unison hoisting sails and securing ropes. Loved the cacophony from the vendors hawking everything from meat pies to bolts of colorful silk. He even loved the harsh medley of smells that combined with the pungent salty air to create a scent that could be found nowhere else in England.

He scanned the faces of the passengers waiting to disembark, but saw no one resembling the smiling young woman in the sketch Elizabeth had drawn. Of course it was impossible to distinguish faces at this distance. Like everyone else meeting passengers, he waited at a safe distance away from the swinging winches unloading the travelers' trunks and the ship's cargo.

Slipping the sketch from his waistcoat pocket, he gazed upon the face that had piqued his interest from the first time he'd seen it months ago, when Elizabeth had given him the drawing along with a request to meet Mrs. Brown at the dock. It was one of the most attractive faces he'd ever seen—lovely not simply because of the pleasing features but due to the joy that flowed from her smile. The warmth and laughter shining in her eyes. And the sense of mischief and fun that seemed to radiate right off the vellum. He would have no trouble recognizing this woman in any size crowd. Indeed, his pulse quickened at the very thought of seeing this lovely creature in person. As he knew Elizabeth had hoped.

Tucking the sketch back in his pocket, he recalled the comment Elizabeth had made just before he'd departed Bradford Hall yesterday. *Perhaps you'll like my friend,* she'd suggested—a phrase he'd heard from the female members of his family more times than he could count. Ever since he had casually mentioned last year that he'd like to settle down and start a family, his sister, sisters-in-law, *and* his mother were only too eager to toss eligible females his way. At first he hadn't objected to their efforts, since his own search for a wife wasn't yielding any results. And he couldn't deny that he'd met an amazing number of charming ladies, some of whom he'd liked quite well, and several with whom he'd discreetly shared far more than a waltz.

However, as time wore on and he hadn't chosen a bride, the introductions had grown awkward, and his family, most especially Caroline, had grown impatient with him. "What on earth is wrong with you?" his sister now demanded every time he didn't fall madly in love with the latest woman she'd brought his way. "She's beautiful, charming, amenable, docile, wealthy, and for reasons I cannot explain, she *adores* you. What the devil are you looking for?"

He didn't know, but he did know he hadn't yet found "the one." The one who made him feel that certain something—that elusive spark he saw every time Austin and Elizabeth exchanged a glance. Every time Caroline and her husband Miles were in the same room. Each time his brother William smiled at his wife Claudine. He'd seen it every day growing up, between his parents, until the day his father died. He couldn't name it, couldn't explain it.

But by damn, he wanted it.

Wanted the happiness and completeness his siblings enjoyed. Wanted to bounce his own child upon his knee. Wanted a wife to share his life with and to make love to every night.

Now all he had to do was find her.

But that was proving bloody well difficult. Damn it all, it seemed he'd met every unmarried woman in the entire country. Still, perhaps his luck was about to change. Elizabeth thought he might like the lovely Mrs. Brown. In fact, he recalled her exact words—*I have a feeling you'll find the happiness you seek in London*—and Elizabeth's "feelings" had an uncanny way of coming true. Indeed, the way her intuition, or perception, or visions, or whatever one chose to call it, had led to his brother William's incredible rescue, was legendary in his family—and a closely guarded secret. They'd opted not to tell anyone else so as not to expose Elizabeth to the inevitable curiosity and skepticism her unusual talents would provoke.

Had her words been in reference to Mrs. Brown? Or had she meant he would find some relief, some peace, from the heaviness that lay upon his heart? A series of images flashed through his mind, and he braced himself as if to receive a blow. The fire roaring out of control. The panicked shouts of men, the terrified screams of the horses. Then Nate's face . . .

He squeezed his eyes shut until the disturbing image faded. He'd never discussed that night or Nate's death with Elizabeth, but she did have that unnerving way of knowing things. . . .

When he'd asked her to translate her cryptic comment, she'd merely graced him with one of those indecipherable female smiles that claim *I know something you don't know.* Well, he would know—whatever it was—soon enough. The passengers were making their way off the ship.

He craned his neck, scanning each person's face as they approached. A pair of young men. Definitely not. A middle-aged gentleman followed by a weary-looking couple each holding the hand of a small child. Robert smiled at the children and received gap-toothed grins in response. Returning his attention to the passengers, he clicked off mental "no's" as a clergyman, a portly gentleman, and a gaggle of chatting matrons passed by. Where was Mrs. Brown? It seemed almost everyone had disembarked.

His gaze flicked over a woman swathed head to toe in mourning black, and another mental "no" quickly formed in his brain. Although Elizabeth had told him Mrs. Brown was a widow, her husband had died years ago. She'd no longer wear mourning clothes.

Still, there was something about the woman's face that brought his gaze back to her. Those wide-spaced eyes, and that intriguing dimple in the center of her chin . . . and the way she was looking at him, as if she recognized him.

Confusion assailed him, and he lifted a hand to shade his eyes from the sun. This couldn't be the right woman. Where was the bright smile? The radiating joy? The sense of laughter and mischief? Sadness and seriousness surrounded this woman like a dark cloud. He gazed beyond her, but the only passenger behind her was a plump matron struggling down the gangway with a trio of small, yapping white dogs.

He returned his attention to the woman in black. She walked toward him swiftly, her eyes scanning his face. He caught a brief glimpse of an errant brown curl that escaped her black bonnet. Recognition slapped him, and although he realized she was indeed Mrs. Brown, his mind struggled to equate this woman with the sketch Elizabeth had given him. They were precisely alike . . . yet nothing alike at all.

"You must be Lord Robert Jamison," she said, stopping several feet away from him. "I recognize you from the sketch Elizabeth gave me."

I wish I could say the same. Surely she did not still mourn her husband? Yet that must be the case as Elizabeth had not mentioned that Mrs. Brown had suffered a more recent loss. Sympathy for her washed over him. Obviously she'd adored her husband, as his death had tragically depleted her. Her eyes, the color of fine, aged brandy, appeared haunted and anxious

in her pale face. How sad that mourning had taken such a toll
on her. How unfair that a man she so clearly loved had been
stolen from her, taking all her laughter and joy with him. She
looked tiny and frightened in her stark clothing, as if her state
of grieving had literally swallowed her whole. He shoved aside
the disappointment and pity he hoped didn't show on his face,
then offered her his most charming smile and a formal bow.

"I am indeed he. And you must be Mrs. Brown."

"Yes." Not even a ghost of a smile touched her lips. Her
expression grew even more grave as her gaze darted about
their surroundings. He watched her, feeling uncharacter-
istically short of words. He racked his brain for something to
say, but she surprised him into further silence by stepping
closer to him. So close, in fact, that the tips of her shoes
touched his boots and her black skirt brushed his breeches. So
close that her scent drifted over him, a tantalizing combination
of sea air and—he inhaled deeply—some sort of flower. Before he could identify the delicate, elusive fragrance, she
rested her gloved hand on his sleeve and rose up on her toes,
leaning toward him.

Egad, she meant to kiss him! Was this how things were
done in America? The only other American he'd ever met was
Elizabeth, and he couldn't deny she possessed a forthright,
friendly manner, although not quite *this* forthright. Still, he
didn't want to hurt Mrs. Brown's feelings by rebuffing her
very un-British greeting.

Lowering his head, he brushed his lips over her mouth. And
everything in him stilled. For the space of several heartbeats,
he couldn't move. Couldn't breathe. Couldn't do anything
save stare down into her shocked eyes while two impossible
words pounded through his brain.

At last.

A frown yanked his brows downward, and he stepped back
from her as if she'd turned into a pillar of fire. At last? Bloody
hell, he'd gone mad. The next stop for him was Bedlam.

Two bright crimson spots stained her cheeks. "What on

earth are you doing?" she asked in a voice that trembled with unmistakable outrage.

Now he'd done it. Whatever she'd been about, clearly she hadn't intended for him to kiss her. And he wished to hell he hadn't. His mouth still tingled with the hint of her taste, and he barely resisted the almost overwhelming urge to lick his lips. Or lean down and lick hers.

Undeniably unsettled, his gaze roamed her face, taking in her becoming blush, the dark lashes surrounding her golden-brown eyes, the pert nose painted by a smattering of pale freckles, the dimple gracing her chin, and then her mouth . . . such a lovely, plump mouth. Moist, deliciously pink, the bottom lip lusciously full, and the top lip, impossibly, even fuller.

Good God, what sort of cad was he to entertain even the hint of a lustful thought toward her? The woman was in *mourning*. Not that he'd had a lustful thought. Certainly not. That inexplicable tingle he'd felt had merely been . . . surprise. Yes, that's all it was. She'd surprised him. And that jolt he'd felt? Nothing more than embarrassment. Yes, he'd simply made an ass of himself. Not the first time, and unfortunately, most likely not the last.

Relieved that he'd settled everything back into the proper perspective, he took another step backward. "My apologies, madam. I meant no offense. In truth, I thought you'd meant to kiss *me*."

"And why would I possibly want to do *that*?"

Amusement, rather than offense at her question and tone, nudged him. "Perhaps an American greeting custom?"

"Absolutely not. I'd merely intended to ask you something, in a discreet manner."

"Ah. You wished to whisper in my ear."

"Precisely."

"And what did you want to—"

"Alberta! There you are, my dear."

Robert turned toward the high-pitched voice. A short, plump, fashionably dressed matron walked crookedly toward them, trying without much success to control three small white dogs that seemed intent upon jerking her in three different directions. Even if he had not recognized the formidable Lady Gaddlestone, there was no mistaking her dogs, those mischievous little charmers he clearly recalled from the last time he'd seen them when he'd mentally dubbed them Sir Piss-a-lot, Sir Bite-a-bit, and Sir Hump-a-leg.

"Tedmund! Edward! Frederick! Cease at once!" The baroness pulled back on the leads, barely halting the trio before they dragged her past him and Mrs. Brown. One of the beasts promptly lifted its leg and watered a weed that had sprouted between the cobblestones. The other two pranced about, one eyeing his ankle as if contemplating a nibble, while the other regarded his calf with an unmistakably lustful gleam.

Raising his brows, Robert intoned, "Sit." Three canine bottoms instantly hit the cobblestones, and three sets of shiny black button eyes gazed up at him.

"Marvelous, Lord Robert," the baroness said, her breath puffing in exertion. "Although I must say it is *quite* vexing that the boys will listen to a near stranger rather than their mama."

"Ah, but Teddie, Eddie, Freddie, and I are old friends, are we not?" Robert crouched down and tickled his fingers over their silky fur and was promptly presented with three tummies to rub. "We enjoyed several invigorating strolls during your last visit to Bradford Hall." He arose, much to the boys' dismay, and made the baroness a formal bow. "A surprise and pleasure to see you again, Lady Gaddlestone. I was not aware you'd sailed on this ship. I see you are already acquainted with my sister-in-law's friend, Mrs. Brown."

"Indeed. Alberta proved a wonderful traveling companion. A stroke of genius on my part, hiring her."

Hiring her? What was the baroness talking about? He glanced at Mrs. Brown and noticed that although a blush stained her cheeks, she lifted her chin and regarded him with an expression that would have done Prinny proud, almost daring him to look upon her with disfavor for undertaking employment. Which he did not. Still, the fact that she *had*, surprised him. And whetted his curiosity.

Before he could think upon the matter further, the baroness continued, "I would have been utterly inconsolable if she'd drowned this morning."

Robert stared at the baroness. "Drowned?"

"Yes. La, it was frightful!" A shudder shook Lady Gaddlestone's ample frame. "The dear girl was hit in the back with a runaway winch, and over the side she went. Thank heavens the boys saw the entire incident. They nearly barked themselves into apoplexy. Captain Whitstead performed a brilliant maneuver and the crew pulled dear Alberta from the sea. Bless the saints she can swim like a fish."

The baroness waved her hand in front of her face, and Robert prayed she wasn't about to swoon. He recalled that the baroness was not prone to draping herself artistically over a fainting couch and ringing for her hartshorn—thank goodness—and true to his memory, she rallied. Once assured that she was steady on her feet, he turned his attention to Mrs. Brown. "I'm sorry you suffered such a terrible ordeal. Were you hurt?"

"No. Just frightened."

"Oh, but you never would have known she was!" Lady Gaddlestone interjected. "She was utterly marvelous, remained perfectly calm, bobbing on the surface like a cork. Heavens, I would have screamed like a banshee, then sunk like a rock. Captain Whitstead was most impressed. As for me, I'm certain I'd have succumbed to the vapors for the first time in my life if I hadn't needed to rescue one of the other passengers from the boys. All three of them quite inexplicably threw themselves upon Mr. Redfern's ankles! Oh, such snapping and snarling as I've never witnessed from my babies! Luckily Mr. Redfern was very understanding when I explained that all the excitement had adversely affected the boys' delicate constitutions. Of course, his trousers will never quite be the same, I'm sure."

She drew a quick breath, then plunged on, "Now we can only pray that dear Alberta does not suffer any lingering affects, such as a congestion in the chest." She pinned a stern glance on Mrs. Brown. "You must take a hot bath the minute you're settled, then take yourself off to bed."

Mrs. Brown nodded. "I—"

"And *you*," the baroness intoned, swinging her gaze to Robert, "shall make certain she is well taken care of until she is in the duchess's care."

"Of course."

"Excellent." Lady Gaddlestone nodded, clearly satisfied that her dictates would be obeyed. "Now I understand the duchess is close to giving birth. Has the child arrived yet?"

"Not as of this morning." A laugh rumbled in Robert's throat. "But Austin has already paced a ditch in the drawing room."

"Well, I shall expect to be informed when the babe arrives so I may schedule a visit. I just *adore* purchasing baby gifts." She gave Robert a thorough up-and-down inspection. "You're looking quite fit, young man," she proclaimed with an approving nod. "Hard to believe, but I dare say you're even more handsome than when I saw you last. You've the look of your father about you. That same devilish gleam in your eye."

"Thank you, my lady. I—"

"Perhaps you can cheer up Mrs. Brown a bit," the baroness plowed on. "Poor dear is still in the doldrums over losing her beloved David. Laughter is what she needs. I've told her at least a dozen times that she's far too serious by half, have I not, Mrs. Brown?"

Mrs. Brown had no opportunity to reply, for the baroness continued, "She enjoyed the boys, however. They managed to coax a number of smiles from her. Remarkably pretty woman when she smiles, which is of course not to insinuate that she isn't remarkably pretty when she isn't smiling, which is sadly most of the time, but when she smiles she is *very* remarkably pretty. Tell me, dear boy, don't the duke and duchess have a dog?"

"Yes. They have—"

"Excellent. Canine company will do Mrs. Brown a world of good. And now, dear boy, tell me, are you married yet?"

"No."

"Betrothed?"

"I'm afraid not."

The baroness raised her brows and pursed her lips, and Robert could almost hear the gears turning in her head. "Excellent" was all she said, and Robert was not certain he wanted to know what she meant by it. She glanced beyond Robert and waggled her gloved fingers. "My carriage is ready to depart." She extended her hand and Robert obligingly bent and brushed a kiss over her fingertips.

"Always a pleasure, Lady Gaddlestone. Welcome home."

"Thank you. I must say it is a relief to have both feet planted back on English soil." She turned to Mrs. Brown. "I shall see you again before you return to America, my dear."

"I hope so," said Mrs. Brown.

"You may count upon it." Giving the leads a slight tug, she set her brood in motion and was nearly yanked off her feet. "Good-bye for now," she huffed as she staggered away.

The instant he judged her out of earshot, Robert turned to Mrs. Brown and offered her a sheepish grin. "I rather feel as if I were rolled over by a runaway carriage."

Allie looked up at him, at his striking countenance, lopsided grin, and mischievous eyes, and her throat tightened. With his ebony hair and dark blue eyes, he looked nothing like blond, brown-eyed David, but his teasing manner, his easy smile . . . they were so achingly, hauntingly familiar. Clearing her throat, she said, "Lady Gaddlestone is really very kind."

"I would never imply otherwise. She could, however, talk a saddle off of a horse." His gaze roamed her face, his eyes reflecting concern. "You're certain you're all right after your accident?"

Accident. "Yes, thank you."

"Now that the baroness had departed, perhaps you will tell me what you'd been about to say before she arrived." A teasing light sparkled in his eyes. "Something you'd wanted to whisper in my ear?"

Heat suffused Allie's face. Did this man take nothing

seriously? Not only had he had the temerity to kiss her but now the gall to tease her about it! She clutched her gown to keep from touching her lips where he'd kissed her. How could such a feathery touch, one that had lasted less than a second, have affected her so? *He surprised me, that is all. That rapid beating of my heart . . . merely the result of the unexpected. And the unwanted.*

She cast a glance around the bustling dock area and another chill crept down her spine. Someone was watching her. She knew it. Biting back her unease, she said, "I'd simply planned to discreetly ask you if we could leave here as soon as possible. I'd noticed Lady Gaddlestone coming toward us—"

"Ah. Say no more. I quite understand. Even people we like can sometimes prove exhausting. We shall depart immediately." He smiled at her and offered his arm, tilting his head with another David-like gesture that made her teeth clench. "My carriage is right this way."

When she hesitated to take his arm, he simply grabbed her hand and settled it in the crook of his elbow. "See there?" he said. "I don't bite. Hardly ever."

She fell into step beside him, trying to reconcile the impulse to snatch her hand away from him and the undeniable relief the safety of his presence offered. His arm felt firm and muscular beneath her fingers, more so than David's had. And although Lord Robert was several inches taller than David, he matched his longer strides to her shorter ones, unlike David. She'd always felt as if she had to run to keep up with her husband.

When they arrived at a handsome black lacquered carriage, Lord Robert instructed the waiting footman to fetch her trunk. He then handed her into the carriage and settled himself on the plush, gray velvet squabs across from her. Deciding the time had arrived to tell him, she cleared her throat.

"I'm afraid I owe you an apology, Lord Robert. You traveled all this way to escort me to Bradford Hall to see Elizabeth, but I'm afraid I must remain in London for at least a day or two. I have some business affairs to see to." She forced her hands to stay still and not pluck at the material of her gown. "There are several matters regarding my late husband's possessions that I must take care of. He'd resettled in America, but he was English, you know. From Liverpool."

"No, I didn't know." He glanced down at her mourning gown. There was no mistaking the sympathy in his gaze. "I'm very sorry for your loss."

She lowered her lashes so he couldn't read her eyes. "Thank you."

"Although it's not exactly the same, I know what it's like to lose someone you love. My father died several years ago. I miss him every day."

He looked as if he were about to say something more, but when he remained silent, she said softly, "I understand. I think about David every day." Drawing a deep breath, she continued. "I'm certain you're anxious to return to Bradford Hall to await the birth of your niece or nephew, and I've no wish to inconvenience you further. If you could recommend a reputable inn, I'll arrange my own transportation to the estate when my business is completed."

He was clearly surprised, but he did not question her. Instead, he offered, "An inn is not necessary, Mrs. Brown. Elizabeth and Austin would insist you stay at their London town house."

"Oh, but I couldn't—"

"Of course you can. Elizabeth would have my head if I allowed you to put up at an inn. And as I have several business affairs that could stand my attention, I have no objection to remaining in London until you are ready to travel to Bradford Hall. I have rooms on Chesterfield, which is only a short distance from the town house."

She studied his face, and a warning tension gripped her stomach. Something had flashed in his eyes when he'd said *several business affairs* . . . that same evasiveness she knew all too well, thanks to David. But the look had been so fleeting. Had she imagined it?

"That is a very kind offer, Lord Robert, but—"

"Kindness has nothing to do with it, believe me. It is simply a case of self-preservation. If I were to show my face at Bradford Hall without you, after giving my solemn vow to bring you there, my honor would be irreparably impinged." A slow grin lit his face. "And Elizabeth would harangue me until my ears fell off."

For the briefest instant, Allie felt herself involuntarily responding to that grin, allowing its warmth to wash over her. It was so like David's grin . . .

His expression turned to one of concern. "Are you all right, Mrs. Brown? You suddenly appear a bit pale."

"I'm fine. I was simply thinking . . ."

"Yes?"

"That you remind me very much of my husband."

He seemed surprised at her words. Then he smiled gently, his eyes full of sympathy. "Thank you."

At that moment, the footman arrived with her trunk. After it was secured to the top of the carriage, they departed, leaving the scents and sounds of the docks behind. As they moved farther away from the riverfront, Allie relaxed a bit, until she glanced at the man sitting across from her. The man who was another David, only this time wrapped up in an even more attractive package. He'd thanked her for the comparison to David. He'd thought she'd paid him a high compliment.

If you only knew, Lord Robert. If you only knew . . .

Lester Redfern emerged from the long shadows cast by the wooden hull of the *Seaward Lady.* He narrowed his eyes at the departing black lacquer carriage, then spit onto the cobblestones. Damn it all, the woman possessed the devil's own luck. How the blazes were he supposed to kill the chit when she were always surrounded by chattin' old biddies and yappin' dogs? He glanced down at his torn trouser cuffs. Bloody stupid beasts. They ruined wot would have been a perfect murder. And weren't it just his rotten luck that the Brown woman could swim?

And now she'd gone off with that fancy toff. He set off swiftly on foot to follow the carriage carrying his quarry. Curse the saints, his employer would not be pleased that she weren't already dead. *But I'll see to it that she's taken care of. I've never failed in a job before, and I ain't about to start now. By this time tomorrow, she'll be dead. And I'll be a very rich man.*

Chapter 2

As the carriage slowly wended its way through the crowded streets toward Mayfair, Robert observed his companion, wondering at her demeanor. She sat ramrod straight, her gloved hands clenched in her lap, and although her eyes were trained on the passing shops, it seemed as if she looked through them. He noticed a muscle jumping in her cheek, indicating she was clenching her jaw. It struck him that she was more than merely sad. She appeared genuinely distressed.

He recalled Lady Gaddlestone's comment about Mrs. Brown being her companion during the voyage. Was Mrs. Brown suffering financial problems that would necessitate hiring herself out? His gaze roamed over her mourning gown. The garment was well made and of good material, but showed subtle signs of wear. He had no way of telling if it was fashionable, as he knew nothing about American styles. Still, based on English fashion, he judged the garment to be several years old.

Curiosity pulled at him, but he firmly tamped it down. Her financial status was none of his business, and he sensed she would not welcome any inquiries. Nor would he under similar circumstances. His duty was merely to look after her and make her feel welcome until he delivered her to Elizabeth at Bradford Hall. And the sooner he accomplished that, the sooner he could resume his search for a wife. Certainly he could make good use of this unexpected time in London. A visit to his solicitor to go over the latest accounting for the payment of reparation monies . . .

Determined to play the perfect host to his reticent companion, he cleared his throat and forced a smile. "Other than today's mishap, did you enjoy your ocean voyage?" he asked.

She continued gazing out the window. "Yes."

"Did you encounter any bad weather?"

"Some."

"Were you frightened?"

"No."

His lips twitched. "Do you think if I keep trying I'll hit upon a question that you'll answer with more than one syllable?"

Finally she turned and looked at him. "Perhaps."

"Ah, see there? I've already succeeded." He smiled at her, but she merely looked at him, studied him actually, and he wondered if she were again thinking that he reminded her of her husband. "Is there anything besides your business that you'd like to do while you're in London?" he asked. "Attend the opera? Visit the shops?"

He'd hoped that the mention of the shops might spark interest in her eyes, but she merely murmured, "No, thank you," then returned her attention to looking outside.

Pity hit him again, lodging a lump in his throat. Within months of each other, he'd lost his beloved father, and then Nate—a man who'd been more than a longtime family servant. He'd been a dear friend. Yes, he knew the horrible, aching loss that death brought. But how wrenching it must be to lose the one person you love above all others. What had she been like before her husband's death?

He tried to force his gaze away from her, but in truth, he found her appearance unexpectedly . . . compelling. Something about those huge, dark-lashed, brandy-colored eyes, with their golden depths reflecting such haunted melancholy—it was almost painful to look at her, yet impossible to look away.

His gaze drifted down to her mouth, and he watched in fascination as she worried her full bottom lip between straight, white teeth. Bloody hell, the rest of her might look like a grieving widow, but that incredible mouth looked stolen from a courtesan. He instantly recalled brushing his lips over hers, and that punched-in-the-gut sensation he'd experienced.

An aberration, he told himself firmly. Any man with eyes would agree her lips were lovely. Besides, he always felt that way when he kissed a beautiful woman. *No, you don't. You've never felt anything like that before.*

A frown creased his brow, and he forced his gaze away from her to stare at the passing scenery. Damn it all, this was turning into one bloody long ride. And he suddenly had a sneaking suspicion that this day or two in London with Mrs. Brown was going to feel more like a decade or two.

When they arrived at the elegant Bradford town house, Allie breathed a sigh of relief. Normally she did not mind silence, but somehow the lack of conversation with Lord Robert had become uncomfortable. The blame, of course, rested squarely on her shoulders, and she made a mental vow to be more polite once she'd taken care of her business and could concentrate on something else. Of course the "something else" would certainly not be Lord Robert, but she would at least find it easier to make conversation once her mind was free.

After alighting from the coach, he escorted her through an elaborate wrought-iron gate, then into the stately brick town house. Standing in the black-and-white marble-tiled foyer, Allie tried not to gape at the luxury and elegance surrounding her, but she was not the least bit successful. Hundreds of glittering prisms reflected from where the sunlight touched the largest chandelier she'd ever seen, casting the cream, silk-covered walls with tiny starbursts of sunshine. Corridors fanned off to the left and right, and a wide staircase curved gracefully upward. It was incredible to think that her hoyden-ish childhood friend now lived amidst such luxury

An image of the lovely house she'd shared with David flashed in Allie's mind. The high ceilings, freshly painted walls, the unexpected nooks tucked into cozy corners. Nothing as grand as this, but she'd loved every inch of it . . . until she'd learned it was bought with lies and deceit.

The sound of Lord Robert's voice yanked her attention back to the present. "Mrs. Brown will be a guest for several days, Carters," he was saying to the butler who stood at stiff-shouldered attention. "I'll send off a note to the family informing them of the change in plans."

"Yes, Lord Robert. I shall have Mrs. Brown's belongings placed in the green guest chamber. Shall I arrange for tea?"

"Yes. In the drawing room, please. And please see to it that water is heated for a bath for Mrs. Brown."

Carters bowed, then turned smartly on his heel and departed.

"This way." Lord Robert inclined his head toward the right, then led her down the corridor. Her head bobbed back and forth, trying to take in the exquisite porcelains set on cherry-wood tables and the collection of paintings lining the walls.

"This is a beautiful home."

He grinned. "It keeps the rain off Austin's and Elizabeth's heads." He halted at a wide oak door, turned the knob, then indicated she should enter.

Allie stepped over the threshold and a pleasure-filled sigh escaped her. Sunshine poured into the room from the tall windows on the far wall, highlighting the warm, golden hue of the entire room. Her gaze skipped around, absorbing everything at once. Pale yellow walls. A brocade settee and a pair of gilded wing chairs arranged around a marble fireplace. Gleaming oak parquet floor dotted with two spacious Persian rugs. An ivory-and-gold escritoire. A pianoforte nestled in the corner.

"Lovely," she murmured, her shoes tapping against the polished floor, then sinking into the carpet as she crossed the room. Her gaze riveted on the gilt-framed painting hanging above the fireplace, and a lump lodged in her throat. It was Elizabeth, wearing a simple ivory gown, sitting in the midst of a lilac-strewn meadow, with several kittens and a puppy prancing around her. An auburn tendril drifted across her cheek, as if blown by a spring breeze, and her face expressed sheer happiness along with an unmistakable whiff of mischief.

"That is exactly how I remember her," Allie said softly. "Happy. Playful. And surrounded by animals. Was this painted recently?"

"Last year. Elizabeth had it done as a birthday gift for Austin. And surrounded by animals she is. Each of those devilish kittens has gone on to either father or produce several litters, and that puppy could now easily be declared the Largest Dog in the Kingdom. His name is Pirate, however I call him B.H."

She dragged her gaze away from the portrait and looked at him. "B.H.?"

"Short for Barking Horse. You'll understand the moment you meet the beast, I assure you." He flashed her a grin, then glanced at the mantel clock. "If you don't mind, I'm going to leave you for a while. I need to stop by my rooms, and I must send off that note to Austin and Elizabeth. Then, if you'd like, I could return and we could dine together."

Allie hesitated, studying his handsome face. What manner of deceit lurked behind the warmth radiating from his dark blue eyes? What secrets did his friendly smile mask? She did not know, but experience had taught her to suspect that some sort of deception or insincerity must lie beneath his charming manner. Still, she could hardly refuse him to dine in his brother's home.

"Dinner together would be fine, Lord Robert."

"Excellent. In the meantime, if you require anything, simply tell Carters, although he is so frighteningly efficient, he'll no doubt know what you want and need before you realize it yourself. And don't let his manner intimidate you." He leaned forward, as if to confide a secret, and Allie inhaled the refreshing fragrance of newly laundered clothing, mixed with another woodsy, fresh scent she could not name, but that was undeniably pleasing.

"In case it escaped your notice," Lord Robert imparted in a conspiratorial tone, "Carters is *excruciatingly* serious. Austin swears he's witnessed the man *laughing* with Elizabeth, to which I can only respond that Austin must be daft, because in my entire life I've never seen the man so much as crack a grin. And believe me, it is not for lack of trying on my part. Getting Carters to smile has become something of a quest, yet I am so far unsuccessful. I therefore dubbed him Sir BUB." At her questioning look, he clarified, "Sir Bunched-up-Brows." He flashed her a grin she imagined few women were immune to, then bowed. "Good afternoon to you, Mrs. Brown. I shall look forward to dinner this evening." He quit the room, closing the door behind him.

Allie pressed her hands to her midsection and breathed a sigh of relief. Thank goodness he was gone. The man somehow managed to make her feel crowded even when several yards separated them. And she refused to be amused by the outrageous sobriquet he'd assigned Carters. Or Elizabeth's dog.

She could not decide which was worse—his gentle teasing, which had filled her with unexpected, unwanted warmth, or his sympathetic compassion, which had riddled her with guilt. She glanced down at her black dress. Like everyone else, Lord Robert had assumed that her widow's weeds meant she still mourned David. As with everyone else she met, she had not disabused him of that notion.

How could she possibly share the humiliating fact that she still wore mourning clothes because she could afford no others? That she could afford no others because her husband had turned out to be a common criminal, and all her funds were exhausted by her determination to repay the people he'd cheated?

Of course, wearing the mourning gowns provided another advantage in addition to saving her money. They repelled any possible suitors. Another man was the absolute *last* thing she wanted.

Still, she hated dishonesty, and remorse filled her at her deception. But she firmly shoved the guilt aside. There was no doubt that Lord Robert Jamison was nothing more than spun glass—lovely to look at, able to hold one's attention for a short period, but without the slightest bit of substance behind his shiny exterior. The hint of secrets shadowed his eyes, and according to Lady Gaddlestone, some misconduct clouded his past. Yes, she knew his sort, and she was an expert at dealing with men like him.

But she needed to banish him from her thoughts. First on the agenda was a bath to rinse away the remnants of seawater.

Then she needed to hire a hack.

In his town house in Grosvenor Square, Geoffrey Hadmore, earl of Shelbourne, sat behind the mahogany desk in his private study. He slowly alternated his gaze between the tarnished silver ring resting upon the highly polished wood and the man who had just given it to him, all the while fighting to tame the tempest brewing inside him. He prided himself on always presenting a calm exterior, unlike many of his peers who were given to vulgar outbursts of emotion.

Still, it cost him not to reach out and wrap his hands around Redfern's scrawny neck. His scrawny, *stupid* neck. Picking up the ring, he held it between his thumb and forefinger, then pinned Redfern with his iciest glare. "What is this, Redfern?"

Redfern had the temerity to look at him as if he were the village idiot. " 'Tis the ring you bid me to steal from Mrs. Brown."

"Tell me, Redfern," Geoffrey said in a deadly calm voice, "does this in any way resemble a *coat-of-arms* ring?"

Redfern scratched his sparse gray hair. "Not a bit. But this were the only ring the lady had. I searched her cabin real careful-like."

"Was this ring in a box?"

"No, my lord."

"Well, *this* is *not* the correct ring," Geoffrey said in frigid voice. "You have failed miserably at a very simple assignment: get the ring and its matching box, then get rid of the woman. Did you get the ring and its box?"

Ruddy color suffused Redfern's cheeks. " 'Parently not."

"And did you get rid of the woman?"

"No, but not fer lack o' tryin'. The bloody woman was always with that infernal baroness biddy and her yappin' mutts. But don't you worry, my lord. I'll off Mrs. Brown before tomorrow's done."

Damn it, he supposed he should be thankful Redfern's attempts to kill Mrs. Brown had proved unsuccessful. He needed her alive until he had the ring—and its box. But the question that plagued him daily rushed into his mind. *What if she did not have it?*

If she did not have the ring . . . he squeezed his eyes shut, trying unsuccessfully to hold back the barrage of hideous possibilities. What if she'd lost it? Or sold it? What if it was sitting in some dusty pawnshop in America, just waiting for someone to purchase it and discover the secret that could ruin his life?

A sharp pain throbbed behind his eyes, and he clenched his teeth, forcing himself to concentrate on the immediate problem at hand. He needed to ascertain if she had the ring, and if so, get it back. And if she did not have it, he still needed to know if she was aware of his secret.

"You will not kill Mrs. Brown. Not until I have my ring. Where is she now?"

"I followed her to a right fancy town house. In Mayfair, on Park Lane. Number six."

A frown pulled down Geoffrey's brows. "That is the duke of Bradford's residence."

Recognition lit in Redfern's eyes. "That's the name of the bloke I heard Mrs. Brown and the old biddy talkin' 'bout on the ship. 'Parently Mrs. Brown is great friends with the duchess. Grew up together or some such. Believe she even mentioned they're distant cousins."

Geoffrey rose, pacing across the maroon-and-gold Persian carpet to the crystal decanters near the window. He poured himself a brandy, then stared into the liquor's amber depths, his stomach cramping at Redfern's news. Rotten piece of luck that Mrs. Brown had a connection to the Bradford family. If the duke were ever to get wind of any of this—

He sliced the thought off, discarding the possibility. If Mrs. Brown planned to extort funds from him, she wouldn't be likely to share that information with Bradford—or anyone else. Everyone knew the duke and duchess were at their country estate awaiting the birth of their child. If Mrs. Brown had come to England to visit the duchess, then why hadn't she gone on to Bradford Hall? Had she remained in London to see *him*? To blackmail him? If so, she certainly must have the ring. *If so, you won't have it much longer, Mrs. Brown. And once the ring is in my possession, your usefulness will be finished. And so will you.*

He tossed back his brandy, savoring the slow burn down his throat, then turned to Redfern. "I hired you, Redfern, because I thought you both discreet and capable."

Unmistakable anger flared in Redfern's eyes. "I'm both, my lord. Don't you doubt it. Just had a bit of bad luck and circumstances. That'll change."

"See to it that it does. I believe Mrs. Brown has the ring. Search her belongings again. Thoroughly. It should pose no problem, as the duke and duchess are not in residence. Get Mrs. Brown away from the house. Then find that ring." He pinned Redfern with a stare. "And if you do, I want her gone."

"Yes, my lord."

"And Redfern? Do it tonight."

Allie stepped from the hack and looked up at the painted sign hanging above the door of the Bond Street establishment. Fitzmoreland Antiques.

"Fitzmoreland's the best antiques man in London," the

hackney said from his driver's perch, jerking his head toward the sign. "Shall I wait fer ye?"

"Yes, please. I'll only be a few minutes." She entered the shop, blinking to adjust her eyes to the dimly lit interior. Neat rows of books, vases, and porcelains lined floor to ceiling shelves, while tables and larger pieces of furniture were tastefully scattered about, lending the shop the appearance of an elegant sitting room. An impeccably dressed, middle-aged gentleman with graying hair approached her.

"May I assist you, madam?"

His gaze swept over her black gown, and although he was very discreet, he was clearly taking her measure. No doubt he was accustomed to dealing with wealthy clientele, and she was thankful she'd taken extra time after her bath to arrange her hair and dress in her best gown. Raising her chin, she said, "I am looking for Mr. Fitzmoreland."

He bowed his head. "Then look no further, madam, for I am he. How may I help you?"

No other customers were in the shop, and Allie relaxed a bit. Opening her reticule, she withdrew a piece of vellum and handed it to him. "I need to identify the coat of arms depicted here. I was informed you are an expert at such matters."

His brows lifted. "Your accent indicates you are American. May I ask who recommended me?"

His question was spoken in a perfectly polite tone, but Allie easily heard the tinge of underlying scorn. No doubt he thought her some destitute foreign widow, desperate to sell him some cheap baubles. *If only I had some cheap baubles to sell . . .*

She lifted her brows exactly as he had. "The duchess of Bradford—"

"The duchess recommended me?" His demeanor instantly transformed, and he seemed to grow two inches taller. " 'Twas very kind of her."

Allie suppressed the urge to inform him that it was actually the duchess's *butler* who had recommended him, and that if he'd allowed her to finish her sentence, he would know that.

Instead, she pushed aside her guilt for allowing him his incorrect assumption and asked, "Do you think you can help me?"

Mr. Fitzmoreland studied the drawing for several seconds, then nodded slowly. "I'm certain I can. It may take several days, however."

"I'm more concerned with discretion than speed."

"Of course."

His keen eyes seemed to bore through her to see all her secrets, but she forced herself not to avert her gaze. "My name is Mrs. Brown and I'm staying at the Bradford town house here in London."

He inclined his head. "I shall report my findings to you as soon as I know anything."

Thanking him, she exited the shop, breathing a sigh of relief at having chipped away another small piece of the burden she carried.

With any luck, she'd soon learn to whom the ring belonged. She would return it, and then, for the first time in three years, she'd be free.

Chapter 3

Shortly before eight that evening, Robert arrived at the town house for dinner. As the night air was delightfully cool and the usual fog had not yet rolled in, he'd walked from his rooms on Chesterfield.

"Good evening, Carters," he said, handing the butler his walking stick, hat, and cape. "How is our guest faring?"

"When I last saw her, as she returned from her errand, she appeared quite well."

"Errand?"

"Yes. Late this afternoon Mrs. Brown asked if I knew a reputable antiquities expert in the city. I of course directed her to Mr. Fitzmoreland."

Curiosity raised Robert's brows. "Did she say why she required an antiquities expert?"

"No, Lord Robert. She merely asked for a referral, then inquired about transportation. I arranged for a hack and a footman to escort her."

"I see." Annoyed at himself for not thinking to do so earlier, he made a mental note to arrange for a carriage to be placed at Mrs. Brown's disposal. "And where is Mrs. Brown now?"

"In the drawing room."

"Thank you." Robert headed down the corridor, his strides slowing as the sounds of piano music drifted toward him. He silently entered the room, then leaned back against the door, observing Mrs. Brown in profile.

She sat at the pianoforte, her head bent over the ivory keys, her brows and lips puckered in concentration. She was again dressed in stark black, making the curve of her smooth cheek appear impossibly pale, like fragile porcelain. The waning vestiges of daylight glowed through the tall windows, bathing her in a subtle stream of gold. Without her bonnet, she proved incorrect his earlier impression that her hair was merely brown. Indeed, her shiny tresses were a deep, rich chestnut, shot with streaks of red. She'd arranged her hair in a simple chignon at her nape, lending her a regal air.

Her fingers continued to caress the ivory keys, but he did not recognize the tune she was playing. Of course, that may have been because—his face puckered in a grimace—she was appallingly bad.

Her hands suddenly stilled, and she turned her head. When she saw him, she snatched her hands away from the keys as if they'd bitten her. A rose-hued blush colored her cheeks, and he bit back a smile. Except for the mourning gown, she looked like a child caught snitching sweets from the kitchen.

"Lord Robert. I did not hear you come in."

He crossed to the pianoforte, then made her a bow. "I was listening to your concert. I was not aware you played."

She looked up at him, and his breath caught when he detected a tiny flash of what appeared to be mischief in her eyes. "How polite you are. If you'd been listening, however, you would know without a doubt that I can*not* play. I've always wished I could." She cast a wistful glance at the keys. "I love music."

"As do I. Unfortunately, not one member of my family possesses an iota of musical talent, neither for the pianoforte nor singing, and I fear I am the most tone-deaf of us all. However, my philosophy has always been that if you cannot play well, play with enthusiasm, and if you cannot sing well, sing loud. A source of great embarrassment for the entire family, I'm afraid." He smiled at her, but she did not smile back. Not even the slightest twitch of her lips. Making this woman laugh was fast becoming a quest, just as it was with Carters. He was suddenly overwhelmed with the desire to see the joyful woman from Elizabeth's sketch. "Tell me, Mrs. Brown, can you sing?"

"Worse than I play the pianoforte."

"Excellent. Shall we have a duet?" He perched himself next to her on the bench and made a great show of flexing his fingers. "I can only play one song. It's all my family would allow me to learn. For some inexplicable reason, some emergency or another always seemed to pop up whenever I sat down to play as I was growing up." He looked around, as if to ensure no one could overhear, then confided *sotto voce,* "Actually, the truth is that, in spite of the family's best efforts to squash my budding talent, I did manage to learn a few other ditties, but I fear that as I learned them in pubs, they are not suitable for a lady." He cleared his throat and nodded toward the music. "I'll play the upper notes, and you can play the lower. Ready?"

She hesitated, her serious gaze roaming his face as if looking for something. After several seconds, she nodded. "I'll try."

They each played their parts, most often with her several notes behind him. Instead of improving as the song went on, however, it seemed their efforts yielded worse results. By the final verse, their voices were raised in jarring harmony:

The sunlight reflected her features so fair
As she waited and wondered, to see if he'd dare.
And he did not disappoint his lovely young miss,
For upon her sweet lips he did bestow a sweet kiss.

The final discordant note lingered, then faded into silence. With laughter rumbling in his throat, Robert shook his head and turned toward her. "Egad, that was stupendously awful."

"Awful, indeed," she agreed in a somewhat breathless

voice. "I don't believe I played one correct note. And I am forced to admit you were correct."

"Of course I was. About what?"

"You, sir, are indeed tone-deaf."

An oh-so-brief, yet this time unmistakable, spark of mischief gleamed in her eyes and his pulse jumped. A tingle started in the region of his heart, and zoomed down to his . . . feet.

He pulled himself together and smiled. "And you, madam, cannot play worth a jot." He rubbed his hands together, then offered forth his most evil chuckle. "I cannot wait for us to entertain the family with this song."

"They'll run from the room screaming."

"Then we shall simply have to play and sing louder."

The slightest twitch touched one corner of her mouth, and he stared at her, his heart thumping at twice its normal rate. His gaze lowered to those incredibly full lips, and another tingle shot through him, this one settling directly in his groin. His attention riveted at the beguiling dimple gracing her chin, and his thumb itched to trace the shallow indentation.

Drawing in a much-needed breath, his head filled with her delicate scent, shooting heated awareness through him. She smelled lovely. Like some sort of flower, but not one familiar to him. He inhaled again, straining to catch the elusive fragrance, somehow resisting the growing urge to lean forward and simply bury his face in her enticing neck.

She blinked several times, then her expression went blank as if she'd drawn a curtain, and she abruptly stood. Crossing to the fireplace, she stared into the flames.

He remained seated, pulling in several unflowery-scented deep breaths, and mentally berated himself. *Not well done at all, you nitwit. Finally get her to give you a tiny twitch of the lips, then what do you do? Stare at her mouth as if you're starving and she were a meat pie. Then sniff at her as if you're a hound and she were a lamb chop.*

Bloody hell, where had his finesse disappeared to? Not to mention his decency. Good God, he'd never before considered himself a cad, but who else but a cad would feel lustful urges for a grieving widow? And as much as he hated to admit it, he could not deny that what he'd experienced was lust. Certainly he was familiar enough with the feeling to recognize it when he felt it. Yet the smacked-in-the-head sensation this woman gave him was definitely unfamiliar territory.

So, perhaps it *wasn't* lust. Perhaps he'd merely been . . . charmed. And . . . pleased to see the beginnings of a smile from her. The poor woman needed to laugh. Hadn't Lady Gaddlestone said as much? And even if she hadn't, a blind person could see Mrs. Brown needed a bit of fun.

He just hadn't planned that the merest hint of a grin from her would impact him like a punch to the heart.

Allie sat at the long, mahogany dining-room table, trying to do justice to the delicious meal of creamed peas and savory beef, but her thoughts were too jumbled to concentrate on her dinner. Peeking up from under her lashes, she covertly observed the man sitting across from her.

Lord Robert was engrossed in cutting his meat. Her gaze settled on his hands, holding his silver cutlery. Large, long-fingered, strong-looking hands. She'd noticed them when they'd played the piano. They looked like they belonged to someone accustomed to the outdoors rather than a gentleman of leisure.

Warmth suffused her cheeks as she recalled their impromptu duet. She'd been unable to resist his teasing invitation, yet she'd allowed herself to get far too carried away, singing with such abandon. But it had been so long since she'd done something silly. For just a moment, exhilaration had filled her and she'd forgotten whom she was with.

A charming, handsome man. A man she barely knew. A man who laughed easily, but whose gaiety did not always reach his eyes . . . eyes she recognized as guarding secrets. A man who'd looked at her in a way that made her heart pound.

Just like David.

David and Lord Robert were so obviously cast from the same mold. How could she have forgotten herself that way? But even as she asked herself the question, the answer came to her. *Because David never let you play the pianoforte. And he never would have encouraged you to sing.* Indeed, David had laughingly told her she sounded like a frog in the meadow, and she could not disagree with him. Still, her family had not minded, and except for her mother, they were all dreadful singers. Yet that had not stopped them from singing together every Tuesday evening, which they'd designated as "music night." David had hated music night, and after they'd married, he'd found any number of reasons to tempt her to stay home on Tuesdays. Most often he'd bring her to their bed and—

She sliced off the thought and ruthlessly buried it. She'd enjoyed the marriage bed, at least in the beginning, but that part of her life was over. Scooping up a forkful of peas, she again peeked at Lord Robert. And discovered his dark blue gaze upon her.

"Is the meal to your liking?" he asked.

Hoping she didn't appear flustered, she said, "Yes, thank you."

"I seem to recall Elizabeth mentioning you have a brother and sister?"

"Two brothers and a sister. All younger." A wave of love washed over her. "The boys are twins, and we call them the identical devils."

"How old are they?"

"Sixteen. My sister will turn twenty this month." A wistful sigh escaped her. "I miss them very much. Miss the noise and happy chaos that always reigned at our house. It's been . . . too long since I saw them."

He sipped his wine and nodded. "I understand. Although I keep my own rooms here in town, I cannot go too long without seeing my family. They occasionally drive me mad, especially Caroline, but they are also my greatest source of joy. And if it's noise and chaos you want, you'll get more than you ever hoped for at Bradford Hall."

She swallowed to relieve her tight throat. "I'm looking forward to it."

He looked toward the ceiling and shook his head. "You may change your mind once you arrive. Indeed, I can just picture what's happening there right now. Austin is glowering and pacing the floor, his hair standing up at odd angles due to his ramming his hands through it, demanding every eight seconds to know when Elizabeth is going to give birth. Caroline is telling her two-year-old daughter Emily to stop chasing the kittens, and Emily is completely ignoring her and looking to her father Miles, who, with a sly wink, will encourage her to continue.

"My brother William, his wife Claudine, and their daughter Josette are drawing pictures, which won't bode well for William, for he is a miserable artist. And my mother has undoubtedly taken Austin and Elizabeth's son James out into the garden where his chubby little hands will decapitate all her best roses for his 'mummy' while his grandmother beams at him." He made a comical face. "Humph. Mother used to fly into the boughs when Austin, William, and I so much as *glanced* at her roses."

A poignant ache filled Allie at the picture he'd painted for her. "It actually sounds much tamer than what I was accustomed to," she said. "Jonathan and Joshua routinely brought home injured animals, until Papa finally turned over a small barn to them that he called the healing room, all the while grumbling he'd never seen so many hobbling pigeons, ducks, and squirrels in his life. And don't ask about the toads, snakes, and ant farms.

"My sister Katherine looks like an angel, but she was forever skinning her knees and elbows as she joined in all Jon and Josh's adventures. Mama simply smiled through it all, bestowing hugs and kisses, applying bandages as needed, and delivering the occasional stern lecture. She loved to see us running about, swimming, and playing. She had an older sister who was bedridden most of her life, so she did not like to rein in our hoydenish activities." A wave of homesickness washed over her. "Mama always smelled like freshly baked bread."

"I suppose you were the reserved member of the family who kept the others in line," he said with a grin.

She shook her head. "Actually, I believe I was the most unruly of the bunch. I forever had twigs in my hair, grass stains on my dresses, dirt on my face. And as I was the eldest, I'm afraid I set the precedent for the others." She set down her fork, her meal forgotten. "Tell me, if you were with your family right now, what would you be doing? Playing with the kittens, drawing pictures, or beheading roses?"

He stroked his chin and pursed his lips. "Hmmm . . . I'd have to say none of those. Most likely I'd be challenging Austin to a game of billiards in a vain attempt to get his mind off Elizabeth for a bit before he wore out Mother's favorite Axminster."

"And would you succeed?"

"Eventually. But not until I'd riled him by calling his bravery into question for refusing to play an astute player"—he cleared this throat with exaggerated modesty—"such as myself."

"I see. And would you win?"

A slow, devastating smile creased his face, and a bolt of heat shot through her. "Of course. I always play to win."

It suddenly felt as if the room had grown ten degrees warmer, and Allie barely resisted the urge to dab at her heated face with her linen napkin. "And after defeating your brother at billiards, then what would you do?"

"Well, assuming that the new babe had not yet made his or her appearance, I suppose I'd round up Lady Giggles, Lord Mischief-Maker, and Miss Tickles for a quick game of 'Guess the Number' before their governesses whisked them off to the nursery."

"I take it you're referring to your nieces and nephew?"

"Indeed." His grin widened. "My mother, brothers, and sister are hardly ever whisked away by their governesses anymore."

"And do you assign these nicknames to everyone?"

"I'm afraid so. Bad habit of mine. I'm sure I'll come up with one for you before long. So you'd better be on your best behavior."

"Indeed. I'd hate to end up Miss Falls-in-Mud. Or Lady Trips-over-Tables."

He chuckled, and she very nearly smiled in return, a fact that disturbed her. Dear Lord, it was not easy keeping this man at a distance. After his laughter tapered off, he remarked, "Carters mentioned you ventured to Mr. Fitzmoreland's shop this afternoon. I hope you were able to find what you were looking for."

His casual statement returned reality with a jarring thump, snuffing out her frivolity like water to a flame. She studied his face for signs of a hidden meaning behind his casual comment, but saw nothing save mild curiosity. "Mr. Fitzmoreland was quite helpful."

"You know, you really shouldn't travel about the city in a hired hack, even with a footman in attendance."

She lifted her chin. "As I told you, I have business I need to conduct here."

"Yes, but you must have proper transportation. I shall arrange for a carriage to be at your disposal starting tomorrow morning. And I shall be happy to accompany you on any errands you need to run."

She clenched her hands in her lap. "That is unnecessary. I'm quite accustomed to fending for myself."

His gaze drifted to her black attire, and his eyes filled with sympathy. "I'm only doing what I know Elizabeth would do if she were here. In the note I sent her this afternoon, I gave her my solemn promise to look after you until we reach Bradford Hall." He shook with an exaggerated shiver. "Please accept the carriage. I've no desire for Elizabeth to scold me for the rest of eternity for allowing you to travel about without proper transportation."

Silence stretched between them for several seconds while Allie struggled with the desire to refuse his offer, and the knowledge that not having to pay for hacks would help preserve her meager resources. Finally, practicality won out.

Pushing back her chair, she stood. "In that case, I thank you. And now, if you'll excuse me, I'd like to retire. It's been a long and exhausting day."

He instantly rose, his eyes reflecting concern. "Of course. I shall see you tomorrow."

She inclined her head in reply, then strode swiftly from the room, overwhelmed with the need to escape his disturbing presence. She made her way quickly up the stairs, yet even after she'd closed her bedchamber door firmly behind her, she still did not relax.

Pacing around the room, she tried to collect her scattered thoughts. Lord Robert had unsettled her. For a brief moment she'd lowered her guard, and he'd managed to burrow beneath the carefully built fence she'd constructed around herself. And she did not like it one bit. Her defenses were hard-earned, her independence hard-won. She did not require a man to look after her, to arrange transportation for her, to escort her on errands. And she most emphatically did not need a man to smile at her, or play silly duets with her, or look at her in a way that resurrected long-buried feminine yearnings.

She wrapped her arms around her midriff and continued to pace. Dear God, the man was even *more* charming than David. All devilish grins and teasing blue eyes. Yet in a flash those eyes could convey sympathy and warmth and concern. Still, she'd seen that hint of secrets behind his charm and smiles. And not every smile reached his eyes.

Just like David. And everything with David had been lies.

But she was no longer a naïve miss. She would not make the same mistakes again.

She stopped pacing and pressed her fingertips to her temples, where a headache was rapidly forming. Her glance wandered to the large bed, but she instantly rejected the idea of retiring. In spite of the fact that her body ached with weariness, sleep was nowhere in her immediate future. And as she well knew, the only thing to cure this restlessness was fresh air.

Crossing the room, she pushed aside the forest-green velvet draperies and looked down at a small, square garden surrounded by a tall stone wall. Taking her shawl, but forgoing a bonnet, she slipped from her bedchamber, quickly exiting the dark, quiet house through the rear door.

The instant Allie's lungs filled with the cool night air, her shoulders relaxed. Staying close to the stone wall, she slowly walked around the garden, enjoying the nighttime chirping song of the crickets, the silver slash of moonlight upon the grass, the smell of burning fireplaces mixed with the pungent scent of garden soil. By her third trip about the perimeter, she'd firmly rebuilt her teetering defenses. Thanks to David, she'd learned, albeit too late, about the inner ugliness a handsome exterior could hide. Of course, it was just as possible for an unattractive man to be evil, but unfortunately, she clearly harbored a distressing weakness for beautiful men, a character flaw she refused to fall victim to again. She'd discovered the hard way that the more beautiful they were, the worse they were.

In which case, she needed to avoid Lord Robert as if he harbored the plague.

That decided, she turned to cross the grass to return to the house. Before she'd taken a step, however, strong arms grabbed her from behind. She gasped, and a beefy hand clapped over her mouth.

"Keep quiet," a guttural voice growled in her ear.

Panic along with fury raced through her. She fought against her captor, kicking her legs, trying to disengage his hand from her mouth. She managed to get out a half-cry before he stuffed a foul-smelling rag between her lips. Twisting around, she freed one hand and slashed it down his face, her nails raking his skin. Before she could enjoy her triumph, however, something hard smashed down on her head and her world faded to black.

.   .   .

Robert was halfway back to his rooms when he realized he'd
left his walking stick at the town house. He debated whether to
return for it, or simply fetch it tomorrow, but decided that as
the weather was cool, and the fog had yet to engulf the streets,
he could use the extra walk. He certainly had no desire to return to his empty rooms and lie in his empty bed, for he knew
damn well that sleep would not come. No, all he would think
about was *her.*

And that was the last thing he wanted to think about.

Her and her big golden-brown eyes. And her silky hair. And
the teasing hint of her smile. And what appeared to be an utterly lush figure underneath . . .

Her mourning clothes.

Disgusted with himself, he purposely turned his thoughts
to the tasks he planned to perform tomorrow before calling
upon her. The visit to his solicitor. Then perhaps a quick stop
at his club.

Taking a shortcut, he slipped into the mews behind the row
of Park Lane town houses. His footsteps faltered when what
sounded like a muffled cry echoed in the air. Before he could
decide if the noise had been a sound of passion or one of distress, or even made by a human, he spied a man with a sack
flung over his back entering the mews from—he leaned forward and squinted into the darkness—damn it, from what very
well could be Austin's garden. Bloody hell, what was this
about?

Keeping to the shadows, he hunched over and ran swiftly
through the mews. The man dashed to a waiting hack, tossed
his bundle inside, then clambered in himself. The hack instantly took off, moving swiftly into the darkness.

Straightening, Robert took off at a dead run. He arrived at
Austin's gate several seconds later. His lips tightened into a
grim line. The gate was ajar. After assuring himself that his
knife was secured in his boot, he ran after the hack. When it
slowed at the corner, he jumped onto the back.

The hack left the fashionable West End, moving east toward the docks. Robert held on tight, deciding that he would avoid confrontation with the bastard who'd stolen from Austin, if possible, but if it were necessary to pound the bloody piss out of the man to regain Austin's belongings, he would. And he had his knife should he need it.

The hack led him through a labyrinth of alleys, and he knew they were nearing the docks when the smell of rotting fish filled the air. When the vehicle slowed to a crawl, Robert jumped down, quickly hiding in the shadows cast by the brick buildings, and continued to follow on foot. Several minutes later, the hack drew to a stop. Pressing himself into the darkness, Robert watched the burly man exit the vehicle with the bundle thrown over his shoulder, then disappear between two buildings. The hackney flapped the reins, then moved off. The instant he was gone, Robert emerged from the shadows and swiftly entered the alleyway the burly man had entered.

He saw the man not far ahead of him. It appeared as if something fell out of the man's sack before he disappeared, turning into what looked like a doorway. Robert moved ahead cautiously, straining his senses to see or hear anything besides the distant shouting of men and wailing of infants. Bending down, he picked up the article that had fallen from the man's bundle.

It was a shoe. A woman's black shoe. A frown yanked his brows downward. It looked like Mrs. Brown's shoe! Could that muffled cry he'd heard have been *her*?

A noise sounded nearby and he froze. Just as he realized the sound came from behind him, something struck him on the back of the head, and then he felt no more.

Chapter 4

Robert came awake slowly, and quickly regretted doing so. He was lying on his side on the hardest, most uncomfortable bed he'd ever had the misfortune to lie upon. And everything *hurt*. Arms, legs, shoulders . . . they all ached as if seized by vicious cramps. Except his hands and feet. He couldn't feel them at all. Nor his arse . . . it seemed as if his buttocks had somehow fallen off.

But his head . . . bloody hell, if only *it* had become detached instead. A gang of demons hammered upon his skull with oversized mallets, and he silently vowed to kill the bastards the moment he found the strength to do so. Good God, whatever liquor he'd overindulged in, he'd never touch again.

He remained perfectly still, breathing slowly, willing the swimming feeling in his head to pass. When it had somewhat abated, he gritted his teeth, pried open one eye, then the other. Complete blackness engulfed him. Where the devil was he? His rooms were never this dark. He tried to turn his head, but instantly abandoned the plan when a shaft of white-hot pain shot outward from his skull. A low moan rumbled in his scratchy, dry throat. Snapping his eyes closed, he concentrated on defeating the waves of nausea rolling through him.

After what seemed like an eternity, but was probably no more than a minute, his insides settled and he drew in a cautiously relieved deep breath. His befuddled senses registered the briny odors of seawater and fish, and his stomach again threatened to rebel.

Another groan rumbled in his throat, but he slowly forced his eyes open. It took a moment for his sight to adjust to the darkness. He couldn't discern very much, other than the outlines of what appeared to be stacked crates. And he wasn't lying on a bed at all, but the rough-hewn planks of a wooden floor.

He frowned, then winced as pain ricocheted behind his eyes. Where the hell was he? This dank place was completely unfamiliar. The fishy odor indicated the river, but why and how had he arrived here? He forced himself to concentrate, to try and remember. And suddenly he did.

Someone stealing from Austin. Following the culprit. Near the docks. Picking up a shoe. Then feeling no more. Until now . . . when body parts he hadn't even known he possessed ached and throbbed.

Picking up a shoe . . .

The cobwebs rapidly cleared from his brain and he drew in a sharp breath. That shoe . . . it had fallen from the sack slung over the thief's shoulder . . . and it looked exactly like Mrs. Brown's shoe. A shoe that had most definitely been attached to her foot when he'd left the town house shortly before returning for his walking stick. Which meant that the brigand hadn't stolen candlesticks and silver . . . he'd stolen Mrs. Brown!

A host of grisly scenarios regarding her fate flashed in his mind, and a film of cold sweat coated his skin. She might be robbed. Or worse. Raped. Murdered . . . her body dumped into the Thames . . . or had she fallen prey to one of the growing number of grisly thieves who sold corpses for medical study? Outrage and something akin to panic pumped through him. He had to find her. Help her. God only knew what horrible circumstance might have already befallen her while he was unconscious. *Don't let me be too late . . . not again.*

Spurred to action, he tried to sit up.

And discovered he couldn't move.

It was as if a weight were attached to him, holding him in place. Gritting his teeth, he tried again. To no avail. He attempted to move his arms, and realized the problem. He was bound.

Although his hands and fingers remained numb, it registered with him that the ache in his wrists was caused by the rough rope digging into his skin, and the pain in his shoulders was from having his arms bound behind him. He tried to move his legs. His ankles were as securely bound as his wrists. Looking down, he saw that ropes crisscrossed his chest and torso.

Damn it all! He had to free himself! He redoubled his efforts, and after what seemed like a decade-long struggle, managed to drag himself into a sitting position. Panting, grunting, and sweating, he fought to catch his breath and prayed for his strength to return. What the hell was tied to his back? It felt like the dead weight of a body. . . .

His blood froze. Turning so swiftly his head swam, he tried to peer over his shoulder, but saw nothing save black. At that instant a low moan came from directly behind him. A soft, *feminine*-sounding moan. He sucked in a much-needed breath and caught a whiff of her elusive scent . . . that soft flowery fragrance. It had to be her. Had to be. Tied to him, back-to-back. And if she were groaning, she was alive. Hope surged through him.

He wriggled his shoulders. "Mrs. Brown," he said in an urgent whisper. "Can you hear me?"

Another soft groan filled the air and relief nearly rendered him light-headed. Jiggling his shoulders more firmly, he repeated, "Mrs. Brown? 'Tis I, Robert Jamison. Can you hear me? Please, speak to me."

An urgent-sounding voice filtered through Allie's mind, a tide expanding and receding in a deep, echoing cave. *Can you hear me? Please . . . speak to me.* Slowly, painfully, she emerged from the black abyss she'd fallen into. She hurt everywhere. Her head felt as if it had exploded and was preparing to erupt again. The world tilted behind her closed eyes, a sickening kaleidoscope of swirling colors that turned her stomach over. Her head fell forward on her limp neck, and sweat blanketed her skin. A long moan rumbled in her dry, sore throat.

'Tis I, Robert Jamison. Can you hear me? Please, speak to me. Confusion spilled through her addled senses. Lord Robert? He sounded so close . . . close enough to touch. She forced her eyes open. Blackness surrounded her. Pain sizzled through her head, and she gasped, squeezing her eyes closed. Where was she? Surely not the drawing room or her bedchamber at the Bradford town house. How had she gotten here . . . wherever here was? And why did she hurt so much? She licked her parched lips and grimaced at the foul taste coating her mouth. That awful taste. How—?

Memory flooded back as if a dam had burst in her mind. Walking in the garden . . . accosted by a man . . . that dreadful rag stuffed in her mouth. Then darkness. The truth hit her like a bucket of icy water, reviving her from her stupor. Someone had tried to abduct her. No, someone *had* abducted her. And had left her in this awful, stinking darkness

Fear seized her, snatching her breath. She tried to move, and discovered she was bound. Fear threatened to turn into panic. Who had done this? Who wished her harm? Why? *Why?* This incident could not be passed off as an accident. But right now, she had to—

"Mrs. Brown, can you hear me? Please wake up."

A layer of relief tempered her fear. She hadn't imagined his voice. She licked her parched lips. "Lord Robert?" Her voice came out in a cracked whisper. "Where are you?"

A rush of air that sounded like a heartfelt sigh of relief brushed by her ear. "Thank God you're awake. I'm here. Right behind you. We're bound together." He jiggled his shoulders, arrowing a shaft of pain up the back of her head.

"Where are we?"

"I'm not certain, but I think we're near the docks. This seems to be some sort of warehouse."

She felt him squirm behind her, and realized that the warm, solid mass pressing against her from shoulder to waist was his broad back. She swallowed, then asked, "How did we get here?"

"I returned to the town house for my walking stick and saw someone sneaking out of Austin's garden, carrying a sack. I followed, hoping to retrieve his stolen goods, never imagining *you* were what was stolen. I'd no sooner realized it when I was coshed from behind, and now here we are." He shifted again. "I've no wish to alarm you, Mrs. Brown, and I've plenty of questions myself, but they'll have to wait. We must free ourselves and get away from here before whoever put us here returns. How do you feel? Are you injured?"

She experimentally moved her bound legs and flexed as much as the tight bindings confining her chest and midriff allowed. "A bit sore all around, but nothing broken as far as I can tell. How are you?"

"Judging by the colossal pounding in my head, I'd say I have an egg-sized lump on my noggin, but otherwise I'm fine." He shifted a bit and grunted. "These ropes are secure. I can't move them." Another series of grunts and what sounded like a muffled obscenity escaped him. "Of course, the fact that my fingers have gone numb doesn't help. How are your hands?"

She wriggled her fingers and they brushed against his. "Cramped, but not numb."

"Excellent. I have a knife in my boot, or at least I did . . . one moment . . ." She felt him shifting. "It's still there," came his triumphant whisper several seconds later. "I can see the tip of the hilt."

Hope bloomed in her heart. "Can you remove it?"

"Yes, but it will require some shifting about . . . for both of us."

"Just tell me what do to."

"I'll try to be as gentle as possible—"

"Lord Robert. While I appreciate your concern for my sensibilities, I am not a fragile hothouse flower, nor am I the sort of woman to fall victim to fainting spells or gasps of horror. This is a matter of life and death. I'm as anxious to depart this place as you are, so let's get on with it. Do whatever you must. I shall cooperate fully."

"All right. On the count of three, I am going to lean forward and pull out the knife with my teeth. I need you to assist me by leaning back, then keeping a steady pressure. Ready?"

"Yes."

"One, two, three."

She leaned back, arching her spine as he leaned forward. The position was uncomfortable, but she held it steady, scarcely daring to breathe lest she move in a way that would break his concentration or cause him to fail. In less than a minute she heard the quiet *swish* of metal being unsheathed, then a muffled *thunk*.

"Got it," he reported in a terse whisper. "I dropped it onto the floor next to me. My hands are useless, therefore we need to shift so you can reach the knife. Then all you need to do is cut the ropes."

"Without amputating our fingers in the process, I suppose?"

"That would be the preferred method, yes."

"In that case, I shall try to be as gentle as possible," she said, using the same words he'd employed earlier.

She felt his head turn, and she turned hers as well, looking over her shoulder. She could see the outline of his profile, and she fancied that his teeth flashed white in the darkness with a quick grin.

"I think our best bet is to use leverage. The floor is wood and that will aid us. Bend your knees, plant your heels, then push against my back while shifting your, ah, bottom. I'll do the same. We'll go about three or four inches at a time. Do you understand?"

"Perfectly."

"On three, we'll move to my right, your left," he said.

He counted, and she dug her heels into the rough wood. Sharp pain stabbed her heel and she clamped her jaws to keep from crying out. She'd obviously lost a shoe, because the wood cut directly into her skin.

"Problem?" he asked over his shoulder.

"No."

She pressed against his back and scooted her bottom several inches to the left.

"Excellent," he said. "Now we need to move me forward. You push and I'll pull."

They accomplished the move, with Allie biting her lip against the pain from the deep splinter in her heel.

"Now just a little more to your left," Lord Robert said, "and the knife will be directly beneath your fingers."

They shifted again, and Allie's fingertips brushed against smooth metal. "I feel it," she whispered.

"Grab the hilt so you don't cut yourself. It's very sharp."

By squirming and maneuvering her hands, she determined which end was the hilt. She wrapped her fingers around it and barely suppressed a whoop of triumph. "I've got it!"

"Good girl. Now cut the ropes and we'll be off."

His tone was breezy, but Allie heard the tension beneath the lighthearted words. He clearly didn't want to sound afraid, didn't want her to be afraid. But she was. With each second that passed, the man who'd abducted her and bound them might return. And hand them a fate far worse than what they'd been dealt so far.

As if to prove her thought correct, the distant sound of muffled male voices interrupted the silence, icing her blood.

"Hurry," Lord Robert urged. "I don't know if that's our man, but I'd rather not find out."

"I couldn't agree more." Gripping the knife's handle and concentrating for all she was worth, while furiously praying she left their limbs intact, Allie sawed at the ropes. The position was awkward and progress so slow that the urge to scream in frustration nearly overwhelmed her. She strained her ears, listening for the male voices, but she heard nothing other than her own sharp breaths and the pounding of her heart. She pushed the blade at the ropes, fighting the desperation and panic clawing at her. *Stay calm. Breathe steady.*

"They're loosening," Lord Robert reported tersely. "Keep going. We're almost there."

Spurred on by his words, she continued to saw at the ropes, nicking the rough hemp deeper each time. A trickle of something warm and wet slithered over her fingers, loosening her hold on the hilt. A faint metallic scent filled her nostrils. Blood. Dear God. His? Hers? She didn't know. She didn't feel anything, and he hadn't complained. Of course, with his hands rendered numb, she could have sliced off a half dozen of his fingers and he wouldn't feel it. *Don't think about it. It's just a nick. Keep going. You're almost there.*

And suddenly she was free. With a final stroke of the blade, the ropes fell from her wrists. A sob bubbled up in her throat and she nearly choked swallowing it. With her hands liberated, she quickly wiped her slippery fingers and the knife's hilt on her gown, then cut the ropes binding their chests. As soon as her body was free, she turned and carefully cut the ropes binding his hands. The instant the cut ropes fell away, a low groan escaped him and he moved his arms forward, across his chest.

Allie made quick work of the ropes binding her feet, then scooted around to cut the last of the ropes securing Lord Robert's ankles. She ventured a quick peek at his face. Even the dim light couldn't hide the grimace twisting his features as he flexed his fingers.

"How are your hands?" she asked, returning her attention to her cutting.

"Deader than stone. My legs as well. But I'm working on it."

"There. You're free. Let me help you." Setting the knife beside her, she reached out for his hands. She quickly ran her fingers over them in as thorough an exam as she could manage in the darkness.

"No cuts or bleeding," she murmured, relieved. Then with sure, deft strokes, she massaged his palms and each finger. He had big hands. Broad-palmed and long-fingered. Surprise raised her brows at the calluses that roughened those broad palms. She'd thought his gentleman's hands would have been smooth.

After a minute, a low groan emanated from him. "Feeling is coming back. In my legs as well. Much as I'd like to give you several hours to continue that marvelous rubbing, we'd best be off. Can you—?"

The squeak of a door creaking on its hinges cut off his words. Allie's gaze flew to his. He laid one finger across her lips, indicating silence, and she nodded. Slow, heavy footsteps sounded in the distance, pausing, then starting again, growing louder with each footfall.

He helped her rise, then gave her a questioning look of unmistakable concern. She nodded. Her cramped legs protested and it was nearly impossible not to stamp her feet to return some feeling to her limbs, but she was fine. And very anxious to leave. The footsteps grew closer.

Reaching down, he picked up his knife. He then grasped her hand, pulling her close. So close they touched from chest to knee. A flash of heat rushed through her. Leaning down, he whispered directly into her ear.

"Don't let go of my hand."

Moving with a catlike silent grace, he pulled her deeper into the shadows of the stacked crates, then paused, listening for the footfalls, which had again stopped. Allie heard the rustle of her petticoat and grimaced. To her ears it sounded as loud as the clanking of a cowbell. And her one shoe was more a hindrance than a help, the heel making her feel lopsided, and sounding an unwanted tap against the wood. Reaching down, she pulled off the shoe, stuffing it into the pocket of her gown. No sense leaving it behind when it might prove useful as a weapon.

With her hand firmly clasped in Lord Robert's, he led her slowly forward through the shadows, keeping close to the stacked crates. The footfalls sounded again, closer this time. Lord Robert halted, then pulled her close against him. He pressed them as far back into the shadows as possible, one arm wrapped around her waist, the other holding her head against his chest, shielding her between the wooden crates and his body.

Heat surrounded her like a velvet blanket. His heart beat hard and fast beneath her ear, and his warm breath touched her temple each time he exhaled. And with each breath she drew, the masculine, musky scent of him filled her head.

The footsteps continued. Closer. Closer. Dear God, was it the man who had abducted her? What would he do when he discovered them gone? Well, he'd have a devil of a fight on his hands if he attempted to take her again. Slipping her hand into her pocket, she wrapped her chilled fingers around her shoe. She prayed she wouldn't be forced to help defend them with such a meager weapon. But she would if she had to.

Closer. Heart pounding, she stood perfectly still, listening to Lord Robert's thudding heartbeat, feeling his chest rise and fall. Closer. Until she was certain they were about to be discovered.

But then, miraculously, whoever it was moved on, passed them, the footfalls diminishing. It must not have been her abductor. A watchman perhaps? A moment later, the squeak of unoiled hinges rent the air, then all was silent.

She locked her knees to fight the limb-weakening relief rushing through her. Lord Robert exhaled a long breath that ruffled her hair. His arms tightened around her and in that momentary respite from her fright, she was suddenly very much aware of him. Not as a protector, but as a man. A brave man whose hard, masculine body was pressed intimately against her, his fingers tangled in her hair where his hand cradled her head to his chest, his warm breath touching her.

A wave of heat scorched her. . . . Heat that had nothing to do with the embarrassment she should have felt. But before she could react, he released her body, gripped her hand, and began leading her silently along. The splinter jabbed deeper into her heel, but she forced the discomfort from her mind. If a sore foot was the worst memento she garnered from this evening, she'd consider herself very fortunate indeed. Less than a minute later they reached a large wooden door.

Keeping her behind him, he cracked the door open. Allie nearly jumped out of her skin when the hinges growled with a noise resembling the cry of a wounded animal. Lord Robert's head and shoulders disappeared through the opening. Seconds later he leaned back.

"This leads to an alleyway," he reported in a low voice. "I'm not certain of our exact location, but I have a general idea. We need to get to a more crowded area, then we can hail a hack." He squeezed her hand in what was clearly meant to be a reassuring way. "Not to worry."

Worry? That was a lukewarm description of her feelings. She'd never been more frightened in her life. "I'm not worried. Do I *look* worried?"

"I don't know. It's too dark to tell. Just don't let go of my hand."

He slipped out the door and Allie gripped his hand ever tighter, needing no urging to follow him out of the dank warehouse. Let go of his hand? Not if her very life depended on it.

Unfortunately, she was terrified that it might.

When they reached the end of the alley, Robert looked both ways. A glimmer of relief edged down his spine, even as dread coursed through him. Fortunately, he did indeed know where they were. Unfortunately, it was one of the worst sections of the city. Getting them home unaccosted would take a miracle. He gripped the hilt of his knife tighter. And prayed for a miracle.

Keeping to the deep shadows, he moved swiftly along, holding tight to Mrs. Brown's small hand. They zigzagged through trash-strewn, rat-infested back streets. The stench of filth and poverty and unwashed humanity mingled with nearby cries of women and harsh shouts of men. A series of deep grunts and moans emanated from a darkened doorway, and he quickened his pace. He expected her to falter, to squeal in dismay, to gasp in horror, to cry out, or to succumb to the vapors, but she kept pace with him, never uttering a sound. Indeed the only reason he even knew she remained behind him was the feel of her palm pressed firmly to his and the slight rustle of her petticoats.

They were close now . . . close to a place where they'd be able to hail a hack. Just two more turns and he'd get her to safety. He would not fail. Not like he had with Nate. . . .

They rounded the second turn and a pent-up breath whooshed from his lungs. There, under the dim circle of light cast by a gas lamp, stood a hack. It was easily the most welcome sight Robert had ever seen.

Both driver and horse appeared to be dozing, but they roused as Robert and Mrs. Brown approached. He called out the direction of the Bradford town house to the sleepy-eyed driver as he helped Mrs. Brown into the carriage.

Settling himself on the seat opposite Mrs. Brown, Robert drew in what seemed like his first easy breath in hours. They were safe. On their way home. He briefly squeezed his eyes shut as a combination of relief, triumph, and exhaustion surged through him. He hadn't failed.

But by damn he wanted to know the whys and whats of how he and Mrs. Brown had ended up trussed like turkeys on a dockside warehouse floor. Setting his knife on the hard seat beside him, he raked his hands through his hair, wincing when his fingers encountered an egg-sized lump.

"Are you all right?" came her soft voice.

"Just a bump. How are . . . ?"

His voice trailed off as they passed under the light of a gas lamp and he got his first good look at her. Her eyes were huge, her face chalk-white. She lifted a visibly trembling hand to brush away a tangled curl clinging to her pale cheek, and his heart seemed to stutter to a stop.

Her hand was covered with blood.

Chapter 5

God, he hated the sight of blood. Always had. Even as a child. He vividly recalled cutting his foot on a sharp stone when he was six years old. He'd watched the blood ooze from the wound and had nearly passed out cold. The only thing that had kept him from doing so was the knowledge that Austin and William would have teased him unmercifully if he'd swooned like a girl.

One look at Mrs. Brown's hand and the crimson streak of blood now marring her pale cheek, and his stomach turned over. "You're hurt," he said. Damn it all, his voice sounded positively feeble. Why hadn't he felt the blood while he'd pulled her along? Had he caused her further injury? Hurt her? No, he realized. Her right hand was bleeding. He'd been holding her left hand.

Clearing his throat, he reached out and gently grasped her forearms. He eased her hands over, and his lips flattened into a grim line. Even in the dim light he could see that her wrists were rubbed raw. Numerous oozing nicks marred her palms and fingers, but it was the long cut running across her right hand that concerned him the most. A drop of blood dripped off her fingertip, and he swallowed hard. "These wounds need to be seen to. Immediately."

His mind raced. It would take at least thirty minutes to make their way through the labyrinth of streets back to the town house. His own rooms were farther away still. He couldn't stand the thought of her waiting, bleeding, for all that time. Dear God, the woman hadn't uttered a word of complaint and she had to have been in agony. Sympathy crowded him, and he barely resisted the urge to pull her onto his lap and cradle her like a broken child. For God help him, that's exactly what she looked like.

An idea popped into his mind, and he seized it like a starving dog pouncing upon a bone. He signaled the driver, then shouted out a different direction for him.

"A sovereign for you if you deliver us there within five minutes," he yelled. The hack surged forward, nearly tossing him off his seat.

"Where are we going?" Mrs. Brown asked, her eyes appearing even larger and more haunted than a moment ago.

His gaze riveted on the streak of blood staining her cheek. "A friend's home. He lives close by. These wounds need immediate attention." Reaching into his pocket, he withdrew his handkerchief, then gently dabbed at her palms. "I'm so sorry . . . these must hurt terribly."

When she didn't reply, his attention returned to her face, and his heart nearly broke when her bottom lip trembled. "To be perfectly honest," she whispered, "they don't hurt nearly as much as my feet."

"Your feet?" His gaze dropped to the floor, but he could see nothing but his boots and her black skirt.

"Yes. As I'd somehow lost a shoe, and it was difficult to run with only one, I removed it. I'm afraid my stockings provided little protection."

A muscle jerked in his jaw. "Good God. Let me see."

She hesitated for several seconds, then slowly raised one foot. He reached out and gently grasped her ankle through the wool of her skirt. She sucked in a sharp breath.

"Forgive me," he said. He slowly eased the material upward until her foot appeared. He barely stifled the moan that rose in his throat. Hell and damnation. Her stocking had torn completely away, its ragged ends dangling about her delicate ankle. Dirt and mud and God knows what else caked her bare foot. She groaned and his gaze shot to her face. Her eyes were squeezed shut, her lips pressed tightly together. There was no doubt she was in pain.

Sympathy and hot anger surged through him. "That fiend who absconded with you will pay for this. I give you my word."

She opened her eyes, and for the space of several heartbeats they silently regarded each other. It appeared she was about to say something, but before she could reply, the hack jerked to a halt. Robert looked outside and saw that they'd arrived at the correct place. "Don't move," he instructed her in a terse voice.

He opened the vehicle's door, then stepped down onto the cobblestone street. Withdrawing two gold coins from his pocket, he tossed them up to the hackney. "Do not depart until we're safely inside," he told the man, who nodded in reply, his eyes round as he stared at the amount of money in his hand. Robert then leaned into the hack and met Mrs. Brown's pain-filled, questioning gaze.

"I'm going to carry you," he said in a tone that brooked no argument.

Yet she argued. "But I cannot go—"

"Yes, you can. Your injuries need attention, and I'll not risk further harm to you by allowing you to walk. This is the home of my friend, Michael Evers. He is knowledgeable in such matters and is discreet." He fixed her with a penetrating look. "I realize this is out of the ordinary, but so are our present circumstances."

She met his gaze steadily, and he wondered what was going through her mind. He hoped she wasn't going to allow a misplaced sense of propriety to rear its head now. Not after all they'd been through. Tied together . . . pressed against each other. An image of her flattened against him in the warehouse flashed through his mind and he firmly pushed it aside.

Finally she nodded. "All right."

Without further delay, he slipped one arm beneath her knees, the other across her back. "Wrap your arms about my neck," he instructed, and to his relief she did as he bid. He gently eased her from the hack, then walked swiftly up the stone steps leading to the modest residence. She felt small and soft and fragile in his arms. His heart skipped with a combination of fear and something else he couldn't define when a low groan pushed past her lips while her head lolled sideways, nestling against his neck. A hint of her flowery scent still clung to her underneath the overpowering smells of blood and dockside alleys.

"Hold on," he whispered against her forehead.

When they reached the oak door, Robert pounded upon it with his boot, praying Michael was home. Less than a minute later a palm-sized panel at eye level in the door slid open. "What the bloody hell?" growled a deep, familiar voice, laced with a hint of Irish brogue. "State your name and business, and it'd better be—"

"Michael, it's Robert Jamison. Please open the door."

The panel slid back into place and the door opened. "What the hell, Jamison—?"

Robert pushed his way into the small foyer. "She's hurt."

Michael's sharp eyes raked over the bloody hands, and the feet exposed under her gown. "How bad is it?"

"I'm not certain. She was abducted. Knocked out. Tied up. Her wrists and hands were cut by the ropes and possibly by my knife. Her feet were injured during our escape."

Michael's dark brows shot upward. *"Our?"*

"I'll explain later. Where can I put her?"

Jerking his head to the left, Michael indicated a short corridor. "Bring her into my study. First door on the right. A fire's already burning and you'll find plenty of brandy. Give her some. There's also a bowl and pitcher of water. I'll get bandages and supplies and join you in a moment."

Robert didn't hesitate. Entering the room, he made directly for the long leather sofa in front of the fireplace and gently laid her down. Then he leaned back, looked at her, and stilled.

He'd half-expected her eyes to be closed, but they were open, looking at him with a steady expression that somehow echoed both fear and strength. Dark hair surrounded her pale face in a matted tangle, with one curl stuck to her cheek by the streak of now dried blood. He reached out a hand that wasn't quite steady and brushed the tangled strand away. Her lower lip trembled, and he brushed his fingertips over her smooth cheek. Something flashed in her eyes. Pain? Fear? He wasn't certain, but he vowed to erase both.

Dropping to his knees beside her, he quickly shrugged out of his jacket, rolled it into a ball, then tucked it behind her head as a pillow. "How do you feel?"

"A bit undone, I'm afraid." She raised her injured hands. "Although I suspect these look worse than they really are. Even the smallest cut can sometimes bleed dreadfully." She stared at her hands for several more seconds, then lowered them once again to her lap. A rueful expression washed over her features. "I'm afraid I do not very much care for the sight of blood."

"Indeed? Doesn't bother me a bit." He cast a quick glance upward to see if he were about to be smote dead with a lightning bolt. "You're in good hands, I assure you. Now, I'm going to give you some brandy. It will help ease the pain. Then we'll get your feet and hands bandaged up." He offered her what he hoped was a reassuring smile. "You'll be running about and will once again be an H.P.P. in no time."

"H.P.P.?"

"Horrid Pianoforte Player."

She raised one eloquent brow. "I believe that is rather like the ocean calling the sea salty."

A grin pulled at his lips and his fingers slid from her face. Her skin felt like velvet, another thought he shoved firmly aside. Clearing his throat, he rose and crossed the room to the decanters resting on a piecrust mahogany table near the window. He poured two fingerfuls into a crystal snifter and tossed it back in a single gulp. Welcome, bracing heat burned down his insides to his belly. He blew out a long breath, poured another portion, then returned to her side.

Holding the snifter to her lips, he helped her drink. After the first sip, her face puckered into a grimace.

"Yeck," she said, turning her face away from the snifter. "What vile stuff."

"On the contrary, I found it to be extraordinary. Knowing Michael, it probably came from Napoleon's private stock."

She turned back to him, her eyes narrowed with clear suspicion. "How would that be possible?"

"Michael is acquainted with people from, shall we say, all walks of life."

"Including scoundrels like you, Jamison," came Michael's deep voice from the doorway.

Turning, Robert watched Michael cross the room, his arms laden with supplies and a bucket of water. He moved like the athlete he was, with a predator-like grace that Robert knew was one of the secrets of his success.

Michael joined them, setting the supplies on the floor. "How do you feel, Miss . . . ?"

"Mrs. Brown," she replied softly. "Alberta Brown."

Michael offered her a solemn nod. "Michael Evers. Glad to make your acquaintance. Now why don't you relax, and Robert and I will take a look at these injuries."

At Mrs. Brown's nod, Michael passed Robert a handful of snowy linen strips with a meaningful look. "I'll take her hands," he said. "You take her feet."

Robert instantly agreed, realizing Michael was assigning him the more intimate task. And hopefully the less bloody one. Rising, he brought the pitcher of water from Michael's desk over to the sofa, then filled two bowls.

Without another word, each man went to work. Robert knelt on the polished wood floor and gently pushed up her skirts until her feet and ankles were exposed. His stomach tightened at the sight. She was a mess, and he prayed that once the filth was cleaned away, he'd discover that that was all she was—merely dirty—and not seriously injured.

He closed his mind to everything but the task at hand. He dipped strip after strip of linen into the water, gently cleansing away the dirt. A sense of amazement rippled through him at what she'd done. Running all that way, over those rough stones and wood, without a word of complaint. She had to have been suffering, and frightened to death as well. Yet even now, when he knew by the tight set of her lips and the pain shadowing her eyes that she was hurting, she didn't utter a word of protest.

He heard the soft rustle of material as Michael folded back her sleeve. "How serious is it, Michael?"

"Wrists are rubbed pretty raw. A fairly deep slash across the base of her right palm. Doesn't need stitching, but it will sting like a bast . . . er, the devil, for a few days. Everything else is small. Little nicks. They'll sting as well, but heal quickly." He glanced at Robert. "How are her feet?"

Robert looked down at the now clean, delicate foot cupped in his palm. He gently manipulated it around in gentle circles, watching her face for signs of pain. "Some bruising around the ankles from the ropes. A few shallow cuts on the bottom." He checked the other foot and frowned. "There's a good-sized splinter in her heel here."

Allie reclined on the sofa, silent and still, watching as they cleansed and examined her, pretending that she wasn't mortified to have a complete stranger and another man she barely knew tending to her. Once they'd determined that she wasn't seriously injured, Lord Robert tersely related to Mr. Evers how she'd come to be a guest at the Bradford town house, and how he'd returned there for his walking stick only to discover a thief departing the garden, and then realized he'd stumbled upon a kidnapping.

Gratitude and amazement washed through her as she listened. Although Lord Robert had told her as much earlier, now that the danger to them was over and she could think clearly, the full import of his words sunk in. Dear God, what would have happened to her if he hadn't followed? A shudder shook her shoulders and she purposefully pushed the question away. She didn't even want to consider the possibilities. But there was no escaping one certainty: Lord Robert had saved her life, risking his own in the process. And now, within minutes he was going to start asking her questions, wanting answers and explanations he might well deserve but that she wasn't prepared to give.

Opening her eyes, she looked toward the end of the sofa and was met with the most disturbing sight of Lord Robert, head bent low, gently removing the splinter from her heel. He looked big and strong and capable, and a wave of heat shot through her, settling in her midsection. A lock of ebony hair fell forward, hiding his upper face from her view, but she could clearly see his mouth. His firm lips were pressed together with obvious concentration. His touch was tender and gentle and sent pleasurable tingles racing up her legs. He'd rolled up the sleeves of his once pristine shirt, exposing muscular forearms. Her gaze drifted lower, and she drew in a sharp breath. Reddened, angry skin banded his wrists.

His head jerked up and their eyes met, his filled with concern. "I'm sorry . . . but at least the splinter is out. Did I hurt you?"

"No. I . . . I just noticed your wrists. You're hurt."

He shook his head. "Scratched. Nothing more." One corner of his mouth pulled up. "Michael will doctor me when we're finished with you."

An inelegant snort sounded from Michael. "What makes you think so?"

"Because I'm one of your best customers. Wouldn't want to lose me."

"Customers?" Allie echoed.

"Michael owns what is arguably the finest boxing emporium in London. And he is, inarguably, the best pugilist in the country."

Allie turned her attention to Michael Evers, who was bandaging her wrist with a gentle deftness that bespoke experience in such matters. His features were bold and possessed a roughness to them, as if they'd been hewn from granite. It was obvious by the crooked shape of his nose that he'd broken it at one time—not surprising given his profession. Nor was the small scar bisecting his left eyebrow. His hair was thick and dark and badly in need of a trim. He was a large man, yet his movements held an almost catlike grace. And in spite of his size, his touch was gentle. With his rough features, husky brogue-flavored voice, and predilection toward swearing, he looked and sounded nothing like a gentleman, yet clearly he and Lord Robert were friends.

At that instant Michael Evers turned toward her, and her face heated at being caught staring at him. Onyx-colored eyes assessed her thoughtfully.

"You're fortunate that Robert returned for his walking stick, Mrs. Brown," he said.

"Indeed I am, Mr. Evers."

"Which brings me to my first of many questions," Lord Robert said. "How did that man get hold of you? Was he in the house?"

Clearly her reprieve from the inevitable questions was over. She drew a deep breath, then said, "No. I was in the garden—"

"The garden?" Lord Robert broke in, his brows lifting.

"Yes. I couldn't sleep. I felt the need for some fresh air."

Their eyes met and she could almost feel something pass between them. Something heated and knowing and intimate. Warmth crept up her neck and she averted her gaze, not wanting to risk that he might read in her eyes that *he* was the reason for her restlessness.

"I don't know how things work in America, Mrs. Brown," Mr. Evers said, "but you should know that it is unsafe for a woman to be out alone. Especially at night."

"An error I won't make again, I assure you."

"So you were walking in the garden," Lord Robert said, "and he grabbed you?"

"Yes. From behind. I never saw his face. I tried to scream, but before I could get out a good yell he stuffed a rag in my mouth. I remember a pain in my head, then nothing else until I awoke, tied to Lord Robert."

"Did your abductor give you any clue as to what he wanted?"

"No."

Lord Robert turned to his friend. "Your ear is always to the ground, Michael. What do you think? I know London is rife with crime, but still, the audacity to abduct a lady? In Mayfair? From a duke's residence? Have you heard of any similar crimes?"

"No. Which makes me wonder if this was a random act or if perhaps someone from the duke's residence was specifically targeted."

A grim expression came over Lord Robert's face. "Austin needs to be informed. I'll write him—" He broke off, then shook his head. "No, I'd best wait and tell him in person. Elizabeth is safe, as I'm certain he's never farther than three paces away from her. And with the baby's imminent arrival, he's already worried. I don't want to unduly alarm him further."

"A smart strategy," said Mr. Evers, "especially considering that it's also possible Mrs. Brown was the intended victim."

Both men looked at her. Allie strove to keep her face expressionless, but was not certain she succeeded. "I cannot see how that could be possible," she said, proud that her voice didn't waver. "No one knows me here. I only just arrived today. I'm certain it was simply an unfortunate accident. One caused by my own stupidity in wandering about alone at night. And one that could have ended tragically if not for Lord Robert's brave intervention." Her eyes met his. "I thank you." She turned to Michael Evers. "And you as well, Mr. Evers, for your assistance."

"You're welcome," Mr. Evers murmured. He watched her for several long seconds, and Allie forced herself to meet his sharp gaze. Finally he resumed bandaging her hands while Lord Robert bandaged her feet. To Allie, the silence felt thick and heavy with tension and she longed to break it. Yet, as she had no wish to initiate a conversation that might lead to more questions, she said nothing.

Several minutes later, Mr. Evers rose. "Finished," he said. "You'll be sore for a few days, but fine." He turned to Robert. "Make sure those bandages are changed once a day. And now let's have a look at you."

Despite Lord Robert's grumbling, Mr. Evers quickly cleaned and bandaged his wrists. "You'll live," he stated. Then, jerking his head toward the corridor, he said, "Let's give Mrs. Brown a moment alone to collect herself. We'll see to transportation to get you home."

Lord Robert and Mr. Evers quit the room, shutting the door softly behind them. Allie closed her eyes and exhaled a long breath. Her wrists hurt, as did her foot where she'd been stabbed by the splinter. And her head still ached, but not nearly as much as it had earlier. All in all, she felt quite well, considering the fact that she could just as well be seriously injured. Or dead.

There was no doubt in her mind that whoever had abducted her hadn't chosen her at random. Between the accidents she'd suffered on the ship and tonight's events, there was clearly someone who wished her harm. But who? The only logical explanation was that the person had to somehow be tied to David's unsavory past. But what did they want from her? She possessed nothing of value. Or did they simply want her dead? A cold chill rippled through her. They'd nearly succeeded tonight. Would they try again?

And tonight, Lord Robert's life had been threatened as well. Her circumstances could be placing him in danger. She should warn him . . . tell him . . .

But tell him what? That some unknown person from her husband's shady past might be after her for a reason she could not possibly guess at? Her insides cramped at the mere thought. She hadn't admitted David's criminal past to anyone. Not to her family, or to Elizabeth through their correspondence. The shame and humiliation, not to mention the scandal that would attach itself to her and her family . . . no, she couldn't tell Lord Robert. She barely knew him. Her life and mistakes with David were none of his or anyone else's business. Besides, she had no desire to become any more involved with Lord Robert than she already was. Sharing her most intimate secrets with him was not something she would even consider.

Intimate . . .

A shiver ran through her as she instantly, vividly recalled the feel of him surrounding her, his heat and strength as he held her against him, protecting her. At the time, her fright had prevented her from focusing on his disturbing nearness, but now . . .

A long sigh escaped her. The sort of breathy, feminine sigh she hadn't indulged in for years. Warmth swept through her, kindling a spark she'd ruthlessly extinguished when David died.

A sudden chill replaced the unbidden, unwanted heat, and her eyes popped open. God help her, she was losing her mind. How could she possibly, even for an instant, entertain such . . . unacceptable thoughts about Lord Robert? He possessed so many traits and characteristics she'd painfully learned to detest and distrust in a man . . . a friendly, teasing manner that could foster undeserved trust. A handsome face to mask inner dishonor. Warm eyes that hid secrets. Winning smiles to conceal lies. Intense looks and touches that inflamed the senses.

Yet tonight, with his heroic rescue of her, his concern for her injuries even though he himself was hurt, he'd shown a side of himself she hadn't anticipated. And it was a side she did not want to see. She did not want to think of him as possessing any admirable qualities. He was already too physically attractive by far. If she were to like him—

She cut off the thought. Like him? Impossible. So he'd done something admirable. Even the worst sort of person normally had *one* good aspect to their character. Surely he did not possess any others. Why, look at how he'd known his way around those disreputable sections of London. Surely no decent gentleman would be familiar with such surroundings.

And the company he kept! This Michael Evers was a suspicious character if she'd ever seen one. A fighter by trade, one who obviously mingled with persons of low society. No telling what manner of nefarious business Lord Robert conducted with such a man. Yes, their friendship merely confirmed her belief that there was darkness lurking behind Lord Robert's casual, fun-loving demeanor. Indeed, Lady Gaddlestone's words on board the ship, concerning the transgression in Lord Robert's past, verified as much—a fact she'd momentarily forgotten. But just like walking about in the garden at night, it was a mistake she would not make again.

Robert stood in the oak-paneled foyer watching Michael lean his head out the front door and emit a trio of piercing whistles. Closing the door, he said, "A trusted man will be here within five minutes to take you home."

"Thank you, Michael. I owe you a boon."

"You damn well owe me several. And don't think I won't collect."

"Since I'm already in your debt, I might as well add to my tally. I've another favor to ask you." He paced across the parquet floor. "I'm very concerned about tonight's happenings. I shudder to think what might have happened to Mrs. Brown. I'm afraid I find it difficult to credit that someone in Austin's household was targeted, yet I'm not entirely convinced that this abduction was random."

Michael crossed his arms over his broad chest and regarded him with an indecipherable expression. "So you think Mrs. Brown was who they wanted, then? Why?"

He shook his head, blowing out a frustrated breath. "I cannot say for certain. But there is something about her manner. . . . I sense fear in her. And that she is hiding something. I felt it when I met her at the docks. Then, this afternoon, when any other lady would have been resting from her journey, she visited an antique shop."

"Seems innocent enough."

"Yes, yet she was decidedly evasive when I asked her about it. She claims she has business affairs to settle on behalf of her deceased husband, which is naturally none of my affair, but she was very secretive. Overly so." He raked his hands through his hair, wincing when he encountered the bump on the back of his head. "Of course, I might be imagining things. I'm so accustomed to Caroline and Elizabeth chattering away like magpies, I wouldn't recognize natural reticence and reserve if it slapped me in the face."

"When did her husband die?"

"Three years ago."

Michael cocked a single brow. "Yet she still wears mourning."

"Clearly she remains devoted to him." For some reason, those words tasted bitter in Robert's mouth.

"Yet that hasn't curbed your interest in her. Indeed, I suspect all this vagueness and secrecy surrounding her has piqued your interest."

He stopped pacing and fixed a glare on his friend. "I'm not interested in her. I am *concerned* about her. She is my responsibility until I deliver her, safe and sound, to Bradford Hall. You can imagine the hue and cry should I allow harm to befall her."

"Yes. I'm certain that is all there is to it. Now, what is this additional favor you wish to ask?"

"Just to keep your eyes and ears open. You've contacts all over town. If you should hear anything regarding tonight's abduction—"

"I'll inform you at once."

Three shrill whistles pierced the air. "Your transportation has arrived," Michael said. "Shall I carry the lovely Mrs. Brown out?"

Lovely? The thought of Michael's strong arms cradling *the lovely* Mrs. Brown tightened Robert's shoulders. He shot his friend a chilly look. "Thank you, no. I can handle her."

Amusement gleamed in Michael's eyes. "I'm not certain I agree, but it will be interesting to watch you try."

.   .   .

Allie spent the twenty-minute ride back to the Bradford town house looking out the carriage window in an attempt to ignore her companion.

She failed utterly.

She'd never been so completely *aware* of a person in her entire life. Even more vexing was the fact that *he* apparently had no trouble ignoring her. On the two occasions when she'd peeked at him from the corner of her eye, he'd seemed engrossed in his own thoughts, his brows pulled down in a frown, his sight set out his own window.

She could hear him breathing. Slow, steady breaths that she knew raised and lowered his chest. She could smell the faint scent of starch that still somehow clung to his clothing. Could feel the warmth emanating from his body. The memory of the sensation of his body pressed to hers filled her mind, and she squeezed her eyes shut to block it out.

When they arrived at the town house, she nearly jumped for joy. Until he announced his intention of carrying her inside.

"You'll do nothing of the sort," she replied in her most prim tone. "What on earth would Elizabeth's staff think?"

"They're all sleeping. But even if they weren't, you're not wearing shoes."

She opened her mouth to argue further, but he forestalled her by placing a single finger over her lips. "It's four A.M. The servants haven't arisen yet, and the members of the *ton* who live nearby aren't home yet from their round of parties. No one will see you."

With that, he slipped his arms beneath her, removed her from the carriage, then, holding her close against his chest, strode up the walkway.

She held herself rigid in his arms, refusing to admit for even a second that his touch was comforting. Pleasing. Exciting.

No, it was unwanted. Embarrassing. And the instant he released her, she silently swore that she would never allow him to touch her again.

Opening the door, he strode with her into the foyer, closing the door with a bump of his hip. Then he climbed the stairs, strode down the corridor, finally placing her gently on her feet outside her bedchamber door.

"Shall I ring for a maid to help you undress?" he asked.

Heavens, the man wasn't even out of breath, while she, who had been carried the entire way, could barely catch hers. "N-no. I can manage."

"In that case, I shall leave you. I'll stop round in the morning after I've visited the magistrate to report this evening's events." He looked down at her with a serious expression, and she instantly wished for him to smile or make a jest. His grin had made her heart flutter, but this unexpected, intense look nearly stuttered it to a halt.

Her mouth went dry. She tried to look away from his compelling stare, but could not.

"I'm glad you're all right," he said in husky whisper.

She licked her dry lips. "Yes. You, too."

His gaze dropped to her mouth and her breath caught. For one insane, breathless second she thought he meant to kiss her. She stood still as a statue, terrified he would. Terrified he wouldn't.

But then a lopsided grin eased across his face, breaking the spell. "Quite an adventure we shared. Most ladies I know prefer the opera or the shops. I must say, you proved to be most skilled with my knife." He waggled his fingers in front of her. "Not a single one missing."

Something warm spread through her. Warm and entirely unwelcome. She tried to stop it, but it came just the same. "I owe you my deepest gratitude."

He swept downward in a deep bow. "A pleasure, my lady." He stood and gazed down at her, an unmistakable twinkle in his eye. "This has undeniably been an evening I won't soon forget." His amusement faded, replaced by another intense look that froze her in place. "But you mustn't venture out again without an escort. There are dangerous men lurking all about."

Dear God, didn't she know it. And the most dangerous one of all stood right before her.

"Good night, Mrs. Brown."

"Good night." She entered her bedchamber, closing the door behind her with a soft click. Then, leaning back against the wooden surface, her eyes slid closed and she drew in a much-needed breath. In fact, the first easy breath she'd drawn in hours. He was gone. She should have been elated. Relieved. Surely she shouldn't be feeling . . . bereft.

Bereft? Nonsense. She was simply tired. She needed sleep. To say that today had been trying was an understatement of gargantuan proportions.

Opening her eyes, she walked toward her bed, anxious to remove her dirty gown and crawl between the sheets. Halfway across the room, she froze.

The wardrobe door stood ajar. She hadn't left it so. Had she?

Slowly her gaze panned the room. Her bed was neatly turned down, but the pillows appeared mussed. And there, on the dresser . . . hadn't she set her bottle of scent in the *right hand* corner? Yes, surely she had. But there it was, in the left corner.

Crossing to the wardrobe, then the dresser, she searched through her things. Nothing was missing. Had one of the servants moved the bottle and left the wardrobe ajar? Most likely . . . when they'd turned down the bed. She pressed her fingers to her temples where the remnants of a headache still lingered. Or perhaps she herself had been careless. Given her distracted state of mind . . . yes, that was certainly possible.

Still, she couldn't shake the unnerving sensation that someone had searched through her belongings.

Chapter 6

Noon the next day found Allie finishing a late, informal breakfast of eggs, ham, and thinly sliced pheasant. The hearty meal, as well as the much-needed sleep and a hot bath upon rising, left her feeling refreshed and rejuvenated. Her wrists and feet were still tender, but so much improved that she pushed the mild discomfort away. Just as a footman was filling her china cup with a second serving of coffee, Carters entered the room bearing a silver salver.

"A message for you, Mrs. Brown," he said in his sonorous voice, holding out the gleaming tray. "The messenger indicated no reply was expected."

Allie accepted the missive. Was it from Elizabeth? Turning over the ivory vellum, she broke the wax seal and read the contents.

Mrs. Brown,
    I have traced the coat of arms you gave me. It is the
family crest belonging to the earl of Shelbourne. The
title dates back to the sixteenth century, when the
first earl was given the title and familial holdings in
gratitude for his service to the Crown. The current earl,

*Geoffrey Hadmore, is undoubtedly known to your good
friend the duchess of Bradford and her husband.*

    *I hope this information proves useful to you, and I
again thank you for your patronage and for the kind
recommendation of the duchess. Please let me know if I
may be of any further assistance to you.*

                  Sincerely yours,
                  Charles Fitzmoreland

    Allie reread the letter, her heart speeding up with anticipa-
tion. This news brought her one crucial step closer to ending
her quest. With any luck, she would soon return the last of
David's pilfered goods to its rightful owner, thus ending this
long, arduous, humiliating chapter of her life. *Thank God.*
    The earl of Shelbourne. All she needed to do now was lo-
cate this man and—
    "Good morning, Mrs. Brown."
    She jerked her head up. Lord Robert stood in the doorway.
Dressed in a dark brown cutaway jacket and buff-colored
breeches, he looked every inch the English gentleman. And
much too handsome by half.
    "Good morning," she echoed, slipping her missive into the
pocket of her black bombazine gown.
    He approached her slowly, stopping when he stood directly
across the table from her. Cupping his chin in his hand, he
made a great show of looking her over, inclining his head left,
then right, like an art critic studying a sculpture.
    "Hmmm. Just as I suspected. You're looking V.M.I." At her
questioning look, he shot her a jaunty grin. "Very Much Improved. How do you feel?"
    "As you say, V.M.I. Head, hands, feet—they barely hurt at
all. And you?"
    "Vastly better than when I saw you last. Amazing what
wonders a few hours' sleep, a substantial breakfast, and a chat
with the magistrate will wrought."
    "What did he say?"
    "He found the case most puzzling." Moving to the side-

board, he helped himself to a plate of ham and eggs, then sat opposite her at the long mahogany table. "While he assured me he'd do his utmost to locate the man responsible, he also warned me that it is unlikely the perpetrator will ever be found. Unless, of course, he was to strike again." He fixed her with a serious dark blue stare. "Which he won't do at *this* town house since there will be no one to abduct as there will be no one wandering about in the gardens. Correct?"

She inclined her head in acquiescence.

"Excellent. Now, regarding your plans for today . . . I've arranged for a carriage to be at your disposal. I am also at your disposal, available to squire you around town, or escort you to the shops, assist you with any errands . . . whatever you'd like."

Her fingers brushed the edge of Mr. Fitzmoreland's letter. "Actually, there is something you might be able to help me with. Do you know the earl of Shelbourne?"

His brows lifted in obvious surprise. After what seemed to be a prolonged silence, he said, "I am acquainted with him, yes."

Questions clearly lurked in his eyes, but he said nothing further, just watched her in a way that left her wondering if he and the earl were on bad terms. When it became obvious he wasn't going to elaborate, she pushed on, "Do you know where he lives?"

His egg-laden fork froze halfway to his mouth. A wary expression, filled with something else she couldn't define, came over his face. "His family seat is in Cornwall."

"I see. Is that far from here?"

"Very. At least a week's traveling time."

Robert watched her expression turn crestfallen, and a dozen questions buzzed through his mind. Why on earth would she inquire about Geoffrey Hadmore? How had she even heard of him? Clearing his throat, he added, "He also keeps a residence here in town."

Unmistakable hope leapt into her eyes. "Do you think it possible he is in London?"

"I think it most likely. He detests the country. Why do you ask about him?"

She leaned forward and a tantalizing whiff of her flowery scent drifted across to him. While she did not smile, there was no denying this was the most animated he'd seen her features, a fact that both confused and, irrationally, annoyed him. Her eyes were all but sparkling. Bloody hell, why was she so . . . whatever she was, at the prospect that Shelbourne was in town?

"I wish to meet him. As soon as possible. Could you arrange the introduction?"

He leaned back, studying her. An introduction? To one of the worst rogues in London? Good God, Elizabeth would have his head. Not to mention the tight feeling that cramped his stomach at the thought of the very eligible earl meeting the lovely widow. True, he didn't know Shelbourne very well, but the man's reputation with women was well known. He charmed them, bedded them, then discarded them frequently, with a cold dispassion that Robert neither liked nor understood. There was no doubt in his mind that the beautiful Mrs. Brown would capture Shelbourne's interest. *As she's captured yours.*

His teeth clenched at his inner voice's unwanted opinion, and he refocused his attention to the matter at hand. What possible reason could she have for wanting to meet such a libertine? He suddenly stilled. Was there a chance she was already aware of Shelbourne's reputation? Could she possibly be contemplating a *liaison* with the man?

His hands fisted at the mere thought. Instead of answering her question, he posed one of his own. "I wasn't aware you knew anyone in England save Elizabeth. How did you come to hear about Shelbourne?"

"He . . . he knew my husband."

Some of the tension drained from his shoulders, and he mentally chastised himself for his unwarranted suspicions. She simply wished to become acquainted with a friend of her husband's. Perfectly understandable. And as long as he accompanied her, Shelbourne would behave. "In that case, I shall send round a note to his town house requesting an audience. If he is in town, I'll escort you."

A curtain seemed to fall over her expression. "Thank you. I appreciate you sending the note, however, I do not require an escort."

Something that felt suspiciously like jealousy, but couldn't possibly be, rippled through him, a feeling made all the more pronounced by the crimson blush staining her cheeks. Perhaps his suspicions weren't unfounded after all. Forcing a smile, he said, "I'm afraid I must insist. English protocol and all that, you know."

A frown creased her brow, and she worried her lower lip between her teeth, clearly torn between not wanting his company and not wishing to flout propriety. And if he weren't so distracted by the sight of her nibbling on her full lip, he'd no doubt be colossally annoyed at her not wanting him around.

Finally, she nodded stiffly. "Very well. You may accompany me."

In spite of his annoyance, he couldn't help but be a tiny bit amused at her disgruntled tone. "Why, thank you."

She rose. "I shall leave you to attend to your correspondence to the earl."

"Again I thank you. However, I hardly ever write letters in the breakfast room. Nothing worse than eggs on the vellum. As soon as I finish my meal, I'll compose a note."

Her blush deepened. "Forgive me. I'm merely anxious to . . ."

Her words drifted off, and he found himself very much wanting her to finish the sentence. *Yes, Mrs. Brown . . . what exactly are you anxious to do?*

But instead of satisfying his ever-growing curiosity, she inclined her head. "As I have my own correspondence to see to, I shall bid you good day, sir."

She swiftly departed the room before he had a chance to reply. Clearly she considered him dismissed—at least until such time as he received a response from Shelbourne. And if not for the events of last evening, he might have left her to her own devices. Indeed, he had planned to visit his solicitor today.

But last night had changed his plans. He could visit his solicitor another day. Until he delivered her safely to Bradford Hall, he intended to keep a very close eye on her.

Her lovely face rose in his mind's eye and he stifled a groan. He'd claimed when he'd arrived that a few hours' sleep had wrought wonders, but his sleep had been anything but refreshing.

Indeed, the moment he'd climbed into his bed his thoughts had been filled with her. The feel of her soft body pressed against him. Her scent curling around him. Her eyes, wide with a combination of fear and strength, that filled him with both concern and admiration. And something else. Something warm that spread through him like honey. And something heated that fired his blood and left him restless and frustrated and aching. He'd lain in his bed unable to erase her from his mind. And when he'd finally drifted off, she'd invaded his dreams. She'd shed her black clothing and beckoned him. He'd reached for her, filled with hunger, but before he could touch her, she'd vanished, like a wisp of smoke. He'd awakened feeling empty and bereft. And aroused as hell.

No, keeping an eye on her wouldn't pose a problem.

Unfortunately, he suspected that keeping his hands off her would.

Geoffrey Hadmore paced the length of his private study. Afternoon sunlight cut a bright path across the Persian carpet, faint dust motes danced in the swatch. Pausing at the fireplace, he glared at the mantel clock. Half past one. Exactly three minutes later than when he had last glared at the damn instrument.

Where the hell was Redfern? Why had he not heard from the bastard? There could only be one reason: He had failed. Again.

Or perhaps Redfern has it in his mind to cross me somehow? A combination of unease and fury tightened his hands into fists. Surely Redfern wouldn't be stupid enough to attempt such a thing. Geoffrey forced his hands to relax, then flexed his stiff fingers. No, Redfern might not be a scholar, but he was no fool. He knew better than to cross him. Yet if he *were* foolish enough . . . well, then, it would be the last foolish thing Redfern ever did.

Bending down, he gently petted Thorndyke's silky, fire-warmed brown fur. The dozing mastiff lifted its massive head. "Ah, Thorndyke, if only Redfern were as trustworthy as you, I'd not be in this mess."

Thorndyke made a sympathetic noise deep in his throat. Geoffrey patted his smooth head one last time, then rose to once again pace the room. This time he halted at his desk. Grabbing a piece of vellum, he composed a quick note. Not bothering to summon Willis with the bellcord, he strode into the foyer and handed the note to the butler.

"I want this delivered. Immediately." He rattled off Redfern's direction. "If he's there, wait for a reply. If not, leave it."

"Yes, my lord."

"I'll be at my club. Bring any correspondence from him there as soon as you have it."

Redfern held the wax-sealed letter in his hand. He knew who it was from. He didn't even need to read the bloody thing to know what it contained. He hadn't answered the persistent knocking on his door, not retrieving the note until the man had finally left.

But now the hour of reckoning were at hand. And he'd failed. Failed to find the ring, failed to get rid of Mrs. Brown. How had his plan gone so awry? Oh, things had started off swimmingly, with Mrs. Brown even presenting herself in the garden, like a gift, saving him the trouble of snatching her from the house. Even coshing the bloke in the alley hadn't proved much of a problem.

Yes, with the two of them well out of the way and tied up nice and pretty, he'd nipped back to the town house. Only had to find the ring. Then he could finish off Mrs. Brown. Would have to get rid of the bloke as well. The earl surely wouldn't want any witnesses flappin' their gums. Maybe he'd even ask the earl for a bonus, seein' as how he had to kill two people instead of one. Yes, things were lookin' rosy indeed.

But after searching for over an hour, he hadn't found the ring. Panic edged down his spine. If he didn't find that ring, he wouldn't get his blunt. But he'd looked everywhere. Had even put everything back in its place so no one would suspect anything. He'd just have to tell the earl there just weren't no ring—a prospect that cramped his belly.

The earl's final words had echoed in his mind. *Find that ring. And if you do, I want her gone.* Well, what the bloody blue blazes were he supposed to do with Mrs. Brown if he *didn't* find the ring? Kill her? Let her go?

He'd think about it on his way back to the warehouse. Surely by the time he arrived he'd know what to do.

Yet when he'd returned, all that were left of Mrs. Brown and the bloke had been a pile of cut ropes. Bastard must have had a blade on him. Bloody rotten bit o' bad luck that was. Never in his entire career had circumstances thwarted him so. But the earl wouldn't be interested in hearin' about no unforeseen circumstances.

Now, with a trembling hand, he broke the seal and read the terse message. Sweat broke out on his brow. There were no mistaking the earl's meaning.

He had to find that ring. Today.

If he didn't, he were a dead man.

And Lester Redfern had no intention of dying.

Allie exited her bedchamber clutching the letter she'd just sealed. Walking quickly down the curving staircase, she entered the foyer. She'd expected to see Carters, but instead a young footman stood near the door.

"I'd like to have a letter delivered," she said. "To the earl of Shelbourne's London residence."

"Of course, ma'am." He held out his gloved hand. "I'll see to it at once."

Allie handed over the missive with a prayer that the earl was indeed in town. Hopefully Lord Robert had already sent off his note. He should have . . . she'd left him in the breakfast room over two hours ago. Surely enough time for him to go home and compose a short letter.

"Was there something else, Mrs. Brown?" the young man asked.

"No, nothing. Thank you." She looked both ways down the corridors fanning out from the foyer. How best to spend her time while she awaited a reply? She needed a diversion, something to keep her mind occupied. Otherwise she'd simply resort to pacing.

"If you're looking for Lord Robert," the footman said, "he's in the billiards room."

"Lord Robert is *here*?"

"Yes, ma'am. In the billiards room." He pointed down the left corridor. "Second doorway on the right. If there's nothing further, I'll see to your letter."

"Thank you," she murmured.

She looked down the left corridor. He was here. In the second room. She should avoid him and his disturbing presence. His laughing eyes that held secrets. Yes, she should return to her bedchamber and read. Take a nap. Something. Anything. Her mind knew it, as did her heart.

Her feet, however, knew nothing of the sort and promptly headed down the left corridor.

The second door was ajar. Pushing it open a bit more, she stood frozen in the threshold and simply stared. Lord Robert stood with his back to her, clearly studying the billiards table, a long tapered, highly polished stick in one hand. He wore the same buff breeches as earlier, but he'd discarded his jacket. A snowy-white shirt stretched across his broad shoulders. Her gaze wandered slowly downward, taking in his trim waist and the snug fit of his breeches. Her gaze settled on his backside and she swallowed. No matter what else she might think of

him, there was no denying that Lord Robert was very . . .
finely put together.

An involuntary sigh of pure feminine appreciation sneaked
past her lips—a sigh he apparently heard, for he turned
around. And instead of staring at his buttocks, she suddenly
found herself staring at his . . .

Oh my. He was indeed very nicely made. She'd suspected
so after their close touching last evening, but now there was no
doubt.

"Good afternoon, Mrs. Brown."

His huskily voiced words yanked her from her stupor, and
her gaze snapped up to meet his. Dark blue eyes assessed her
with a questioning, yet somehow knowing look. Heat rushed
into her face, and she barely resisted the urge to clap her palms
to her flaming cheeks. Perhaps if she prayed hard enough, the
parquet flooring would yawn open and swallow her. Dear God,
he'd caught her staring. And not simply staring, but staring at
that.

Determined to regain her composure, she lifted her chin
and raised her brows. "Good afternoon, Lord Robert. I didn't
know you'd returned."

"Returned? I never departed."

"I thought you'd left. To write the letter you promised."

"I wrote it and sent it off ages ago. Borrowed a sheet of
Austin's stationery. I trust you completed your own correspondence?"

"Yes."

"In that case, perhaps you'd care to ride through the park?
The weather is exceptionally fine."

The thought of sharing a carriage with him, sitting close
enough to breathe in his masculine scent, near enough to study
his teasing eyes, and watch his lips curve upward with that
devastating, devilish grin, was terrifyingly tempting. And
therefore absolutely out of the question.

"No, thank you," she said. "But please don't let me stop
you from enjoying the afternoon." She inwardly cringed at her
stiff tone. She hadn't meant to sound so abrupt.

But instead of taking offense, he laughed. "Ah, but I am enjoying myself, honing my game." He nodded toward the baize-covered table. "Do you play?"

"I'm afraid not."

"Would you like to learn?"

An automatic "no" rose to her lips, but she hesitated. She desperately needed some diversion, and she was very fond of games. Her gaze drifted over the table. It was easily twelve feet long and six feet across. Certainly big enough to maintain a safe distance from him . . . much more distance than a carriage could provide.

"Why, yes, I believe that would be lovely." *And safe.*

"Excellent. It's a very simple game. Only three balls—one red and two white—and a few rules. All the rest is practice, skill, and a bit of luck." Striding across the room, he lifted another tapered stick from a holder on the wall, then returned to her.

"This is a cue," he said, handing her the stick. "The object of the game is to be the first to score the number of points we agree upon."

"How does one score points?"

"Several ways." He went on to describe the game, explaining unfamiliar terms such as "potting," "cannons," and "in off." Leaning over the table, he demonstrated as he spoke, educating her regarding cushions, pockets, the balk line, and the "D."

"Any questions so far?" he asked when he finished.

"Not yet, but I'm certain I'll have dozens once we begin." In truth, the game sounded quite simple.

"Then let's start you off with some practice shots. The proper way to hold the cue is like this. . . ." He demonstrated, and she mimicked him. "Good," he praised. "Now line up your shot, slide the cue stick back, then bring it forward, nice and smoothly." His actions mirrored his words. The tip of his stick hit the cue ball, knocking it into the red ball, which rolled across the baize surface and fell into the corner pocket. "That shot would earn me three points for potting the red ball." He retrieved the ball from the pocket and placed it back on the table. "Now you try."

Holding the stick as he had, she leaned over the table. Taking careful aim, she slid the cue stick toward the cue ball. And missed it completely.

Humph. She tried again. This time she firmly struck the ball. It shot up and forward, sailing off the table, and landed on the carpet with a dull thud.

"Oh, dear," she said, dismayed. "This is more difficult than it looks. I'm sorry. As much as I enjoy games, I fear I do not excel at them." A memory suddenly assailed her, tightening her grip on the cue stick. She and David, sitting in their parlor near the fireplace. He'd tried to teach her to play chess, but quickly lost patience with her when she moved her pieces incorrectly. Shaking his head, he'd heaved a long sigh. "Obviously the game is beyond you, Allie."

She shook off the remnants of the past and looked at Lord Robert. Not the tiniest hint of impatience glimmered in his eyes. In fact, he appeared wholly amused.

"Quite good for a first attempt," he said with an approving nod. "Much better than mine. I broke a window my first game. To this day Austin is fond of telling anyone who will listen about my 'shatteringly' poor performance. And I tell anyone who will listen that my performance was merely a reflection of my teacher's dubious talents." He retrieved the ball and set it back on the table. Then he walked around the table to stand behind her. "Try it again. I'll help you." Reaching around her, he placed his hands over hers on the cue stick. "You just need to get the feel of it . . . like this."

And suddenly she did get the feel of it . . . of his warm, hard body pressing against her back from shoulder to thigh. Of his large, callused hands covering hers.

"You're gripping the stick too tightly. Just relax."

If her lungs hadn't ceased functioning, she would have huffed out an incredulous breath. Relax? How could she possibly hope to do so while his body surrounded her like a heated blanket, cloaking her in an onslaught of sensation?

"Ease up your grip, and move your arm smoothly. Like this." His breath ruffled the hair at her temple, rippling tingles down her spine. With his hand covering hers, he moved her arm slowly forward and back, demonstrating the motion. But all she could concentrate on was the feel of his muscles bunching against her arm and back. The sensation of his skin touching hers. He'd rolled back his shirtsleeves, and her gaze riveted on his strong, sinewy forearms, dusted with dark hair. A brush fire of heat rushed through her, overwhelming her with its intensity.

Step away . . . get away from him! Her inner voice all but screamed at her. But it had been so long since anyone . . . a man . . . had touched her. Held her. She simply couldn't deny herself the pleasure. Her eyes drifted closed, and for one insane instant she allowed herself to absorb the feel of him. *Just one more second . . . he's behind me . . . can't see me . . . he won't know. . . .*

Robert raised his gaze, intending to adjust his stance to offer further instructions, when his eye was caught by a movement across the room. There, reflected in the small mirror hanging on the opposite wall, he saw her. Standing in the circle of his arms, her eyes closed, her face flushed, her full lips slightly parted. She looked beautiful. Sensual. And aroused.

Everything inside him stilled. Heart, pulse, breath. A delicate shudder ran through her, a feather-soft vibration against his chest that reverberated through him.

Her silky hair tickled his jaw, and he had only to turn his head to touch his lips to her temple, yet he didn't dare move. Couldn't move. He was spellbound, riveted by the sight of her, of them, together. He drew in a slow, shaky breath and his head filled with her delicate floral fragrance.

Desire hit him low and hard. His jaw clenched, and he tried to will away the heat coursing through him, but there was no stopping it. Damn it, he shouldn't be feeling this toward her. He barely knew her. She lived an ocean away. She remained in mourning. . . . Her heart belonged to another man.

Another man? Perhaps. Yet as he watched the color rising

in her cheeks, felt the quickening of her breath, there was no denying that her body responded to *him*. He'd seen it earlier, when he'd turned around and caught her staring at him, but he'd convinced himself that that was an aberration. But this . . . this heat they clearly both felt, was very real. Frighteningly so. And if he didn't move away from her, she would be left in no doubt exactly how much heat she inspired in him.

With an effort that cost him, he released her. Stepping back two paces, he watched her in the mirror. Her eyes opened slowly, then she blinked several times. She swayed slightly, and he fisted his hands at his sides to keep from reaching for her. Her tongue peeked out and moistened her lips, and it was all he could do to swallow his groan of longing.

In that instant, however, she clearly recalled herself. Her eyes widened, and crimson flooded her cheeks. Her back went ramrod stiff, and her knuckles turned white around the cue stick. There was no mistaking her distress, and guilt slapped him, branding him a cad. *You have no business touching her. Smelling her skin. Desiring her.*

Hoping to put her at ease and dispel the tension thickening the air, he said, "I think you've got it now." Damn it, his voice sounded like he'd swallowed a mouthful of gravel. Clearing his throat, he moved to the end of the table, putting more distance between them. "Try it again."

She stared at the table. What was she thinking? Was she angry with him? Should he apologize? He hadn't meant to touch her—

Liar. His inner voice sliced off the falsehood before his mind could even finish the thought, and shame filled him. Indeed, he rarely indulged in the useless exercise of lying to himself, and there was no point in doing so now. He'd wanted to touch her. Desperately. And billiards had offered him a seemingly innocent excuse to do so. But God help him, the lust she inspired was the furthest thing from innocent he'd ever experienced.

Well, he'd simply have to stop touching her. Yes, that should be simple enough. No more touching. He drew in a much-needed deep breath, and her scent wafted into his head. Hmmm. Breathing around her was not a good idea. Unfortunately, that would be harder to avoid. His gaze skimmed over her and his jaw tightened. She was bent over the table, her full lips pursed with concentration. Desire skidded through him and he looked away. No more looking, either.

Yes, that was his plan. No more touching, no more breathing, no more looking. Or at least, no more breathing than absolutely necessary.

Cheered by his ingenious plan, he forced himself to focus on the game and his role as teacher. Keeping his distance and his gaze firmly trained on the table, he offered pointers and advice. Within an hour, she'd improved immensely and he suggested they begin a game.

"It's the best way to develop your skills," he assured her.

She agreed, and they began. Thirty minutes later, after he'd made an exceptionally tricky shot, she remarked in a dry voice, "I believe someone spends entirely too much time playing this game."

For the first time since enforcing his ingenious plan, he looked directly at her. It proved a mistake. Her full lips were pursed in a way that immediately generated thoughts of kissing, and a gleam of wry humor sparkled in her golden-brown eyes. His heart thumped, then galloped. And now that he'd looked at her, he couldn't look away.

Slowly straightening from his position leaning over the table, he raised his brows and arranged his features into an exaggerated, haughty expression. "Too much time?" He affected a sniff. "Sounds like the sort of comment a player who was lagging in the score would mutter."

"Hmmm. Exactly how much behind am I?"

"You've scored a total of twelve points. Very impressive for a beginner."

"And your score?"

"Three hundred and forty-two."

She nodded her head solemnly. "I haven't a prayer of winning, do I?"

"Not this game, I'm afraid. But you show great promise."

"I'm abysmal."

"Merely inexperienced."

"Awkward."

"Unpracticed," he corrected.

An expression he couldn't decipher came into her eyes. She studied him for several seconds, then said, "You're remarkably patient."

And you're remarkably lovely. He shoved the unbidden thought away and offered her a lopsided grin. "I'm certain you don't mean to sound so surprised."

A delicate blush colored her cheeks and she averted her gaze. "Forgive me. It's just that . . ."

He waited for her to continue, but she merely shook her head. Setting her cue stick on the table, she made him a bow. "In light of the news that I trail you by three hundred and twenty points—"

"Three hundred and thirty, actually."

"—and that my chance of winning is slim—"

"Nonexistent."

"—I suggest we call this game a draw."

"Very generous of you, I'm sure."

She shot him an arch look. "Although my performance to-day indicates otherwise, I am not completely inept. Observe." Reaching out, she scooped up the three billiards balls and tossed them into the air. The trio of spheres rotated around as she juggled them with deftness and skill.

"Very impressive," he said. "Who taught you that?"

"My father. It is a skill that proved quite useful for enter-taining and distracting my rambunctious siblings. I remember one afternoon when Joshua was four," she said as she tossed the balls ever faster, "he'd fallen down that morning and scraped his elbows and knees. Poor darling, he was so miser-able and sore. To divert his attention, I brought him outside. We walked to the chicken coop, where I decided to entertain him by juggling . . . with the nearest available objects, which happened to be eggs."

An odd feeling invaded his chest at the incongruous but utterly charming picture she made—a grown woman garbed in mourning, her face flushed with unmistakable pleasure, juggling billiards balls. "Was your brother entertained?"

"Oh, my, yes. Especially when I missed."

"The egg fell on the ground?"

"No. It fell on my face. The second hit my shoulder, and the third landed on top of my head."

Laughter rumbled in his throat. "You must have looked quite the sight."

"Indeed. Joshua, of course, nearly split his sides laughing. And his hilarity only increased when the egg began to dry. Do you have any idea how uncomfortable it is to have hardened egg on your face?"

"I'm afraid not. While I've frequently suffered from having egg on my face, it's been strictly of the figurative, as opposed to the literal, nature."

"Well, it's horribly uncomfortable," she informed him. "I'd strongly advise against it."

"And this egg-on-the-face miss you made . . . was it deliberate?"

He fancied she shrugged. "It was a small price to pay to see him smile. And now, to end the show . . ." She tossed the balls high in the air, spun around in a quick circle, then expertly caught them.

"Bravo," he said, clapping. "Very well done."

"Thank you, kind sir. That is exactly what Joshua said . . . once he ceased laughing." A faraway look entered her eyes. "I remember that afternoon so vividly. It was lovely. A very happy day. . . ."

Her voice trailed off, and she was clearly lost in her memories. Robert watched her, imagining her as a young girl, irrepressible and full of fun, mischief, and laughter, letting eggs fall upon her to entertain an injured boy. *That* was the woman in the sketch Elizabeth had drawn of her. Where had that woman gone? Was she so far lost as to be beyond recall?

His question was answered at that exact instant when she looked at him.

And smiled.

A beautiful, full smile that bloomed on her face like an unfurling flower. It was like the sun appearing from behind a dark cloud. It embraced her entire face, etching a pair of tiny dimples near the corners of her mouth, lighting her eyes, and casting her features with pure pleasure and a hint of deviltry. It was, without question, the most winsome, enchanting smile he'd ever seen.

The impact was like a punch to his heart. Yet before he could gather himself, she dealt him another reeling blow. She laughed. A delighted, mischievous, full-bodied laugh that surely would have beckoned him to join in if she hadn't already struck him senseless.

"Oh, you should have seen Mama's face when she saw me," she said, shaking her head. "It was priceless."

He managed to find his voice. "She was shocked?"

"Shocked?" An enchanting sound that could only be described as a giggle escaped her. "Heavens no! With four boisterous children, nothing shocked Mama. She didn't even turn a hair. But when I entered the house, Mrs. Yardly, the nosiest, most disagreeable woman in the village, was visiting." She screwed her face into a comical pucker, stuck her nose in the air, and mimicked in a high-pitched tone, " 'What unladylike *mess* has your *hoyden* daughter gotten herself into *now*?' "

Her features relaxed and she continued in her normal voice, "I wanted to crawl under the braided rug, but Mama, bless her, simply looked at Mrs. Yardly as if she'd grown another head. 'Why, Harriet,' Mama said, 'I'm stunned that *you* do not know that dried egg on one's hair and face is the secret to shinier curls and smoother skin. You'd best start using it, immediately, every day. Unless, of course, you *want* more lines on your face.' "

She covered her lips with her fingertips, but there was no containing her merriment. "Mama could be quite wicked, I'm afraid."

His lips curved upward in a grin, and although he knew he appeared perfectly relaxed on the outside, a maelstrom of feelings swirled inside him—all of them warm and aching. Unsettling. And unexpected in their intensity.

"Actually, she sounds delightful," he said. "And very much like my own mother, who can somehow convey more with the simple lift of her brows than most people can with an hour of oratory. Fabulous talent, but quite frightening." He looked heavenward and affected an angelic expression. "I, of course, being a perfect child, rarely was the victim of Duchess Lifts-the-Brows." He made a *tsk*ing noise. "Sadly, I fear my brothers did not fare as well."

She shot him a clearly dubious look, laughter still dancing in her eyes. "I believe you are telling me what Lady Gaddlestone would refer to as a Banbury tale."

"*I?* Never. What makes you suspect such a thing?"

"Several anecdotes Elizabeth shared with me in her letters."

He waved a dismissive hand. "Can't believe a word she says, as she obviously hears these tales from Austin, who of course would repeat them in a wholly fictitious manner in order to show himself in the best light."

"I see. So you didn't try to scare off Caroline's governess by rigging a bucket of water and barrel of flour over her bedchamber door?"

"Well, yes, but—"

"And you didn't dare your brothers to shuck their clothing and swim in the lake?"

"*Dare* is a rather strong word—"

"Banbury tale," she decreed. "I suspect your poor mother has a permanent wrinkle etched on her forehead from all the brow-raising you induced."

"To match the one you gave your mother, I'm sure."

They simply stood there, smiling at each other for the space of several heartbeats, and Robert could almost feel something pass between them. A sense of kinship and understanding, yet something more . . . an intimate awareness that sent a fissure of heat through him.

"I'll acknowledge that Lady Gaddlestone's saying is apt," he said. "As were other words I recall her saying."

"Indeed? What were those?"

"She said you need laughter. And that you're far too serious by half." He walked slowly toward her, drawn like a moth to flame, stopping when only two feet separated them. All vestiges of amusement faded from her eyes, replaced by the guarded, wary expression normally there. The urge to reach out and glide his fingers over her silky cheek nearly overwhelmed him, as did the desire to see her laugh again.

The happy, smiling woman she once was clearly still dwelled within her. A mere glimpse of her had utterly captivated him. And by damn, he wanted to see her again.

But it was obvious from her expression that she'd once again retreated behind the walls she'd erected around herself. His heart protested, swelling in sympathy for her.

"I know all too well what it is like to have your laughter stolen, and a heavy weight upon your heart," he said softly, unable to stop the words.

Something that looked like anger flashed in her eyes, but it disappeared before he could be certain. "You don't understand—"

"I do." Reaching out, he gently squeezed her hand. Nate's death would haunt him for the rest of his life. The only difference between his sorrow and hers was that she wore her sadness and loneliness on her sleeve—literally with her mourning clothes—whereas he'd learned to hide his inner sadness from the world.

Damn it, she was young. And lovely. And had suffered the same sort of deep, personal loss as he. She deserved some fun. And by damn, he was going to provide it.

He pulled her toward the door. "Come. It's far too lovely a day to remain indoors. Let us ride through the park. There's something I want to show you. . . . Something you'd enjoy."

She hesitated and he tugged gently on her hand. "Please. It

is one of my nieces' and nephew's favorite things to do when they're in town. One of Elizabeth's as well. She'd never forgive me if I neglected to show you."

"What is it?"

"That would spoil the surprise." He smiled at her. "Trust me."

The expression that passed over her face made him wonder if he'd mistakenly suggested they chop the furniture to pieces with an axe. Her features cleared, but then she studied him for so long he was prompted to tease, "I promise not to try to extract national secrets from you, Mrs. Brown. I've suggested a ride in the park, not high treason."

A blush stained her cheeks. "Of course. I'm sorry. It's just that for a moment, you very much reminded me of . . . my husband."

She'd said as much to him once before. Compassion for her filled him, along with pride at the compliment she'd bestowed. To be compared to a man she clearly adored was an honor, and one that filled him with warmth, and something else he couldn't name.

"Thank you. And now, let us be off."

Geoffrey Hadmore sat in the plush leather wing chair at White's, nursing his third brandy. His reflection in the mirror across the richly paneled room indicated an outward calm he was far from feeling. Pain thumped behind his eyes and rage seethed just beneath the surface, churning in his gut. *Where the hell are you, Redfern?*

He rolled the crystal snifter between his palms, staring into the brandy's gently undulating amber depths. A plan took shape in his mind, and he slowly nodded to himself. Yes, if he didn't hear from the bastard by the end of the day, he'd simply take matters into his own hands.

Lester Redfern watched Mrs. Brown and a gentleman settle themselves in a fancy black lacquer carriage led by a handsome set of matched grays. They entered the park, then disappeared from his view. About bloody time she'd gone out.

He patted his jacket. Pistol and knife were in place. His mouth flattened with grim determination. Pulling his hat low over his brow, he made his way toward the town house.

Chapter 7

Allie sat on a curved stone bench in Hyde Park under the shade of a massive willow and drew in a deep breath that did little to calm her.

She should not have come here.

Oh, yes, the weather was indeed lovely. A warm, summer breeze ruffled her hair, and ribbons of late afternoon sunshine filtered down through the leaves, casting striped shadows upon the ground. In the distance she could see handsome horses and carriages moving slowly around the park, and fashionably attired ladies and gentlemen strolling along the cobbled paths.

Less than thirty feet away stood the elegant black carriage that had brought them here. The coachman tended to the gray mares, offering them each a carrot he pulled from his pocket. While she couldn't deny she'd enjoyed the ride, the fresh air, and the sunshine, neither could she deny that Lord Robert's presence unsettled her in a way that was becoming more and more disturbing. Despite her best efforts to stop it, he was awakening feelings in her she'd thought she'd buried long ago. Spending more time in his increasingly pleasurable company was a very poor idea. Yet she'd been unable to resist his invitation for a ride in the park.

Holding up her gloved hand to shield her eyes from a swatch of sunlight, she observed a footman near the carriage hand Lord Robert what appeared to be a pouch. Lord Robert then walked toward her, pouch in hand, crooked grin curving his lips.

She tried to force her gaze away, but could not. He moved with lithe grace, his long, powerful boot-clad legs eating up the distance between them. An involuntary hum of pure feminine appreciation tickled her throat. Heavens above, he was truly heartstoppingly attractive. Dozens of female hearts no doubt littered his doorstep. His tailored clothing fit him to perfection, accentuating his muscular thighs and the broad expanse of his shoulders . . . shoulders that she vividly recalled the warmth and strength of.

Her fingers clenched in her lap, and she firmly pushed the disturbing image away. She hated that she was so intensely *aware* of him. What character flaw, what weakness of spirit did she possess that wouldn't allow her to strike the man from her mind? The mere thought of him made her skin tingle. And he had a way of looking at her that rendered her flustered and confused. And aching. The way he laughed one minute, then regarded her with the most serious of expressions the next, utterly confounded her. *The problem is that he is just like David.*

The thought stilled her. *Was* that the problem? Or was it perhaps the even more disconcerting possibility that he *wasn't* exactly like David. Certainly, in many ways he was—his easy charm, the secrets flickering in his eyes—yet in other ways he was nothing like her husband. He appeared not to possess David's impatience. And while Lord Robert was solicitous of her, he somehow did not make her feel like a useless, fragile piece of china as David often had. And his willingness to laugh at his own expense, well, that was something David never would have done. Yes, if he were just like David, she could guard herself against him. But it was these differences she sensed—

The realization of what she was doing slammed into her and she froze. Dear God, she was finding excuses to . . . *like* him. Rationalizing this impossible, unwanted attraction toward him. Convincing herself it was acceptable.

This had to stop. Immediately. She'd allowed one charming, attractive man to sweep her off her feet and he'd nearly destroyed her. She would never allow herself to fall victim to another such man or those feelings again.

"Are you ready?" Lord Robert's voice dragged her from her thoughts. He stood before her, a broad smile on his face. "This is a favorite activity of my nieces and nephew. Watch."

He set the pouch down on the bench beside her, then reached inside, pulling out two large handfuls of what appeared to be bread crumbs. He then spread his arms straight out and opened his hands, palms upward.

"Whatever are you doing?" she asked, curious in spite of herself. "You look like a scarecrow."

"Just watch. You'll see."

A trio of pigeons fluttered down. One landed on Lord Robert's outstretched right arm, the other two on his left, then proceeded to feast upon the bread crumbs in his palms.

Before she could stop it, a giggle bubbled up in her throat. "Now you *truly* resemble a scarecrow . . . a decidedly unsuccessful one."

He grinned. "I'm about to become even more unsuccessful."

Several more birds joined the fun, and in less than a minute, the very finely garbed Lord Robert Jamison had cooing pigeons resting all along his arms and shoulders. Just when she thought another bird couldn't possibly fit on him, a particularly plump, gray-breasted pigeon fluttered in. And perched itself on Lord Robert's very elegant black hat.

"Oh, my!" A burst of uncontainable merriment erupted from her, and she pressed her hands to her cheeks. "I believe the one on your hat is settling in for an extended stay."

"No doubt. Care to try it?"

She pursed her lips. "Thank you, but I'm not particularly

fond of the taste of bread crumbs, and in truth, I don't believe you have any more room on your arm, or your hat, for me."

He chuckled and several pigeons ruffled their feathers. "They're very gentle. Take a handful of bread crumbs and join us."

It instantly occurred to her that David never, ever, would have suggested such a thing. And his disapproval would have prevented her from doing so. *David is gone. I can do as I please.*

With an almost defiant air, she rose, reached into the pouch, and grabbed two handfuls of bread crumbs. She then spread her arms as Lord Robert had done.

"Prepare yourself," he said with a chuckle. "Here they come."

A fat pigeon landed on her right arm and delicately pecked crumbs from her gloved hand. "Oh!" Before she could recover from her surprise, two more landed on her other black sleeve. The overwhelming urge to giggle seized her, yet she tried her utmost to contain it, not wanting to startle the birds. But the endeavor proved hopeless, and a fit of laughter seized her. Gray feathers ruffled a bit, then quickly settled back in place, the birds clearly not overly concerned about a chuckling perch.

"I wish Elizabeth was here," she said. "I would love for her to capture this moment in her sketchbook. You look so funny with that pigeon on your hat!"

"You're looking rather comical yourself. Brace yourself. One is heading for your bonnet."

"Oh, my . . ." She felt the weight settle on top of her head, and merriment simply consumed her. Bit by bit, the mantle of her concerns slipped from her shoulders, falling into a heap at her feet. She laughed until her sides ached and tears streamed down her cheeks. Dear God, how long had it been since she'd laughed like this? Enjoyed herself so thoroughly? Years . . . although it seemed like decades.

"A suitable sobriquet for you suddenly occurs to me," he

said, blowing a pigeon tail feather from his chin. "I dub you Madam BOB, short for Bird-on-Bonnet."

"Very well, Sir FOF."

"I beg your pardon?"

"Feathers-on-Face. There's a small one clinging to your cheek, and a particularly lovely one attached to your earlobe."

The laughter continued for several more minutes, then, when the supply of bread crumbs was eaten, the pigeons departed one by one. Except for the one on Lord Robert's hat.

"I think she likes you," Allie said with a laugh, as she brushed off her sleeves and resettled her bonnet.

"Either that or she's made a nest. I hope not, as this is my favorite hat." He made gentle shooing motions, but the pigeon remained. "It appears we have an extra passenger for the time being. Do you mind?"

She pressed her lips together to contain her amusement at the picture he made with that pigeon perched on his hat, but wasn't the least successful. "Not at all."

"Excellent." He extended his elbow with regal solemnity, and with equal pomp, she accepted. "I suggest we make our way to Regent Street," he said as they stepped onto the tree-lined, cobbled path leading back to the carriage. "No visit to London is complete without sampling the shops."

She hesitated, overcome with a sense of wistful nostalgia. At one time she'd have accepted the invitation with alacrity. She'd adored perusing the shops, choosing lovely gowns and frivolous hats. But now, with no excess funds to spend, the prospect was nothing short of depressing. He glanced down at her, and she instantly wondered what he'd discerned in her expression, for a look that could only be described as chagrin passed over his face. Before either could speak, however, a familiar voice hailed them.

"Alberta! Lord Robert!"

They turned in unison and were greeted by the sight of Lady Gaddlestone bearing down upon them, with Tedmund, Edward, and Frederick straining at their leads. A harried-looking footman trotted behind the baroness, his arms laden with a trio of colorful fabric-covered pillows that clearly belonged to the Maltese brood.

"Guard your ankles and skirt," Lord Robert warned in an undertone. "Here comes Sir Piss-a-lot, Sir Bite-a-bit, and Sir Hump-a-leg."

Laughter gurgled in her throat, and she coughed to cover it. Good Lord, the man was outrageous!

"What a delightful surprise," the baroness exclaimed as she and the boys drew near. She pulled back on the leather leads, but the dogs forged ahead, poufy tails wagging, heading straight for Allie and Lord Robert while emitting sharp *yips* of unrestrained glee. "Tedmund! Edward! Frederick! Cease at once!"

The pigeon nesting on Lord Robert's hat clearly disliked the din and flew off with a loud flapping of feathers. He turned to Allie, and she bit her lip to keep from laughing aloud. The pigeon's takeoff had pushed his hat askew and it now rested on his head at a precarious angle, completing hiding one eye.

"You're not *laughing* at me, are you, Madam BOB?" he asked in a mock severe tone.

She windened her eyes. "I, Sir FOF? Certainly not."

One mischief-filled, dark blue eye blinked at her. "Banbury tale," he decreed.

The baroness finally managed to halt her barking brood, her plump face red with exertion. Lord Robert straightened his hat, then looked down at the boys. "Sit," he commanded. The boys instantly obeyed, looking up at him with button-eyed devotion.

"You really *must* show me how you do that," the baroness panted, dabbing her glistening brow with a delicate lace handkerchief. "The wicked darlings simply *refuse* to obey me when they're excited. Now tell me, my dears, why are you still in town? I thought you'd have traveled to Bradford Hall by now." A look of concern passed over her face. "I hope there is no problem with the duchess and the babe?"

"All is well," Lord Robert assured her. "And as far as I know, I am not yet an uncle again. Mrs. Brown needed to remain in London for several days to settle some business affairs. I shall escort her to Bradford Hall when she is finished."

The baroness looked back and forth between them, her face alive with interest. "I see. I would ask if you are enjoying your London stay, Alberta dear, but I can clearly see that you are. Why, I don't believe I've ever seen you looking quite so . . . animated." She leaned toward Lord Robert and whispered loudly, "Did I not tell you that she is *very* remarkably pretty when she smiles?"

"You did indeed."

For several seconds, Allie held her breath, waiting to see if he'd say more . . . if he'd agree with Lady Gaddlestone's opinion. But he said nothing further, rendering her strangely disappointed. Sanity returned, along with a strong flare of self-directed annoyance. For heaven's sake, why would she care if he thought her pretty? Desperate to change the direction of the conversation, she quickly asked, "How are you faring now that you're home, Lady Gaddlestone?"

"Very well, my dear. I've had dozens of callers and am nearly all caught up on the latest *on dits*." She shot an arch look at Lord Robert. "Although I've heard nothing about this apparent trend of gentlemen wearing pigeons upon their hats."

"Indeed? How shocking, for it is the very latest in manly headgear."

"Humph. You wouldn't have thought so had that feathered beast ruined your hat."

"Ah, but it would have been a small price to pay."

Allie felt his gaze shift to her, and he flexed his arm where her hand rested in the crook of his elbow, lightly squeezing her fingers. A frown tugged at her brows. Those words sounded very familiar. . . .

Realization hit her. He'd repeated her own words about juggling the eggs for Joshua. *It was a small price to pay to see him smile.* His meaning was suddenly perfectly clear.

He'd brought her here and risked his clothing for one purpose. To make her smile.

She turned swiftly and discovered his gaze resting upon

her. Such beautiful eyes, filled with mischief and warmth, made all the more alluring by the small smile playing around the corners of his mouth. A river of feeling cascaded through her, simultaneously warming and confusing her.

Before she could even think of a reply, he returned his attention to the baroness. "Mrs. Brown and I were just about to visit Regent Street. I thought she might enjoy a visit to the confectioner's and then tea at The Blue Iris. Would you care to join us? I'd love to hear about your travels in America."

The baroness beamed a smile at him. "My dear boy, I'd love nothing better."

Comfortably ensconced in a plush, indigo velvet chair near The Blue Iris's massive brick fireplace, Lady Gaddlestone sipped her tea and chatted gaily about her adventures in America, all the while thanking her lucky stars for her most useful ability of requiring only half her attention to be engaged to carry on a conversation. Because the other half of her attention was riveted on the absolutely fascinating tableau unfolding right before her very eyes between dear Alberta and Lord Robert.

While she regaled her audience with tales of elegant soirees, her mind made avid notations. *Heavens, the way he just looked at her! With that teasing, yet somehow heated expression.* She fought the urge to fan herself with her linen napkin. *And look at that blush creeping over Alberta's cheeks. And that delighted smile she just gave him!*

Oh, there was no doubt Lord Robert was smitten. And clearly dear Alberta was far from immune to Lord Robert's undeniable charm. She'd suspected such might be the case, and allowed herself a mental pat on the back. Of course, she was rarely wrong in such matters. She paused for a sip of tea in order to hide the satisfied smile she could not suppress behind her porcelain cup.

With her facial expressions once more under control, she continued her tale. "Yes, the costume ball hosted by Mr. and

Mrs. Whatley in Philadelphia was all great fun, but it could have been a complete disaster. I found out that the very next night after the ball, the Whatley mansion caught fire!"

Lord Robert's hand jarred to a halt halfway to his lips, sloshing several drops of tea over the edge of his cup. Something the baroness could not decipher flashed in his eyes. "Was anyone hurt?" he asked tightly.

"No, thank goodness," the baroness said. "Mr. and Mrs. Whatley were not at home, and the servants all managed to escape. The house, however, was completely destroyed." A shudder passed through her. "If the fire had occurred the night before, with all those guests in the house, why there's no telling how many people might have been hurt or lost their lives."

Another odd expression passed over Lord Robert's face, and his jaw appeared to tighten. It also looked as if his face paled, but surely that was just a trick of the tea room's subdued lighting? Still, he seemed somehow distressed. Her gaze shifted to Alberta, who also seemed to note Lord Robert's sudden tension. But then, in the blink of an eye, his expression cleared, leaving her to wonder if she'd imagined his momentary discomfort. She shook her head. Gracious, it was a trial to get on in years. Perhaps she needed spectacles.

Well, she may have imagined his reaction to her story, but there was no mistaking his reaction to dear Alberta. Settling herself more comfortably in her chair, she launched into another account of her travels, all the while planning the dress she would have made to wear to the undoubtedly upcoming wedding.

By the time Robert settled himself on the gray velvet squabs across from Mrs. Brown for the carriage ride back to the Bradford town house, shadows of twilight were darkening the sky. After signaling the driver to depart, he smiled at his companion. To his immense satisfaction, her lips curved partially upward in return.

"Did you enjoy your afternoon?"

"Very much. Indeed, I'd be hard-pressed to choose what I liked more—the delicious confections you very generously purchased for us all—"

"Only a cad would buy just enough for himself."

"—the divine tea, or the stimulating conversation."

"The baroness *is* quite talkative."

"Yes. But you well knew that when you asked her to join us and regale you with stories of her travels. You knew it would please her immensely to tell you." She gave him a look he couldn't decipher, then she added softly, "And I suspect you would have sat there without complaint until midnight listening to her."

He felt an odd urge to squirm under her steady regard, as if he were a green boy and she'd caught him at a falsehood. "As I enjoy traveling myself, I like hearing about such adventures."

"As do I. However, I do believe that my favorite part of the afternoon was seeing you with all those pigeons perched upon you." Her lips twitched. "It is an image I shall never forget."

"As I shall never forget the sight of you, weak with laughter, with a pigeon on your bonnet."

Their gazes held for several seconds, and his heart performed a crazy roll. Such lovely eyes. Their deep, golden-brown depths reminded him of fine brandy: warm and intoxicating. Indeed, he could almost feel himself growing befuddled just looking at her.

"I realize," she said softly, "that the only reason you made such sport of yourself was to amuse me. It was a very kind gesture." Her gaze fell to her lap. "It felt good to laugh. Thank you."

His fingers twitched with the desire to lift her chin, but he clenched his hands, resisting. Damn it all, did she have any idea how expressive her eyes were? How they glowed when she smiled? Or how they so heartbreakingly reflected the sadness she clearly felt? Did she know that the painfully obvious fact she harbored secrets was shadowed in them?

God help him, every time their eyes had met during tea, his heart had pounded in a way that indicated he'd just run a mile, as opposed to sitting in a chair. And her lips . . . his gaze riveted on them and he swallowed a groan. Her lovely, full lips had curved upward in a smile four times during tea. He'd counted. And all four times his pulse had raced.

Recalling his reaction, annoyance edged through him. Ridiculous. His physical response to her absolutely bordered on the ridiculous. Perhaps that blow to the head he'd suffered had damaged him in some way. A fine theory . . . until faced with the fact that she'd affected him from the moment he laid eyes on her.

No, if he were to be scrupulously honest with himself, she'd affected him even *before* he saw her. His interest, or whatever name he chose to put to this preoccupation, had started when Elizabeth had given him the sketch of a beautiful, laughing, vibrant young woman.

Damn it all, if a mere charcoal image of her had fascinated him, he should have known that the actual woman would affect him profoundly. And perhaps, in the inner recesses of his mind, he had. But he hadn't known she would make him feel like . . . this. So unsettled and frustrated.

His gaze skimmed over her black mourning dress and his jaw clenched. Bloody hell, those morbid clothes irked him. She should be garbed in pastels and airy muslins. Rich silks and satins. Yet there was more to it than that. The fact that after three years she still proclaimed her devotion to a dead man through her attire disturbed him in a way he was reluctant to examine. He did not consider himself a saint by any reckoning, but he did pride himself on being a man of integrity. A man of decency. And surely a decent man of integrity would not harbor lustful urges for a grieving woman. Wouldn't long to erase the image of her dead beloved from her mind, or be so utterly, painfully attracted to her that he'd rack his brain for any excuse to touch her.

The carriage jerked to a halt, and he expelled a breath of relief when he saw they'd arrived at the town house. He helped her from the carriage, noting that she did not look at him, and pulled her hand away from his the instant her feet touched the cobblestones—facts which surely should have pleased him, not left him feeling both irritated and mildly hurt. He led the way up the walkway, chiding himself the entire distance. *She doesn't feel it, you dolt. Clearly she has no trouble resisting you.* But what about that moment in the billiards room this morning? She'd sure as hell felt something then. *'Twas obviously just a momentary lapse of judgment on her part. She's forgotten it.* Now he needed to do the same.

Just as they climbed the steps, the double oak doors flew open. Robert's greeting to Carters died on his lips when he saw the butler's stricken face. Striding into the foyer, he grabbed the man's upper arm. "What's happened? Is it Elizabeth?"

Carters swallowed hard, then shook his head. "No, Lord Robert. No one is injured."

"But something is wrong."

"I'm afraid so. I'm sorry to tell you, but the town house has been robbed."

Darkness had fallen by the time Geoffrey walked with deliberate calm up the brick steps leading to his town house. The instant he set foot on the top tread, the oak-paneled front door opened inward on silent, well-oiled hinges. Willis bowed from the waist as Geoffrey entered the foyer.

"Any messages arrive for me?" he asked the butler.

"Two arrived earlier this afternoon, my lord," Willis said, accepting his hat, coat, and walking stick. "But I did not forward them to you at White's, as neither was from the gentleman you were expecting to hear from. The letters await you on your desk."

His hands clenched. "I'll be in my study. Unless another message arrives, I do not wish to be disturbed."

"Yes, my lord."

Seconds later, Geoffrey entered his private study and headed directly for the decanters. The pain in his head had swelled to an unbearable, rhythmic pounding that set his teeth on edge. He tossed back a fingerful of brandy, relishing the slow burn edging down to his belly. The liquor did little to ease the thumping behind his eyes, but it helped settle his nerves, which teetered dangerously close to the edge.

Damn Redfern to hell and back! He'd give the bastard one more hour. If he had not heard from him by then, he would be forced to put his plan into action. This uncertainty had dragged on far too long. The possibility that he could be destroyed . . . sometimes he felt as if he were going mad.

No! Not mad. It's simply the strain. This impossible state of suspense. Wincing, he pressed his palm to his temple in a useless attempt to stem the relentless banging. He would not, could not, lose what was his.

He looked around the room, at the opulent cream silk wall coverings, the handsome furnishings, the priceless works of art, and a red haze seemed to envelop him, cloaking him in a dark rage that thundered through his veins and threatened to suffocate him. *This is mine. All of it. Every bloody last bit of it. I sold my soul for it . . . and I'm not the only one who did so. Like father like son. . . .*

That bastard David Brown had stolen the ring and its box—had discovered the truth. Had blackmailed him. And now the ring and the proof that could cast doubt on the validity of his parents' marriage was God only knew where. If the truth were discovered . . .

Sweat broke out on his forehead, and he clenched his snifter, the cut glass digging into his fingers and palm. His heart pounded so hard he could feel it beating in his ears. Forcing long, deep breaths into his lungs, he strove to compose himself. *Can't lose control. Must remain calm. Focused.*

He wiped his damp brow with his handkerchief, then, with jerky steps, crossed the maroon-and-gold Persian rug to his desk, where his gaze fell upon the two letters resting on the polished cherry-wood surface. Picking up the top one, he broke the seal and scanned the brief contents.

Dear Lord Shelbourne,
    I am in possession of a ring that belongs to your

*family. I would very much like to return this ring to you
at your earliest convenience. Please contact me at the
Bradford town house on Park Lane to set up a meeting.*
                                        Yours truly,
                                        Mrs. Alberta Brown

Stunned, he reread the missive, then crumpled it in his fist.
A maelstrom of thoughts and emotions twisted through his
mind, and he fought to sort them into some semblance of
order.

She *did* have the ring. Thank God. He no longer needed to
agonize over its whereabouts. Relief smacked him like a blow,
only to be immediately replaced by fury at her gall.

She wanted to *return* his ring? A humorless laugh erupted
from his lips. Of course she did—but at what exorbitant price?
No doubt more than her bloody husband had demanded.

He heaved her letter into the hearth with a vicious oath,
then watched the flames consume it. Redfern had failed yet
again. Damn it all, why couldn't the man manage to steal one
small ring from one small woman? Surely that was not too difficult a task!

Dragging his hands through his hair, he turned, and his
gaze locked on the other note on his desk. What was this, a
blackmail request? Snatching up the vellum, he ripped open
the seal and quickly read the few lines.

A frown pulled down his brows and he pursed his lips. With
the duke and duchess still in Kent awaiting the birth of their
child, clearly Robert Jamison was serving as Mrs. Brown's escort during her London stay. And Jamison wished to introduce
him to an American woman named Mrs. Alberta Brown whose
deceased husband David—how had he put it? He scanned the
letter again. Ah, yes. . . . *Whose deceased husband was an acquaintance of yours.*

Bitterness burned Geoffrey's throat. Oh, he was *acquainted*
with David Brown, all right. He recited a silent prayer of
thanks every day that the bastard was dead. His only regret
was that he hadn't had the pleasure of wrapping his hands

around Brown's miserable neck and squeezing the life out him himself. If not for Brown, he'd not be in this damnable mess. And what about Jamison? What did he know? Was he somehow involved as more than Mrs. Brown's escort? Damn it all, he couldn't risk anyone in the duke's family finding out—

A knock sounded at the door, jerking him from his disturbing musings. "Come in."

Willis crossed the room, holding out a silver salver. "This just arrived, my lord."

Geoffrey accepted the missive. Anticipation curled through him as he saw his name scrawled in Redfern's familiar, coarse scrawl. The instant Willis quit the room, he tore open the seal.

I've got the ring. Expect me tomorrow.

He stared at that single line, his jaw working. Obviously either Redfern or Mrs. Brown was lying. Or foolishly attempting to play an elaborate game with him. Or perhaps not. . . .

Willis had said the other two notes had arrived earlier this afternoon. Realization dawned, and a bark of laughter burst from him. Mrs. Brown must have sent her note *before* Redfern stole the ring. She no longer had it. But just as quickly as relief came, it vanished like a puff of smoke.

She might no longer have the ring, but that didn't mean she hadn't discovered its secret. She still might know . . . might know that another could rightfully lay claim to his title.

Pitching Jamison's and Redfern's notes into the fireplace, he grasped the mantel with a white-knuckled grip. He watched the flames lick at the vellum, his mind working at a feverish pace. There was only one answer. He'd have to meet with her. Get to know her. Find out what, if anything, she knew about his secret. Discover if she planned to blackmail him. Did she know the identity of the man who could destroy his life and take *everything* from him? *If only I knew who he was. I could destroy him first.*

He *had* to get that ring.

Walking to his desk, he composed a note inviting Mrs. Brown and Robert Jamison to call upon him the next morning.

He folded the vellum, then pressed his seal into the wax with far more force than necessary.

He debated sending a note to Redfern, but decided against it. Now that the whereabouts of the ring was assured, if Redfern killed Mrs. Brown before Geoffrey met with her, so be it. In fact, so much the better.

By this time tomorrow, he would be a free man. His gaze narrowed and drifted to the fireplace, where nothing but ashes remained of the letters from Mrs. Brown, Robert Jamison, and Redfern.

And all the loose ends would be eliminated. Permanently.

Leaning against the thick, polished oak mantel in the library, Robert listened to Eustace Laramie, the magistrate, recite what he knew of the crime, much of which Robert had already heard from Carters.

"A maid discovered the theft when she entered Mrs. Brown's bedchamber. Found the room all torn apart, garments and bedding shredded and strewn all around. Carters conducted a thorough search of the house and reported Mrs. Brown's bedchamber was the only room disturbed. The thief most likely climbed the trellis, then entered through the French windows leading to her balcony. According to Carters, a number of the Bradford family's possessions are missing from the bedchamber. They include a sterling hairbrush and comb, as well as two silver candlesticks and several figurines from the mantel. Mrs. Brown will be able to tell us what, if any, of her belongings are missing once she's finished looking through the mess." He fixed a penetrating look on Robert. "First the abduction you reported to me only this morning, and now this. Odd how you and Mrs. Brown have suffered from such a recent spate of crime."

"Indeed." Robert scrubbed his hands down his face. "Have there been any other reports of thefts in the immediate area?"

"No."

"Do you think the same person is responsible?"

Laramie stroked his chin and nodded thoughtfully. "It's certainly possible, although we're talking about two different sorts of crimes. And what with so many thieves about, it could just as easily be two different dirty dogs." He waved his hand and made a disgusted sound. "Damn bastards. Seems like for every one you send to Newgate, a dozen more take his place."

Robert fixed a meaningful look on the man. "Two different crimes, but the same victims. It certainly gives one pause."

"Indeed, it is something to consider. I'll—"

A soft knock sounded at the door. "Come in," Robert said.

Mrs. Brown entered, closing the door behind her. She crossed the Axminster rug, stopping in front of the fireplace. In spite of clearly trying to appear calm, Robert could tell she was shaken. Her complexion resembled chalk, and he detected a tremor in her walk, as if her knees weren't quite steady. Her hands were clasped tightly in front of her, and there was a haunted look in her eyes. She reminded him of a piece of glass about to shatter.

He could understand her being upset—he was so himself—but she seemed even more tense and afraid than she had when they'd escaped from the warehouse.

"Have you determined if any of your belongings were taken?" Laramie asked.

She hesitated, then jerked her head in a nod. "Yes. There is one item missing. A ring."

"So jewelry was what he was after," Laramie said, nodding. "Typical. But I'm surprised he stole only the one bauble. Are you certain that's all that is gone?"

"Positive. It was the only piece of jewelry in my possession."

"I see. Was it valuable?"

Again she hesitated. "It was my husband's . . ." Her voice trailed off, then she cleared her throat. "There was more sentimental value attached to it than anything else, Mr. Laramie."

"Mr. Laramie and I were just discussing the possibility that this robbery is linked to last night's events," Robert said.

Her gaze flew to his. Was that alarm that flashed in her eyes? It disappeared so quickly, he couldn't be certain.

She returned her attention to the magistrate. "I understand there is a very high rate of crime in London, Mr. Laramie. Surely these are just random acts. Unfortunate and coincidental, but random just the same."

"That is possible. However, it is also possible that someone is targeting the duke's household." Laramie's eyes took on a keen edge. "Or you, Mrs. Brown."

She raised her chin. "I think that extremely unlikely, for as you know, I just recently arrived and am completely unknown in London."

"Have you experienced any other problems or unusual occurrences since arriving?"

"No."

A determined look gleamed in Laramie's eyes. "Rest assured we'll do what we can to find him, but I must warn you against getting your hopes up for recovering your possessions. These blokes strike quick as that"—he snapped his fingers—"then disappear like rats scurrying into holes. Your belongings have probably been sold three times over by now, I'm sad to say. But if there's any news, I'll contact you immediately." He nodded to them both, then quit the room, closing the door with a quiet click.

Robert's attention turned to Mrs. Brown. She stood in front of the fire, perfectly still, her face ashen. She stared into the flames, her lips pressed into a grim line. After several seconds, however, she seemed to recall herself.

"If you'll excuse me," she murmured, turning toward the door.

"Actually, I'd like a word with you, Mrs. Brown," he said, unable to keep the edge from his voice. "In fact, I'd like more than a word with you."

She turned so swiftly her skirt billowed out. "I beg your pardon?"

He walked toward her in measured steps, not halting until

he stood directly in front of her. "I want to know exactly what the devil is going on here."

Color suffused her pale cheeks. "I'm certain I don't know what you mean."

"Indeed? Then allow me to enlighten you. Since your arrival here *yesterday*, you have been coshed, abducted, trussed up like a goose, and robbed. These same unfortunate circumstances have befallen me. It certainly makes one wonder what circumstances might greet us after you've been here a *week*."

Her gaze remained steady, and he had to applaud her show of bravery. The effect would have been perfect except for the slight trembling of her lower lip. "I'm sorry—"

"It is not your apology I seek, Mrs. Brown. What I want is an explanation and the truth."

"I don't know—"

"You lied to Laramie. I want to know why. And you are not leaving this room until you tell me."

Chapter 8

A knot tightened in Allie's stomach. She needed only to glance at the grim set of Lord Robert's features to know he meant what he said. He would keep her in this room until she offered him some sort of explanation for the extraordinary events that had befallen him, and her, since her arrival.

In truth, she could not blame him, although providing such an explanation placed her in an awkward position. How to tell him enough to satisfy him, yet not tell him so much as to compromise herself? And what exactly had he meant when he'd accused her of lying to Laramie?

She looked away from his far too penetrating gaze to stare into the flames dancing in the hearth, trying to assimilate the conflicting emotions battering her.

Cold, stark fear shivered down her spine. There was no longer even the shadow of a doubt that someone had meant her serious harm all along. And it was now clear that the reason was the coat-of-arms ring. But why? And who? The person responsible had clearly sailed with her from America. It had to be someone who had known David, who'd been involved in his shady dealings. And clearly this person believed the ring was valuable.

But what now? Now that the person—or persons—had gained possession of what they wanted, would they leave her alone? *Please, God, let it be so.*

Anger collided with her fear, and she pressed her lips together. *Damn you, David!* Even three years after his death, he continued to wreak havoc in her life. A sudden wave of weariness crashed through her, draining her, and her eyes slid closed. God, how many days and nights had she spent hovering on the brink of despair? Sitting alone, so tempted to give up. It would be so easy to simply stop this quest . . . to let him win.

She pulled in a deep breath and gritted her teeth. No. She would *not* give up. She refused to be a victim again. David would not steal anything else from her.

Steal. Guilt hit her like a slap. Even though she'd tried her best to keep it safe, she'd lost possession of Lord Shelbourne's ring. She dreaded meeting the earl now, having to tell him that she did not have his ring after all.

And not only the ring was gone. Valuables belonging to Lord Robert's family had been taken, and her bedchamber was a shambles. In spite of her best intentions, she'd certainly proven to be a less than stellar houseguest. And it was now time to make some amends.

Drawing a bracing breath, she turned to Lord Robert. He stood with his arms folded across his chest, watching her with a piercing intensity that curled her toes inside her shoes.

"I'm not quite sure where to begin—"

"You can start by telling me why you lied to Laramie," he said in a tone that brooked no argument. "You told him nothing else unusual had happened to you, yet I recall that you fell overboard several hours before arriving in London."

She lifted her brows. "I did not lie to him. He asked if I'd experienced any other problems since *arriving*. I haven't. That incident occurred *before* I arrived."

Unmistakable annoyance flashed in his eyes. Reaching out, he grasped her upper arms. The heat of his hands pressed through her bombazine sleeves. "I'm not in a mood to play word games or split hairs, Mrs. Brown. Perhaps, by some miracle, you might have convinced me that the kidnapping and today's robbery were unrelated, but falling overboard as well?" His fingers tightened briefly. "No, I'm afraid you haven't a prayer of persuading me that the *three* occurrences are unlinked. Tell me, were there any other incidences *during* your journey?"

She tried her best to keep her features expressionless, but clearly she failed, for a muscle in his jaw ticked. Realizing there was no point in hiding them, she told him about falling down the stairs and becoming ill after eating on the ship.

Concern darkened his eyes. "Surely you cannot believe that all these disturbing occurrences are unrelated?"

"No . . . not any longer." Then, in an effort to forestall the barrage of questions she sensed about to burst from him, she added, "I'll try to explain, but I'm afraid I do not know very much."

He slowly released her arms, but his gaze never wavered from hers. "The fact that you know anything about these events puts you at an advantage over me. I'm listening."

Pressing her hands to her jittery stomach, she said, "After David died, I found a coat-of-arms ring among his effects. I was curious about the piece as I'd never seen it before. A jeweler in America told me he believed it was English in origin. When I decided to visit Elizabeth, I brought the ring along, hoping to learn more about it. I gave Mr. Fitzmoreland, the antiquities expert I spoke with here, a drawing of the coat of arms. I received a letter from him this morning informing me that the coat of arms was that of the Shelbourne family."

She paused to draw a much-needed breath and to gauge his reaction thus far. Understanding was dawning in his gaze.

"This was the business you wished to conduct in London."

"Yes."

"And that's the reason you requested an introduction to Shelbourne."

She nodded. "I wished to return the ring to him. I had no

use for it, and I thought it might hold some sentimental value for him."

"How did it come to be in your husband's possession?"

"I'm not certain. David was a . . . collector. No doubt he purchased it in some dusty little treasure shop he discovered during his travels."

"The ring was no doubt quite valuable. You planned to simply *give* it to Shelbourne? Why not sell it to him?"

She raised her chin a notch. "I didn't feel it was mine to sell." Before he could question her motives further, she plunged on, "For reasons unknown to me, it appears that someone wanted that ring—desperately enough to try to harm me, then to steal it. I didn't believe the incidents were connected because I couldn't imagine what anyone would want from me."

"But now it is clear they wanted the ring. And were quite willing to harm you in order to get it." He frowned with obvious concern. "Since the attacks began on board the ship, this person must have followed you from America. Who knew you had this ring in your possession?"

"The only person I ever told or showed it to was the jeweler."

His frown deepened. "Perhaps the ring was more valuable than this jeweler led you to believe and he wanted it for himself. Did you mention your travel plans to him?"

"No. And I can assure you he was not on board the *Seaward Lady*."

"He could have hired someone to follow you."

She mulled that over for several seconds, then nodded. "I suppose that is possible. But now that whoever wanted the ring has it, I'm certain they will no longer bother with me."

She looked into his eyes. His expression was unreadable, but very intense. After a long moment, his gaze lowered to her mouth. His eyes seemed to darken, and a look she'd have sworn was desire flared in their depths.

Heat rushed through her like a brush fire. She imagined him stepping closer, leaning forward, brushing his lips over hers. Her mouth tingled, as if he'd actually caressed her, and she bit her bottom lip to stem the unsettling sensation.

Unable to stand the intensity of his regard, she stared down at the carpet and endeavored to regain her equilibrium. "I'm very sorry that you became involved in this, Lord Robert," she said quietly, "and I'm equally sorry that your family's belongings were stolen as a result. I don't know how I will replace them, but—"

His fingertips touched under her chin, cutting off her words. He gently raised her chin until their eyes met. "They are merely *things*, Mrs. Brown, and of no importance. We must be grateful that neither of us was seriously injured. Things can easily be replaced. People, however, cannot. . . ." A muscle jumped in his jaw, and something else flickered in his eyes. Something dark, haunted, and full of pain. Then, as quickly as it appeared, the expression vanished. It was the same expression she'd seen flash in his eyes at The Blue Iris.

Curiosity she could not shove aside pulled at her. What secrets was this man hiding? What was the transgression in his past that Lady Gaddlestone had alluded to? Was his misconduct of the same sort as David's?

Part of her instantly rejected the possibility that Lord Robert was capable of criminal deeds, but she forced herself to ignore that involuntary softer leaning. After all, she barely knew the man. And indeed, it didn't matter what his secrets entailed or what he'd done—just the fact that he obviously *had* secrets and had done *something* was reason enough to be wary and keep her distance from him.

His hand slid away from her chin, and he stepped back from her. "Tell me, were all your garments destroyed?"

She fought the urge to lay her fingers over the spot where his had just touched her, to hold in the warm imprint he'd left upon her skin. "Not all of them. I still have two gowns—the one I'm wearing and one other."

He nodded in a preoccupied fashion, his thoughts clearly elsewhere. She took advantage of his distraction to edge toward the door. With any luck, she'd quit his company before he thought to question her further. "If you'll excuse me, I'd like to retire now."

He turned back to her, surprise flickering over his face, as if he'd momentarily forgotten she was in the room. "Of course. I'm certain your bedchamber has been put back to rights by now. Good night, Mrs. Brown."

She murmured good night, then quickly exited the room. She'd half-expected him to leave the library with her, to prepare to return to his own rooms, but clearly he intended to stay for a while. There was no denying his presence in the town house made her feel safe, yet at the same time it left her achingly unsettled. And increasingly frightened of her own reactions.

Of its own volition, her hand rose to her face, her fingertips lightly brushing over her chin. Dear God, he'd barely touched her, yet she'd felt that gentle caress as if lightning had struck her. And the way he'd looked at her. . . .

Her fingers moved up to her mouth. He'd wanted to kiss her. There was no doubt. She'd seen it in his eyes. A sigh whispered past her lips, blowing warm against her fingertips. What would she have done if he had?

Melted. Into a quivering puddle of want. And then—

She caught herself and, with an exclamation of disgust, yanked her hand down to her side. With unease cramping her insides, she walked briskly down the corridor to the stairs.

Heaven help her, these feelings he inspired in her terrified her. They were exactly the same dreamy, impractical emotions David had aroused . . . except for one thing.

The feelings Lord Robert aroused in her were even stronger.

Robert stared at the flames, memories overwhelming him. He tried to stop them, but the danger facing Mrs. Brown, coupled by Lady Gaddlestone's tale at The Blue Iris and his own earlier words, brought the past flooding back like a giant wave, drowning everything in its path. *Things can easily be replaced. People, however, cannot. . . .*

She had offered him an explanation, but damn it, he strongly suspected she had not told him the entire story behind that ring. He'd chosen not to press her any further, sensing she would not tell him anything more. But she had been in real danger. And she very well might still be. The thought of anything happening to her . . .

His hands fisted and his jaw tightened. No! No harm would befall her. He would personally see to it. He'd failed Nate. He would *not* fail again. Straightening, he paced in front of the fire.

The hell with propriety, he would remain here at the town house instead of returning to his rooms. After all, Elizabeth would never forgive him if anything happened to her friend. *You'd never forgive yourself,* his inner voice informed him.

Well, of course he wouldn't. He wouldn't wish harm on *anyone* . . . not just specifically *her*.

A groan escaped him, and he raked his hands through his hair. Who the bloody hell was he trying to fool with that cock-and-bull nonsense? Of course he wouldn't want anyone to suffer harm, but damn it, it was vital, *crucial* that no harm befall *her*.

Another groan eased past his lips. Walking to the leather settee, he sat wearily upon the cushion, then rubbed his tired eyes with the heels of his palms.

Damn it, he'd almost kissed her. Had wanted to so badly he could all but taste her upon his tongue. . . . Had wanted to with an intensity that had actually frightened him because he somehow knew that something much more than a simple touching of lips would occur.

Blast it, she appealed to him more with each passing moment. He admired her courage and grit. Not once during any of their mishaps had she complained. He respected the great lengths and expense she'd gone to in order to trace the ring to its owner and attempt to return it, without any gain to herself. And the fact that someone had tried to hurt her, that she might still be in danger, called out to all his protective instincts.

And then there was simply the look of her, which attracted him in a way he'd never before experienced. He knew dozens of beautiful women, yet none affected him as she did. There was something in her eyes . . . in spite of her brave words and actions, there was something haunted and lonely, sad and vulnerable in her gaze that simply grabbed him by the heart. The contrast between the real woman and the woman in the sketch fascinated him.

"Argh!" Tipping his head back, he squeezed his eyes shut and expelled a long breath. Damn it, he did not want to feel this way. Not with this woman whose heart belonged to another man and whose home was on another continent. Why the bloody hell couldn't he be feeling all these things for an uncomplicated English girl?

And just what the bloody hell was he going to do about it?

Allie stepped into the breakfast room just after dawn the next morning, and halted as if she'd walked into a wall of glass.

Lord Robert sat at one end of the polished mahogany table, drinking from a china cup and perusing a newspaper.

Good Lord, what was he doing here so early? She'd known that he would come to the town house today, yet she'd hoped to have the morning hours to mentally prepare herself to face him. Obviously she was not to have that luxury, for there he sat, looking strong and masculine in a dark blue jacket, snowy shirt, and perfectly knotted cravat.

He looked up from his reading and their eyes met over the rim of his china cup. Heaven help her if he looked at her as he had last evening. . . .

But her worries were for naught, as he merely smiled at her in a friendly manner. "Good morning, Mrs. Brown. You're up bright and early today."

She swallowed to moisten her dry throat. "I could say the same to you, Lord Robert."

"Ah, well, I've always been a morning sort of person," he

said, lowering his cup to the saucer. "Please join me for breakfast. The poached eggs are especially good."

Breathing in the heavenly scent of coffee permeating the
air, she walked to the sideboard where she filled a china plate
with two eggs, several pieces of thinly sliced ham, and a thick
slice of fragrant, freshly baked bread.

Sliding into the chair across from him, she heard him
chuckle. "It must run in the family," he said.

"I beg your pardon?"

"I know you and Elizabeth are distant cousins." He nodded
toward her stacked plate. "Clearly your love of a healthy-sized
breakfast runs in the family. We all tease Elizabeth unmercifully about her fondness for the morning meal."

Settling her linen napkin in her lap, she said, "It has always
been my favorite. One day, when Elizabeth and I were eight
years old, we engaged in a contest to see which of us could eat
the most eggs for breakfast."

He smiled. "Ah, so you did more with eggs than juggle
them and splatter them upon your face, I see."

"I'm afraid so."

"And who won this competition?"

The memory washed over her, filling her with wistful nostalgia. "Neither of us. As we both attempted to force down our
seventh egg, Mama put a stop to it. We both suffered dreadful
bellyaches the rest of the morning, to which Mama was totally
unsympathetic."

He laughed, and her eyes were drawn to the way his firm
lips stretched over his even, white teeth. "At least your competition was with eggs. I recall issuing a similar challenge to
Austin over pies."

She raised her brows. "That sounds quite fun, actually."

"Not when the pies are made of mud." Pure deviltry glinted
in his eyes. "Of course, Austin wasn't aware of that when he
accepted me."

"Oh, dear. How old were you?"

"I had just turned five. Austin was nine." A chuckle

sounded from his throat. "I won. Didn't have to eat more than a spoonful, as Austin gave over after the tiniest taste."

"Yet I somehow have the feeling that you would have eaten much more than a spoonful in order to best him."

He inclined his head in agreement. "Absolutely. I always play to win. Although to this day I vividly recall how utterly foul that dirt tasted." He pulled a comical face and shuddered dramatically. "Never again."

A footman appeared at her elbow, and she gratefully accepted coffee. She could feel the weight of Lord Robert's stare upon her, but as she did not wish to become lost in his dark blue gaze, she applied her attention to her breakfast with the zeal of a scientist to a microscope.

"Did you sleep well?" he asked after a moment where the only sound was her cutlery tapping against her plate.

No. I tossed and turned most of the night, and it's entirely your fault. "Yes, thank you. Did you?"

After a full minute passed without him offering a reply, she risked prying her attention from her thinly sliced ham to peek up at him. And nearly choked on her food.

His gaze was riveted on her breasts.

All the tension that had drained away after his easy greeting and companionable conversation, came roaring back, bringing with it a storm of heat. To her horror, she felt her nipples harden. And to her utter mortification, it was obvious from his quick intake of breath and the way his eyes darkened that he noticed.

She felt color climbing up her neck. She needed to lift her napkin, or cross her arms—*something*—yet she found she couldn't move. Aching need rushed through her, sparking to life nerve endings that had lain dormant for three years.

He suddenly looked up, and her breath stalled at the unmistakable desire emanating from his eyes. "No," he said, his voice low and husky. "I didn't sleep well at all."

"I . . . I'm sorry to hear that." *Please, please stop looking at me like that. It makes me feel things I don't want to feel. . . . Makes me want things . . .*

He reached for his coffee, breaking that hypnotic stare, and relief relaxed some of her tense muscles.

"But then, I rarely sleep well when I'm not in my own bed," he said. "I spent the night here."

Her heart skipped a beat. No more than a few feet had separated them last night. "You did?"

"Yes. Given the dangers you've faced, coupled with the fact that we don't know if there might be further threats to you, I thought it best. I sent a footman round to my rooms last night to collect my essentials. I plan to remain here until we leave for Bradford Hall, which may be happening quite soon." Reaching into his jacket, he withdrew a note. "This arrived last night after you'd retired. It's from Shelbourne. He's invited us to call upon him this morning. I haven't responded yet, as I didn't know if you still wished to meet him in light of the fact that you no longer have his ring. Since he never knew you had it—"

"He knew. I wrote to him yesterday, telling him. I wanted him to know I had the ring and wished to return it to him." She blew out a breath. "I feel dreadful having to tell him it is no longer in my possession, but there is no alternative."

He rose, setting his napkin next to his plate. "In that case, I shall write him immediately, telling him to expect us. If you'll excuse me . . ."

Although she tried not to, she watched his reflection in the huge gilt mirror hanging above the mahogany sideboard. When he disappeared through the doorway, a breath she hadn't realized she held, expelled from her lips, and she fought the urge to fan herself with her napkin.

There was no doubt about it—Lord Robert looked as fine exiting a room as he did entering one.

Robert fought the urge to scowl as he watched the earl of Shelbourne bow low over Mrs. Brown's hand.

"A pleasure to meet you," the earl said. "Jamison here always seems to be acquainted with the loveliest women. I'm honored that he would introduce us." Tucking Mrs. Brown's hand through his arm, he led her across the well-appointed drawing room to an overstuffed settee. He sat next to Mrs. Brown, angling himself in such a way that Robert was forced to sit several yards away in a wing chair.

Settling himself in the chair, which he grudgingly admitted was quite comfortable, he silently observed Geoffrey Hadmore and Mrs. Brown. With her golden-brown eyes wide and full of distress, she explained, as she had to him last evening, how she'd found the ring among her husband's possessions and traced it to him. Then she related the story of the robbery, apologizing profusely, and promising to return the ring to him immediately if it was found.

Shelbourne, his dark eyes full of admiring warmth, clasped her hand between his. "My dear, undoubtedly this ring was nothing more than an inexpensive bauble an uncle or cousin sold or gave away. And I can hardly miss something that I never even knew existed. While I greatly appreciate your efforts to restore it to me, you mustn't give it another thought. Now, you must tell me about America. Fascinating place. I'd love to travel there someday. . . ."

Robert shifted in his chair and turned a deaf ear to Shelbourne. Bloody hell, it was an effort not to roll his eyes at all the palaver flapping from the earl's lips. Indeed, if it had been directed at anyone other than Mrs. Brown, he would have ignored it and simply enjoyed the tea and what looked like excellent biscuits resting on the ornate silver tea tray. But as the full strength of Shelbourne's attention and charm *was* directed at Mrs. Brown, Robert's teeth ground in annoyance.

At that moment Shelbourne's mastiff walked into the room, the *thump* of his massive paws silenced by the maroon-and-blue Persian rug. Robert patted his knee in invitation to the beast, who he recalled from walks in the park was named Thorndyke and whose enormous size hid a kittenlike temperament.

Clearly sensing a friend, Thorndyke trotted over and plopped his huge head on Robert's thigh, looking up at him with a woebegone expression. Robert stroked the dog's warm fur, then shared a biscuit with him. Thorndyke gazed at him with pure canine devotion that proclaimed them to now be lifelong friends.

He glanced over at the couple on the settee and his annoyance instantly multiplied when he observed an attractive blush staining Mrs. Brown's cheeks. "That is very kind of you to say, Lord Shelbourne," she murmured.

Damn it, what the hell had the bounder said? He'd been so disgruntled, he'd missed it. He did not, however, miss Shelbourne's low-pitched reply.

"Please, call me Geoffrey." A slow, admiring smile, the likes of which Robert had seen Shelbourne bestow on numerous other women, eased over the earl's face. "I see no reason for us to be so formal, do you? And may I call you Alberta?"

"By God, look at the time," Robert said, jumping to his feet, brushing biscuit crumbs from his breeches, which Thorndyke immediately licked up. "Had no idea it was so late. Really must shove off. Important appointment, you know."

Mrs. Brown appeared surprised by his announcement, but she quickly gathered up her reticule. Shelbourne rose and shot Robert a look that was no doubt meant to be pleasant, but which didn't quite cover up the annoyance simmering in his eyes.

"If you must go, Jamison, of course I won't detain you. There is, however, no need for Mrs. Brown to depart so soon. I'd be delighted to escort her home after we've finished getting acquainted."

I'll just wager you would be. Curving his lips into a smile that precisely mimicked Shelbourne's, Robert shook his head regretfully. "A generous offer, Shelbourne, but I'm afraid that's impossible. The appointment is Mrs. Brown's, and therefore she must be present."

Shelbourne stared at him for the space of several heartbeats. Robert kept his expression perfectly bland. Clearly the earl wished to pursue the matter, but instead he turned to Mrs. Brown, who had risen and stood near the edge of the settee.

Taking her hand, Shelbourne raised it to his lips and pressed a decidedly prolonged kiss to her fingertips, edging Robert's irritation up several more notches.

"I am bereft that you must leave so soon," Shelbourne said, "but I am delighted we were introduced. It is not often that my home is graced with such beauty."

Robert fought the urge to drag Shelbourne outdoors and introduce him to the cobblestones. Headfirst. Damn it all, he was looking at Mrs. Brown as if she were a sugarcoated morsel he wished to nibble upon.

Tucking her arm through his with a proprietary air that curled Robert's hands into fists, the earl walked with Mrs. Brown toward the foyer. As the corridor was only wide enough to accommodate two people, Robert was forced to trail behind.

"I would like very much to continue our conversation . . . Alberta. Would you do me the honor of allowing me to escort you to the opera this evening?"

"Thank you," came Alberta's soft reply, "but as I'm in mourning, I'm afraid I cannot accept."

Ha! See there, she's in mourning, you reprobate, so just cast your roving eye elsewhere. The opera, indeed. Robert knew Shelbourne well enough to know that singing was the last thing on the man's mind. He recognized that lustful gleam in Shelbourne's eye. *And well you should,* his inner voice taunted. *It's the same gleam you have in your own eye for the lovely Mrs. Brown.*

His irritation pumped up yet another notch, and he consigned his inner voice to the devil. Yes, she inspired lustful urges in him. But at least he knew *he* wouldn't *act* upon them. Shelbourne, he knew, wouldn't hesitate. Yes, unlike Shelbourne, he most certainly would not foist his lust upon a woman who still mourned her dead husband. No, he'd take such urges to a mistress.

A frown tugged down his brows. Fustian. He did not currently have a mistress. He'd been so busy trying to find a *wife* . . .

Well, he'd simply double his efforts to find a wife and bring his lustful urges to *her*. He'd find a beautiful young English girl and marry her and—

At that moment Mrs. Brown turned around, and their eyes met. The effect was like a blow to his midsection. His jaw clenched as the truth settled upon him like a death knell. It was going to be bloody hard to search for a bride when he could not even entertain the thought of any woman except the one looking at him right now.

Pushing aside the burgundy velvet drapery in his private study, Geoffrey watched the black lacquer coach carrying Jamison and Mrs. Brown disappear from view. For the first time in what seemed like decades, he allowed himself to draw an easy breath.

Mrs. Brown had not given any indication, by her manner or conversation, that she knew his secret. Of course, she might simply be a consummate actress, but once the ring was in his possession, it wouldn't matter what she might know. He'd destroy the evidence. And then get rid of the loose ends.

At that moment he caught sight of Lester Redfern walking swiftly toward the town house. *Speaking of loose ends . . .*

Ah, yes, within a matter of minutes, the ring would be his, thus ending the nightmare that had hovered over him for so long.

"I wasn't aware I had an appointment," Allie said as the carriage moved slowly down the crowded street. Indeed, she would have contradicted Lord Robert's obvious falsehood on principle if she had not been anxious to depart. No doubt she should have been flattered by the handsome earl's obvious interest, but instead his attentions had repulsed her. Now, if only the man sitting across from her repulsed her. . . .

A boyish smile lit his features. "Of course not, this appointment is a surprise."

Dear Lord, it was difficult to resist that smile, but she had to. For her own peace of mind. "I'm afraid I do not care over-much for surprises," she said stiffly. "Where are we going?"

"Nowhere sinister, Mrs. Brown, I give you my word. I simply scheduled an appointment for you at the modiste. I thought you might wish to replace your destroyed gowns."

An embarrassed flush crept up her face. Heaven knew she did not wish to spend the next weeks and months with only two gowns to her name, but she simply could not afford to purchase new ones. And how humiliating to have to admit as much to him, especially when his gesture was so kind and thoughtful.

Raising her chin, she said, "While that was very considerate of you, I'm afraid I only brought limited travel funds with me."

"I do not know how clothing is priced in America, but I believe you'll find that it is quite inexpensive here in London. Remarkably so. Especially wools. All those sheep wandering about the countryside, you know."

Although she suspected that what constituted inexpensive to him would differ vastly from her definition, a spark of hope kindled in her. If what he said was true, perhaps she could afford *one* new gown.

The carriage halted. "Here we are," Lord Robert said with a winning grin. "Let us see what fabulous bargains Madame Renee has to offer."

Geoffrey looked at the ring resting in his palm, then raised his gaze to Redfern.

"There it is," Redfern said. "Had it sewn into her petticoat, she did. Right clever hiding spot. But not clever enough." He grasped his lapels and rocked back on his heels, a smug grin creasing his face.

"Where is the box?" Geoffrey asked in a perfectly controlled voice.

The smug grin faltered. "Box?"

"The ring box." A slow thumping commenced behind his eyes. "You were to retrieve the matching box as well. Was the ring not in a box?"

"Yes, but—"

"So where is the box?" He enunciated each word very clearly, striving to ward off the red haze he felt draping over his vision.

"I suppose it's still in Mrs. Brown's bedchamber."

"You left it behind."

A flash of unease flickered in Redfern's eyes at his glacial tone, but then a defiant look crossed his ruddy face. "I left it behind," he concurred. "Took the ring out of it to make sure it were the right bloody ring this time, then tossed the box on the floor like the piece of trash it were. All rusty and dented it were—not any sort of a matchin' box to that fine ring. You said *nothin'* about a bloody dented, rusty box. 'Get the ring and its *matchin'* box' is wot you said, and there"—he jabbed a stubby finger at Geoffrey's palm—"is the bloody ring. There weren't no *matchin'* box." He jutted out his chin. "I held up my end, and now it's time for you to hold up yours. I want my blunt. And I want it now."

Geoffrey's fingers curled around the ring, the cool metal digging into his palm in an effort not to wrap his fingers around Redfern's throat. With studied nonchalance, he crossed to the fireplace, then crouched down to affectionately stroke Thorndyke's fur.

"Tell me, Redfern, do you value your life?" he asked in a soft, conversational tone.

When he did not receive a reply, he looked up at Redfern, who stood still and silent as a statue near the French windows, his jaw tightly clenched.

Finally Redfern answered, " 'Course I value my life. But I ain't takin' all the blame here. You should have been more specific about the damn box."

"You will recall to whom you are speaking, Redfern, and guard your tone as well as your insolent tongue." Geoffrey forced in a deep breath to calm his fury. "Clearly I overestimated your capabilities."

"You did not. Just some unfortunate circumstances—"

"Have thwarted you, yes, so you've said. Well, allow me to explain this, and I shall endeavor to put it in terms even you can understand. I want the box the ring was in. I don't care how you get it. You will receive not so much as a farthing from me until I have it. If you fail to get it for me, you will die." With a final fond pat to his pet's head, Geoffrey rose. "Any questions?"

A muscle in Redfern's jaw ticked. "No, my lord."

"Excellent." He inclined his head toward the door. "Willis will show you out."

The instant Redfern quit the room, Geoffrey walked to his desk, forcing his steps to remain calm and measured. Slipping a small silver key from his waistcoat, he unlocked the bottom drawer. Then, opening his fist, he dropped the ring inside. It hit the wood with a hollow thud. He then relocked the drawer and pocketed the key.

Crossing to the decanters, he poured himself a brandy. To his disgust, his hands shook, sloshing several amber drops onto the rug. He quickly tossed back the potent liquor, swallowing the obscenity that threatened to roar from his throat. The urge to break something, to throw something, to destroy something with his hands nearly strangled him, and he quickly poured himself another drink. He then wrapped his hands around the crystal snifter to keep them still. *Calm. Must remain calm.*

With the second brandy burning down to his gut, he started to feel a bit steadier, regaining the control that imbecile Redfern had nearly disrupted.

The box. Sick panic clutched him and he squeezed his eyes shut, beating it back, forcing himself to think rationally and plan his next move.

Had Mrs. Brown discovered the secret of the box? Exactly how much did she know? It had *appeared* she knew nothing about his secret, but he had to *know*. And if she didn't already know, might she not still learn the truth? What if she discovered the false bottom in the box now that the ring was gone? What if she gave the box to someone? Or threw it away and it was found by one of the servants? The only way he could be assured that his secret would never come to light would be to destroy the box and its hidden contents himself.

Still, why had she not returned the box to him? Did she realize its value? Did she indeed intend to blackmail him? But if so, why had she not already made a demand? Or was that her ploy—to bide her time, like an animal stalking its prey, waiting to strike. *She's trying to drive me mad.*

Well, she would not succeed. And he'd not leave his future up to chance with Redfern. He needed to take action. Immediately.

Crossing to his desk, he withdrew a sheet of ivory vellum and composed a quick note.

Dear Alberta,

   I cannot tell you how much I enjoyed our conversation this morning, and how much I appreciate the efforts you went to on my behalf regarding the Shelbourne ring. Although the ring is gone, I was wondering if perhaps there might have been a ring box? Other pieces in the Shelbourne collection are housed in boxes fashioned specifically for the piece, and it occurred to me that the ring might have had such a box. If so, I would like very much to have that, as a memento.

   I would be honored if you would join me for dinner this evening at eight o'clock. This would give us an opportunity to become better acquainted, and you could bring the box along with you, assuming it exists. I anxiously await your reply.

Yours,
Geoffrey Hadmore

He sealed the letter, then rang for Willis. Handing over the missive, Geoffrey said, "See to it that this is delivered at once. The messenger is to await a reply."

As Willis quit the room, icy determination settled over Geoffrey. Either he or Redfern would get that bloody box. And by this time tomorrow, Mrs. Alberta Brown would no longer be a problem.

Chapter 9

Two hours after leaving Mrs. Brown in Madame Renee's expert hands, Robert reentered the modiste shop, a tinkling chime above the door announcing his arrival. He'd spent the intervening time with his solicitor. Assured that the rebuilt smithy was thriving and Nate's family provided for, eased, just a bit, the vise of guilt squeezing him.

The front of Madame Renee's was empty. Clearly Mrs. Brown and Madame Renee were in the rear, which, as he knew from previous visits with Caroline and Mother, housed the dressing and alteration areas, as well as two large sewing rooms. Removing his hat, he opted to stand rather than attempt to settle himself on one of the horribly uncomfortable chairs. He shot a baleful glare at the tiny lavender velvet seat cushion. He knew from experience that his buttocks would hang over the side. Good God, how did women manage to perch themselves upon such ridiculous furniture? It seemed fashioned more for a canary than a human.

Wandering about the bolts of colorful material, he noticed a deep sapphire-blue satin. Knowing it was Caroline's favorite color, he made a mental note to mention it to her. He'd passed stripes and solids, patterns and prints, when his gaze was caught by a striking coppery-bronze color. Pausing, he ran his hand over the luxurious material. Silk, exceptionally fine and delicate. And the color . . . bold yet delicate, shimmering with gold highlights. It was truly extraordinary.

An image flashed through his mind . . . of *her* . . . wearing a gown fashioned from the material, the color glowing against her creamy skin, accentuating her golden-brown eyes and the rich chestnut of her hair.

As if the mere thought of her conjured her up, she entered the room through the curved archway leading from the back, Madame Renee directly behind her. The shop owner's sharp eyes glanced down at the silk bolt his hand still rested upon.

"Is eet not *tres magnifique*? Zee finest silk, and zee color!" Madame Renee kissed her fingertips in dramatic fashion.

Mrs. Brown's gaze wandered to the material, and Robert caught the glimmer of wistfulness that flickered in her eyes. "Gorgeous," she agreed with a sigh. She then appeared to regain herself. "But not for me."

"Were you able to find something to suit you?" he asked, sliding his hand from the soft silk.

Before Mrs. Brown could reply, Madame Renee raised her brows. "Surely you did not doubt zat Madame Renee could assist her?"

He held up his hands in mock surrender. "Not I. Never."

"Actually, I was very fortunate," Mrs. Brown said. "Madame had two black bombazine gowns that someone had ordered, then canceled."

"Most annoying," Madame said, making a *tsk*ing sound. "But my loss is Madame Brown's gain. Because zee client cancel, I am forced to sell at a large discount. Zee gowns require only minor alterations and will be sent to her later today."

He was disappointed but not surprised that she'd opted to purchase only black gowns. His glance wandered back to the bolt of coppery silk. She'd look breathtaking . . .

He gave himself a mental shake. Good God, having her look any more breathtaking was the last thing he needed. Indeed, he'd be wise, and certainly better served, to imagine her with a sack over her head rather than draped in low-cut, sheer material.

After saying good-bye to Madame Renee, they climbed into the carriage. "I'm sorry you had to wait so long," Mrs. Brown said as they settled themselves on the gray velvet squabs. "I'd thought to perhaps purchase *one* gown, but her prices were so reasonable, I decided to buy two." She offered him a half-smile, and his heart, quite ridiculously, thumped in response. "Thank you very much for bringing me there."

"My pleasure. And don't apologize for me waiting. Indeed, it was a fraction of how long Caroline and Mother normally take. I made good use of the time by attending to some business matters that required my attention. And speaking of business matters . . . was there anything else besides seeing Shelbourne that you needed to do in London?"

"No. My business here is finished."

"Then I propose we depart for Bradford Hall tomorrow morning. That would allow for the delivery of your gowns, give us both sufficient time to pack our belongings, and allow me to send off some correspondence that needs seeing to. Does that meet with your approval?"

"Yes, that is fine."

"Excellent. And that also gives us the rest of this lovely afternoon to enjoy. Given the exceptional weather, I thought you might like to see Vauxhall."

Mischief flickered in her eyes. "Vauxhall? Is that a breed of hat-nesting pigeons?"

He laughed. "No. It's a pleasure garden across the Thames. Acres of shady walking paths, and particularly nice this time of year with so many flowers in bloom. Would you like to go?"

"I'm very fond of flowers. A visit to Vauxhall sounds . . . lovely."

Another smile touched her lips, and his idiotic pulse galloped away. *Lovely,* his inner voice repeated as his gaze roamed her face. *My thought exactly.*

.   .   .

Strolling along a wide graveled walk, Allie breathed in the cool, earth-scented air, then heaved out a sigh of pleasure. Stately elms lined both sides of the avenue, forming a delightful canopy of shade through which fingers of sunlight filtered. Birds flitted from branch to branch, warbling their summertime songs.

"This is called the Grand Walk," Lord Robert said. "Running parallel on our right is South Walk, with Hermit's Walk to the left. Up ahead we'll come to Grand Cross Walk, which runs through the entire garden. We'll turn there to go to the Grove."

"What is that?"

"A square surrounded by the principal walks." He pointed through the trees. "You can see it over there, where those pavilions are. There's also a colonnade in the event of inclement weather, and dozens of supper boxes."

Intrigued, she mused, "So people come here in the evenings to stroll among the lighted trees and dine. . . . What a delightful thing to do."

"Indeed, but there is also entertainment. Orchestras, singers, fireworks, battle enactments, grand parties. Several years ago I saw a woman named Madame Saqui walk along a tightrope affixed to a sixty-foot pole, all to the accompaniment of a fireworks display."

"It sounds marvelous. And exciting." Looking up, she noted the hundreds of globe lamps placed in the trees. "It must be lovely when the lamps are illuminated."

"Very striking. Elizabeth says it looks as if glowing faeries hover in the trees." He looked down at her and smiled. "Perhaps you'd like to return this evening? To experience the garden's nighttime splendor?"

She hesitated. The thought of seeing the lights, hearing the music, was so incredibly tempting. . . .

Yet she could vividly imagine the intimacy and romance such a setting would induce. And the temptation of the man next to her . . .

At Madame Renee's, she'd nearly succumbed to the desire

to splurge her meager funds on something colorful, or even a pastel—knowing in her heart that even more than wanting to wear something pretty for herself, she wanted *him* to see her garbed in something pretty. She'd resisted—but barely. The black gowns were the most affordable, and they would serve to discourage male attention, as they had for the past three years. Add to that the fact that her heart's rate tripled at the mere idea of strolling with him through the darkness, the only light coming from the shimmering lit trees . . . no, it was not a good idea.

"Thank you, that is very thoughtful, but I'll need this evening to prepare for our journey tomorrow."

She fancied she saw relief flash in his eyes at her refusal. Did he feel it, too, this disturbing awareness that held her firmly in its grip? Had he realized the folly of them being alone together in the dark?

They turned a corner, and a large grouping of rosebushes caught her eye. Grateful for the distraction, she said, "I don't know where I've ever seen such a colorful profusion of roses." Attracted by a particularly vivid pink bud, she paused to bend over and breathe in its heady scent.

"Wait until you see the formal gardens at Bradford Hall. They're really quite spectacular, and contain what seems like miles of roses. Whenever I smell the flower, I am reminded of Caroline and my mother. They both wear the scent."

Straightening, she fell back into step beside him, nodding. "I understand precisely what you mean, associating certain smells with certain people. Whenever I smell freshly baked bread, I think of Mama. The aroma of tobacco always brings Papa to mind. And whenever I breathe in lilacs, I think of—"

"Elizabeth," they said in unison, then both laughed.

Lord Robert shot her a quick smile that set her heart to fluttering. "Whenever I smell leather," he said, "especially a leather saddle, I think of my father. My very earliest memory is sitting in front of him on his horse, Lancelot. Father was an expert horseman, not to mention incredibly patient. Taught all of us how to ride. Even Caroline."

There was no mistaking the affection in his tone. "Tell me more about your father."

All hints of amusement slowly faded from his expression, leaving behind an unmistakable melancholy. "I don't know quite how to describe him other than to say he was a great man, and noble in a way that had nothing to do with his title. He was well respected by his peers, adored by his wife, and loved by his children. Strict, yet reasonable. Generous with his time, funds, and affection, and fair with his tenants. Slow to anger, quick to laugh, and unlike many men in his position, devoted to his family."

Her fingers, resting on his forearm, flexed in sympathy. "He sounds like a wonderful person."

He nodded. "William, Austin, and I . . . even as boys we always strove to emulate him. To this day, I believe we still do. I know I do, although if I'm able to be half the man he was, I'll consider myself blessed." He paused for several seconds, then continued, "His death was so sudden, so unexpected. So horribly shocking. He appeared in perfect health, yet his heart just . . . stopped."

The husky emotion in his voice swelled something inside her . . . sympathy, yet something else she could not quite define. Something unsettling. Until this moment, she'd believed that he was not a serious man, that he was merely frivolous and carefree. Yet the way he spoke of his father, of wanting to be like him, bespoke a depth she hadn't considered he'd possess. A depth she found dangerously, disturbingly attractive.

"Do you know," he said, pulling her from her thoughts, "my father asked my mother to marry him, right here in Vauxhall? It was a favorite family story, told every year on their anniversary." He pointed to a stone bench under a majestic elm. "Father swore they were sitting on that bench. Mother, however, always corrected him, saying it was a seat near the north border of the gardens." A chuckle rumbled from him. "It was a continuous source of good-natured ribbing between them, an argument that always ended with Father winking at Mother and saying, 'It matters not *where* I asked, only that the lady said yes.' "

She couldn't help but smile at the loving picture his words painted in her mind. The wistful sadness in his eyes called out to her, urging her to replace it with the mischievous laughter she was used to seeing there.

"Very romantic. Very unlike *my* parents." Leaning closer, as if she were about to impart the most confidential of matters, she asked in an undertone, "Can you keep a secret?"

His brows rose. "Of course."

"My *mother* proposed to my *father*."

He stared down at her for several seconds, then, as she'd hoped, his lips quirked upward. "Never say so."

She laid her free hand over her heart. "I tell you the truth, sir. Mama and Papa had known and loved each other from childhood. The summer Mama turned seventeen, she waited and waited for Papa to propose to her, but he was waiting for the perfect moment. Deciding she'd grow old before his idea of the perfect moment ever arrived, Mama took matters into her own hands and asked him."

"Obviously he said yes."

"True, although Papa still claims he was quite disgruntled about her stealing his big romantic moment, to which Mama always replies, 'If I'd waited for you, Henry, we still wouldn't be married. Why, I would have had to marry Marvin Blakely instead.' "

She laughed, then continued, "That's when Papa would mutter something uncomplimentary under his breath about Marvin Blakely. Then he and Mama would share what I called their special smile . . . the one that made it so obvious that they still loved each other after all these years."

He paused, drawing her to a stop. Surprise flickered in his eyes. "My parents often exchanged that same sort of look. They could have been standing in a room filled with dozens of people, but it would suddenly seem as if they were alone. As if no one else existed."

"Yes, that's precisely the look."

They stood there, in the middle of the path, looking at each other, and once again, as she had the day before, she swore something passed between them. A subtle, unspoken understanding—silent, yet nonetheless real.

Forcing herself to look away from him, she shook her head and sighed. "I'm so sorry for your mother. It must be terrible to lose a husband you love so much. . . ."

She felt him start, and she looked up at him. He was staring at her with an odd expression. "But of course you would understand how that feels . . ." he murmured. He didn't ask *wouldn't you*, yet she clearly heard the question in his voice, saw it in his frown.

Heat suffused her face, and she started walking again, turning away from his penetrating, inquisitive stare, afraid that he would read the truth in her eyes.

While she could not deny that she had loved David when he'd died, her discovery of his true nature had extinguished her love like a snuffed-out candle. She tried to conjure David's likeness in her mind's eye, to forcibly remind herself of what she never wanted to suffer through again, but the handsome face that filled her mind wasn't David's.

God, help me. She squeezed her eyes shut, trying to erase Lord Robert's image, but failed utterly. He filled her mind completely. But worse, she suspected that if she let her guard down at all, he would fill her heart.

Grateful to be back at the town house, Robert handed his hat and walking stick to Carters. He couldn't have endured one more minute confined with her in that carriage, breathing in her hypnotic flowery scent, racking his brain without success for something to say. Nearly the entire journey from Vauxhall was made in silence. He'd sat across from her, tongue-tied like a green schoolboy.

Damn it, they'd enjoyed such camaraderie during their walk, but then it had suddenly vanished, replaced with an uneasy tension that emanated from her in waves. Half of him had

longed to break that tension, but the other half told him it was
better this way. For the more he spoke to her, shared with her,
the more enchanted he became with her. The more he wanted
to know everything about her.

Carters' voice yanked him from his musings. "A package
from Madame Renee's establishment arrived for Mrs. Brown
while you were out. I placed it in her bedchamber." Reaching
into his coat pocket, he withdrew a sealed letter and handed it
to Mrs. Brown. "This arrived as well. There's a lad waiting to
bring a reply back to Lord Shelbourne."

Robert's shoulder's stiffened. What did Shelbourne want
now? With a nod of thanks, she broke the seal and read the
contents. A tapping echoed in the foyer, and to his annoyance
he realized it was the toe of his own boot striking the marble
floor. Nearly a minute passed with her silently reading. What
the devil had Shelbourne written her? A bloody novel?

Clearing his throat, he adopted a casual tone in marked
contrast to his annoyance and remarked, "Nothing amiss, I
hope."

She glanced up from the vellum. "Lord Shelbourne wishes
for me to dine with him at his home this evening."

Robert's hands fisted. Bloody hell! Clearly the rogue
sought to pursue her in the privacy of his home as she'd
refused his invitation to go out publicly. Well, Mrs. Brown
was no foolish, naïve miss. Of course she would divine
Shelbourne's intent and refuse him.

"May I use the carriage tonight?"

He stared at her. Much as he tried to will it away, he
couldn't stop the jealousy pumping through him. Nor the hurt.
Damn it, she'd turned down *his* invitation for an evening at
Vauxhall. No matter that the instant the invitation had passed
his lips he'd regretted it. The intimacy of the setting would be
pure torture for him, and he'd been more than a little relieved
when she'd declined. But now . . .

"You intend to accept him?" he asked, much more stiffly
than he'd intended. "I thought you required this evening to
prepare for tomorrow's journey."

"In truth, I do, but I really cannot refuse the earl's invitation. See for yourself," she said, handing him the missive.

He scanned the few lines, his jaw tightening at the phrase "opportunity to become better acquainted." "Do you have this box he mentions?"

"Yes. I suppose I should have brought it to him this morning, but I never thought of it. Indeed, I most likely would have thrown it away when I packed up my belongings this evening. The box is rusted and dented on the top. I'm certainly happy to give it to him, especially since I cannot return his ring."

"So you wish to accept his invitation simply to return this rusty, dented box."

"Yes. I consider it an errand of honor. Wouldn't you?"

Marginally cheered, he admitted, "Yes, I suppose I would. However, I must warn you that Shelbourne has . . . something of a reputation with the ladies." He nearly choked on the mild description, but he did not feel the need to prejudice her against the man with the unvarnished truth—that Shelbourne was a jaded libertine without a single scruple in regards to women—although he would if he had to. "Elizabeth would have my head if I allowed you to spend time alone with someone who could damage your reputation. Therefore, I insist upon accompanying you."

She appeared relieved. "Thank you. While I feel I must go, I've no wish to dine alone with the earl."

Hmmm. Clearly Shelbourne was the only one who wished to become better acquainted. Excellent. And while it was hardly polite to invite himself to dinner, under the circumstances, he had little choice. Just knowing it would irk Shelbourne cheered him even further.

"Then I'll send off a reply for him to expect two dinner guests." He consulted his timepiece. "We have almost two hours before we must depart. As we'll be out this evening, I suggest we use this time to prepare for tomorrow's departure."

"An excellent plan." With a nod, she climbed the stairs, disappearing from his view when she turned down the corridor leading to her bedchamber. Turning on his heel, he walked

to Austin's study, intent upon making use of his brother's
stationery. He had to send off his reply to Shelbourne.

And then he had another, more important letter to write.

Allie entered her bedchamber, heading directly toward the mahogany dresser. She picked up the rusted ring box, setting it in
the palm of her hand.

"I will be very relieved to see the last of you," she whispered to the dented piece. "Once you are returned, I will be
free." David and the damage he'd wrought would finally be ex-
orcized from her life, although she suspected that a few
demons would always remain.

Still, profound relief washed through her. With her quest
completed, she could fully enjoy her visit with Elizabeth. Six
lovely weeks in the English countryside, with nothing more
pressing to do than to catch up with her childhood friend, and
put the last bits of the past behind her. Then she'd return to
America and—

Never see Lord Robert again.

The unwanted words popped unbidden into her mind.
Thoroughly irritated that he'd once again invaded her
thoughts, she set the box back down on the dresser, but clearly
with more force than she'd intended, for she heard a slight
cracking sound.

Picking up the box, she examined the dresser's polished
surfaced, relieved when she noted no damage. Then she held
the box up to eye level.

The bottom appeared to be separating. She attempted to
gently snap the bottom back into place, but the instant she applied pressure, the entire affair broke into two pieces.

"Oh, dear." She gazed at the pieces in dismay, a feeling that
was quickly replaced by surprise. It appeared the one section
was a false bottom. With a piece of folded paper secreted in
the small space.

Chapter 10

Moving to catch the swatch of fading sunlight pouring through the window, Allie frowned at the yellowed paper tucked into the broken piece. Could this be something that belonged to David? Determined to find out, she carefully pried out the paper, then gently unfolded it. She could make out some writing, but it appeared badly faded. Holding the paper up to the light, she squinted at it, trying to make out the words. It seemed to be written in a foreign language—one she did not recognize. While she was not a linguist, it didn't appear to be French, Spanish, or Latin.

She peered at the note again. Could the words possibly be Gaelic? David had been familiar with the language, she knew. Many times, during moments of passion, he'd whispered to her in the dark—enchanting, romantic-sounding words she hadn't understood. They were Gaelic, he'd said. Phrases he'd learned during his numerous trips to Dublin, sailing across the Irish Sea from his native Liverpool.

A sense of dismay that had nothing to do with breaking the box washed through her. If this note had anything to do with David, she might not yet be able to put the past behind her. The temptation to refold the note and stuff it back into the box, or better yet, to destroy it—simply toss it into the fire—nearly overwhelmed her. *No one would know.*

The words reverberated through her mind, irresistibly coaxing her. *No one would know.* What did it matter if the note concerned David? He was dead. She owed him nothing. *Destroy it. No one would know.*

Yet something held her back. No one would know—except her. As much as she wished it otherwise, her conscience, not to mention her curiosity, would plague her if she did not at least attempt to discover the contents of the note. And perhaps it did not concern David at all. Perhaps it belonged to Lord Shelbourne—after all, the ring and box belonged to him. And if this note were the earl's property, she could not destroy it. She would have to return it to him.

But the fact that David knew Gaelic, coupled with everything else she knew about him . . . no, she could not dismiss the very real and disturbing probability that the note in some way involved her late husband.

She drew in a shaky breath. Discovering the contents . . . that meant the need to face the possibility that this note might very well yield information about more people he'd cheated. And if she were successful in deciphering the words, and it indeed listed more of David's victims, she would have to—

No! The word roared through her mind, and she pressed her fingertips to her temple. God help her, she wouldn't, *couldn't*, spend any more time righting any more of his wrongs—yet how could she not? But the mere thought of enduring more financial hardships and personal humiliations such as she'd endured for the past three years—especially when the end had seemed so close—nearly suffocated her. *Don't think about it now. It might not even be an issue. And if it is . . . you'll decide then.*

She couldn't destroy the note. Not until she knew. Nor could she return it to the box. She couldn't risk Lord Shelbourne finding the note—of potentially damaging information falling into his or anyone else's hands. Heaving a weary sigh, she carefully refolded the note, then secreted it in a small pouch in the lining of her reticule, all the while damning the fact that she'd found it. Freedom had been so close. But at least she'd be rid of the box. Settling herself on the edge of her bed, she set about fitting the two pieces back together.

Geoffrey leaned against the marble mantel in his drawing room, watching a footman serve his guests an aperitif. It was nearly impossible to maintain his air of detached outer calm. She'd handed the box to him a quarter hour ago, when she'd first entered the room. He'd given it a quick glance, then laughed. "Not a particularly handsome piece, is it?" After thanking her, he'd casually slipped it into his pocket, where it now all but scorched a hole through the material.

Finally, unable to stand the suspense one second longer, he said, "If you'll excuse me for a moment, I must have a word with Willis." Maintaining a slow, even stride, he left the room, then entered his private study where he locked the door behind him.

He crossed to his desk, slowly withdrawing the box from his pocket, biting back the overwhelming urge to pounce upon it like a mongrel on a bone. With his heart slamming against his ribs, he pulled the box apart and stared in the bottom.

The empty bottom.

Panic seized him and he ran shaking, frantic fingers all over the rusted metal surface. Was there another opening? But after several minutes of desperate searching, he was forced to admit the nightmarish truth. The paper was missing.

A barrage of obscenities exploded from his lips, and he hurled the useless box across the room. Fisting his hands in his hair, he paced furiously around the room, his breath expelling from his lungs in painful gasps.

Where the bloody hell was it? She must have it. Must have found it. Or at least must know its whereabouts.

He had to find out. Had to. Had to. Now. He halted and squeezed his eyes shut. Damn it, his head felt about to explode. *Have to pull myself together. Must find out what she knows. Then get rid of her.* He hadn't worried about Redfern finding the letter, as the man did not know how to read—a fact that Geoffrey had been careful to ascertain before hiring him. It wouldn't do to have Redfern find the note by chance and be able to extort money from him as David Brown had done. Although Redfern's greed would keep him from showing the letter to anyone to read and risk having to share his blunt. But Mrs. Brown . . . he suspected she was neither illiterate nor stupid. And she was no doubt as greedy as her husband had been.

Drawing deep breaths until he steadied, he then walked slowly to the mirror and smoothed his hair back into place. He jerked his lapels back into perfect alignment, then made a minute adjustment to his cravat. Satisfied that his appearance was once again flawless, he quit the room to return to his guests.

Alberta Brown clearly thought herself clever. *A mistake, my dear. A fatal mistake.*

Allie immediately sensed something odd in the earl's demeanor when he reentered the drawing room. From her seat facing the doorway, she watched him pause on the threshold, his gaze riveted on her. A chill of apprehension slithered down her spine at his glacial expression.

"Everything all right?" Lord Robert asked, looking at their host with a puzzled frown. Clearly he also sensed all was not well.

"Of course." The earl waved his hand in a dismissive manner. "A tiny miscalculation in the kitchen apparently, but Willis assures me all is well. Shall we adjourn to the dining room?"

Allie accepted his proffered elbow, praying her reluctance did not show. Perhaps she was imagining his disquiet.

But by the second dinner course of delicately poached turbot, Allie knew she was not imagining things. The way he kept staring at her, as if he were attempting to see into her mind . . . yes, something was definitely amiss. Was he ill? She dismissed the notion as quickly as it occurred to her. No, it seemed as if repressed *anger* bubbled just below the surface of his flawless manners.

Could he possibly know about the note? Know it was missing and that she had it? She instantly discarded that theory as well. How could he know about the note when he had not even known that the ring or the box existed until she came to England?

No answers presented themselves, yet his manner disturbed her in a way she could not put her finger on. Some instinct, however, cautioned her that it might behoove her to find out more about this man. And surely the best way to do that was not to remain silent.

Raising her chin, she offered the earl a smile. "Your home is lovely . . . Geoffrey."

His expression relaxed. Then his lips curved slowly upward, while his gaze drifted leisurely downward to rest on her mouth. "Thank you."

She indicated the gilt-framed still life adorning the wall behind him. "You're clearly a lover of art. That is a beautiful piece."

Robert's jaw froze in midchew, and he stared across the table. Mrs. Brown was looking at—no, *smiling* at—Shelbourne—no, *Geoffrey*—with an interested warmth that simultaneously stunned and irritated him. Damn it all, he'd been in another brown study and had clearly missed something. And the way Shelbourne was looking at—no, *ogling*—her. . . . When the bloody hell had all this warm coziness started?

Pretending to be fascinated with his turbot and peas, he covertly observed their interchange, but it quickly became apparent he did not require the ruse, as they both had seemingly forgotten his presence.

"Do you like art, Alberta?"

"I very much enjoy looking at it, but I'm afraid I possess little knowledge on the subject."

"Then after dinner, I shall show you the gallery. While it's quite modest in comparison to the one at Shelbourne Manor, there are some . . . exquisite pieces."

The inflection in Shelbourne's tone when he said "exquisite pieces," not to mention the way his gaze boldly roamed over her breasts, tensed every muscle in Robert's body. Bloody libertine. How dare he look at her like that? *You mean, in the exact way you've looked at her?* his inner voice taunted.

No! He fought the urge to tunnel his hands through his hair in exasperation. He couldn't deny he'd looked at her with desire, but there was a calculation in Shelbourne's eyes . . . a predatory gleam that edged more than jealousy through Robert. It made him distinctly uneasy.

"Lord Robert showed me through Vauxhall Gardens this afternoon," Mrs. Brown said to their host. "A lovely place."

Shelbourne cocked a brow. "In the afternoon, yes, but it is especially so at night." He leaned closer to her, his voice dropping to an intimate level. "All those dark, private walkways make for some very . . . stimulating evenings."

Robert gritted his teeth and fought the nearly overwhelming urge to plant the blackguard a facer. Yet more disturbing than Shelbourne's behavior—which was at least expected— was Mrs. Brown's. Instead of appearing outraged, a delicate peach blush colored her cheeks, and what appeared to be a suppressed grin twitched her lips. . . . Lips that Shelbourne's gaze seemed plastered to.

A change in conversation was most definitely in order. "How are things at your Cornwall estate, Shelbourne?" he asked.

Shelbourne did not even glance at him. "Spendid. Tell me, Alberta—"

"Have you implemented any upgrades? I understand from Austin there's been recent improvements in both irrigation systems and farming techniques."

Shelbourne finally turned toward him, a lazily amused smile lifting one corner of his mouth. "My irrigation systems are in excellent condition, Jamison, thank you for asking. As for my techniques . . . I've heard no complaints."

"Indeed? Perhaps you are not listening closely enough."

A long, measuring look passed between them. Then, with a careless shrug that set Robert's teeth on edge, Shelbourne's gaze swiveled back to Mrs. Brown. He launched into a lengthy description of his Cornwall estate, his attention remaining almost exclusively on Mrs. Brown, who seemed not to mind at all. Indeed, if her blushes were any indication, she was quite enjoying Shelbourne's address. Deciding the meal would end more quickly if he did not prolong the conversation, Robert remained mostly silent.

The instant the interminable meal ended, Robert rose, intending to depart, but Shelbourne smoothly reminded him that he'd promised Mrs. Brown a tour of the gallery.

"I'd love to see it," Mrs. Brown said.

Left with no option that did not leave him appearing churlish, and not about to allow Shelbourne to be alone with her, Robert accompanied them, his mood growing more grim each time Shelbourne touched her, which seemed to be constantly. Brushing his fingers against her arm to gain her attention. Resting his palm on the small of her back to lead her to the next painting. Tucking her hand through his elbow. Jealousy ate at him, made worse—and damn it, more hurtful—every time she offered Shelbourne one of her rare smiles.

Six, damn it. She'd smiled at Shelbourne six times since they'd entered the gallery. And eight times during dinner. Not that Robert was counting. But she hadn't offered *him* so much as a glance. Her obvious pleasure in Shelbourne's company concerned and genuinely confused him.

What about her devotion to her husband? Had Shelbourne's attention encouraged her to step out from her mourning? While he would be happy to see her abandon the outward signs of grieving, he found it hard to accept that Shelbourne would be the man to make her want to do so. *Me. I want it to be me.*

As much as he hated to, he was forced to admit that Shelbourne possessed the qualities that most women admired: He was wealthy, titled, and handsome, his dark good looks

tinged with an edge of danger. But Mrs. Brown did not strike
Robert as falling into the category of "most women."

Still, perhaps all she'd needed was for a man to court her.
To sweep her off her feet. To show her, without a doubt, that he
found her desirable. *Me. I want it to be me.*

His footsteps faltered at the thought, precipitously so, as
he'd been about to plow into Shelbourne's back where he and
Mrs. Brown had paused before what was, thankfully, the last
painting.

"She's beautiful," Mrs. Brown murmured.

"Yes," Shelbourne agreed. "But she pales in comparison to
you."

Robert's gaze flicked over the painting. A Gainsborough,
he noted. Quite a nice one. And the subject, a young woman
standing in a field of wildflowers, was undeniably beautiful.
And she did indeed pale in comparison to Mrs. Brown.

And damn it, *he* wanted to be the one telling her so. Wanted
her gaze directed at *him*.

Me. I want her to want me.

And it was about time he did something about it.

"Given your interest in art," Shelbourne was saying, "you
must see the Elgin Marbles while you're in town. Why don't I
call upon you tomorrow—"

"Impossible," Robert interjected, not even attempting to
hide the edge in his voice. "We depart for Bradford Hall at first
light. Indeed, it's time we take our leave of you."

Shelbourne led them down the corridor toward the foyer,
his gaze never leaving Mrs. Brown's face. "I am desolate,
Alberta. How long will you stay in Kent?"

"Six weeks."

"And then?"

"Then I sail home," she said softly.

Something squeezed in Robert's chest at her words.

"I may be traveling through Kent in the next few weeks. If
so, I shall make a point to call at Bradford Hall. It would be a
pleasure to see Bradford and the duchess again." Shelbourne

leaned down, his lips nearly brushing Mrs. Brown's ear. "And a great pleasure to see *you* again."

Luckily they arrived in the foyer just then, for Robert felt like a teakettle about to spew a stream of steam.

"Thank you for dinner," Mrs. Brown said, tying her bonnet strings in a small bow beneath her chin. "I enjoyed the food and your artwork very much."

"As I enjoyed your company, Alberta." Lifting her hand to his lips, he kissed her fingertips—for much longer than necessary—and with a heated look in his eye Robert recognized all too well.

His hands fisted inside his gloves. The manners drummed into him since childhood were the only thing that kept him from dropping the man like a stone. Inclining his head in Shelbourne's direction, he said, "Lovely meal. My thanks." Then, before Shelbourne could so much as look at her again, he angled himself between them and swiftly escorted her to the waiting carriage.

After assisting Mrs. Brown to step up, he murmured, "Excuse me, I forgot my walking stick." He strode back to the town house, where Willis admitted him. Shelbourne still stood in the foyer.

"A moment of your time, Shelbourne," he said.

Shelbourne raised his brows at his sharp tone, but merely said, "Of course. My study?"

"The foyer is adequate."

With an almost imperceptible nod from Shelbourne, Willis left them alone. Then Shelbourne regarded him through narrowed eyes. "What on earth could be so important, Jamison, that you would leave that ravishing creature alone?"

"*She* is what I wish to talk about. Leave her alone."

"Surely that is something the lady can decide for herself. And I must tell you, Jamison, she did not give me the impression that that was what she wanted."

"She doesn't know your reputation as I do."

Shelbourne appeared amused. "Oh, but by all means, tell

her. My wicked reputation is often half the attraction. And I've a particular fondness for experienced widows."

Robert favored him with his most frigid, unwavering glare. "Cast your jaded eye elsewhere, Shelbourne."

"She doesn't belong to you, Jamison." Cunning speculation flickered in his eyes. "Or does she?"

It took every ounce of Robert's willpower not to wipe that smug expression from Shelbourne's face—with his fist. "All you need to know is that she will *never* belong to you. Have I made myself clear?"

"I don't believe I care for your tone, Jamison."

"I don't believe I give a damn, Shelbourne." He took one step closer to the earl. Shelbourne was tall, but Robert had him by an inch, a fact he took full advantage of. "I've said what I came here to say. You'd be wise to not give me cause to ever repeat it."

Without waiting for Willis, Robert let himself out, striding quickly down the walkway to the waiting carriage.

From the narrow foyer window, Geoffrey watched the carriage depart. Hmm. Jamison clearly harbored a tendre for Mrs. Brown. Pity. The woman was not long for this world. And if Jamison got in the way, his days were numbered as well.

Chapter 11

The moment the carriage halted in front of the Bradford town house, Robert knew something was amiss. It appeared as if every chandelier and candle in the entire household were lit, for light blazed from every window. Before he and Mrs. Brown had made it halfway up the cobbled walkway, the double oak doors opened. Carters stood in the swath of light, his normally blank features lined with distress.

Fear hit him. Now what? Had something happened to Elizabeth? To the babe? He all but propelled Mrs. Brown up the steps and into the foyer. "What's wrong?" he asked Carters, forcing himself not to shake the man by his lapels. "The duchess?"

"No, Lord Robert." Unmistakable anger flashed in Carters' eyes. "But someone has attempted to rob us again."

"Was anyone hurt?"

"No, sir. Indeed, nothing was taken. The scoundrel tried to enter Mrs. Brown's bedchamber from the balcony, but was scared off when Clara screamed. She'd just turned down Mrs. Brown's bed and was seeing to the fire when the French windows leading to the balcony opened. And there he stood, dressed head to toe in black, she said. Never heard a woman scream like that in my entire life. Gave all of us quite a turn, of course, not so much of a turn as poor Clara suffered."

"Then what happened?" Robert asked.

"I was the first to arrive in the bedchamber, where I found Clara still screaming and brandishing the fire poker. Apparently she'd scared off the brigand. He'd vaulted over the railing to the ground. By the time I'd gotten the story from her, the bloke had vanished."

"Where is Clara now?"

"Gone to bed, sir. Cook prepared her a restorative toddy to calm her nerves. Nearly fell to pieces afterward, but Clara quite saved the day."

"Indeed she did," Robert murmured. "When did this happen?"

"Not more than half an hour after you departed, sir. As soon as I'd turned Clara over to Cook, I sent for the magistrate. Mr. Laramie interviewed Clara, then departed. He advised me to tell you that he'd inform you of any news, and to make certain all the doors and windows are locked. I've already been through the entire household checking. We are all secured."

"Thank you, Carters." Robert turned to Mrs. Brown, who had remained silent throughout his exchange with Carters. She stood still as a statue, her face devoid of color, her eyes twin pools of distress. He noted the slight tremor of her bottom lip, and the way her fingers were twisted together.

She was hiding something, damn it, and he'd had quite enough of it. He hadn't pressed her last evening, but tonight things would be different.

"I believe we need to have another conversation, Mrs. Brown," he said softly.

Allie stood in front of the drawing-room fireplace, staring at the flames, trying to absorb the heat to chase away the chill that had invaded her bones at Carters' disturbing news.

Dear God, it wasn't over. The ring, the box, they were both

gone, yet still someone wanted something from her. Or simply wanted her . . . gone.

She clasped her hands tightly in front of her but could not stop their trembling. She could not recall a time in her life when she'd been more frightened. Or felt more alone. And not only frightened for herself. This menace no longer threatened just her. Lord Robert had already been hurt, and the town house ransacked and robbed. If she traveled to Bradford Hall, could her presence there bring danger to Elizabeth and her family?

She couldn't risk such a thing. The best thing would no doubt be for her to return to America. Immediately. Her heart balked at the idea, but she wouldn't forgive herself if further harm befell someone because of her. Because of her connection to David. For that was the only explanation. This person who wanted something from her had to be someone from David's past. Someone must have followed her from America. A sense of weary bitterness invaded her. *So now you will steal something else from me, David. My chance to see Elizabeth.*

Hot tears pressed behind her eyes. Dear God, she felt so alone—with a stabbing ache she'd never before experienced. And she was so tired of being alone.

"Are you all right?"

Lord Robert's deep voice sounded directly behind her. Turning, she found herself staring up into eyes not dark with anger, as she'd anticipated, but steady with unmistakable concern.

Reaching out, he cupped her shoulders. Warmth from his wide palms seeped through her gown. "It is obvious that you are *not* all right," he said softly. "It is also obvious that there is more going on here than you've told me." His fingers tightened and an edge entered his voice. "Whatever is going on, it's placing not only you, but me and everyone and everything in my brother's household, at risk. I do not want anyone to get hurt."

"Neither do I," she whispered. "Which is why the best

thing is for me to return to America. On the first available ship."

He seemed to freeze for several seconds. An indecipherable look flashed in his eyes, then his fingers tightened on her shoulders. "No," he said in an emphatic tone. "That would *not* be best. We can solve this problem. Whoever is behind this will be apprehended. In the meanwhile, Bradford Hall is very secure, and once we arrive, I'll see to it that extra safety precautions are taken."

His confidence wavered her resolve. God knew she did not want to leave. Of course, if she were to go, she wouldn't be forced to confide the humiliating details of her marriage. She could simply sail home without him ever having to know.

He lightly shook her shoulders, regaining her attention. "You must abandon this idea of leaving. Not only would Elizabeth never forgive me if I allowed you to do so, but you cannot make such a trip alone. If, after seeing Elizabeth, you are still determined to cut your visit to England short, we will arrange for a traveling companion to accompany you." His compelling blue gaze bore into hers. "But you do not strike me as the sort of woman who would run away."

His statement struck her as both compliment and challenge, strengthening her determination not to allow David to rob her of anything else. All of Lord Robert's arguments to stay were sound, while the thought of leaving filled her with an ache she could not name.

"I'll stay," she said. The instant the words passed her lips, it felt as if a weight had been lifted from her heart.

Lord Robert expelled a long breath, and his grip on her shoulders relaxed. "Excellent. Now you must tell me what is going on. I've pledged to do my utmost to protect both you and my family, but I cannot do that until I know everything."

Everything. He was right, of course. There was more at risk here than simply her own safety. Her silence might be placing him in danger. Indeed, it already had. If further harm were to befall him—

No. She couldn't allow that to happen.

He gave her shoulders another tiny shake. "Let me help you. Trust me."

She swallowed the humorless laugh that rose in her throat. Yet even as her mind scoffed at the notion of trusting him, her heart reminded her that this man had proven himself trustworthy, at least as far as protecting her was concerned. He'd rescued her from her abductors, and had watched over her since she'd arrived.

Let me help you. She briefly squeezed her eyes closed. To have an ally . . . someone to talk to. Confide in. Lean on. But what would he think of her once he knew the truth? The thought of seeing the warmth and admiration fade from his gaze saddened her. But she owed him the truth. With his safety at risk, she had no choice.

"It's rather a long story," she said.

His gaze never wavered. "I have as long as you need." His hands slid down her arms, and he clasped her hands in a reassuring grip. "Come. Let's sit." He led her to the settee, and once they were settled, she drew a deep breath.

"Did Elizabeth tell you anything about . . . my husband?"

He appeared surprised. "No. Only that he'd died."

"She didn't mention *how* he died?"

"No. I assumed an illness of some sort."

"David was killed in a duel." She longed to look away from his penetrating gaze, but forced herself to look him straight in the eye. "By his lover's husband."

It clearly took several seconds for her words to sink in, but then there was no mistaking his stunned reaction. Unable to stand the pity she saw brewing in his eyes, she rose and began to pace in front of the fire.

"I had no idea," she said. "One minute I thought I had a husband who loved me as much as I loved him. The next minute I found out he was dead. Before I could even assimilate that news, I learned he'd been unfaithful to me . . . almost from the moment we'd wed."

Now that she'd begun, the words seemed to pour from her, as if she'd lanced a wound, letting out the poison. "I was still reeling from that blow when I realized that adultery was the least of David's sins. While packing away his belongings, I discovered a journal. After reading it, I learned exactly what sort of man I'd married."

She pressed shaky hands to her stomach in a vain attempt to calm her inner trembling. "He was a thief. A blackmailer. A criminal. The journal listed, in great detail, hundreds of items he'd stolen and then sold. Of sums he'd extorted." A fresh on-slaught of pain rushed through her at the memory, tightening her throat. "I was sick. Literally sick. Every comfort I'd en-joyed as his wife—our fine home, the beautiful furnishings, my exquisite wardrobe—were all at the expense of other people."

She turned to him and spread her hands. "I didn't know," she whispered. "I didn't know. And once I found out, it nearly destroyed me. So many emotions churned through me, I thought I might lose my mind. I spent an entire week locked in my room. First crying over what I'd lost—my husband, my se-curity, my future. Then I cried over what a fool I'd been. I'd trusted David absolutely, with my whole heart. He'd fooled me so completely. Had fooled everyone. Except Elizabeth. She'd tried to warn me. Cautioned me I didn't know him well enough, but I wouldn't listen. . . ."

Pausing long enough to draw several deep breaths, she con-tinued, "After a week of indulging in tears and self-pity, I couldn't stand myself anymore. That is when anger replaced the self-pity. Anger at myself for being such a naïve fool. And with David for all his lies and deceit."

Turning from him, she started to pace once again, the words flowing even faster. "Once I stopped feeling sorry for myself, I decided I would not, could not, allow David to rob me of my self-respect. He'd stolen everything else, but he wasn't going to have that. And there was only one way I would ever have a chance of feeling good about myself again. I de-cided to return all the monies he'd stolen.

"To that end, little by little, I sold everything. The house, the furniture, my jewelry, and eventually even my clothing. As soon as the house sold, I moved away. The gossip and scandal surrounding David's death at the hands of his lover's husband . . . well, you cannot even imagine how unbearable it made my life. I settled in a small town outside Boston. David had lived in the city for several years, and according to his journal, the majority of the people he'd stolen from were from that area. Living close by enabled me to ensure that the funds safely reached those I needed to repay. As Brown is a common surname, and I did not tell anyone my husband's name had been David, everyone simply regarded me with the respect due a young widow. I earned a bit of money taking in sewing. With that independence, and the feeling of doing something useful to right the wrongs David had wrought . . . I eventually started to heal."

Memories flashed through her mind. Her modest rooms. Long nights that had eventually ceased to seem quite so lonely. Her self-respect slowly seeping back as, one by one, she anonymously paid back David's victims.

"I found one item among David's belongings," she continued, "that was not mentioned in his journal. It was a small rusted box containing a coat-of-arms ring. I thought it odd that there was no mention of the piece, especially given how meticulously all the other ill-gotten items were listed. Candlesticks, jewelry, snuffboxes. With the exception of perhaps a dozen items, he'd sold the wares as fast as he stole them, therefore I could only return the money he'd sold them for, rather than the actual goods." Another humorless laugh escaped her. "While I couldn't explain why there was no mention of this ring in the journal, I of course had good reason to assume it was stolen. If it was, I wanted to return it to the owner. If it actually had belonged to David, I planned to sell it, then donate the money to charity. I wanted all traces of him gone."

She stopped pacing and glanced at him. He sat on the settee, leaning forward, his forearms braced on his spread legs, his hands clasped, watching her intently. Questions lurked in his intense gaze, but he said nothing, clearly waiting for her to continue.

Clearing her throat, and pacing once more, she plunged on. "I consulted with an antiquities expert in Boston, but was only able to learn that the ring was old, of English origin, and probably belonged to a member of the peerage. Which meant, of course, that David had almost certainly stolen it, no doubt before he sailed to America. I left the ring as my final item to return, deciding to combine my search for the owner with a visit to Elizabeth. It took me three long years to locate, then repay, David's victims, but I finally succeeded. The only things I kept were my silver wedding band, which I no longer wore, and my mourning gowns, which I wore every day. I couldn't afford other clothing, and the black kept any suitors at bay. And both the wedding band and the gowns served as daily reminders of what I'd lost . . . and a harsh warning to never allow myself to be put in a similar situation again." She stopped in front of the fire and stared into the flames, her hands fisted at her sides. "Never again," she whispered fervently. "Never again."

"Does Elizabeth know all this?" he asked.

Turning to face him, she shook her head. "*No one* knows. All Elizabeth knows is what I wrote to her in my very first letter where I told her that David had been killed in a duel. Because she deserved to know she'd been right about him, I informed her about the circumstances surrounding his death. I begged for her forgiveness and I asked her if I could visit her, to apologize in person. She wrote back, readily offering her forgiveness and inviting me to come to England."

"What about your family? Did you not tell them?"

"Only about David being unfaithful, which of course *everyone* learned about upon his death. No one knows the rest." She raised her chin a fraction. "Except you. Nor does anyone else know of my financial situation. If I'd told my family, they would have insisted upon helping me. But paying those people back . . . it was something I had to do on my own." She slowly shook her head. "I do not expect you to understand. . . ."

A shadow passed over his face. "Actually, I understand perfectly."

She sincerely doubted he could, but when their eyes met, there was no mistaking the empathy in his gaze. Curiosity nudged her, but she forced herself to push it aside and finish her own tale. "By the time I was ready to travel to London, I could barely afford the passage. But I didn't wish to delay my trip any longer and be forced to endure a winter ocean crossing. And I *had* to come. I had to find out more about the ring so I could put the last remaining piece of the past behind me, and I needed to see Elizabeth. To make amends to her. Through the letters we'd exchanged, I knew she generously forgave my horrible treatment of her, but I wanted, needed, to express my sorrow in person." She pressed her hands tighter against her middle. "I was hateful to her. She was my best friend, with nothing but my best interests at heart, and I pushed her away. That's the reason she came to England, you know. She'd been living with my family after her father passed away. But when she warned me about David, told me not to marry him, I told her to leave."

Her voice dropped to a whisper, and she could barely speak around the lump that settled in her throat. "I accused her of wanting David for herself. Accused her of being jealous of my happiness. I told her that I did not want her at my wedding or to be a part of my life any longer. When she left my family she had nowhere to go, so she sailed to England to visit her aunt." She closed her eyes. "She warned me . . . dear God, if I'd only listened to her."

She heaved a deep sigh. "Because my funds were so limited, I hired myself out as a companion to Lady Gaddlestone to pay for the voyage. But once on board the ship, the mishaps I told you about occurred. When you met me at the pier, I was terrified. I had the strongest feeling someone was watching me. I couldn't wait to get away from there." A shudder ran through her. "Yet the strange happenings followed me here, as you know. I thought it was over—the coat-of-arms ring is gone, as well as its box."

"Yet clearly it's not over," he said, his voice grim. "The fact that someone tried to break in this evening clearly indicates that whoever it is still wants something. Do you have any idea what it could be?"

She briefly considered not telling him, but decided there was no point, as he already knew all her other humiliating secrets. "There's nothing left . . . except this." Crossing to the settee, she opened her reticule and withdrew the folded paper. "I found this just today. Hidden in a false bottom in the ring box."

"What does it say?"

"I don't know. It's written in some foreign language. I'm afraid it might have information about David . . . information I wouldn't want anyone else to know, which is why I did not put it back before I gave the box over to Lord Shelbourne."

"May I take a look at it?"

She wordlessly handed him the delicate paper. Moving to the fireplace, he crouched on the stone hearth and held the note at the best angle to capture the light. After a minute he remarked, "I think this might be Gaelic."

Her stomach knotted. "I thought so as well, in which case it most likely does concern David. He was familiar with the language."

He nodded in an almost absent manner, then said, "This word . . . how odd." He pointed to a word. "That looks like 'Evers.' "

Crouching down beside him, she squinted at the cramped, faded letters. "Yes, it does," she agreed. Something tickled her memory, but remained just out of reach. "Does that mean something to you?"

"Only that it is my friend Michael's surname."

Recognition hit her. "The pugilist fellow who bandaged us."

"Yes." He continued to examine the letter. Nearly a minute passed where the only sound breaking the silence was the snapping of the orange-red flames in the hearth.

"Look at this word," he finally said, pointing to another faded group of letters. "I swear it looks like the name of the town in Ireland where I recall that Michael grew up." He turned to her, his eyes dark and serious in the firelight. "I'd like to show this letter to Michael."

She opened her mouth to protest, but before she could utter a word, he said, "Being from Ireland, he might be able to translate the words. I give you my word that he is discreet."

She debated saying no, but a wave of weariness washed over her, nearly drowning her in its wake. She wanted so badly for this to be over. . . .

"Very well," she agreed in a tired voice.

Robert watched as the strength seemed to simply seep out of her. Setting the note on the mahogany end table, he stood, then reached down to help her up. She stared at his hands for several seconds, and he thought she was going to refuse his help. But then she grasped his palms and allowed him to assist her to her feet.

No more than two feet separated them. Her hands felt small and cold clasped in his, and her eyes . . . they appeared enormous in her pale face, shadowed with ghosts of the past and inner weariness. She looked emotionally and physically spent.

His chest tightened, and all the anger he'd held steadfastly at bay while listening to her tale bombarded him. A violence such as he'd never before experienced rose in him, and he deeply regretted that he'd never have five minutes alone with David Brown. Now he knew where the girl in the sketch had gone. And he couldn't help but marvel at the determination and inner strength that had kept even a tiny flicker of that girl alive.

Looking at her now, however, his anger faded as quickly as it had flared, snuffed out by a swell of sympathy. Bloody hell, what this young woman had endured . . . and how she'd fought back. And how difficult it clearly had been for her to tell him.

She suddenly stiffened and pulled her hands from his grasp.

"Another reason I moved away," she said, "was to distance myself from my family. Not only did I not want the scandal to touch them any more than it already had but I simply couldn't stand their pity any longer. I knew they loved me, yet every time they looked at me, all they saw was 'poor Allie.' They all stared at me with that same expression that's on your face right now." She lifted her chin, her gaze steady. "I do not want your pity."

"I understand. Yet I cannot help but feel sorry for what you've suffered. If it makes you feel better, I can tell you that pity is actually only a small part of what I'm feeling right now."

She pressed her lips together, then raised her chin another notch. "I imagine you're quite disgusted."

"Indeed, it disgusts me to know that not only do people such as David Brown exist but they hurt people . . . kind, trusting people, like you."

"I meant disgusted with me. For being so stupid as to love such a man. For not being able to see his true nature."

"No. God, no." Reaching out, he cupped her shoulders. "You did nothing wrong. You were victimized—in the cruelest of ways. I feel the deepest admiration for you, for the way you paid back his other victims. You're very brave."

A short, humorless laugh blew from between her lips. "Brave? I'm frightened all the time. Unsure of . . . everything."

"Yet you go on. Trying your best. Bravery isn't being without fear—it's overcoming your fears. Moving forward in spite of them. Facing them down." When she continued to look unconvinced, he continued, "I cannot tell you how much I admire your strength. How you've worked so hard to right wrongs that weren't even yours."

Confusion flickered in her eyes. "Giving back things that did not belong to me, returning money that David had stolen, that did not take strength."

"Didn't it? How many other people do you honestly think would have done it? Especially if it left them on the brink of financial ruin?" His gaze roamed her lovely, pale face, and his heart, quite simply, turned over. "I believe you're the bravest and strongest woman I've ever met. And I give you my word that whoever is behind these 'accidents' and abductions and robberies will be apprehended. I'll not allow anyone to harm you again."

A wealth of expressions flitted across her features. Surprise. Doubt. Uncertainty. Then gratitude. And all of them shadowed by an underlying vulnerability that made him want to wrap his arms around her and protect her from anyone or anything that would be foolish enough to attempt to hurt her again. Her bottom lip trembled slightly, drawing his attention to her mouth . . . her full, beautiful mouth.

Desire slammed into him—low, hard, and undeniable. She was so achingly beautiful. A sudden flush of color washed over her cheeks. Clearly she'd recognized the hunger he knew burned in his gaze. He remained perfectly still for several seconds, giving her the chance to move away, but she stood her ground. That beguiling blush beckoned him like a siren's call, and slowly, as if in a trance, he raised his hand to her face and gently brushed his fingertips over her cheek.

Velvet. Her skin was like cream velvet. Or was satin softer? Or silk? He didn't know, but she was most definitely whichever was the softest. A tiny, breathy sound escaped her, once again drawing his gaze to her lips. And suddenly he could not recall one reason why he shouldn't give in to the longing that had plagued him since even before he'd met her, and kiss her. She didn't mourn. . . . Her heart was free.

Wrapping one arm around her waist, he slowly drew her to him until they touched from chest to knee. Her eyes widened slightly, but there was no mistaking the awareness glimmering in her golden-brown depths. Or the stirrings of desire. He inhaled, and her scent wrapped around him like a seductive vine. Lowering his head, he brushed his mouth over hers.

At last.

That same intense rush of feeling he'd experienced at the pier enveloped him, and for several seconds he couldn't move as the words reverberated through his mind. If it had been possible, he would have laughed at his strong reaction. Bloody hell, he'd barely touched her. . . .

He pulled her tighter against him. No woman, ever, had felt

this right. As if she'd been fashioned precisely for him and no one else. Rising up on her toes, she strained closer to him, pressing her lush curves against him, instantly evaporating any hopes he might have foolishly harbored about remaining in control. A low growl rumbled in his throat. He touched his tongue to the seam of her lips, and she opened for him with a husky sigh of want that ignited him, racing his blood through his veins.

She tasted like heated wine. Smooth and warm, delicious and intoxicating. While he explored the dark mysteries of her mouth, she explored his with equal fervor, her tongue rubbing against his with exquisite friction. Need, hot and increasingly demanding, ripped through him, and if he'd been able to think clearly, he would have been appalled at his lack of subtlety.

He tunneled impatient fingers into her soft hair, scattering pins, until a curtain of flowery-scented tresses rained over his hands. Soft. God, she was so soft. And smelled so damn good. Her thick hair rippled through his fingers like cool silk, a stunning contrast to the fire burning through him. A fire made all the more intense by her reactions. For as impatiently as his mouth claimed hers, she pressed against him. For as eagerly as his hands combed through her hair, her fingers raced through his.

A moan vibrated between them. Him? Her? God help him, he didn't know anymore. Desperate to feel more of her, his hands smoothed down her back until he cupped her rounded buttocks. Every muscle strained with wanting her closer, and he cursed the barrier of their clothing that kept their skin from touching.

He didn't know how long that frantic mating of lips and tongues continued before a semblance of sanity returned, along with a modicum of finesse. He gentled his kiss, somehow finding the strength to abandon her lips and explore the delights of her slender neck. He ran hot, open-mouthed kisses down her jaw to the rapidly quivering pulse at the base of her throat. He gently touched his tongue to the spot, savoring the long, low moan vibrating in her throat.

"That fragrance," he whispered against the shell of her ear. "What is that incredible scent you wear?" He captured her lobe between his teeth and lightly tugged.

"Honeysuckle," she breathed, the word ending on a husky groan.

Honeysuckle. The luscious aroma that had embedded itself in his mind had a name. Honeysuckle. Hell, it even *sounded* luscious. Sensual. Like the woman in his arms.

Slowly he raised his head and looked at her. Shiny strands of chestnut hair lay about her shoulders in wild abandon. Her eyes were closed, her face flushed with arousal, her full lips damp and swollen from their frantic kiss. Next time he would go slower. Savor her. Take the time to memorize every exquisite nuance of her. He would certainly have been appalled at himself for all but devouring her if not for the fact that she'd been as voracious as he. Indeed, they'd fed each other's hunger. But next time he would—

Next time? He paused to consider the import of those words. Yes, next time, for he knew, without a doubt, there would be one. To consider not touching her again . . . unthinkable. Kissing her had felt like coming home after a long journey. Like finding shelter after being lost in a storm. He'd once doubted, indeed had scoffed at the notion that this woman made him feel that "certain something." By God, he couldn't doubt it or scoff any longer. One kiss had practically brought him to his knees. He wanted her. With an intensity that, quite literally, left him shaking.

Her lids fluttered open, and he swallowed a groan at her dreamy, languid expression. Her eyes looked like brown velvet, their depths soft with sexual want. For the first time he could recall, he was utterly speechless. No jest or joke sprang to mind, no laughing remark tripped off his tongue. He'd suspected—no, damn it all, he'd *known*—that kissing her wouldn't be just a simple kiss.

Allie slowly emerged from the sensual fog enveloping her, with a sigh of pure pleasure. She felt so wonderfully *alive*. Every nerve ending tingled, pulsing need through her. It had

been so long since she'd been kissed. And she'd never been
kissed quite like that . . . like he'd wanted to simply absorb
her. Like he couldn't hold her close enough. Taste her deeply
enough. And Lord help her, she hadn't wanted him to stop.
The instant he'd touched her, after telling her how brave and
strong he thought her, it was as if she were dry kindling and he
were a match. She'd flared to life under the onslaught of a kiss
that changed in a heartbeat from gentle to devouring.

His large hands still cupped her buttocks, while her fingers
remained tangled in the thick hair at his nape. Her eyes finally
focused on his, and her breath stalled at the intense heat blast-
ing from his gaze. She shifted slightly in his embrace, the
movement rubbing her against his arousal. He inhaled
sharply, and heat flared in her. Fierce and aching.

And unwelcome.

Sanity returned like the slap of a cold, wet blanket. What on
earth was she doing? *Kissing him. As you've wanted to since
that first evening, when he coaxed you into that amusing duet.*
Yes. And giving in to the temptation only proved how unwise a
decision it was. For with one mere kiss he'd inflamed her, resurrected tormenting needs and desires she'd thought she'd
buried. Thoughts and feelings she never wanted or expected to
experience again. But here they were, pounding through her,
harder and stronger than she ever recalled them being in the
past. And God help her, that frightened her.

Disentangling her fingers from his hair, she took two shaky
steps back, away from him. His hands slid slowly from her
buttocks. It was nearly impossible to stand her ground and
look at him when everything cautious inside her screamed at
her to flee. Now. Before she gave in to her body's cravings and
threw herself against him.

The coward in her longed for him to speak first. To say that
what had passed between them was a mistake . . . a lapse in
judgment that would not be repeated. But when silence
stretched between them, she decided it would have to be her.

"Lord Robert—"

"Robert." One corner of his mouth lifted. "I believe we are officially on a first-name basis now . . . Allie."

The way he said her name, in that husky voice, rippled a warm shiver down her spine. Clearing her throat, she said in what she hoped passed for a brisk tone, "I accept my full share of the blame for what just happened. I think we can both agree that it was a mistake. One that will not be repeated."

"Oh, but it was not a mistake," he said in a soft voice completely at odds with the dead seriousness in his gaze. Reaching out, he clasped her hands, shooting tingles up her arms. "And it will happen again. Surely you realize that."

She wanted to deny it, to open her mouth and refute his frightening statement, but the words refused to form in her throat.

"You felt it, too," he whispered, his eyes steady on hers. "Just as I did. That 'certain something.' I know you did. You might not want to or be ready to admit it to yourself, but I felt it in your response. Tasted it in your kiss. It's there, between us. And it's not going away. Indeed, it's only gaining momentum."

His honesty and obvious acceptance of something so completely *un*acceptable stilled her. She moistened her dry lips. "If we ignore it—"

"Impossible." He squeezed her hands and stepped closer to her. "And why would you want to?"

"Why? How can you even ask?" There was no disguising the anguish sneaking into her voice. "To involve myself with another man . . ." Her words trailed off, and a shudder ran through her.

"But I am *nothing* like David." A muscle jerked in his jaw and his eyes narrowed. "But you think I am. You've told me so. Twice. And I believed you were paying me a tremendous compliment." An incredulous sound burst from his lips, and he released her hands, stepping back from her with a half-baffled, half-angry expression. "May I ask exactly what I've done to give you any reason to think so badly of me?"

"I did not mean that I believed you to be a criminal—"

"Very kind, I'm sure," he murmured dryly.

"But you do remind me of him in other ways. Ways that are difficult to describe."

"We resemble each other?"

"Physically, no. David was very handsome."

"Ah. I see. Well, that splat you just heard was my manly ego hitting the floor."

Embarrassment flooded her. "I did not mean to imply . . . what I meant was . . . oh, botheration." Annoyance shoved her embarrassment aside. "The truth of the matter is that while David was very handsome, you are even more so. But it's your *manner* that is just like him. You possess the same carefree, fun-loving, never-take-anything-seriously personality."

"I'm afraid I must beg to differ. There are a number of things I take very seriously."

"Perhaps. But it matters not. I refuse to risk myself again. To any degree. For any man. Clearly no one has ever betrayed your trust."

"Not in the way yours was betrayed, no."

"Then you cannot possibly understand the humiliation and despair."

Something flashed in his eyes. "I know despair," he said quietly. "But what either of us has experienced in the past has no bearing on this . . . attraction we feel for each other. I want to show you something." Reaching into his cream brocade waistcoat, he withdrew a piece of vellum, which he carefully unfolded and handed to her.

Allie looked down and stilled. It was a sketch. Of her.

"Elizabeth gave this to me," he said, "so I would recognize you at the pier. I believe she sent you one of me for the same reason."

"Yes." *And I've looked at it every day.*

"I've looked at that sketch every day, Allie," he said softly.

Her gaze snapped back up to his. Before she could react to his words, which so eerily mirrored her own thoughts, he went on, "I've been enchanted by that woman from the moment I saw her."

Allie stared at the laughing young woman in the sketch, and a lump settled in her throat. Handing him back the drawing, she said, "She doesn't exist anymore."

"Yes, she does. She's just hiding." He reached out and trailed a single fingertip down her cheek. "We simply need to coax her to come out and play."

A confusing mixture of fear and longing shook her. "Why would you want to?"

"Because I want to know her. I think I'd like her. . . . Indeed, I already do. And I think she'd like me."

God help her, she already does. Far too much.

He refolded the sketch, then slipped it back into his pocket. "You are welcome to try to ignore your feelings, resist them, if you like, but I can promise you won't be able to. Not for long."

The sheer arrogance of his statement—combined with the fact that she feared he was correct—irked her. A pique of pride lifted her brows. "How can you be so certain?"

"Because unlike you, I'm not afraid of how our kiss made me feel. Because I cannot even imagine not exploring those feelings further. Because you think I'm handsome, and I think you're absolutely beautiful. And because, if it's the last thing I ever do, I will make you realize that I am *nothing* like David." He stepped toward her until they almost, but not quite, touched. Then he leaned down to whisper directly in her ear, his warm breath tickling across her sensitive skin, "You won't be able to ignore what's between us, Allie, because I won't let you. And you'll never again doubt that I can be a *very* serious man."

Closing his bedchamber door behind him, Robert leaned back against the oak panel and drew in a much-needed deep breath. Her luscious taste lingered on his tongue, and the memory of her flowery scent teased his senses. God help him, he wanted her. And was determined to have her.

But her words drifted back to him. *I did not mean that I believed you to be a criminal. . . .*

He squeezed his eyes shut against the guilt battering him. What would she say, how would she react, if she knew about his own criminal past? Images of the fire, the damage he'd caused, of Nate, all collided in his mind, and he dragged his hands down his face. He'd denied he was anything like her thieving late husband, and he wasn't—but would she believe that if she knew about his darkest hour?

The years rolled away, and he vividly recalled that night. Visiting a pub on the outskirts of London. His surprise at seeing Cyril Owens, the blacksmith from the village near Bradford Hall. Cyril drunkenly bragging to a group of sailors about a girl he'd recently had, and how he'd used his own brand of charm to "convince" her. Filled with disgust, Robert had turned away. But then Cyril had said her name. Hannah.

He'd realized with horror whom Cyril meant. Hannah Morehouse, Nate's daughter. Nate Morehouse was more than just of one of Bradford Hall's longtime grooms—more than just a servant. Robert admired and respected the man; he considered him a friend. He recalled Nate mentioning how concerned he was about Hannah, how withdrawn and quiet she'd become over the past several weeks. And now Robert knew why.

The urge to wrap his hands around Owens' neck was strong, but he managed to control the impulse. There were better ways to see justice served. So he'd gone to Nate. Told him what he'd overheard. He'd then assured the stricken man that he would handle the situation, in his own way, vowing that justice would be done. Dear God, he'd been such a young, impetuous fool. *All my fault . . .*

He dragged his hands through his hair and blew out a long breath. His stomach clenched as he imagined Allie's reaction to the story, given her disastrous history with David.

It was not a chance he was willing to take.

Not yet. Damn it, he wished he could tell her the truth. Wished he wasn't bound by his promise. He couldn't avoid forever telling her the version of the story everyone knew, but surely he could put it off a while longer.

Yes, surely there was no harm in waiting a while longer.

Chapter 12

Redfern limped up the cobbled walkway leading to the earl's house, cursing his rotten luck. Blast that screamin' banshee of a maid. If it weren't for her, he'd have the bloody box. And he wouldn't be sportin' a sore ankle from leapin' over the damn balcony rail. Bad enough he'd landed with a bone-jarrin' thud, turnin' his ankle, but he landed with that bone-jarrin' thud right in some sort of thorny bush. Now his ankle throbbed, his best breeches and jacket were torn all up, and his arse hurt like hell. Were there any bones in a man's arse? 'Cause if there were, he knew he'd broken the bastards. All 'cause of that screamin' wench. Typical woman. Never knew when to shut up. Maybe when he'd washed his hands of the nightmare this job had become, he'd pay that screamin' wench a little private visit.

But for now, the earl were not going to be pleased he'd failed to get the box. Why the devil would he want the piece of junk? He'd considered avoidin' the earl, not reportin' in until he had the goods, but decided it were better to let Lord Shelbourne know he were on the job and huntin' for that box. Otherwise Shelbourne might get it into his head to kill first, ask questions afterward. *I'll get the box tomorrow. Without fail.*

He knocked on the big double doors. Shelbourne's uppity butler Willis opened the door. Damn, Redfern hated the way that pompous bloke looked at him—down his long, skinny nose as if he were his bloody majesty and Redfern were a piece of flotsam on his shoe. Devil take it, the man somehow seemed to *sniff* all his comments. He were nothin' but a servant! Well, when Refern collected his blunt, the first thing he were going to do were hire himself a fancy butler *he* could sniff orders at.

After a quarter hour wait, where he were forced to stand on his throbbing ankle—'cause in spite of all the hoity-toityness of his lordship's fancy house, there weren't one single chair in the bloody foyer—Willis finally led him down the corridor. Well, when Redfern collected his blunt, the second thing he were going to do were buy himself a fine house and fill the bloody foyer with bloody chairs so a bloody body could sit itself down. Yes, he'd set himself up right nice, and never again take orders from any nose-in-the-air nobleman.

Seconds later Willis opened a door. Redfern offered him his best sneer, then limped across the carpet. The door closed behind him with a firm click.

The earl sat in a brown leather chair near the fireplace, a brandy snifter cradled in one hand, the other hand resting on his mastiff's enormous head. Both the earl and the dog watched his hobbling progress across the room through narrowed eyes, and Redfern weren't certain which made him more uncomfortable—the man or the beast. He weren't particularly fond of dogs, especially dogs wot looked like they could chew his arm off with one bite. Shelbourne certainly seemed to love the monstrous beast, always pettin' it. He'd even heard the earl talkin' sweet to the beast several times, in a silly high-pitched voice like one would use with a tyke. He indulged in a mental shrug. Just no figurin' the Quality.

Redfern halted in front of the earl. The heat from the fire only partially eased the chill of unease snaking down his back.

No, the earl didn't look happy—and he hadn't even told him the bad news yet. Maybe this was a bad idea.

"Well?" the earl asked in that icy tone of his.

Trying to inject confidence into his voice, Redfern said, "I've got me some good news, my lord. That box you want? You'll have it by this time tomorrow. You've got me word on that."

"Really? Unless you intend to rob *me,* I do not see how that is possible. You see, Redfern, *I* have the box."

"You?" Redfern repeated, confused. "How'd—"

"Mrs. Brown gave it to me."

Although muddled by all the whys and what-fors, Redfern instantly understood the ramifications. Relief relaxed his shoulders. "Well, fine, then. You've got what you wanted. Now, about my blunt—"

"I'm afraid there's a problem, Redfern. You see, the box contained a note I wanted. The note is no longer in the box, leading me to believe Mrs. Brown still has it."

"Bloody hell, wot's this now? First you wanted the ring. Then the box. Now this note. Why the blazes, if all you'd wanted was this foolish note all along, hadn't you just said so?" He clenched his hands to curb the overwhelming desire to plant the earl a facer. "You blame me for botchin' a job, but how can you expect me to succeed when I don't have all the bloody facts?"

The look the earl leveled upon him was no doubt meant to freeze his blood, but there was no cooling the anger bubbling in Redfern's veins.

"I wanted all of them," the earl said. "The ring, the box, and the note were together until *you* separated them. My error was in assuming you were intelligent enough to carry out the simplest of orders."

He took a leisurely sip from his brandy, then continued, "I want that note, Redfern. And you're going to get it for me. Do you understand?"

"I understand." *But it's the last bloody thing I'm doin' for the likes of you.*

"Good. Mrs. Brown is traveling tomorrow to the Bradford country estate in Kent. I'm certain she'll have the note with her."

He hesitated. Blast and be damned, hopefully the earl weren't going to want him to *read* this bloody note. Well, if so, he'd figure some story. He'd gotten himself this far without knowin' how to cipher words. 'Course, the earl didn't know that. And none of his business it was, either. "How will I know which note you're lookin' for? You know how ladies are, always keepin' letters and such."

"This letter will be old, and will have been folded many times so it would have fit in the ring box. It will be hidden somewhere—she wouldn't keep it out in the open. Bring me the letter, and I'll make you rich beyond your wildest dreams. If you fail . . ." The earl shrugged. "I believe I've already made myself clear regarding that scenario."

Very clear. Still, nothin' but anticipation surged through Redfern. He would indeed be a rich man. Because the blasted earl were going to have to pay a king's ransom before Redfern would surrender that letter.

Robert eyed the rough-looking character who answered his knock on Michael Evers' door. Although properly garbed in servant's attire, the man looked more like a cutthroat than a butler. No doubt because of the huge muscles evident beneath his black jacket, his shaved head, the scar that diagonally bisected his forehead, and the small gold hoop earring dangling from his left lobe. He looked as if he could pulverize stone without breaking a sweat.

"Bloody early fer a visit, ain't it?" the giant growled. He crossed his beefy arms over his massive chest and regarded Robert from his extraordinary height with an obsidian-eyed glare.

Robert handed the man his calling card, which was swallowed up in his ham-sized palm. "I need to see Mr. Evers. Immediately." Although he favored the man with his best aristocratic stare, it was damned difficult to peer down his nose at someone who stood a foot taller than him.

"Well, we'll just see if Mr. Evers needs to speak to *you*." With that, the door slammed in Robert's face.

Momentarily stunned, he stood on the porch, a cool gust of early morning air blowing about him. Then amusement tickled him. Damn, but Michael certainly employed a colorful group, both at his boxing emporium and his home, and it seemed some new face or another was always popping up. This giant was unfamiliar to Robert. As he recalled, Michael's last butler had been thin as a stick and sported a patch over one eye.

Robert knew his friend could afford properly trained servants, as well as a much grander residence, thanks to his lucrative career. But Michael preferred to live simply, in a part of town that, while decent, fell short of being fashionable. And he'd once told Robert that he liked to hire people who needed a second—or in some cases a third or fourth—chance in life. An admirable and noble sentiment to be sure, and Michael could certainly defend himself against any ruffian who might be foolish enough to cross him.

The door swung open. With a jerk of his head, the giant indicated he should enter. "This way," he growled, leading Robert down a short corridor. Opening a door, the giant shouted across the threshold, "Here's the bloke wot came to see ya."

Robert entered the breakfast room. Michael looked at him over the rim of a steaming cup of what, based on the redolent scent in the air, was strong coffee.

"Good morning, Jamison. You're looking a mite better than when I saw you last."

"Feeling better, too."

"No more being bashed on the head, then?"

"No. Although I suspect your, er, butler would be happy to oblige."

"Don't worry about Crusher. His bark far outweighs his bite."

"I don't believe I'd care to experience either his bark or his bite. Do I want to know why he's called Crusher?"

"Probably not." He waved Robert forward. "Sit down. Enjoy some coffee. Would you care for some food?"

"No, nothing, thank you. I cannot stay. We are leaving for Bradford Hall as soon as I return to the town house."

"We?"

"Me and Al—Mrs. Brown."

"Aye? And how is the lovely widow? Fully recovered, I hope?"

To Robert's annoyance, warmth crept up his neck. "She is very well."

Michael studied him for several seconds with a penetrating, inscrutable look, then slowly nodded. "So it's that way, is it? I suspected so."

He didn't even attempt to deny it. "Yes. It's that way. But she's in danger—there's no doubt of it. Other things have happened since the night she was abducted, and I need your help." Sitting down across from Michael, Robert filled him in on the disturbing events that had occurred since he'd last seen him— the robbery, the attempted break-in, and finally the discovery of the note. At the end of his recitation, after stressing the need for discretion, he carefully withdrew the fragile note from his waistcoat pocket.

"Can you read this?" he asked, handing Michael the missive.

Michael gently unfolded the paper, then spent several minutes studying it. "I would agree with you that this is Gaelic," he said. "Unfortunately, except for a few words, I cannot read the language. I was always more a fighter than a scholar."

Reaching across the table, Robert pointed to the two words he'd deciphered. "Do you not agree that is 'Evers' and that is the name of the town where you grew up?"

"Yes." A puzzled frown creased Michael's brow, and he leaned closer to the paper.

"Do you recognize something else?" Robert asked.

"It looks like this says 'Brianne,'" Michael said slowly. "That name's bloody odd."

"Odd? Actually, I think it's rather a nice name."

"It is." Michael looked up at him, a combination of confusion and suspicion flickering in his eyes. "It's my mum's name."

Robert raised his brows and stroked his chin. "Bloody odd, indeed. Granted, there's probably thousands of women named Brianne in Ireland—"

"But it's peculiar that my surname, the town I lived in, *and* my mum's name are all in this note," finished Michael. A troubled frown pulled down his brows. "I wonder if this could explain . . ."

When he did not elaborate, Robert leaned forward and prompted, "What?"

"I don't know . . . it's probably nothing."

"*What* is probably nothing?" When his friend again remained silent, Robert's patience slipped. Reaching across the table, he grasped his friend's forearm. "Damn it, Michael, you must realize how important this is. Tell me."

After another long hesitation, Michael finally said, "When I was a lad, I used to tell my mum that her eyes were 'secrety.' A silly, childish word, but I didn't know any other way to describe what I read in her eyes. To this day, I still don't. She told me that everyone has secrets. . . . And it was always evident to me that she herself had some."

"Surely you don't think this note has something to do with your mother?"

"Brianne's a common name, but I don't recall any others called that in our small village. Impossible as it seems, I can't dismiss the possibility. Can you?"

Robert raked his hands through his hair. "I suppose not. Can your mother read Gaelic?"

"Yes." His steady gaze met Robert's. "I'd like to show her this. I understand Mrs. Brown's desire for discretion. You have my word I'll show it to no one else but my mum."

A long silent look passed between them, then Robert

nodded. "All right. But I'd like this matter resolved as quickly as possible—before any further strange incidents or accidents occur. When can you depart for Ireland?"

"I'll make arrangements to leave today."

Robert rose, then extended his hand to his friend. "I'm grateful."

"I'll report back to you at Bradford Hall as soon as I can."

"Thank you. And Michael—be sure to watch your back."

Unobtrusively lifting his gaze from the book he'd been trying to concentrate on for the past several hours, Robert ventured a look across the seat at his traveling companion. She sat perfectly composed, holding a book she appeared completely engrossed in.

He swallowed a disgruntled sound. She'd kept herself busy from the moment she'd settled herself in the carriage. First she'd sewn tiny buttons on several pairs of black gloves. Then she'd pulled out an embroidery hoop, which had occupied her for over three hours. Now her nose was buried in a book. He'd twice tried to engage her in conversation, but she'd answered in monosyllables, never looking up from her stitching or reading, and he'd finally turned his attention to his own book—with miserable results.

How could she concentrate on such mundane matters when all *he* could do was think of her? The feel of her. The taste of her. He inhaled and the flowery scent of her skin . . . that luscious honeysuckle, wrapped around his senses. How was it that while she clearly found him completely resistible, he found her completely *ir*resistible?

And just what the bloody hell was she reading that was so fascinating? They'd both chosen volumes from the town house library before departing, but he had not asked what she'd selected. Shifting slightly forward, he squinted at the title printed in gold leaf on the leather spine of her book. His eyes widened.

She was reading *The Taming of the Shrew*.

Upside down.

He stilled, then pressed his lips together to contain the broad grin that threatened to spread across his face. Clearly she wasn't quite as engrossed in the Bard as she'd like him to think.

Considerably cheered, he gave up all pretense at reading. Snapping his book closed, he laid it on the velvet squabs next to him and indulged in a long, leisurely look at her.

She was dressed from head to toe in unrelenting black. The gown she wore looked new, and he surmised that it was one of those she had purchased from Madame Renee. The stark color contrasted with her creamy skin, lending her an alluring air of delicacy. Her black bonnet covered nearly all of her hair, and his fingers itched with the desire to untie the ribbons and remove it. He recalled the silky, thick texture of those chestnut strands sifting through his fingers. With her eyes cast downward on the upside-down words, he noted the length of her lashes casting crescent shadows on her smooth cheeks.

His gaze lowered to her lips and he stifled a groan. The feel of that luscious mouth crushed beneath his came roaring back with a vengeance that swelled him against his breeches. Such a delicious mouth. And bloody hell, she knew how to use it.

Wrapped in mourning from her neck to her toes, she looked like a remote, black-garbed island—untouchable, and lonely. Yet he knew the passion that hovered beneath the surface of her quiet exterior. And he was determined to share and experience that passion, in all its forms, with her. For after a sleepless night spent pacing and thinking, he'd finally, as dawn approached, accepted the irrefutable truth.

Allie was *The One.*

The one he'd been searching for. The one who made him feel that "certain something." The one he wanted.

Oh, he'd tried to talk himself out of the realization as he'd paced a trough in his bedchamber last night. Ticking off the reasons on his fingers. He'd known her less than a week. She lived an ocean away. She did not trust men. In her own words she'd said she refused to risk herself again. To any degree. For any man.

But as quickly as the obstacles rose, he felled them. It did not matter that they had not known each other long. Every member of his family had married after brief, whirlwind courtships. He'd always known that when love hit him it would, in the family tradition, resemble the strike of a lightning bolt—fast, hard, furious, and sizzling. As for living in America, she could simply do as Elizabeth had done—resettle in England. And while her aversion to involvement and marriage was justified, he would just have to find a way to overcome it. She might not want to risk herself for any man, but damn it, he wasn't just any man. He was the man who loved her.

But how to convince her to change her mind-set? To make her want him as he wanted her? How to get her to give up the past and embrace a future with him?

He shook his head at his own conceit. He had never even considered the possibility that when he found "the one" she might not fall in happily with his plans—might not feel exactly the same way about him. No, he'd simply assumed that Cupid's bow would strike them both simultaneously, and there would never be any question that they were made for each other.

He swallowed an ironic snort. Of course, he'd always thought he'd fall in love with an uncomplicated English girl who would worship the ground he walked upon. Instead, Fate had presented him with an American widow whose life was in danger, who adamantly wanted nothing to do with men or marriage, and who compared him to her criminally-minded, adulterous late husband.

A bloody tall mountain to climb was what Fate had given him.

Luckily he enjoyed a challenge.

And he always played to win.

Yet he clearly sensed that if he simply laid his heart out for her, told her his feelings and asked her to marry him, she would bolt like a fox chased by a pack of hounds. No, he needed to move slowly. Cautiously. Let her realize, on her own, that she felt all the same wondrous things for him that he felt for her. Because he knew she did. Fate would never be so unkind to allow it to be otherwise. Besides, he clearly recalled Elizabeth's prediction—that he'd find the happiness he sought in London. There was now no doubt in his mind that she'd meant Allie. Well, he'd found her. Now all he had to do was keep her safe from the maniac who was after her, and convince her that she wanted to give up her life in America and stay in England to marry a man she barely knew.

Bloody hell.

Allie felt the weight of his stare, and fought to retain her outward air of calm. It had been nearly impossible to ignore him while he was engrossed in his book, but now, with his volume set aside, it was painfully obvious he was engrossed in *her*.

An unwanted, heated thrill coursed through her. Within seconds her face would flush and he'd know . . . know she was aware of him and his regard. Would he also know she'd spent a sleepless night, her thoughts in turmoil, her body aching with long-forgotten needs? Needs that she feared would demand to be met now that they were reawakened?

Images flashed through her mind. The early days of her marriage. She'd gone to her marriage bed self-conscious and unsure, but David had quickly cured her of her insecurities. He'd introduced her to passion, and for all his other faults, she could not deny he was a wonderful lover. He'd taught her how to please him and to learn what pleased her. During their first four months as man and wife, not a night had passed without them making love, endlessly exploring each other's body. And while she had never failed to find physical release and satisfaction during their lovemaking sessions, something was missing . . . something she could not put a name to. Physically, David gave her everything she craved, yet every night she'd go to bed hoping to capture that elusive missing element, but it somehow remained out of reach.

They'd spoken briefly about children. . . . She'd wanted them desperately, and the fact that she had failed to conceive was the only cloud on her otherwise sunny horizon. When she'd expressed concern to David that she might be barren, he'd agreed that she must be, crushing her hopes of becoming a mother. But he'd told her it did not matter, that they had each other and that was all that mattered. He'd been so convincing, she'd done her best to bury her disappointment and concentrate all her energies on him. Even though there would be no children, she had David, and he made her happy.

A bitter sound rose in her throat. She'd been such an incredible fool.

When David's passion had started to wane after those first few months, she'd accepted without question his increasingly frequent explanations of being tired, or not feeling well. *Such a fool.*

After he'd died, she'd ruthlessly banished every feminine urge and longing he'd awakened in her. And dormant they had lain. Until this man sitting across from her had roused them from their hibernation.

She'd tried mightily, as she'd paced her bedchamber floor last night, to plow through her warring emotions and make sense of them . . . to talk herself out of this impossible attraction, but to no avail. Her inner battle had continued during this seemingly endless carriage ride, but now it was time to surrender and face the truth.

Robert aroused feelings in her she'd thought long dead, but now that they'd returned, she could not ignore them. She would never marry again, but her status as a widow did give her some advantages.

She could take a lover.

Fiery heat rushed through her at the mere thought. The idea had occurred to her during her endless pacing last night, but she'd thrust it away in fear. But now, after spending the last several hours sitting only several feet away from him, breathing in his musky, masculine scent every time she inhaled, being so painfully aware of him her skin tingled, she could not run from the truth any longer. She wanted him. In a way that exhilarated and frightened her all at the same time. In a way she could not ignore. And based on what they'd shared last night, it was obvious he wanted her as well. They were both unmarried adults; no one would be hurt. She did not need to worry about conceiving a child. As long as they were discreet . . .

She'd be leaving England in six weeks, if not sooner. They could enjoy each other during that time. Then a nice, clean break. No messy emotions. She would allow him to engage her mind and her body, and leave her heart untouched. It wouldn't matter if he was devil-may-care, or if his past held secrets. Theirs would be only a *physically* intimate union.

Her inner voice tried to interject, to object, but she squashed it soundly. Yes, an affair might be just the thing.

But how to broach such a subject? Should she simply ask him? Offer it up like a business proposition? What if he refused? She pressed her lips together. Dear God, as embarrassing as it might prove to ask him to become her lover, it would be utterly humiliating were he to turn down her offer. Well, she'd just have to make certain he could *not* turn down her offer.

The hint of a smile pulled at her lips as she imagined herself in the role of seductress. What would he do if she slid across the seat to sit upon his lap? Sifted her fingers through his thick, dark hair? Brushed her lips over his lovely, masculine mouth?

He'd kiss you senseless. Then he'd touch you . . . in all the spots that ache for him. He'd strip off your gown and then—

"How is your book?"

The huskily spoken words jerked her from her sensual thoughts. She raised her head, and her gaze collided with his. It was the first time she'd looked directly at him since last night, and the effect of his dark blue eyes, of the unmistakable desire brewing beneath his innocuous question, wreaked havoc upon her already heightened awareness of him.

Heat rushed into her cheeks and her heart skipped one, perhaps two, beats. She swallowed to locate her voice. "I beg your pardon?"

"Your book. Are you enjoying it?"

Book? She glanced down and sanity returned. "Oh! Yes. It's wonderful."

A slow, devastatingly attractive smile lifted one corner of his mouth. "That is an incredible talent you possess. Did your father teach you that as well as juggling?"

"What talent?"

Instead of answering, he reached across the space between them, then plucked the book from her fingers. Without breaking eye contact, he turned the slim volume upside down, then handed it back to her.

Puzzled, she looked down. At the correctly printed words.

Surely the hellfires burning in her cheeks would simply scorch her and leave her in a pile of ashes. She raised her gaze once again, and their eyes met, but instead of the humor and teasing she'd expected to see, his gaze was intense. And completely serious.

"I'm suffering from the same affliction, Allie," he said quietly.

That softly spoken admission arrowed straight through her heart. And erased any doubts she might have possessed. Closing the book with a snap, she carefully placed it on the cushion next to her. Then, gathering her courage, she drew a deep breath and jumped off the cliff into the black abyss of the unknown yawning before her. "I believe I've thought of a solution to cure our mutual . . . affliction."

"Please, do not keep me in suspense."

Adopting what she hoped was a businesslike tone, she said, "I think we should become lovers."

Surprise flashed in his eyes, followed instantly by a flare of fire, then a flicker of something else that passed too quickly for her to read. He said nothing for several seconds. Then, just as he opened his mouth to speak, the carriage jerked to a halt. They both turned toward the window. A palatial gray stone home stood before them.

Before she could assimilate her scattered thoughts, a footman opened the carriage door and announced, "We have arrived at Bradford Hall."

Chapter 13

It took every ounce of Robert's concentration and will to act normally as he escorted Allie to the massive oak doors. With six softly spoken words she'd literally knocked him sideways. *I think we should become lovers.*

He simultaneously cursed and blessed the fact that they'd arrived just then—cursed it for preventing him from reaching for her and taking her up on her offer right then and there. Yet blessed it for saving him from saying or doing the wrong thing, granting him a reprieve to gather his thoughts—which would surely be easier once his brain commenced functioning again.

God knew he wanted to be her lover. But he wanted much more than that. The fact that she'd suggested such an arrangement both pleased and aroused him—almost unbearably. Yet it also somehow left him with a distinctly uneasy feeling he could not identify. The irony of the situation hit him full force, and he shook his head. He'd paced a ditch in the floor last night, then sat for five hours in that bloody carriage trying his damnedest to think of a way to get her to want him, only to discover that she did. He stifled a frustrated groan. If only she'd voiced her heart-stopping suggestion five hours earlier . . .

The doors opened, and they entered the foyer. "Good afternoon, Lord Robert, Mrs. Brown," Fenton said with a bow. "Everyone has been anxiously awaiting your arrival."

"All is well with the duchess, I trust?" Robert asked, handing his hat to the stately butler.

"Yes, sir. The duchess's . . . pains," he colored slightly, "started this morning. The last report sent down indicated all is moving along nicely. Her Grace is most robust."

"Ah. So the babe will most likely make its appearance today. Excellent news. And the duke?"

A slight wince creased Fenton's thin face. "About as well as can be expected, sir."

Amusement lifted Robert's lips. "Ranting, raving, pacing, and scowling at the clock, is he?"

"That sums it up nicely, sir."

"His hair?"

"Quite standing on end."

"Cravat?"

"A disaster. Kingsbury is most distraught."

Robert leaned toward Allie. "Kingsbury is Austin's valet. The man simply cannot abide untidy neckwear. What about everyone else?"

"Lord William departed yesterday to oversee a business matter in Brighton for His Grace. Lady William and their daughter accompanied him," Fenton reported, taking Allie's bonnet and spencer.

Robert laughed. "Managed to escape, did they?"

"Yes, sir. The children are napping in the nursery, and your mother and Lord and Lady Eddington are in the drawing room"—he coughed discreetly into his hand—"with His Grace."

"Egad. How long have they been stuck in there with him?"

Fenton consulted his timepiece. "One hour and thirty-eight minutes."

"Good lord, they deserve a medal." He turned to Allie. "Would you like to freshen up, or simply jump into the fray?"

"I'd like to meet everyone first . . . unless I look in dire need of repair?"

His gaze traveled slowly downward, then back up to her face. "You look lovely." *And I want nothing more than to muss you up.*

A delicate blush colored her cheeks. "Then by all means, on with the introductions."

"Lead the way, Fenton." He extended his arm to Allie and bludgeoned away the image of them, naked, entwined in each other's arms. "You can meet the family and help rescue them all in one fell swoop."

She curved her hand around his arm, and he clenched his teeth, banishing another heated image of them in his bed. Maintaining his outward composure was going to be a challenge indeed. He could not recall the last time he'd felt so unsettled and frustrated.

Damn. How long before he'd be able to get her alone again? To finish their interrupted conversation? He did not know, but first he had to greet his family. Perhaps seeing them would distract his thoughts from Allie.

"Lord Robert and Mrs. Brown," Fenton intoned at the entrance to the drawing room.

Allie stepped over the threshold into the spacious, brightly lit room. Two women and a gentleman, all wearing unmistakable expressions of relief, rose from the brocade sofa near the fireplace and made their way toward them. Another gentleman, with badly mussed dark hair and his cravat horribly askew, stood near the French windows on the far side of the vast room.

Allie slid her hand from Robert's arm and stepped away from him, drawing in a much-needed deep breath. It was nearly impossible to concentrate when she touched him, stood close enough to breathe in his heavenly scent of masculine soap and freshly laundered clothing. As much as she wanted to see Elizabeth and meet her family, she wished their arrival could have been delayed just a few more minutes. What had Robert been about to say? Had he been about to accept her offer? Reject it? Nothing in his demeanor or expression since the footman had opened the carriage door had provided a clue.

How could she hope to act normally in front of these people when her thoughts churned in such turmoil? *Just do what you've done for the past three years. Pretend all is well.* Straightening her spine, she offered what she hoped passed for a friendly smile to the approaching group.

A beautiful, regal woman with pale golden hair and dark blue eyes extended her hands to Robert. "Darling, I'm so glad you've arrived."

Robert bent and kissed both of her cheeks. "Mother, you look"—he straightened, a smile dancing around the corners of his mouth—"stunning, as always. Certainly much too young to once again hover on the brink of grandmotherhood."

Her eyes twinkled at him. "Which, of course, I am."

"Mother, may I present Mrs. Brown. My mother, the dowager duchess of Bradford."

She turned to Allie and offered her a welcoming smile. "Mrs. Brown. I am very happy to make your acquaintance. Elizabeth has told us so much about you, I feel I know you already."

Allie bobbed into what she hoped was an acceptable curtsy. "A pleasure to meet you, Your Grace."

A smiling, younger version of Robert's mother joined the group, followed by a handsome, dark-haired man.

"My sister and brother-in-law, Lord and Lady Eddington," Robert said.

The petite blonde waggled her fingers at Robert, murmuring under her breath, "We thought you'd never get here, brother dear." She then grasped both of Allie's hands. "Mother is absolutely correct. We all feel as if we know you already."

"Thank you, Lady Eddington."

"Piffle. You must call me Caroline."

"I am honored. And please, call me Allie." She smiled at Caroline's husband and offered a curtsy. "A pleasure, Lord Eddington."

He smiled and two deep dimples creased his cheeks. "Likewise, Mrs. Brown." He nodded toward Robert, then said in an undertone, "Your presence is most welcome. I've been unable to engage him. Perhaps you can before he wears a hole in the carpet."

Robert's glance flicked toward the approaching duke. "Do I detect a note of desperation in everyone's voice?"

Before anyone could answer, the duke joined the group. Robert extended his hand. As the two men shook hands, Allie took measure of the man who had won Elizabeth's heart. He was, in a word, breathtaking. Tall, handsome, compelling. And clearly in such a state of near panic her heart went out to him. He turned to her and she was struck by his resemblance to Robert. Except that this man's eyes were gray. And worried.

Dropping into a curtsy, she said, "It is an honor to meet you, Your Grace. Thank you for your generous invitation to stay in your home."

He took her hand and bowed over it. "The pleasure is ours, Mrs. Brown. Indeed, the anticipation of your arrival has kept Elizabeth's spirits at an all-time high. She is most anxious to see you." His gaze flew to the doorway. "Did I just hear a cry? Was that Elizabeth?"

Caroline shot Robert a meaningful look. "Austin, calm yourself. There was no cry. The babe won't arrive for hours yet."

He paled and raked his hands through his badly disheveled hair.

"Come on, old man," Robert said, clapping a hand on his brother's shoulder. "Let us repair to the billiards room and allow the ladies to get better acquainted. Before you rip out all your hair and Elizabeth is forced to live with a bald man."

"Thank you, Robert, but I'm not in the mood for billiards."

Robert turned to Lord Eddington. "Since Austin is obviously terrified of losing to my vastly superior skill, might I interest you in a game, Miles?"

There was no missing Lord Eddington's relief. "Certainly. I was hoping for a game earlier, but Austin declined. He clearly also fears my skill at the billiards table."

An inelegant snort escaped Robert. "You have no skill at the billiards table."

Lord Eddington spread his hands and shrugged. "Yet Austin fears losing to me."

The duke bounced an annoyed glance between Lord Eddington and Robert. "Don't imagine for even one second that I don't know what you two are doing. And it is not going to work. I've no desire to play games at a time like this."

"Certainly not," Robert agreed. "But all this hair-yanking and hand-wringing and pacing about is clearly distressing Mother and Caroline. And that Axminster you're trampling into a threadbare state is, I believe, a favorite of both your wife and mother."

"I rather like it as well," Lord Eddington added helpfully.

"You see? It's unanimous," Robert declared. "And just think of how much happier Elizabeth will be when we send up a report that you are frolicking in the billiards room rather than destroying her favorite rug."

The frigid glare the duke shot him could have frozen the air between them. Allie watched Robert and his brother stare at each other for a long moment, and some silent communication seemed to pass between them.

Finally the duke heaved a lengthy sigh. "Very well. I'll go to the billiards room. But don't think you'll have me in there all afternoon." He jabbed a finger at Lord Eddington. "Afraid to lose to you? I could beat you with my eyes closed."

"And *I* could beat *you* with my eyes closed," Robert challenged his brother with a smug smile.

The duke swiveled his gaze to Robert and raised his brows. "You cannot possibly believe that."

"Oh, but I do. In fact, I'd be willing to put a fiver on it. Of course, if you're afraid—"

"It is going to be a great pleasure to relieve you of your five-pound note," the duke said with a grim smile. "In fact, I'd be happy to relieve you of more than that. Shall we say twenty?"

Robert frowned and stroked his chin. "Can you afford to lose that much? You are about to add another mouth to feed, you know."

"I believe the coffers can handle the sum should the need arise, which it won't. The question is, can *you* afford it?"

"Yes, however, I won't need to."

"One of us is incorrect," the duke said.

"Indeed. And you know that I am never wrong," Robert replied. He nonchalantly buffed his nails against his lapel. "Actually, I think my 'always-rightness' is one of my most appealing qualities, second only to my—"

"Inflated pompousness?" the duke broke in.

"Nooo," Robert said in a tone one might use with a small child. "Second only to my extraordinary—and dare I claim unbeatable?—skills with a cue stick."

"You do indeed beg to be beaten with a cue stick," the duke said. "I'll await you in the billiards room." He all but stomped from the room.

Caroline, her husband, and her mother all expelled sighs of relief. "Thank you, darling," the dowager duchess said. "He's been pacing about like a caged bear with a thorn in its paw ever since Elizabeth experienced her first pain. He's driving us all quite mad." Reaching up, she patted Robert's cheek. "A game is just what he needs to distract him. And I'll be certain to replace your twenty pounds."

Robert raised his brows. "Such a lack of faith, Mother. What makes you think I'll lose the wager?"

"I realize you're a good player, darling, but so is Austin. To best him with your eyes closed? Surely you don't think you can."

"We shall see." His gaze rested on Allie's. "You know I always play to win."

Allie spent a few minutes exchanging pleasantries with Caroline and her mother, then asked to be excused. "I'd like to freshen up, if you don't mind."

"Of course you would," Caroline said, looping her arm through Allie's. "Elizabeth has put you in the ivory guest chamber. I'll take you up now."

"I'll stay here," the dowager duchess said with a regal smile, "and enjoy the quiet and lack of pacing."

As soon as they turned into the corridor, Caroline leaned close and confided, "Poor Austin. He has been simply beside himself. Of course the rest of us are just as anxious, but Austin is simply incapable of masking his anxiety."

"There's no problem—?"

"Oh, no. Elizabeth is doing beautifully. The midwife sends down word every quarter hour. If she did not, Austin would simply steam up the stairs and burst into the birthing room. It is the way of men. Miles was precisely the same way when our daughter was born. Mother tells me our father was the same, and Claudine says William suffered more than she did. And I'm certain Robert, for all his jovial calmness, will be a candidate for Bedlam when his turn for impending fatherhood arrives."

A jittery feeling edged through Allie's stomach at the thought of Robert being a father. Having a wife. *Jittery?* her inner voice taunted. *You idiot. That is jealousy.*

" 'Tis a good thing it is women who have babies," Caroline said as they climbed the wide staircase. "Heavens, if the task were left up to men, humanity would cease to exist. At the very first labor pain, *pfft!*" She snapped her fingers. "They would promptly kill themselves."

A chuckle tickled Allie's throat, but she was engaged in trying not to tumble down the wide staircase as she gawked at the splendor surrounding her. "This is the most magnificent house I've ever seen." A tremendous crystal chandelier, which held what appeared to be hundreds of candles, sent rainbow prisms of light bouncing off the cream silk-covered walls. Everywhere she looked, her eye lit on something lovely—artwork, porcelain vases filled with fragrant cut flowers, marble statues. Caroline led her around a corner. They passed by a huge gilt-framed mirror where she caught a glimpse of her dumbfounded expression.

"Elizabeth wrote to me about Bradford Hall," she said, "but her words did not do this justice. It is strange to think of her living in such luxurious surroundings. I am very happy for her good fortune in meeting your brother. She loves him very much."

"And Austin utterly adores her," Caroline said. "Quite unfashionable, you know, for a man in his position to make a love match, but it really was love at first sight." She heaved out a dreamy-sounding sigh. "It was so romantic. And such a whirlwind courtship. But of course that is not surprising, as such breathless courtships are a family tradition." They paused in front of a door, which Caroline opened. "This will be your bedchamber."

Allie crossed the threshold and gasped. The room was simply stunning. Done entirely in ivory, soft green, and gold, it looked as if it belonged to a princess. A thick green and gold Persian rug covered the floor. A cheery fire burned in the marble fireplace, and shafts of sunlight streamed in through the French windows, which were flanked by pale green velvet draperies. A huge four-poster bed dominated the room, the elegant counterpane made of alabaster satin embroidered with gilt thread. An escritoire sat near the window, inviting one to write letters while looking out over the verdant landscape.

"Beautiful," Allie said, turning in a slow circle.

Caroline indicated a long cord near the head of the bed. "If you need anything, day or night, just pull that cord." Caroline's smile dimmed as her glance flickered down to her black clothing. "Elizabeth did not mention you'd suffered a recent loss. . . . I'm so sorry."

Warmth crept up Allie's neck. She hated lying, but in some cases, the truth was worse. "My loss is not recent. It's been three years since my husband . . ." She allowed her words to fade off, rationalizing, as she had for a long time now, that if someone drew the incorrect conclusions, that was hardly her fault, and it kept her from telling an outright lie.

Caroline instantly looked distressed. "Forgive me. I did not mean to pry or bring up sad memories." Crossing the room, she clasped Allie's hands. "But we intend to see to it that you are very happy during your stay. Do you ride?"

"Yes. In fact, I enjoy it very much."

"Then I suggest, given the lovely weather, we take a ride while the gentlemen play billiards. Do you have a riding habit?"

Embarrassment heated Allie's face. "I'm afraid not." She looked down at her black gown. "Can I not wear this?"

"Oh, yes," Caroline assured her hastily. "It's just a shame to risk one's everyday clothing to the dirt and odors of riding." She looked her up and down. "We are of a similar height and size. I would be happy to lend you one of my riding ensembles." Before Allie could object, Caroline added, "While I do not have a black one, I have a dark brown one."

Allie hovered on the brink of indecision. She should not, of course, borrow someone else's clothing. But the temptation to wear something other than black . . . to throw off the outward mantle of mourning, to go out into the sunshine and ride with this lovely, smiling, friendly woman who had the same eyes as Robert, was nearly overwhelming. But something inside her knew that once she took that irrevocable first step, there would be no turning back.

"Thank you, but I'll wear one of my older gowns," she said before she could change her mind and give in to the need.

Caroline squeezed her hands, then headed toward the door. "The offer stands, should you reconsider. I'll change and meet you back here in thirty minutes?"

"All right."

Caroline smiled at her from the doorway. "I'm so glad you're here, Allie. I promise we'll keep you occupied until Elizabeth is back on her feet. Perhaps by the time we return from our ride, the babe will have arrived. Wouldn't that be wonderful?"

A new baby. . . . Allie slapped back the wistful longing that threatened to sneak up on her. "Yes."

With a smile and a wave, Caroline departed and Allie wandered to the window. Her bedchamber faced the front of the estate. Verdant lawns stretched around a seemingly endless curve of tree-lined drive. The cheerful song of chirping birds sounded from the trees, and leaves shimmered with golden strands of afternoon sunshine in the light breeze. *Oh, Elizabeth, I'm so happy for you. That you found this wonderful place and these delightful people. And now await the birth of your second child. You deserve every bit of happiness.* And while it was undeniably odd to imagine Elizabeth among all this opulence, she could easily imagine her fitting in this pastoral country setting.

Her gaze lingered on the cobbled drive below. Less than an hour ago she'd ridden on that very drive and asked Robert to be her lover. A rush of warmth spread through her, filling her with need and longing and trepidation.

What would his answer be? And was he thinking about it right now?

The instant Robert and Miles entered the billiards room, Austin demanded, "All right, Robert. The only reason I'm here is because you gave me 'the look.' Obviously you need to tell me something. What the bloody hell is so important?"

Robert raked his hands through his hair. Indeed, it had nearly taken an act of Parliament to drag Austin away from his self-imposed post in the drawing room. It wasn't until he'd given Austin the wordless signal the siblings had devised in childhood to indicate that something was amiss that Austin had agreed to come to the billiards room. And while he had no desire to add to Austin's worries, he could not delay any longer in telling him about the disturbing incidents in London.

Speaking quickly, he brought Austin and Miles up to date. When he finished his recitation, both men regarded him with grave expressions.

"We experienced no problems on the journey here from London," Robert said, "but I don't feel this is over. With Michael on his way to Ireland with the note and the magistrate looking for the culprit, hopefully the bastard will be caught soon. But in the meanwhile, we need to take extra precautions.

I do not want Mrs. Brown—or any of the women—to go about alone until this mystery is solved."

Austin nodded slowly. "I'll alert the staff, instruct them to report any unusual activities." A determined glint entered his eyes. "No one will be harmed." He then laid a hand on Robert's shoulder. "I'm glad neither of you were hurt. You did well getting Mrs. Brown here safely."

Robert's jaw clenched. "Not good enough. That bastard could have killed her." His hand tightened into fists. "He'll not have another opportunity, I can promise you that."

He watched Austin and Miles exchange a quick, speculative glance. Austin then remarked, as if choosing his words carefully, "Mrs. Brown is clearly a determined woman who stands strongly by her beliefs. A trait to be admired, especially in light of the hardships she's faced doing so. I can understand why she and Elizabeth are so close—they are very much alike in that respect."

"Yes. She is most certainly a woman to be admired," Robert agreed, meeting Austin's gaze steadily, not caring a whit if his brother guessed his feelings for Allie. If he had his way, everyone would know before long. "If you two will excuse me, I'm going to check on the ladies. Make certain Caroline hasn't dragged Mrs. Brown off somewhere." He nodded at Austin. "I'm assuming you won't leave the house."

Austin raked his hands through his hair. "You assume correctly."

He tossed Austin a glossy, polished cue stick. "Practice up, brother. When I return, you're going to owe me twenty pounds."

When Robert found the drawing room empty, he continued out the French windows to the sun-splashed terrace where he was greeted by the sight of his mother enjoying tea and biscuits with her lively grandchildren. Pirate, his giant canine body stationed strategically near the table, gobbled up the biscuit crumbs as quickly as they hit the ground, and in some cases, before they made it that far.

Raising a hand to shield his eyes from the bright sunlight, Robert scanned the area for Allie and Caroline, and was relieved to note their figures in the distance, walking toward the terrace from the direction of the stables.

"Uncle Roboo!" a little voice squealed. Returning his attention to the wrought-iron table, he saw Caroline's two-year-old daughter Emily jump from her chair. She ran toward him, launching herself into his arms.

He caught her, then twirled her like a top, laughing at her delight. "Ah, Miss Tickles, I've missed you," he said as he stopped.

She pressed a sweet, biscuity, giggly kiss to his cheek. "Again!"

Before he could oblige her, Austin and Elizabeth's son James attached himself to Robert's leg like a burr. "Me twirl," James demanded with all the authority of a three-year-old heir to a dukedom.

"Well, if it isn't Lord Mischief-Maker." He scooped up the boy, settling him on his other arm, then circled around with his passengers until they were all breathless. When he finally halted, the world still twirled around him.

James favored him with a lopsided grin. "Feel spinny."

"Me, too," Robert said with a laugh. "How about a biscuit, little man? I'm hungry after all that." He set the child down, and James immediately ran, rather unsteadily, toward the table.

Emily, still in his arms, placed her little hands, fingers splayed, on each side of his face, and turned his head toward her in order to ensure his full attention. Robert couldn't help but smile at the sprite. He made the funny face he knew she loved, then blew noisy kisses into her soft, sweet-smelling neck. She squealed with delight, grabbing two little fistfuls of his hair.

"Oh, you're the biscuit," he said, widening his eyes. "I'll just eat *you* all up!" He burrowed deeper into the crevice between her chin and shoulder, making exaggerated eating noises.

He lowered himself to his knees, and was immediately set upon by James, who, biscuit in hand, climbed on his back and commanded, "Horsey!" Pirate loped toward the trio, tail wagging, following the trail of sugary crumbs James left in his wake. He greeted Robert with a canine grin and a friendly swipe of his tongue across Robert's hand.

Laughing, Robert looked up, then stilled. Allie and Caroline were climbing the stone steps to the terrace. Caroline was chattering away, Allie nodding, one of her rare smiles curving her lips. His heart seemed to stall, then race ahead of itself. She looked flushed and happy, young and carefree . . . the girl from the sketch.

Everything around him seemed to fade away. Except her. And then she turned and looked at him.

Allie's footsteps faltered as she found herself looking directly into Robert's intent gaze. A little girl who looked like a miniature version of Caroline sat in the crook of his arm, her small hands wreaking havoc with his hair. Indeed, the child had raised two tufts of dark hair on his head that resembled devil's horns. A small boy who she knew had to be Elizabeth's son hung on his back, demanding his attention, while a huge dog nudged his hand with its snout.

But his attention was completely focused on her. A frisson of awareness sizzled between them, frightening in its intensity. She pulled her gaze away, looking at the children clinging to him. They clearly adored him, and he them, a fact which brought a hard lump to her throat. This was a man who would someday make a wonderful father.

Caroline's voice sifted through her stupor, breaking the spell. "That little imp is my daughter Emily," she said with a smile. "And the other devil—the *smaller* devil, I should specify," she said, pointing to Robert and the boy, "is Elizabeth and Austin's son James."

"They're darling," Allie said. The dog suddenly raised its head to look at her, and Allie drew in a sharp breath.

"Don't be frightened," Caroline said as the huge beast trotted toward them, tongue lolling. "Pirate may be huge, but he is very gentle."

"I'm not afraid," Allie assured her. She patted Pirate's soft white fur, then gently ran her fingers around the dark brown patch surrounding his left eye—the only spot of color on his otherwise snowy coat. This was clearly the dog Robert referred to as Barking Horse. "Indeed, I feel as if I were greeting an old friend. He looks exactly like Patch, Elizabeth's childhood pet. She left him with our family when she traveled to England. He was too old to make the journey." She scratched behind the dog's ears, and his tail thumped with pleasure. "We loved him dearly."

"Austin knew how much Elizabeth missed her dog, so he searched practically all of England to find one that looked just like her beloved Patch."

"He succeeded," Allie murmured, smiling as Pirate looked up at her with an adoring expression that clearly begged for more behind-the-ear scratching. A feeling she could not describe pulled at her insides at the knowledge that the duke had gone to such lengths to please Elizabeth. Allie well knew how difficult it had been for Elizabeth to leave Patch behind. *She wouldn't have had to do so if not for me . . . if I hadn't made her leave.*

"Well, I believe you've now met every member of the family," Caroline said.

"Not quite," came a deep voice from behind them.

They all turned. The duke stood by the French windows, his smile reflecting joy, relief, and weariness. "I've just come from Elizabeth's chamber. There is now one more member of the family that you all will need to meet."

Chapter 14

After the dowager duchess, Caroline and her husband, and Robert had all visited Elizabeth and the newest member of the family, Allie stood in the doorway of the cozy, walnut-paneled bedchamber, fighting tears at the scene she beheld. Elizabeth sat in the bed, propped up by a mountain of fluffy, lace-edged pillows, the ivory coverlet tucked around her waist. She looked clean and fresh, all the outwardly visible signs of childbirth washed away. Her auburn hair was dressed in a simple braid, and while there was no denying she looked tired, there was a maternal glow about her that lent her an air of serene beauty. Dressed in an exquisite pale yellow bed gown, she smiled down at the tiny pink-blanketed bundle cradled in her arms. The duke sat on the edge of the bed, one strong arm wrapped around Elizabeth's shoulders, their heads close together. The duke's gaze alternated between his wife and new daughter with naked adoration. He was clearly a man truly in love with both the women in his life.

The sun had long since set, the room's only light coming from the warming blaze in the hearth and the candelabra on the bedside table. The flickering glow lit the proud parents in a stunning, golden tableau of happiness that filled Allie with joy and envy at the same time, and made her feel like an intruder trespassing upon the intimate scene. Even though her friend had sent for her, Allie decided to leave and come back after the duke left. She started to back out of the room, but in that instant Elizabeth looked up.

The years melted away as their eyes met, and a kaleidoscope of images flitted through Allie's mind. She and Elizabeth as children, splashing at the lake. Laughing over a meal. Playing with Patch and Allie's unruly dogs. Taking their blankets and sleeping in the hayloft. Sharing secrets and dreams, laughter and tears. And the abrupt end of their friendship. *Because of me.*

She watched Elizabeth hand her precious bundle to her husband. Then, turning back to her, Elizabeth smiled. And held out her arms.

She supposed her feet must have moved, because the next thing she knew, she was leaning over the bed, hugging Elizabeth, both of them crying, then laughing, then crying some more.

Finally Allie leaned back and looked into smiling, tear-drenched eyes whose color matched her own. She could barely speak around the egg-sized lump that seemed wedged in her throat. "Elizabeth . . . it is so good to see you. I . . . I've missed you so."

Elizabeth's smile could have illuminated the room. "I feel the same. I thought you would never arrive, and then when you finally did, I couldn't even receive you."

A trembling smile pulled at her lips. "Perfectly understandable. After all, babies tend to arrive when *they* wish to."

"Indeed they do. And now, I'd like you to meet our daughter . . . Lily."

"Named after your mother," Allie said softly. She moved to the other side of the bed, intending to simply peek into the fluffy pink blanket, but the duke handed her the bundle. Looking down, Allie's breath caught. A tiny angel with a perfect, bow-shaped mouth slept, her eyelashes forming miniature half-moons on plump cheeks. One minuscule hand lay fisted next to her downy face.

Being the oldest child, she was well used to babies, but it had been a number of years since she'd held one in her arms. A rush of warmth and love and longing filled her, and she bent her head to breathe in the one-of-a-kind scent that belonged to infants.

"Well, hello, Lily," she whispered. "I believe you are the most beautiful little lady I've ever seen." Allie touched her index finger to Lily's buttery soft hand. The tiny fingers flexed, then grabbed Allie's finger. Her heart turned over, melting. "Oh, and so strong you are. And so lucky. You have a wonderful Mama and Papa who love you very much." She raised her gaze to Elizabeth and the duke. "She's wonderful. I'm so happy for you both."

The duke stood. "Thank you. And now, if you'll excuse me, I'll give you ladies some privacy to chat. I believe I have a billiards game to win. But first, I'll escort my daughter to the nursery." He looked at his wife, and Allie could easily see he would have preferred not to leave her side. He squeezed Elizabeth's hand, promising, "I'll be back soon." Allie handed Lily over to him, unable to suppress a tender smile at the contrasting, loving picture they made . . . the tall, broad-shouldered man cuddling the tiny pink bundle.

After the door closed behind him, Elizabeth patted the bed. "Sit beside me. We have so much to talk about."

Allie hesitated. "As much as I would enjoy that, you must be exhausted—"

"Tired, yes. But much too exhilarated to sleep just yet."

Allie sat on the edge of the bed, and for a full minute they simply looked at each other. Finally Allie said, "Being a duchess clearly agrees with you."

Elizabeth leaned closer and confided, "Being a duchess is terrifying, but I'm adjusting. Caroline and my mother-in-law are very patient, as is Austin."

"I don't believe I've ever seen a prouder papa."

Elizabeth laughed. "I understand from Robert that Austin

nearly wore a hole in the drawing-room carpet with his pacing."

At the mention of Robert's name, Allie felt heat creep up her neck. "He looked quite undone, yes." Then, before the conversation could wander down a path she did not wish to travel—especially before she said the things she wanted, needed to say—she drew a deep breath and said, "Elizabeth, I need to apologize to you. . . . I don't even know how to express my sorrow."

"Allie, don't," Elizabeth said gently. "You apologized in your letters. I completely understand. You loved David. There is nothing to forgive."

She looked into Elizabeth's eyes, so filled with compassion and understanding. Remorse and shame threatened to choke her and she pressed her hands together to stop their trembling. "Yes, there is. I treated you horribly, and you were right." A tear spilled from her eyes and dripped onto the ivory coverlet. "If only I'd listened to you . . . about David . . ."

Slowly, haltingly at first, but then gathering strength, the entire story of David's betrayal, her discovery of what he really was, and her efforts to correct his wrongs poured out of her. Elizabeth listened intently, saying nothing, yet offering sympathy and encouragement through her expressive eyes. When she finally finished, Allie released a long, weary sigh. Her face felt tight with dried tears, her body exhausted as if she'd run a mile. But her heart felt lighter—as if she'd shed a heavy weight.

"I know you accepted my apology through our correspondence, Elizabeth, but you deserve to hear the words from me in person. You were my closest friend, with only my best interests at heart." She shook her head and looked down. "I'm so ashamed that I failed to be the same to you."

"Allie, please. Listen to me. Look at me."

Allie raised her head and looked into Elizabeth's eyes, which brimmed with compassion. "You've suffered through a horrible ordeal. Let's not compound it by dragging it on any longer. Our differences are in the past, and as far as I am concerned, all is forgiven and forgotten. What you need to do is forgive yourself. And allow yourself to forget." Her gaze wandered pointedly over Allie's black gown.

"But I don't want to forget," Allie said fiercely. "If I do, I stand in danger of making the same mistake again." She drew a deep breath. "Now that I've told you everything, I need to ask . . . how did you know about David, Elizabeth? You wrote that you would tell me when I visited you . . . and here I am."

Elizabeth regarded her through solemn eyes. "I'm afraid it's rather difficult to explain. And it might prove even harder for you to accept."

She reached out and gently touched Elizabeth's sleeve. "I can accept the truth, Elizabeth, whatever it is. I've learned the hard way that it is lies and deceit that destroy . . . not honesty."

"I would not want to risk our friendship again."

Guilt struck her like a backhanded slap. "I doubted you once, Elizabeth. It is a mistake I will not repeat."

Elizabeth nodded, then drew what appeared to be a bracing breath. "Do you recall that sometimes I was rather . . . perceptive?"

"*Rather* perceptive?" In spite of her pensive mood, a smile tugged at Allie's lips. "I'll never forget when Jonathan and Joshua were born. You not only guessed Mama was going to have twin boys, but the day they'd arrive, and the exact time! And that instance where you knew that Katherine was going to fall from her horse. I realize you had an intuition about David, but—"

"It's more than simple intuition, Allie. I *feel* things. *See* things. In my mind. Future events and past events. I cannot explain it, but I swear to you, on my honor, it is true. I never told you—or anyone else—because the visions are erratic and infrequent. And I feared people would think I was insane." Her eyes grew sorrowful. "I knew David would hurt you. I didn't know how, but I knew he would. I could not discern what he'd done, but I knew he'd done bad things. That he was a liar."

Allie listened, absorbing the words. No doubt she should be shocked or skeptical about what Elizabeth had revealed, but somehow she was not. Indeed, so many extraordinary things had happened to her in the last few days, Elizabeth's revelation seemed almost commonplace. She'd always known Elizabeth was keenly perceptive. Now she simply knew *how* keenly perceptive.

Elizabeth reached out and clasped her hands tightly between both her own. Nearly a minute of silence passed, then Elizabeth said gently, "Falling in love is not a mistake, Allie."

A short, bitter laugh pushed past Allie's lips. "I am living proof that it certainly can be."

Something in Elizabeth's intent expression gave her the eerie sensation she was looking directly into her soul, and she suddenly feared what her friend might see there.

"You chose the wrong man, Allie. You wouldn't do so again."

"No, I would not. Because there will not be another man." An image of Robert's laughing face rose in her mind's eye, squeezing her insides. "Not ever."

"But you mustn't give up on love. *That* would be a terrible, sad mistake." She hesitated for several seconds, then asked, "I trust Robert has been a solicitous escort?"

The heat burning her cheeks flared into hellfires. "Yes."

Elizabeth looked directly into her eyes. "He is a very fine man."

Allie's mind raced. Did Elizabeth know what secrets Robert was keeping? *I shouldn't care. His past is none of my concern.* Still, she could not ignore the curiosity nudging her, and this could prove a perfect opportunity to find out. Adopting what she hoped was a noncommittal tone, she said, "A fine man, perhaps, but one with his share of secrets."

Elizabeth's expression was impossible to read. "Yes, I've sensed as much. Has he spoken to you about them?"

So she was correct. There *were* secrets. She'd known as much, yet somehow, having Elizabeth confirm it came as a blow. "No, he has not."

"But you want to know what they are," Elizabeth said quietly.

"No. Yes." She shook her head. "I don't know. It doesn't matter what they are. The fact that he *has* secrets—just as David did—tells me all I need to know." She searched Elizabeth's eyes. "Do you know what Robert is hiding?"

"I don't believe anyone knows the entire story except Robert, therefore it is up to him to tell you. I suggest you ask him." She squeezed Allie's hand tighter, and a troubled frown suddenly creased her forehead.

Something in her expression prompted Allie to ask, "Is something amiss?"

"I . . . I sense danger. Nothing specific, but I feel it." Her grip tightened further. "You must be careful, Allie. Promise me you won't go off alone. Promise me."

Concerned about her friend's unmistakable agitation, Allie patted her shoulder. "I promise I won't wander off, Elizabeth. Please do not worry."

"I've just checked on Lily," came the duke's deep voice from the doorway, "and she is still sleeping like an angel."

Allie gently extracted her hand from Elizabeth's embrace, then eased off the bed. "Thank you for your understanding and forgiveness," she whispered.

Elizabeth looked at her with concern-filled eyes. "You have both. Always. And my love as well."

" 'Tis far more than I deserve, but I shall gratefully accept."

"You'll visit me tomorrow?"

"If you're feeling up to it, of course."

"And you'll remember your promise?"

"Yes." Leaning down, she touched her lips to Elizabeth's forehead. "Good night." She bid good evening to the duke, then quit the room, closing the door with a quiet click.

Austin immediately strode across the room, grabbing up Elizabeth's cold hands. Unease edged down his spine at her strained expression. "Something is wrong," he said. "Are you unwell?"

"No, I'm fine," she quickly assured him.

"But something is amiss." He peered at her face, and tensed. "You've had a vision."

She nodded slowly. "Yes. When I touched Allie's hand." She squeezed his hands, then gave him a searching look. "You know about the danger she and Robert have faced."

"Robert informed me, yes."

"You deliberately kept it from me."

"He only told me this afternoon, Elizabeth." He raised her hand to his lips and kissed her fingertips. "And you were a bit occupied."

"It's not over, Austin," she whispered. "I don't know how, but it's going to happen soon. . . ."

He sat on the edge of the bed and grasped her shoulders. "What's going to happen? What did you see?"

She swallowed, her eyes stricken. "Death."

His heart seemed to stall. When he'd first met her, he'd doubted her bewildering ability to "see" past and future events—but no more. Her gift had saved not only his life, but William's and Claudine's and Josette's as well. Austin well knew the frightening word she'd just spoken would come to pass unless steps were taken to stop the events she had seen.

"Who is going to die?" he asked urgently.

"I don't know . . . it wasn't clear. But I sensed death. Very strongly."

"Did you tell Allie?"

"I told her about my visions, yes. Told her I felt danger. Warned her to be careful." She briefly closed her eyes, then shook her head, clearly frightened and frustrated. "There is a menace approaching. . . . Its exact nature I can't determine. But it's moving closer. And I do know this"—reaching out, she grasped his upper arms—"Austin, Allie is in grave danger. And Robert as well."

Robert stood in the darkened drawing room, staring out the French windows. Clouds obscured the moon, and from the gusts of chill wind rattling the glass panes, he judged a storm most likely on its way. He swirled his brandy slowly in the snifter cupped in his hand, then tilted back his head and drained the potent liquor down his throat. The mantel clock chimed softly, proclaiming the hour. Two A.M. Way past time to retire, as everyone else had hours earlier. But sleep, he knew, would not come, and he could not bear the thought of lying in bed, aroused, thinking of her, lying in her own bed just two doors away. Best he stayed down here, at a safe distance. Closer to the brandy. In fact, another brandy sounded like a capital idea.

As he poured himself another fingerful, Austin's voice rose from the shadowed doorway. "I'll have one as well, as long as you're pouring."

Robert bit back a sigh. Devil take it, there were over fifty bloody rooms in Bradford Hall. Why did Austin have to choose *this* room to haunt? There was only one person whose company he wanted, and Austin wasn't that person. Much as he loved his brother, he'd prefer to be alone with his thoughts. Wordlessly, he poured a second drink.

"To Lily. And her mother," Austin said softly, raising his snifter.

Feeling churlish for wishing his brother out of his own drawing room, Robert touched his glass to Austin's, the chime of crystal tapping crystal echoing through the room. "To Lily and Elizabeth," he repeated. He tossed back his drink with one burning gulp, then returned to the window and stared out at the darkness. "A beautiful wife, a new daughter, a healthy son . . . you're a lucky man, Austin."

"That I am." Robert heard him cross the room. Seconds later Austin joined him at the windows. "Lucky . . . and worried."

Robert turned quickly toward him. "Elizabeth? Lily?"

"No. You. And Mrs. Brown."

"Has something happened I'm not aware of?"

"Not exactly . . ."

"I sense a 'but.' "

"I'm afraid so. Elizabeth had one of her visions earlier. When she touched Mrs. Brown."

The serious look in Austin's eyes, combined with his grave tone, tightened Robert's every muscle. "What did she see?"

Austin's expression grew even more grim. "Death. And danger. Someone is going to die, Robert. She does not know who. But she knows that both you and Mrs. Brown are in danger."

Robert froze. Allie in danger. Austin's words reverberated through his mind. *Someone is going to die. . . .*

Before Robert could fashion a reply, Austin crossed to the sofa and picked up something, then returned to the windows. He held out his hand, revealing a pistol. "Keep this close to you. Do you carry a knife?"

"Always."

"Good. Do not go anywhere alone. If Elizabeth 'sees' anything else, I'll inform you immediately."

Robert took the pistol, balancing the weight in his hand. *Someone is going to die.*

Grim determination filled him. *That someone is going to be you, you bastard, whoever you are.*

Clearing his throat, he looked at Austin. "I thank you for the warning. And the weapon. You have my word that no harm will come to Allie."

Austin slowly raised his brows. *"Allie?"*

There was no misinterpreting the question asked with that single word. Robert's gaze did not waver. "Yes. Allie. I trust you aren't going to voice any objections." It was a statement rather than a question.

"No. No objections. I believe I, more than anyone, can understand the allure of a beautiful American. I'm just a bit surprised, as you haven't known her very long."

"Indeed? And how long did you know Elizabeth before *you* knew?"

A sheepish look crossed Austin's face. "About a minute and a half. Of course, it took me several weeks to admit it to myself."

Robert sighed dramatically. "I've always suspected you

were slow-witted. I calculate it only took me forty-three seconds. But I only just admitted it to myself a few hours ago."

"Still, I believe that is a new family record."

"Yes. One that I'd prefer remain between us, at least until I've declared myself to the lady."

"Understood. But you should know that Elizabeth will probably 'feel' your emotions. And I suspect Caroline will guess. Our sister can ferret out these emotional sort of things with unerring accuracy."

"Noted." The mantel clock chimed the half hour. "If you'll excuse me, I'd best retire now. It's been a long day."

They exchanged good nights, with Austin opting to remain for another brandy. Robert climbed the stairs. He had to keep Allie safe at any cost. And the best way to do that was to be exactly where she was.

He headed for her bedchamber.

Chapter 15

Allie stood in the darkened corner of her bedchamber looking out the window. All she could see was darkness and her own pale reflection. She'd lain in the wide bed for hours, praying for sleep to release her from the maelstrom of thoughts whirling through her mind, but sleep had stubbornly refused to come. Instead, emotions and worries and fears marched through her head like a battalion of soldiers—Robert, the ring, Robert, the note, Robert, secrets, Robert, Elizabeth's warning.

Robert.

She pressed her fingers to her temples and squeezed her eyes shut, trying to banish him, but he remained firmly embedded in her mind. She had not seen him since dinner—a rushed meal, as everyone wished to visit with Elizabeth and Lily. Of course, it had been impossible to speak to him in the dining room about what was uppermost in her mind. *I think we should become lovers.*

And now, Elizabeth's confirmation that he did indeed have secrets had her thoughts in further turmoil. What was he hiding? What had happened in his past? An almost morbid curiosity pulled at her. In spite of the fact that she shouldn't care, that it should not matter, she felt an inexplicable need, an overwhelming urge to know. What would happen if she, as Elizabeth suggested, simply asked him? Would he tell her? Or would he, as David had, lie? Or deny there was anything to tell? *Don't be a fool. If he has not shared his secrets with his own family, why would he tell you? And why would you want him to?*

She opened her eyes, and her breath caught in her throat. In the window's reflection she saw her bedchamber door opening slowly inward. An icy ball of fear bounced through her, and she whirled around.

And found herself staring at Robert quietly entering her bedchamber. She blinked twice, certain he was a figment of her overwrought imagination, but he was very real. And *here.*

A wave of heat engulfed her, instantly melting her fear. From her shadowy corner, she watched him close, then lock, the door. He moved slowly, silently, toward the bed. She knew the exact instant he realized she did not lie beneath the rumpled bedclothes. He froze, then quickly scanned the room.

"I'm here," she said, emerging from the deep shadows.

Robert turned so quickly he swore he almost snapped his neck. There she stood, in the golden glow cast by the low-burning fire in the grate. Relief hit him so hard he felt an actual need to sit down. Instead, he strode across the room and grasped her by her upper arms.

"Are you all right?" he asked in a tight voice.

"I'm fine."

"I was concerned." His voice sounded harsh and more than a little accusatory, even to his own ears.

She raised her brows. "Then we are even. My heart nearly stopped when I saw my door opening in that furtive manner."

"It wasn't furtive. It was cautious. I'm relieved you are all right. When I saw the empty bed I thought . . ." Whatever he'd been about to say evaporated from his mind as his gaze lowered. She wore a cream dressing gown that covered her in unadorned, prim cotton from just below her chin to her toes. A long row of buttons ran down the front, and he imagined an equally plain cotton night rail lay beneath.

He'd never seen her garbed in anything other than black, and the effect was like a punch in the heart. She looked so achingly lovely, and for the first time since he'd met her, he did not feel that the shadow of another man stood between them.

"What did you think?" she asked softly. "That some man had absconded with me?"

He refocused his gaze on her face. Glossy strands of hair had worked free of her braid, lending her a sensually disheveled air. Lifting his hand, he brushed a single fingertip over the smudges marring the delicate pale skin under her eyes, marks that told him without words that she had not slept. Her pupils dilated at the whisper of a touch, and he instantly wondered what her reaction would be to a bolder, more intimate caress.

"I feared some manner of disaster had befallen you, yes," he said. "Based on the events of our acquaintance thus far, you can hardly fault my concern."

"I was not finding fault. Indeed, considering my conversation this evening with Elizabeth, I appreciate your vigilance on my behalf."

His fingers drifted down her smooth cheek. She had no idea how vigilant he intended to be. "What did Elizabeth tell you?"

"That she sensed danger. And that I should not venture off alone."

"So you know about her . . . feelings?"

"She told me this evening, yes. Told me she'd felt something about David . . . that was why she'd tried to persuade me not to marry him." A humorless laugh escaped her. "If only—" She shook her head, then stepped away from him. His hands fell to his sides, and he watched her walk across the room to stand in front of the fireplace. Sensing she needed to put some space between them, he forced himself to remain where he was.

"I cannot change the past," she said. "All I can do is learn from my mistakes."

"That is all any of us can do, Allie."

She contemplated the burning log for several seconds, then

turned back to him. "This ability of Elizabeth's, it's extraordinary."

"Indeed it is," he agreed. "Her 'feelings' saved Austin's life. My brother William's and his family's lives as well. We are forever in her debt."

There was no mistaking her surprise. "I did not know this. It is a story I would be interested in hearing."

"Then I shall tell you. But not now. Now there are other things we need to discuss."

He watched her go still. Then she lifted her chin a notch. "What other things?"

"The fact that there is still danger facing you," he said, walking slowly toward her. Her eyes widened slightly at his deliberately measured approach, but she stood her ground. Good. He liked that she didn't back away. Liked the awareness tempered with caution flickering in her eyes. "There is also the fact that you do not need to worry about venturing off alone because I have no intention of being farther away from you than"—he halted when only two feet separated them—"this."

Reaching out, he lightly clasped her wrists. Her pulse raced beneath his fingers, pleasing him. "Then there is the matter of finishing our conversation from the carriage."

"Have you thought on the matter?" she asked.

"I've thought of nothing else."

"I see. And have you made a decision?" He had to admire her air of calm nonchalance, an effect spoiled only by the rapid quickening of her pulse.

With his eyes steady on hers, he said, "Surely there can be no doubt in your mind that I want to make love to you."

A flicker of what appeared to be relief flashed in her eyes. Yet when he said nothing further, simply stood and watched her, that relief turned to uncertainty. "Not a doubt exactly," she said, "yet I sense a 'but.' "

"I assume you've considered that you could become pregnant." He forcibly pushed aside the incredible, heart-stopping image of her, large with his child.

"Of course I considered it, but it is not a concern." She lowered her chin and stared at the floor. "I am . . . barren."

Everything inside him tensed, and a mental *No!* screamed through his head. Fate would not be so cruel. Swallowing to moisten his suddenly dry throat, he asked, "What makes you believe that?"

She raised her head and met his gaze. "I never conceived during my marriage."

His muscles relaxed somewhat. "You were not married very long."

"Eight months. Certainly long enough, especially considering how frequently we . . . tried."

His teeth clenched at the thought of that thieving scoundrel touching her, and he was glad the bastard would never touch her again. *No man will. Except me.* "Perhaps the fault was your husband's."

She shook her head. "No. The failure was mine. David was quite positive on the matter. So positive, in fact, that given what I now know about him, I would not be surprised if he'd fathered a child at some point." Bitterness compressed her lips. "Indeed, he might have fathered several. Lord knows I was not his first woman . . . or his last. Not being able to have children . . . it was difficult to accept, yet I had no choice but to do so."

Her words cut deep. He wanted children. Lots of them. And Allie would be a wonderful mother.

But what if she were truly barren?

He looked into her eyes, and his heart turned over. Yes, children were important. But *she* was *essential*. If she truly could not bear a child, then they would lavish their love on their nieces and nephews. And in the meanwhile, he'd pointed out the likelihood that her husband could have been at fault for her childless state. If the lady wasn't concerned about becoming pregnant, well, who was he to argue?

The ramifications of that seared through his brain. If she were to become pregnant with his child . . . that would force her to stay with him. Marry him.

Surely that thought should horrify his conscience, yet his inner voice remained silent, allowing him to rationalize that, while he would never want her to be forced into a marriage she did not want, there was not a doubt in his mind that given enough time, she would come to realize they belonged together. Certainly once they'd made love, she would know.

"Was there anything else you wished to discuss?" she asked.

Releasing her wrists, he entwined their fingers. "No. In fact, I believe I'm quite out of conversation."

She stepped forward, erasing the distance between them. The tips of her breasts brushed his shirt, igniting him. "Then perhaps you'd like to kiss me."

His gaze drifted down to her full lips, and he swelled against his breeches. "Yes, I would. For starters . . ."

Bending his head, he captured her mouth in a kiss he'd meant to be tender. But the instant his lips touched hers, it blazed into something hot and demanding, then scorching when she disentangled her fingers from his and ran her palms up his chest and over his shoulders to tangle in his hair.

Wrapping one arm around her waist, he hauled her tightly against him, while his free hand slid up her back, into her soft hair. They strained against each other, her breasts flattened against his chest, his erection cradled in the V of her thighs. Their tongues tangled in a desperate dance to taste more, delve deeper. The taste of her . . . sweet and spicy at the same time, her luscious honeysuckle scent, wrapped around him, invading his senses. He wanted, needed, more of her. Now.

A small inner voice warned him to slow down, but his body was beyond obeying. He felt as if he'd spent months in the desert, deprived of water, and she was an oasis. A desperate need to touch her everywhere at once overwhelmed him, fueling the hunger pounding through him. His hands skimmed restlessly down her back, cupping her rounded buttocks, then wandered up her rib cage and forward, to fill his palms with her full breasts.

She squirmed against him, and a low, animal-like growl

vibrated in his throat. He wanted his hands on her skin. Needed hers on his. Breaking off their kiss, he looked down at her. Her lips were swollen and moist, her color high, her eyes glazed with arousal. Her chest rose and fell with her rapid breaths, no less frantic than his own.

Reaching up, he cupped her face between his none-too-steady hands. "Allie . . ." Bloody hell, he barely recognized that rasp as his voice. "I want to go slow, gently, with you, but God help me, I don't know if I can."

Her warm breath puffed over his lips. "I don't recall asking you to go slow. In fact . . ." She lowered her hand down his body and stroked her fingers over his straining erection.

He sucked in a sharp breath and managed a jerky nod. "Right. We'll save slow for another time." He took one step back and set to work unfastening his shirt with an impatience he could not control. She immediately busied herself undoing the row of buttons on her dressing gown. He mourned the fact that he wasn't removing her clothing himself, but damn it, this was faster. And he wanted, needed, them skin to skin as quickly as possible.

In spite of his shaking hands, and his attention diverted by the arousing sight of her robe slipping off her shoulders, he managed to strip off his clothing in record time. He tossed his breeches aside just as her gown slithered downward to pool at her feet.

For the space of several heartbeats, they stared at each other. She was incredible. Round and womanly, soft and fragrant. Her breasts were high and full, her coral nipples pebbled with arousal. His gaze wandered downward, touching on her curved waist, then the triangle of chestnut curls nestled between her shapely thighs. By God, the instant he did not feel so desperate and about to explode, he would take the time to savor every delectable inch of her.

They reached for each other at the same time, arms going about each other, skin pressed to heated skin from chest to knee. *At last.* She felt so damn good . . . so soft and warm. He captured her mouth in another searing kiss, slipping his

tongue into the silky heaven behind her lips. With his mouth
fused to hers, he cupped her buttocks and lifted her up against
him. She instantly wrapped her legs around his hips, opening
herself, her moist feminine flesh pressing against his arousal.
Bloody hell, he wasn't sure he could make it to the bed. Determined not to disgrace himself, he headed swiftly across the
room, tumbling her onto the mattress, then following her
down.

Again his inner voice yelled for him to slow down, that his
performance here was sadly lacking, and perhaps, if she'd
been docile, he might have succeeded. But she clearly was as
impatient and frantic as he. Spreading her legs wide, she
surged her hips upward, and he sank deep into her body in one
smooth, heart-stopping stroke. Her inner walls clutched him
like a tight, wet, hot velvet fist, and a long moan of pure feminine satisfaction rumbled from her throat.

She undulated beneath him, rubbing her aroused nipples
against his chest, and he lost any semblance of control he
might have imagined he still possessed. His world narrowed to
the place where their bodies were intimately joined. Nothing
existed except her . . . her skin against his, his heart pounding
against hers. Mindless, his muscles moving of their own ac-
cord, he thrust into her with long, hard strokes, touching her
deeper and higher each time. Her hands clutched at his shoulders, and he was vaguely aware of her fingers digging into his
skin.

He felt the spasms pulse deep within her, and her low, guttural growl of pleasure vibrated against his ear. Helpless to
contain his own release any longer, he buried his face against
her neck and throbbed inside her for an endless, intense moment, spilling his seed, and what felt like his soul, inside her.

God help him, he could not move. Could not so much as
flex his fingers. He did not know how long it took sanity to return, but when it did, it smacked him like a brick to the head.

What the devil had happened to him? What had come over
him? He'd totally, completely, lost control of himself. Of his
mind and body. In a way he never had before. He'd shown her

a completely appalling lack of mastery and finesse, and certainly less consideration than he'd ever shown any previous lover, a fact which filled him with self-disgust and guilt.

Summoning what strength he could, he lifted his head and propped his upper-body weight on his forearms. He gazed down at her, and caught his still-not-fully-returned breath.

Her eyes were closed, her sable lashes resting against smooth cheeks hectic with color. Her shiny hair lay in tangled disarray on the sheet, her braid completely undone. Her lips were parted, and he gave in to his urge to drop a soft kiss upon them.

Her eyes opened slowly, and heat rushed through him at her dazed expression. The tip of her tongue peeked out to moisten the lips he'd just kissed. She said nothing, just stared up at him, a kaleidoscope of impossible-to-read emotions flickering in her rapidly clearing eyes.

Unease pulled at him. Damn it, what was she thinking? He knew she'd found her release. He'd felt her orgasm shimmer through her, pulsing around him, driving him mad. But was it possible she had not felt the same magic, the same intensity as he? Everything inside him protested the mere thought. No. She *had* to have felt it . . . that same fire that had damn near incinerated him.

A jumble of feelings crowded into his brain, declarations that demanded to be verbalized, but he pushed them away. For now. It was too soon. He needed to take one step at a time. So far, lacking finesse or not, he'd engaged her body. Her heart would soon follow. He refused to consider anything else. Yet he could not deny that he'd employed all the expertise of a green boy.

Clearing his throat, he said, "I'm afraid I quite lost control of myself. Next time will be better for you. I promise."

Allie's heart lurched at his words, and she remained silent for several breathless seconds, studying him. His hair was disheveled from her frantic fingers, one dark lock dipping over his forehead in a way that begged her to touch the soft strands. His cheeks were ruddy from his exertions, his mouth slightly reddened from their devouring kisses. And his eyes . . . they were so dark and intense, steadily regarding her with a potent expression she'd never seen before. One that made her feel so . . . she didn't know.

Could *this*—whatever it was—be that elusive something she'd unsuccessfully sought during her marriage? The question raised an onslaught of unwanted emotions she was not prepared to examine now. Later . . . she would think later. There would be plenty of time . . . later. Right now, all she wanted to do was feel . . . experience more of the magic he'd wrought with his hands and body.

She stretched like a contented cat beneath him, reveling in the glorious sensation of his weight pressing her into the mattress, his crisp chest hair grazing her sensitive nipples. That brief glimpse she'd been treated to of his naked form, before they'd fallen upon each other like starved creatures presented with a feast, had turned her insides to porridge and shot liquid heat directly to her womb. Tall, muscular, broad shoulders . . . and that fascinating ribbon of dark hair that bisected his ridged abdomen, then spread to cradle his most impressive arousal. A shiver of anticipation skittered down her spine, and a smile born of all the wicked delight coursing through her pulled at her lips.

"*Better* for me?" she repeated. "Oh, my. I wouldn't have thought such a thing possible . . . but if you insist it is, I shall anxiously await next time. Have you any idea when that might be, Sir M.M.Q.?"

"M.M.Q.?"

She brushed a fingertip over his bottom lip. "Makes Me Quiver."

Lowering his head, he traced the sensitive shell of her ear with the tip of his tongue, then whispered, "Actually, I have a very good idea when the next time might be."

Another delicate shiver ran through her. "Hmmm. I hope it's soon."

"I was thinking about *now*."

"*Now* sounds lovely."

"Indeed it does."

Pushing himself up, Robert settled back onto his knees between her splayed legs and took the time he'd been too impatient to take earlier, to savor the sight of her.

She looked like a golden-bronze temptress, bathed in firelight, her skin glowing with the exertion of their frantic mating. His gaze leisurely appreciated her dusky nipples, her abdomen, the charming indent of her navel, then the alluring dark curls between her thighs. He inhaled, and the musky scent they'd created together filled his head.

She regarded him with a half-serious, half-playful sinful expression that fired heat straight to his groin. Reaching out, he touched one finger to the delicate hollow of her throat, then dragged his fingertip slowly downward, arousing one plump nipple, then the other, with a feathery caress, his hand a dark contrast against her pale skin. When her breathing turned into a series of long sighs, he leaned forward and replaced his fingers with his tongue, slowly laving her breasts, then drawing the taut peaks into his mouth. The scent of honeysuckle rose from her damp flesh, mixing with the musk of their joining, intoxicating him.

Her sighs turned into moans, and she combed her fingers through his hair, thrusting her breasts upward, encouraging him to take more into his mouth. Her hips undulated, rubbing her inner thighs against his legs. He discovered an enchanting trio of freckles just below her left breast that occupied his lips for several minutes. Then he explored further, running his tongue slowly downward toward her stomach, savoring every quiver of her skin, every hill and valley of her feminine form, along the way. When he dipped his tongue into her navel, she responded with a husky groan that notched up his temperature several degrees.

"Robert . . ."

Every nerve in his body caught fire at the sound of his name coming from her lips in that passion-roughed whisper. He straightened, settling back on his heels, then looked into her eyes, which seemed to breathe golden-brown smoke. Need, hot and strong and impatient, clawed at him.

Gliding his palms over her smooth thighs, he gently pushed her legs wider apart, revealing her glistening feminine flesh to his avid gaze. Reaching out, he caressed her wet, swollen folds with a gentle circular motion, his gaze alternating between his fingers and her expressive face. Her body writhed sensually beneath his touch, and her uninhibited response aroused him to the breaking point. And that's where he wanted her—at the breaking point. The instant he sensed she was there, he withdrew his hand. Her sharp groan of protest filled the room, spiking his now nearly desperate need.

Leaning over her, his weight supported on his hands, he lightly teased her with the head of his arousal. The satiny, wet feel of her, coupled with her gasp of pleasure, arrowed sensation through him. He looked down, between their bodies, watching as he slowly entered her, sinking into her snug, moist heat.

Her purr of satisfaction brought his gaze back to her face. Their gazes met and held, and he knew that the naked need and want in her eyes was mirrored in his own.

"Allie." Her name whispered past his lips like a prayer, unable to be contained. She reached up, running restless fingers over his face, his lips, before pulling his head down to hers for a deep, intimate kiss. She raised her hands above her head, and he ran his palms up her arms, entwining their fingers. Then, breaking their kiss, he watched her as he moved slowly within her, withdrawing nearly all the way out of her body, only to glide deep again. A dozen expressions of pleasure and wonder flitted across her face, and he mentally recorded each one, as he memorized each of her breathy sighs.

When he increased the depth of his thrusts, her eyes slid closed. "Look at me," he whispered. Her lids fluttered open, and with gazes locked, he stroked her harder, faster, until she tensed beneath him, arching her back, moaning out her release. With a final deep thrust, he buried his face in her fragrant neck and followed her over the edge.

•   •   •

Robert came awake slowly, his senses rousing themselves one
at a time. Sprawled on his back, the first thing he noticed was
silky, warm skin pressed against his side. *Allie.* Satisfaction
eased through him and he drew in a deep, contented breath. A
hint of honeysuckle, mixed with the erotic redolence of spent
passion, brought his sense of smell to life, filling his head with
images of their night together. Opening his eyes, he looked at
his lover.

His heart swelled at the word. *Lover*. His *lover* slept next to
him, on her side, her head nestled in the crook of his shoulder.
One of her slender arms was thrown across his chest, her hand
resting above his heart. The weight of a shapely leg curved to
rest over his thighs.

Her long hair fanned out like a chestnut halo, spilling over
her shoulders, onto his chest. He gently rubbed the silky
strands between his thumb and forefinger. Like the rest of her,
her hair was beautiful. And satiny soft.

Her warm breath puffed against his shoulder, filling him
with a rush of possessiveness unlike anything he'd ever before
experienced. This woman was *his*. They belonged together.
After the passion they'd shared during the night, the emotional
and physical bond they'd forged, she could not possibly refute
it. When she awoke, she would know. With the same certainty
he did.

The sound of rain lashing against glass drew his gaze to the
windows. The storm that had threatened earlier was upon
them. He looked at the mantel clock and sighed. Almost dawn.
The household would soon stir. As much as he hated to leave
her, he needed to return to his own bedchamber. Now—before
he was discovered in a manner that would impinge her honor
and reputation. Now—before he gave in to the temptation to
kiss her awake and continue their sensual exploration of each
other.

Easing himself from the bed, he quickly gathered his clothing. With one last look at her sleeping from, he slipped silently

from the room, secure in the knowledge that he would not have to leave her bed like this for much longer. For soon she would be his wife.

Lester Redfern looked out the dingy window of his small room and uttered a curse. Here it were, rainin' like to make up for a century-long drought. He ground the stubs of his teeth together. He should have left London yesterday, but he hadn't wanted to miss the cockfight at The Hound's Tooth last night. He'd won five quid, but now it seemed liked a poor wager. How the bloody hell were he supposed to know the skies would open up? Now how were he supposed to get to Bradford Hall? The roads would be nothin' but wheel-eatin' ruts. The only other choice were horseback, but he didn't own a bloody horse, and he hated the beasts besides. Nasty, ill-tempered, stupid brutes that bit him and smelled. Not to mention the poundin' his arse would take ridin' all that way. Could things get any bloody worse? The instant the question popped into his mind, he shoved it aside. With the way his luck were runnin', it were best not to ask.

But, if he didn't go, didn't get the earl's bloody note from that bloody woman . . . his eye twitched and he swallowed hard. No, not goin' to the country weren't an option. Rain or no, he had to go. Had to finish this damn business once and for all.

Today.

Chapter 16

Late in the morning following her night with Robert, Allie stood in front of the cheval glass and examined her reflection. Even with the meager light due to the gray, drizzling skies, even garbed in her usual black, she could discern the unmistakable glow. It sparkled in her eyes, glimmered on her flushed cheeks, announced itself in the small, secret smile she could not erase from her lips.

She had not felt so wonderfully alive, so vibrant and exhilarated, in three years. Her body hummed with pleasure, her pulse jumped every time she thought of the previous night . . . which was constantly. Turning, she looked toward the bed, now neatly made. But she instantly visualized herself and Robert among tangled sheets, their limbs entwined, touching, tasting, exploring. And God help her, she could not wait to do it again.

Surely everyone would guess. How could anyone look at her and not know? The look of a well-pleasured woman rested upon her like a cashmere shawl, and nothing—not the long bath she'd indulged in, or the gray weather, or her somber attire diminished it. She did not regret her actions, yet she needed to employ caution. Discretion. It was one thing to take a lover . . . it was quite another to have his entire family know about their liaison.

But how could she hope to be in the same room with him and act normally? Now that she knew how firm and smooth his skin felt beneath her fingers? Now that she'd seen his eyes darken with passion and need as he buried himself in her body? Knew the sound of his voice as he groaned her name in release?

You won't be able to, you fool. You never should have—

Squeezing her eyes shut, she bludgeoned back her inner voice, as she already had more times than she cared to count since she'd awakened. Robert was her lover. Nothing more. They would enjoy the pleasure they brought each other until it was time for her to leave England. And then it would be over.

Once again her inner voice tried to interject, but she forcibly closed her heart and mind to its unwanted warnings. It was time to venture downstairs . . . to visit with Elizabeth's family. And face her lover.

With butterflies of anticipation fluttering in her stomach, she turned toward the door. Before she took one step, however, someone knocked.

Good Lord, could it be him? "Come in," she called, pressing her hands to her midsection to calm her jitters.

Caroline entered, her face wreathed in smiles, her arms wrapped around a large rectangular box. "Good morning, Allie . . . or rather afternoon." She walked to the bed, where she deposited the box. "Did you sleep well?"

Heat rose in Allie's cheeks. "Very well. Just later than I expected."

Caroline waved a negligent hand. "Lounging about in bed until early afternoon is what rusticating in the country is for. I ventured downstairs myself only a few minutes ago, where I discovered *this*"—she pointed to the box—"waiting for you. According to Fenton, it had just arrived from London. Since I could not wait to see what you'd purchased from Madame Renee, I brought it up to you. Her creations are simply divine."

Allie frowned in confusion. "Madame Renee? There must

be some mistake. I did purchase two gowns from her shop, but they were both delivered to me before I departed London."

Caroline's eyes goggled. "Heavens, with you being in town only a few days, you must have paid her a fortune to receive your garments so quickly. It normally takes at *least* three months. She is, after all, the most exclusive modiste in London." She laughed. "Miles cringes in fear for the family fortune every time I so much as mention the woman's name."

"We must be speaking of two different Madame Renees," Allie said. "The gowns I bought were extremely reasonable."

"There is only one Madame Renee," Caroline said positively. "Her shop is located on Bond Street." Her gaze ran over Allie's black gown. "What you're wearing—it is from her shop. As was the gown you wore yesterday. Her flawless workmanship and style are easily recognizable. I'd meant to ask you yesterday how you managed to have her fit you so quickly. You must let me in on your secret."

"But I have no secret. Your brother brought me to her shop and . . ." Her voice trailed off as suspicion filled her. Surely Robert had not . . . no, he could not have.

Caroline's eyes lit up with unmistakable interest. "*Robert* brought you? To *Madame Renee's*? Voluntarily?"

Caroline's incredulous tone left little doubt that such an excursion was extraordinary behavior on her brother's part.

"I'd asked him where I might purchase some new attire," Allie said hastily, squashing her indignant conscience into submission.

"I see," Caroline murmured, but a wealth of curious speculation lurked behind the two innocent words. "Well, let's see what Madame sent you," she urged. "Perhaps it is a shawl or some other accessory for one of the gowns you bought."

"Perhaps," Allie conceded doubtfully. "But I fear there has been a mistake."

Yet the instant she parted the pink-and-white striped tissue paper and caught sight of the shimmering copper-hued material beneath, her breath stalled, and she knew there was no mistake . . . at least not the sort she'd initially suspected.

"How beautiful," Caroline enthused. "What an extraordinary color. It is perfect for you."

As if in a daze, Allie carefully lifted the gown from its bed of tissue. It was the most exquisite garment she'd ever seen, a fluid fall of golden topaz, elegant and understated in its simplicity. She recognized the material as that which she had admired in Madame Renee's shop. And there was only one way a gown such as this could have been commissioned.

Robert.

A myriad of emotions buzzed around her like a swarm of bees, confusing her with their contrariness. Clearly he'd lied to her about Madame Renee and the prices she charged. It was equally clear he'd subsidized her purchases, and based on Caroline's words, it had cost him dearly. And *this* creation must have set him back a fortune.

A part of her heart melted at his thoughtful, gallant consideration in attempting to provide her with the means to purchase new gowns in a way that would leave her pride intact. But then, the very nature of his gesture trod irrevocably upon her hard-earned independence. She did not need him, or anyone, to purchase her clothing. She refused to be in another man's debt ever again.

But what struck the most painful blow, leaving her simultaneously hurt and angry, disappointed and disgusted, was the fact that he'd lied to her. Perhaps his intentions had been good, but damnation, she could not abide being lied to. For any reason. And while she was undeniably angry with him, she was doubly so at herself. For letting down her guard. For allowing herself to believe, to foolishly hope for even one minute, that he would not lie to her as David so often had.

Even though her every feminine instinct longed to don the gorgeous gown, her pride and the keen sense of betrayal knotting her insides forced her to lay the garment gently back in the box.

Offering Caroline a smile she prayed did not appear as tight and forced as it felt, she asked, "Would you know where your brother is, Caroline?"

"I believe he is in the nursery with the children."

"Would you take me there, please? There is something I need to discuss with him."

Allie stood in the doorway of the nursery, riveted by the sight of Robert sitting on the edge of an overstuffed, chintz-covered settee. His long legs, clad in buff-colored breeches, were spread wide. Emily straddled his one knee, while James straddled the other.

"Are you ready for the start of the next gallop around the forest?" he asked the children.

"Ready!" they answered in unison.

"Hold on," he commanded, then proceeded to make loud horselike noises, bouncing his legs to the children's delight. "Here comes the fence," he said. "Jump!" He lifted his legs higher, and they clung to his knees, breathless with laughter. "We're almost at the end. Hold on!"

Seconds later his jouncing halted, and Emily instantly demanded, "Again!"

He laughed and lifted her off his knee to hug her. "Horsey needs to rest first." He kissed her cherubic cheek, then set her on her feet. Turning his head, he caught sight of Allie and Caroline standing in the doorway.

His gaze locked with Allie's, and there was no missing the naked heat that blazed in his eyes. In spite of her anger, warmth raced into her cheeks at that blatantly intimate look. Good Lord, Caroline was standing right beside her. She would certainly see and wonder—

"Mama!" Emily ran toward Caroline on chubby, sturdy little legs. James slid off Robert's knee and galloped toward his aunt as well. Crouching down, Caroline hugged them both.

"Well, if it isn't my two favorite racers," Caroline said with a smile. "Who won?"

"I did!" Emily and James said simultaneously.

"It was a tie," Robert said with a laugh. He rose to stand in front of the settee, his gaze never leaving Allie's. And although half the length of the room separated them, Allie felt as if he'd caressed her.

Caroline straightened, and Allie forced herself to look away from Robert's compelling eyes. Taking each child by a hand, Caroline alternated a bright, innocent-looking smile between her brother and Allie that in no way disguised her open speculation.

"If you two will excuse us," Caroline said, "I will take these expert riders off to help me cajole Cook out of some biscuits as a reward for their endeavors." She glanced toward the window, where rain continued to fall. "Then I propose we visit the conservatory to pick some flowers to bring Lily and her mama."

"Flowers for Mama," James agreed, tugging on her hand.

Allie nodded her thanks, and Caroline herded her excited charges from the room. Their voices grew fainter until silence reigned.

Robert simply stood, studying her for several seconds, his heart quickening from the mere fact that they stood in the same room. He wanted nothing more than to stride across the carpet and drag her into his arms, but there was something in her eyes, in her utterly still and stiff posture, that edged unease down his spine, rendering him reluctant to make any quick moves. As if facing a rabbit about to bolt, he walked slowly toward her. She stood her ground, watching him approach. He halted directly in front of her, then, reaching behind her, closed the door, locking it with a gentle click that seemed to reverberate through the quiet room.

This serious woman was not the same wanton, laughing creature he'd held in his arms last night. And damn it, he wanted that woman back.

Was she experiencing regrets? He hoped not, because he certainly was not. Last night had been . . . perfect. The first of many such perfect nights to follow. Yet by her expression, it seemed clear he would need to convince her of that.

He reached out to touch her, but she instantly moved away,

out of his reach. "I need to speak with you," she said, in a flat voice that doubled his unease.

She stood with her back only a foot from the wall, and he debated moving closer, bracketing her in, but decided to give her the room she obviously wanted. But there was no denying the hurt that pricked him at her frigid composure.

"I'm listening," he said, bracing himself to hear a barrage of morning-after recriminations and regrets.

"You lied to me."

He blinked. "I beg your pardon?"

"You lied to me about Madame Renee. I've just learned that her shop is the most exclusive in London, and that she charges exorbitant prices. That clients must wait months before receiving their garments."

Bloody hell. He clearly had his sister to thank for this. Still, some of the tension left his shoulders that this wasn't about last night. "Allie, I merely—"

"Lied." Twin flags of color rose on her cheeks and her voice vibrated with anger. "And I shall thank you not to continue to do so by denying it." She squared her shoulders. "You will prepare a full accounting of all the funds you spent subsidizing my purchases so I can repay you."

Irritation tickled at him. "I will do nothing of the sort."

"Then I shall be forced to ask Madame Renee herself."

"She will not tell you."

"Then I will ask Caroline to estimate the amount I owe you."

Confusion replaced his irritation. "You do not owe me anything. Your gowns were destroyed by the thief. I simply provided you with a means to replace them in an expedient manner."

"By *lying* to me." Sparks all but sizzled from her. "Do you know what it feels like to be lied to, Robert?" Before he could answer, she continued, "*I* know what it feels like. It's horrible. And I refuse to be taken advantage of in that way ever again."

"Allie . . ." He reached out toward her, but she backed away again, leaving him to rake his hand through his hair in rapidly mounting frustration. Damn it, he'd clearly stepped into it this time. "I was merely trying to help you. Obviously I went about it in a poor way, in a way that has upset you, and for that I apologize. But I think you are making too much out of a few simple gowns."

Her lips pressed into a thin, angry line. "There is nothing simple about it. I did not ask for your help. I neither want nor need your help. I've survived quite well on my own for the past three years, and I shall continue to do so without being in anyone's debt."

Her words stung like a slap. "You are not in my debt. I would have done the same for anyone I care about, without expecting anything in return. I did not want you to know about it only because I sensed your pride would not allow you to accept anything from me—or anyone else, for that matter. And while I can understand, and even admire, such a sentiment, in this instance I wholly disagree with it."

"You made a choice *for me*, a choice I would not have made for myself had I been in full possession of the facts, which I was not because you lied to me. And what of the other gown? The one that just arrived from Madame Renee. How did you arrange *that*?"

"I wrote to her after our visit to her shop."

"I see. So obviously that gown is something you decided I *needed* as well."

He studied her angry face for several seconds before replying. "I think it's time you ceased to wear mourning clothing, yes."

"That is not your decision to make."

No. But damn it, he wanted it to be. The hell with not touching her. Reaching out, he caught her firmly by her shoulders. She stiffened, but did not struggle. "Allie. I just wanted you to have something beautiful to wear. I wanted to see you in something other than black."

"I cannot afford such a gown."

A frown pulled at his brows. "It is a *gift*."

"I do not want it. I can not, and will not, accept a gift from another man who lies to me."

Something inside him snapped and he abruptly released her, stepping back several paces. "Damn it, I am *not* him. I am *not* David."

"Aren't you?"

He erased the space between them with one quick stride. She retreated, flattening her back against the wall, and he slapped a palm against the wood paneling on either side of her shoulders, caging her in.

"Do you have any idea how such a comparison makes me feel?" When she simply stared up at him with wide eyes, he leaned closer to her, not even attempting to hide the anger and hurt he knew showed in his eyes. "Allow me to enlighten you. It is more than insulting. It is extremely hurtful. While I will readily admit that I have faults, cheating, stealing, and black-mailing are not among them. You say you refuse to be lied to? Very well. That is quite understandable. But *you* need to understand that *I* refuse to be further compared to your late husband. I am not normally in the habit of telling less than the truth, but with regard to Madame Renee, yes, I lied to you. I can only say that my intentions were good, and offer you my apology and my promise not to be untruthful with you again."

Allie stared up at him and swallowed hard. He was angry. And hurt. The sentiments all but radiated from his eyes and his body, both of which were too close. Both of which held her captive. She tried to hold on to her own anger, but it began seeping away, like sand sifting through an hourglass, to be re-placed by twinges of guilt for hurting him. She fisted her hands. She did not want to feel this way . . . this softening of her indignation. He'd *lied* to her. She was right; he was wrong.

Yet she was struck by the irony that, while she had indeed compared him to David, he was now behaving in a way David *never* would have. She could not recall David ever admitting he possessed faults. Or apologizing. And she certainly could not imagine him ever openly admitting he'd lied.

A fissure of shame wound through her. She did not like

what he'd done, but his well-intentioned sin could in no way compare to David's transgressions. And while she could not disregard those shadows that lurked in Robert's eyes, could not overlook the fact that he hid secrets, it was increasingly difficult to credit that those secrets involved anything sinister or illegal or bad—not from a man who had the integrity and honor to look her in the eye and admit his mistakes, then apologize for them.

But these realizations . . . that he was a good, decent man, and one who clearly cared for her, filled her with a knee-weakening fear. For if he was all those wonderful things she was beginning to suspect he was, how could she hope to guard her heart against him? Even now her body was betraying her, overwhelmed with the desire to lean into the heat emanating from him, to bury her face against his broad chest and breathe in his clean, masculine scent that teased her senses. *He is your lover. Nothing more. Will never be anything more.*

But if nothing else, she at least owed him the same courtesy he'd afforded her. Lifting her chin, she said, "I appreciate your apology, and hope you will accept my own. I did not mean to insult or hurt you. It was not my intention to insinuate you are a cheater, thief, or blackmailer."

His expression remained fierce for several seconds, then softened a bit. "Thank you."

"Now, about the gowns—"

He cut off her words by laying his fingers over her lips. "Accept them, Allie. Please. In the spirit in which they were intended. The black gowns as a gift from a friend who cares about you." He leaned forward and whispered against her ear. "And the gold gown as a token of the deepest regard from your lover."

Heat whooshed through her as if he'd set her clothing on fire. He flicked the tip of his tongue over her sensitive earlobe, and she squeezed her eyes shut against the pleasure.

"Are you normally so generous with your lovers?" The instant the question passed her lips, she wished she could recall it. His behavior with other lovers did not matter. Yet her inner voice taunted, *It should not matter, but it does.* God help her, she did not want to think of him with other lovers, past or future. Did not want to feel this irrational jealousy pumping through her.

He leaned back and gave her a long, searching look, his eyes serious and intent and questioning. Clearly he wondered why she would ask him. Finally he said, "I'm not certain I understand what you mean by 'generous.' I cannot deny I have given lovers gifts, but they've always been impersonal. Flowers, or the occasional bracelet. Never something as personal as clothing. And never something that I wanted a lover to have more."

She tried to ignore the way her heart jumped at his words, but it was impossible. Even more so when he slid his hands down her arms and entwined their fingers. The warmth of his palms pressing against hers sent rivulets of heat through her veins. He stepped closer. Less than a foot separated them, and his body seemed to surround her like a velvet cloak.

"You say you don't want to insult or hurt me," he said in a husky voice, his gaze steady on hers, "but refusing my gifts will do both. If you do not wish to accept them for yourself, do it for me. Because knowing you don't have to worry about replacing your garments destroyed in the theft makes me happy. Because I want so very much to see you wear that golden gown." He lifted her hand and pressed a kiss against her fingers. "And because I greatly anticipate slipping that shimmery material from your body and making love to you."

Her limbs turned to liquid, and she stiffened her knees to keep from sliding to the floor. "I . . . I don't know what to say." Good lord, it amazed her she was able to even form a coherent word.

"Ah. I am more than happy to help." A flicker of mischief gleamed in his eyes. "Say 'Thank you, Robert.' "

A tiny answering smile jerked at her lips. She should say no. But she simply could not. "Thank you, Robert."

"Say 'I'll wear the golden gown tonight.' "

"I'll wear the golden gown tonight," she whispered.

"Say 'and all evening long I'll think about how you are going to take it off me, then make love to me.' "

God help her, how could she refuse to say something that was so completely, undeniably true? Yet how could she verbalize such a confession . . . words such as she'd never uttered before? Still, almost of their own volition, her lips moved. "And all evening long I'll think about how you are going to take it off me, then make love to me."

His eyes darkened with a naked heat so raw she felt engulfed in flames. Releasing her hands, he slipped his arms around her, pulling her closer, until his hard body touched her from chest to knee.

As he lowered his mouth toward hers, she planted her hands against his chest to halt his progress. "Robert, I feel compelled to point out that this is probably not a good idea."

"On the contrary. I think it is an excellent idea." A mixture of heat and mischief sparkled in his eyes. "And really, quite unstoppable. I simply must kiss you."

"But what if Caroline returns with the children?"

"She won't. They're having biscuits, then picking flowers. Believe me, once Emily and James are in the conservatory, they'll run about the rows of plants for hours playing hide-and-seek. Lily has her own private nursery, near Elizabeth's bedchamber. And the door here is locked. We are very much alone."

"I see. Well, in that case . . ." She rose up on her toes and their lips met in a lush, openmouthed kiss. He tasted of coffee and heat, of man, and his own unique flavor that stirred her senses, bringing a purr of pleasure to her throat.

Everything faded away but him and the delight she felt under the onslaught of his sensual kiss. . . . A kiss that quickly burned into so much more. His hands caressed down her back, then forward to cup her breasts. Her nipples beaded into aching points of need, and she pressed herself closer to him, seeking more of his touch.

Her fingers became restless, frantic things, fluttering butterflies seeking a place to land in a windstorm. His erection pressed against her belly, coiling need straight to her core. She slipped her hand between them and stroked her open palm down the front of his breeches, over his hard ridge of flesh.

He broke off their kiss and sucked in a sharp breath. "Allie . . ." He rested his forehead against hers, his ragged breath beating warm against her face. Feeling wicked and bold and empowered by his response, she ran her hand over him again, slowly. A long, low moan rumbled in his throat.

"I feel it only fair to warn you," he said in a voice rough with arousal, "that if you continue to touch me like that, you will not get out of this room . . . unscathed."

"Oh, my," she breathed, deliberately tickling her fingertips over the head of his erection. "What exactly do you mean by . . . unscathed?"

"God help you, you're about to find out." And with those few words, he simply took her over. His mouth came down on hers with devouring intensity. His tongue slid past her lips, stroking her mouth deeply, slowly, with a devastating rhythm that perfectly mimicked how her body ached to join with his.

Breaking their kiss, he pressed a trail of kisses down her neck, while his hands made quick work of removing her fichu. His lips wandered lower, over the tops of her breasts, and she bit down hard on her lip to keep from crying out in frustration at the barrier of clothing between them. Her hands wreaked havoc with his hair, pressing him closer, while she drowned in sensation.

With a low groan, he lifted her against him, then strode quickly to the sofa where he lowered her to the cushion, following her down. His impatient hands tugged at her bodice, freeing her breasts, and she gasped when he immediately drew one of her aching nipples into his heated mouth, his tongue swirling over her sensitive flesh.

She tried to catch her breath, but it was impossible with his mouth and tongue teasing her breasts while his hand worked its way under her gown and slid up her leg. She squirmed beneath him, spreading her thighs, lifting her hips to give him easier access, while her hands clutched at his shoulders. Her feminine flesh felt hot and heavy and wet, and if he didn't touch her soon—

Robert's fingers skimmed over her swollen folds, and the last remaining ounce of control he'd managed to cling to, vanished. She arched against his hand, a long moan of satisfaction rumbling in her throat. Rising to kneel between her splayed thighs, he pushed her gown to her waist, reveling in the erotic sight of his fingers playing with her glistening flesh, of her hips undulating as passion consumed her, her nipples still wet and erect from his mouth. He eased first one, then two fingers inside her, clenching his teeth when her silky heat surrounded him. The scent of her arousal, mixed with the delicate fragrance of honeysuckle, inundated his senses, and his erection jerked inside his confining breeches. With his other hand, he quickly freed himself.

He wanted to wait, wanted to prolong their pleasure, touch her, taste her, but as it had last night, his mastery over his own body deserted him. He needed to be inside her. Now.

He slipped his fingers from her, and would have smiled at her cry of protest if he'd been able. Surging over her, he slid into her tight, wet heat in a single stroke. Any thoughts he might have entertained of going slowly evaporated when she raced her hands down his back to his buttocks, urging him deeper into her body. Bracing his weight on his forearms, he thrust into her with hard, fast strokes. Sweat broke out along his brow, and he looked down at her. Her head was thrown back, exposing the delicate curve of her throat. Her eyes were shut, her lips parted, her breath a series of ragged pants that matched his own.

"Ohhhh," she breathed, and he watched her orgasm claim her, felt her body tense, her inner walls clutching him, pushing him over the edge with her. With an animal-like growl, he threw his head back and thrust into her, spilling his seed deep in her body. He pulsed inside her for an endless, mindless moment, then collapsed, burying his face in the fragrant curve of her neck, pressing his lips against her jumping pulse.

It took several moments for sanity to return, for him to

garner enough strength to raise his head. Their gazes met and his heart performed a slow roll at the warm, satisfied glow in her eyes.

There were a dozen things he wanted to say to her, tell her, but he hesitated, partly because he was not sure she was ready to hear them, and also because he wasn't yet capable of speech. So he said the one word he could manage to push past his lips.

"Allie."

She blinked twice, then a slow smile eased across her face, reminding him of the sun coming out from behind the clouds. Here was his girl from the sketch. She whispered one word in reply.

"Robert."

He felt himself grinning in return, unable to hide his happiness. She was his. And nothing, no one, would keep them apart.

In her bedchamber, Allie had just finished repairing herself after her sensual interlude with Robert, when a knock sounded on the door.

"Come in."

A middle-aged maid bearing a bright smile and a ceramic pitcher entered.

"Beggin' yer pardon, Mrs. Brown. My name's Mary. I were just wantin' to bring some fresh water and see to tidyin' up. I can come back later."

"Hello, Mary. Please come in." She was about to add that she herself was about to leave the bedchamber, when something stopped her. With her bright cheeks and wide grin, Mary struck her as a friendly sort. Perhaps the friendly sort of woman who might be led to answer some questions. . . .

Her conscience tapped her firmly on the shoulder. *Not even an hour ago you were furious with Robert for being dishonest. Trying to glean information from this woman is hardly honest.*

She slapped back her inner voice, rationalizing that there

was a distinct difference between dishonesty and curiosity about the man she'd taken as her lover. And she was merely . . . curious. Besides, the maid might not know anything.

She engaged Mary in small talk regarding the rainy weather and the new baby, as the woman bustled around the room wielding her feather duster with energetic efficiency. Then Allie led the conversation around to Elizabeth and the duke.

"Fine people. Not hoity-toity as the Quality often can be," Mary said, her mobcap swaying as she fluffed the bed pillows. " 'Course, the whole family is the first water. I've been here at Bradford Hall for twenty years, you know."

"So you've known the duke and his siblings since they were children."

"Indeed. Smart as whips, every one of them." A chuckle passed her lips. "But the youngest, Lord Robert, now he were a caution, that one. Always gettin' into some sort of mischief. But a more lovable boy ye'd be hard-pressed to find."

Allie's heart pounded at the conversational opening Mary had unwittingly handed her. Forcing aside the guilt once again nudging her, she said, "Yes, he's very charming." She lowered her voice and added in a halting voice, "Of course, it's too bad . . . about what happened . . ."

Molly looked confused for several seconds, then her eyes widened. "So ye know about the fire?" She made a *tsk*ing sound and frowned. "Can't believe folks still talk about it, it happened so long ago."

Fire? "A terrible tragedy," Allie murmured.

A disgruntled *harrumph* sounded from Mary. "Don't care what anyone else says, 'twas a youthful indiscretion gone bad, if you ask me. That boy wouldn't hurt no one on purpose, not ever. And he made all the reparations, just like he promised. 'Course, no one hardly mentions it anymore as it's been four years. And the family don't discuss it at all."

"Perfectly understandable," Allie managed to say, her head spinning with Mary's unwitting revelations. Was Robert guilty of some sort of *criminal* act?

"All's tidy here, Mrs. Brown. I'll leave you now."

"Thank you, Mary."

The maid quit the room and Allie pressed her fingers to her temples, where a headache was rapidly forming. Thankfully she was standing close to the wing chair near the fireplace and required only a few jerky steps to sink onto the cushion. Surely she should not feel as if someone had cut her legs off at the knees. Yet she did.

Mary had mentioned a fire. And reparations. What were the details surrounding this incident? And how was Robert involved—for clearly he had been in some way. Something tickled her memory, and she suddenly recalled Robert's odd reaction when Lady Gaddlestone had mentioned a fire during their tea at The Blue Iris. What had he done? A shiver of dread gripped her, and she wrapped her arms around her middle to ward off the sudden chill. Clearly there was more to the man she'd asked to be her lover than she had anticipated. Should she follow Elizabeth's advice and ask him? Did she really want to know the answers? And if she did ask him, would he tell her the truth? Or, like David, would he lie, or evade her questions?

Get a hold on yourself, Allie. It's not as if you're going to marry him. Did his past *really* matter? The man was her lover. Nothing more. It was not necessary to know every facet of his life.

She drew a deep, calming breath. As long as she kept her heart uninvolved, his past and secrets did not matter. She would allow him to engage her body and nothing else.

Geoffrey Hadmore sat in his usual leather chair in White's. He'd just lifted his brandy snifter to his lips when a commotion near the betting book captured his attention.

"The official announcement arrived from Bradford just this morning," proclaimed Lord Astley. "The duchess was delivered of a girl yesterday." A smug smile curved over Astley's face. "Lots of money going to be changing hands on that one."

Geoffrey sipped his brandy and turned a deaf ear to the crowd gathering around the betting book. So the duchess had her baby. Excellent. Everyone's attention at Bradford Hall would be focused on the newest edition, allowing Redfern more freedom to accomplish his task. And allowing Geoffrey himself more freedom to accomplish his.

A slow smile pulled at his lips. Bringing the newest member of the Bradford household a gift was an excellent excuse to visit the estate.

Chapter 17

Dressed in the beautiful golden gown, Allie paused at the top of the wide staircase and pressed her gloved hands against her stomach. Drawing in a deep breath, she tried to calm her inner jitters, but anticipation and excitement and emotions raced through her at a breakneck speed she'd been unable to control all day.

She looked down at the fall of shimmering material and could not suppress the sigh that escaped her. It had been so long since she'd worn anything so bright and colorful. That felt so sinfully delightful against her skin. And she had never owned a more gorgeous gown. It fit her perfectly, from the gathered bodice to the short, puffed sleeves, to the velvet ribbon gathered beneath her breasts. How amazing that one garment could make her feel so wonderful. So feminine and pretty. Like a princess.

And as much as she loved wearing it, she could not wait to see Robert's reaction. His words echoed through her mind, leaving a trail of heat in their wake: *I greatly anticipate slipping that shimmery material from your body and making love to you.*

Good Lord, how would she make it through the evening

without giving herself away? Especially now that she'd finally figured out what that elusive something was that she'd felt was missing in her physical relationship with David.

Realization had dawned this afternoon, as she'd lain beneath Robert on that sofa, recovering from her intense orgasm, aftershocks of pleasure still rippling through her. He'd collapsed against her, his weight pressing her into the cushion, his heart hammering against hers, his breath panting against her neck. His jacket and shirt abraded her tender breasts, his breeches pressed into her splayed thighs. And it came to her in a flash of recognition.

This wild wanting, this intense *need* he clearly felt for her—*this* was what she'd been missing. His total loss of control. His wanting her so much that he simply couldn't wait to undress to have her. Had to just impatiently push aside the barriers keeping their skin apart.

This was what had been lacking between her and David. For while David had been an exciting and proficient lover, he'd *never* lost control like that. She'd never once stripped him of his command over himself. Driven him to such intense physical need. Had never incited him by her words or deeds to simply . . . take her. To want her *that much*. So that his control fled. And she, she now realized, had never truly surrendered her own control. Not completely.

No, she'd never experienced this depth of physical and emotional connection. It was, without a doubt, what she'd been missing. And now that she knew, she wanted to experience it again. . . .

God help her, she had to think about something else. Pressing her hands more firmly against her midriff, she started slowly down the stairs. Perhaps the fact that Elizabeth was joining the family for dinner would save her. Yes, she could concentrate on her friend, and push Robert from her mind completely.

Completely? her inner voice taunted. *Ha! You're a fool. The next time you push him from your mind will be the* first *time you've managed to do so.*

She swatted the voice away as she would a bothersome insect. Nothing was going to spoil this evening. She'd waited too long to share an evening like this with Elizabeth and her family.

Elizabeth? You are indeed a fool. She is not the one who has your heart pounding and your pulse racing and your palms sweating.

She huffed out an exasperated breath. All right, she was a fool. But God help her, it felt so incredibly delicious and free and marvelous being one, she could not deprive herself the pleasure. So, for tonight, and for this brief magical time she was here at Bradford Hall, she would be a fool and allow herself to enjoy every minute of it. Because reality would intrude all too soon.

She stepped into the foyer, and instantly felt his presence. He stepped from the shadows of an alcove, and her breath caught. Dressed in a midnight-blue cutaway jacket that matched his eyes, and cream-colored breeches that accentuated his tall, muscular frame, he was nothing short of magnificent. Her already rapidly beating heart floundered, then sped up, not only at the look of him but at the heat blazing from his eyes as his gaze wandered over her.

Walking slowly forward, he gently picked up her gloved hand then raised it to his lips. "You look stunning," he breathed against her fingertips. "It almost hurts to look at you."

She could not stop the flush of pleasure his compliment washed through her. And surely she should be appalled at the naked desire shining in his eyes, at the possessive way his gaze roamed over her. But instead she felt desirable. And feminine. And practically giddy.

"Thank you," she said, unable to keep the breathlessness from her voice. "The gown is beautiful."

"The woman wearing it is beautiful." He reached out and gently touched one of the tendrils framing her face. "I like your hair this way."

She resisted the urge to pat her artfully arranged curls,

which Elizabeth's abigail had styled into an elegant Grecian-style knot. "My hair is so horribly straight. I'm certain the curls won't last the duration of the evening."

"My darling Allie. I *know* those curls won't last the duration of the evening. The moment I get you alone, they will be M.B.R."

She raised her brows, and he said, "Mussed Beyond Repair."

"I see. Well, in that case, I.C.W." She paused for a second, then clarified, "I Cannot Wait."

"Nor can I." He took her hand and pressed it against his white shirt. His heartbeat slapped against her palm, hard, fast, and intimate. "That is what the sight of you does to me," he whispered, his gaze locked on hers. "I've thought of nothing but you all day." He huffed out a ragged-sounding laugh. "It was nearly impossible to assist Austin with the accounts as he requested. God knows I did not want to leave you for even five minutes, let alone the remainder of the afternoon. Thank goodness Miles was there to correct the numerous mistakes I made."

"I spent a very enjoyable time with your mother and Caroline. They taught me to play piquet, then we roamed about the conservatory." Her gaze settled on his lips, and it struck her just how beautiful his mouth was. Masculine and full, firm, yet somehow soft at the same time.

"If you continue to look at me like that," he said in a gruff voice, "you will not get out of this foyer—"

"Unscathed?" she suggested, raising her gaze to his.

His eyes darkened. "Unkissed. Unscathed is for . . . later."

A delicious shiver curled through her at the mere thought of . . . later. "Although a kiss sounds delightful, I think we'd best not," she said, slipping her hand from the warmth of his chest. "I suspect there would be no way to keep ourselves intact, and I can hardly go in to dinner with my bodice pulled down and my hair all askew."

He cocked a dark brow at her. "Are you insinuating I'm a . . . messy kisser?"

She closed her eyes and breathed out a long, rapturous sigh. "Oh, my. Yes."

At his low rumble of laughter, she opened her eyes. "In that case," he said, "you are correct, and we'd best wait. Now, may I escort you to dinner?" He extended his elbow. Tilting her head in a formal fashion, she placed her gloved hand very properly on his arm and allowed him to lead her down the corridor, while very *im*proper thoughts danced through her head.

Dinner was a gala, celebratory affair, with course after delectable course served while sherry, Madeira, and champagne flowed freely. At the start of each course, beginning with a delicate soup, then turbot with lobster, lamb cutlets with French mustard, and asparagus and creamed peas, everyone raised their glasses and toasted Elizabeth and Lily.

Sitting between Caroline and his mother, Robert ate his fill of each perfectly prepared dish, but the fine meal was truly lost on him. Allie sat directly across from him, and it was nearly impossible to take his eyes off her. Never had he seen her so animated, so full of laughter and fun. He'd long since lost count of her smiles, and he found himself utterly, completely enchanted by her.

And the sight of her in that gown . . . the topaz color glowing against her creamy skin. . . .

Bloody hell, she stole the breath from his lungs.

Elizabeth, resplendent in a pale green muslin gown, sat at the foot of the table. As the dishes were cleared in preparation for the next course, she turned toward Allie and said, "Do you recall the first time we went fishing?"

Allie raised her gaze toward the ceiling. "I shall never forget."

"What happened?" Caroline asked.

"We were twelve," Allie said, "and for some reason I shall never understand, we allowed my father to goad us into claiming that we could certainly fish as well as he could, in spite of the fact that neither of us had ever attempted to fish before.

After all, how difficult could it be to catch a few fish? So off we went to the lake to prove ourselves. Unfortunately, we quickly discovered that neither of us wanted to put the worm on the hook."

"The worms were *slimy*," Elizabeth stressed.

"This from my robust wife?" Austin teased from the head of the table.

"*Slimy* has nothing to do with a robust constitution," she said with a haughty sniff.

"We knew, of course, that it is quite impossible to catch fish without bait," Allie continued. "Unless you are a bear or bird or some such—"

"—which we are not," Elizabeth interjected.

"—so we decided to use something else as bait," Allie said. "Sadly our choices were somewhat limited. But based on our experimentation, I can report that fish do *not* like to eat acorns, leaves, rocks, or cheese."

"Cheese?" asked Robert.

"We'd brought a hunk with us," Allie acknowledged. "Quite a nice cheese, too. You would have thought that there would be *one* fish in that large lake who liked cheese."

"Obviously not the most intelligent of fish," Robert murmured with a smile.

"That is exactly what we said!" Allie replied with a wide smile of her own. "Still, despite our best efforts, we were unable to catch a single fish. But we simply could not go home without one. Papa had teased us unmercifully before we'd set out on our fishing expedition, claiming that we wouldn't be able to catch any fish without his manly presence to help us."

"So he was proven correct?" Caroline said, her disappointment evident.

"Oh, no," Allie said. The devilish gleam in her eyes was at complete odds with her angelic, innocent smile. "On our way home, we detoured through the village. And stopped at the fishmonger."

"By pooling our resources, we were able to purchase a very respectable fish," Elizabeth said with a laugh. "Allie's father never knew that we'd bought the fish instead of catching it. It cost us every bit of money we had between us, but it was well worth it."

"Amazing," Austin said. "Just when I think I know everything about my wife, I learn something new." He made a *tsk*ing sound, his eyes gleaming at Elizabeth down the length of the table. "I never would have suspected her capable of such despicable chicanery."

Elizabeth raised her chin with a regal, duchesslike air. "The dastardly deed was entirely Allie's idea."

An expression of mock shock widened Allie's eyes. "*My* idea?" She frowned, then pursed her lips. "Oh, well, yes, I suppose it was."

Everyone laughed, and Robert spent the remainder of the meal falling more and more in love with her. Every time their eyes met, his heart jumped. Every time she smiled, his heart melted. Every time she laughed, his heart rolled over in his chest. Indeed, by the time dessert was served, he realized with an inward wry smile that his heart stood a good chance of not making it through the evening, what with the beating it was taking.

Bloody hell, she was lovely. Everything he'd always wanted. Everything he'd been searching for. Witty, intelligent, generous, caring, honorable. And she set his blood on fire.

"You're awfully quiet," Caroline said to him in an undertone, leaning toward him as conversation buzzed around them. He looked at her, noting her arch smile. "And you're sporting a very interesting gleam in your eye. I wager I can guess why." She flicked her gaze toward Allie in a totally unsubtle way.

Robert shot Caroline an equally arch look, then flicked his own gaze toward Allie. "I don't believe I'll take that wager, because I'm certain you're correct."

He bit back a smile at her smug expression. She leaned closer to him. "You mean . . . Allie?"

He arranged his features into a look of confusion. "Allie? Whatever do you mean? I thought you were referring to the syllabub. It is absolutely delicious. Cannot possibly speak when eating it, you know. Must concentrate all one's attention on the delicate flavor. And that subtle taste of lemon always puts a gleam in my eyes."

Caroline bared her teeth at him. "Do you know who is more vexing than you?"

"Who?"

"No one."

He threw back his head and laughed. Ah, yes, life was good. He'd found the woman he loved, and could still get a rise out of his sister. And life was very soon to be even better. For he had the entire night planned. Making love to Allie, then asking her to be his wife. His inner voice roused itself, pointing out that she might very well have some objections to his past, but he pushed the bothersome warning aside. Nothing would spoil this evening. Certainly not something that had happened four years ago. *You're fooling yourself. You know how she would react if she knew.* Indeed. Which was precisely why he had no intention of telling her now.

Later. He would tell her later. After she loved him enough to understand. Of course, he would never be able to tell her the whole truth, but surely he could make her understand. But not tonight. Tonight he would propose. She would say yes, and they would announce their betrothal at breakfast tomorrow. The family would welcome her with open arms, for it was obvious, especially after this meal, that she fit like a glove. Elizabeth loved her, and it was clear that Caroline and Mother liked her enormously. And he . . . he was a man deeply in love.

Ah, yes, life was good indeed.

After dinner, Robert suggested they retire to the music room.

"Why?" The question came from the duke, who Allie noted was glaring at Robert with ill-concealed suspicion.

"I wish to entertain you all with a song."

Allie nearly choked with laughter at the range of horrified expressions surrounding her. Caroline and her mother looked as if they'd just spied an insect swimming in their teacups, while the duke and Lord Eddington appeared as if they'd bitten into sour pickles. Only Elizabeth seemed amused.

"Good God, man," the duke said, "if you won't take pity on the rest of us, at least have some consideration for Elizabeth. She's just been through a trying ordeal."

"Nonsense," Elizabeth said, taking Robert's arm and leading the way toward the music room. "You know how robust I am. I should love to hear a song."

A collective groan went up, but everyone followed the duo down the corridor, albeit with obvious reluctance. Allie walked beside Robert's mother, who whispered, "I'm sorry, my dear. He's my son and I love him, but he cannot carry a tune in a bucket. We tried to discourage him, but I'm afraid the dear boy loves to sing."

"I've already heard him sing," Allie confided. "And play the pianoforte. At the town house in London."

"Oh, dear. So you know."

"That he's completely tone-deaf? I'm afraid so. But then again, so am I."

"Ah, then you shall fit in with us quite nicely, my dear. We're all abysmal singers, although Caroline plays the pianoforte passably well."

When they arrived in the music room, Patch raised his head from his cozy position on the hearth rug, and thumped his tail in greeting. Everyone settled themselves on the settees and wing chairs, except Robert, who took his place at the pianoforte. The instant he sat before the instrument, Pirate, clearly sensing what was coming, scrambled to his feet and trotted swiftly from the room, head down, tail tucked between his legs. The duke muttered something that sounded suspiciously like *smart dog*.

Robert smiled at his audience. "Would anyone else prefer to go first?"

"No!" they all answered in unison.

"We want you to get it over with, brother dear," Caroline said with a sweet smile.

"I'll have you know, the piece I plan to play will astound you—"

"Frighten is closer to the truth," the duke said dryly.

Robert lifted his nose into the air in dramatic fashion. "—will astound you because it is a duet. And I'd now like to ask my lovely partner to join me." He turned toward her. "Allie?"

Heat rushed into Allie's cheeks and she shook her head. "Oh, I couldn't possibly."

"Of course you can," Robert said. "We'll perform the song we played in London—to commemorate Lily's birth."

"That would be lovely, Robert," Elizabeth said.

He glared at his audience. "There? You see? Elizabeth thinks it would be lovely."

"Elizabeth is hopelessly polite," the duke muttered.

"Actually," Elizabeth said, her eyes gleaming with unmistakable mischief, "I'm anxious to hear Allie sing and play the pianoforte. These must be newly acquired skills for her. I've known her my entire life and"—she coughed discreetly into her hand—"and a singer and musician she was not."

Forcing herself not to laugh, Allie put on her best haughty expression. She then swept toward the pianoforte like a ship under full sail, and positioned herself on the cushioned bench next to Robert.

"I believe aspersions have been cast upon our musical talent, sir," she said.

"Indeed they have," he agreed. "Therefore, we must, in the name of honor, redeem ourselves."

"I'll pay you twenty pounds if you don't," the duke offered with a hopeful expression.

Robert gave his brother an angelic smile. "You already owe me twenty for the billiards game you lost."

That revelation set up a hum of conversation. Allie turned to Robert and said in an undertone, "You won? With your *eyes closed*?"

"I won. I told you—I always play to win."

"I suppose your brother was quite distracted," she murmured with a teasing grin.

"Yes." In spite of their teasing banter, she clearly read the heat in his eyes. "But taking advantage of your opponent's weaknesses is part of the game."

"Ahem. You can begin anytime now, brother," came the duke's voice. Allie pulled her gaze away from Robert's and realized with no small amount of chagrin that the conversation had stopped, and five pairs of eyes were focused on them with varying degrees of speculation.

Yet instead of appearing embarrassed, Robert grinned broadly. "Well, since you *insist* . . ."

They played the same song they'd played before, and if it were possible, their performance was even more horrendous than the last time. Probably because Allie could not catch her breath from laughing at Robert's dramatic antics, his voice booming, several notes off key.

When they reached the final verse, however, he slowed the tempo and lowered his voice, singing the final words softly, albeit still off key.

The sunlight reflected her features so fair
As she waited and wondered, to see if he'd dare.
And he did not disappoint his lovely young miss,
For upon her sweet lips he did bestow a sweet kiss.

With the final discordant note still echoing in the room, she felt his gaze upon her, and she purposely kept her eyes cast down at the ivory keys, afraid if she looked at him that he and everyone else would see how much she anticipated him obeying the song's words and bestowing a sweet kiss. Only when the applause started did she dare raise her gaze, and then she deliberately focused her attention on the audience.

Elizabeth came forward and hugged Robert, then enfolded Allie in her arms. "That was wonderful," she enthused.

The duke said in a loud aside to Lord Eddington, " 'Wonderful' is an American word that means 'Robert, you are hopelessly tone-deaf and should be ashamed of yourself for dragging poor Mrs. Brown down with your lack of musical acumen.' "

"Perhaps *you* would care to regale us with a song, Austin," Caroline suggested.

A look of pure horror crossed over his handsome face. "God save us, no. I've no desire to see you all jump out the window to escape the cacophony. Indeed, I believe it would be best if Elizabeth and I retire." He looked toward his wife with loving concern. "I would not want you to overtire yourself, darling."

"I am rather fatigued," Elizabeth agreed. She hugged Allie's shoulders. "But this has been a marvelous evening. And thank you both for the song."

As it was nearly midnight, everyone else decided to retire as well. They climbed the wide staircase as a group, then separated to adjourn to their respective bedchambers. Allie was very careful not to look directly at Robert, for she knew her face would give her away. Indeed, even not looking at him, she knew her cheeks flamed crimson. After bidding everyone good night, she walked swiftly to her bedchamber. Closing the door behind her, she leaned against the oak panel and closed her eyes, her heart pounding with anticipation.

How long would it take him to come to her?

In Lily's nursery, Elizabeth stood looking down at her tiny, sleeping daughter. Austin came up behind her, placing his warm hands on her shoulders, and she leaned back into his chest. He pressed a loving kiss to the side of her neck, then rested his cheek against hers as they both admired Lily.

A sigh escaped Elizabeth, and Austin straightened, turning her so they faced each other. "Are you all right?" he asked, his gaze anxiously roaming her face.

She forced a smile to ease his worry. "Yes. Just tired." She shook her head. "No, not just tired. I'm also worried. About Robert and Allie."

"Have you seen something else?"

She looked into his eyes. "He's in love with her."

A tiny smile edged up one corner of his mouth. "Darling, even I, who do not possess your clairvoyant abilities, can see that." When she did not return his smile, his amusement disappeared. "I would have thought a match between them would please you. Indeed, had you not predicted he would fall in love with her?"

"Yes. And it would make me happy, except . . ."

"You're concerned about the danger you sensed?"

"Yes. I still feel that. But I sense something else . . . something even more imminent." She shook her head. "Robert's heart is going to be broken, Austin."

His fingers tightened on her shoulders. "Are you certain? It seems quite clear she cares for him as well."

"I felt it, very strongly, when I touched them in the music room. Heartbreak. For both of them."

Michael Evers settled himself onto the lumpy mattress, his every muscle aching with fatigue. He'd ridden hard with little rest, changing horses frequently, trying to keep ahead of the storm he saw brewing in the skies just south of his route. He'd arrived in Liverpool less than an hour ago. Exhausted, he'd found an inn, eaten some stew, then all but collapsed upon the bed.

Tomorrow morning he would cross the Irish Sea to Dublin, a journey he was not relishing. Damn it all, he hated the water. Hated everything to do with it. Sailing, fishing, all of it. Most likely his intense dislike arose from the fact that he could not swim. Every time he ventured near water, a sheen of sweat broke out over his entire body. Of course, his fear was not something he shared with anyone. *Never show weakness* was his motto. And in his line of work, and given the company he kept, he could not afford to do so. He'd rather ride a bloody horse all day than spend five minutes in a bloody boat. Aye, give him some solid horseflesh beneath him—not some wooden planks at the mercy of unpredictable tides and waves that rolled and undulated in a way that made his stomach feel queer.

In truth, he could have secured passage on a livestock barge scheduled to depart at midnight. But damn it, he couldn't face the prospect of crossing all that water in the dark. Best he spend the night here, rest up, and cross during daylight hours. When he could see what was going on. See where the railings were, so he didn't accidentally fall off the bloody deck.

Besides, for years Mrs. Brown had had possession of the note now secreted in his waistcoat. What possible difference could a few more hours make?

Chapter 18

At precisely half past midnight, Robert slipped into Allie's bedchamber, closing and locking the door behind him. She stood near the fireplace, surrounded by a golden, backlit glow that made her appear ethereal. Except for her eyes. They looked wickedly aware, and full of desire.

A lump lodged in his throat. It seemed as if he'd waited forever to find her, had searched everywhere for her. And here she was. Waiting for him. *At last.*

With his gaze fastened on hers, he crossed the room, his bare feet sinking into the plush carpet. He wore only his royal-blue dressing gown, knotted loosely at his waist, and with each step he took, the silky material abraded his overheated skin. He stopped directly in front of her, his heart slapping against his ribs as if he'd run ten miles.

"I want you to know," he said softly, "that I shall try my best to go slowly this time, but given how I feel right now—without having even touched you—I'm afraid the chances are not particularly good."

She stepped forward, erasing the two-foot space he'd left between them, then splayed her palms against his chest in the V opening of his dressing gown, instantly tightening his groin.

He rested his hands on her waist, sucking in a breath when she leaned forward and pressed her lips against his exposed skin.

"I think," she said, her breath caressing him, "that slowly can wait for later." She replaced her fingers with her warm mouth, flicking her tongue over his nipples, sending a shudder through him. Her hands slid down his abdomen to the tie at his waist. Grasping her wrists, he took a shaky step back.

"*Later* will arrive in mere seconds if you continue to do that," he ground out. Disappointment tempered with unmistakable feminine awareness glittered in her eyes. His own gaze roamed slowly down her golden-clad body. "That is indeed a beautiful gown," he murmured.

"Yes."

"Let's take it off."

Her eyes darkened. "Yes."

Releasing her wrists, he stepped behind her. Resting his hands on her shoulders, he leaned forward and kissed the pale, vulnerable skin at the base of her neck. Honeysuckle teased his senses, and he touched his tongue to the spot, absorbing the delicate shiver that ran through her.

Straightening, he ran his finger along the row of tiny buttons running down the gown from just below her nape to the center of her back. He slipped the top one through its loop, exposing a tantalizing glimpse of creamy skin, which he kissed before slipping the second button free.

"I specifically asked Madame Rence to put these buttons here," he whispered as he undid the third and fourth fastenings, "so that I could do this." The remaining buttons came free, and he slowly parted the material and ran a single fingertip down her spine.

A breath huffed from her. "Most likely I should be appalled at such arrogance and presumption."

"Not arrogance," he whispered against her neck. "Confidence. Knowing when something is . . . right. And inevitable." He gently pushed the gown from her shoulders and down her arms. It slithered over her hips, pooling in a golden puddle at her feet. He turned her slowly around, then took her hand, helping her to step out of the circle of material. He then picked up the gown and laid it over the back of a wing chair, congratulating himself on his impressive show of restraint thus far.

Turning back toward her, he swallowed. Dressed in nothing more than a nearly transparent chemise and delicate stockings tied with lace garters, she stole his breath. And a good deal of the restraint he'd just congratulated himself upon. Coral-hued nipples pressed against her chemise, calling to him like a siren's song.

He started toward her, but she backed up. He raised his gaze to hers and was arrested by the devilish challenge sparkling in her eyes.

"You're looking at me in a very *distracting* way," she said in a raspy voice he could only describe as smoky.

He advanced several more steps, angling himself so that her retreat led her directly toward the bed. "On the contrary, I'm not the least bit distracted. I know *exactly* what I plan to do with you."

"Oh, my. Would you care to enlighten me?"

Her retreat was halted when the backs of her legs hit the side of the mattress. He stalked slowly forward, like a jungle cat preparing to pounce on its prey. Halting directly in front of her, he absorbed the desire and mischief dancing in her eyes, the rapid pulse quivering at the base of her throat, the delicate, unmistakable scent of female arousal rising from her skin.

"My darling Allie, I would be delighted to enlighten you. First I plan to remove the remainder of your clothing." Reaching out, he slid her chemise slowly down her arms, until it fell to her feet, leaving her in just her stockings and garters.

"You are exquisite," he murmured, taking in all of her, every delectable curve from her head to her toes. He then filled his hands with her full breasts, her taut nipples pressing into his palms.

A long sigh escaped Allie, and pinpricks of pleasure raced over her sensitive skin. Her eyes slid shut, and she gave herself over totally to the sensation of his hands on her body, arousing her nipples, then gliding down to caress her buttocks while his lips and tongue laved her breasts. She ran her fingers through his silky hair, thrusting her breasts higher, urging him to take more of her into the wet heaven of his mouth. Desire curled through her, dampening her flesh, pooling an aching, heavy heat between her thighs that demanded his touch. Impatience scraped at her. She wanted, needed, more. Now.

"What do you intend to do next?" she said in a raspy voice she did not even recognize as her own.

He lifted his head from her breast, and the inferno blazing in his eyes stalled her breath. Rising to his full height, he placed his hands on her shoulders and gently pressed her down. With her knees already as limp as overcooked noodles, she sank to sit upon the mattress. He then gently urged her back until she was fully reclined from knee to head, her feet dangling off the side of the mattress. Insinuating himself between her knees, he loomed over her, resting his wide palms on the ivory counterpane on either side of her shoulders.

"Next," he said, his warm breath beating against her face, "I intend to find out if you taste like honeysuckle everywhere."

Oh, my. He leaned down and teased her bottom lip with the tip of his tongue. She tried to capture his mouth in a kiss, but he moved his lips away, across her jaw, then down her neck. She ruffled her fingers through his hair, then raised her arms over her head, and simply gave herself over completely to the magic his hands and mouth wrought so expertly upon her.

For a man who'd claimed the inability to go slow, his exploration of her body was an agony of prolonged pleasure. His fingers and lips glided sinuously over her skin with a devastating combination of feathery caresses and velvety, wet heat. He suckled her breasts until she writhed beneath him, aching for him to fill her, and put out this relentless fire he'd stoked.

Still, his journey continued with a leisure that brought her to the brink of desperation. His tongue dampened a trail down her abdomen, then dipped into her navel. Feeling him shift lower, she forced her eyes open and propped herself up on her elbows. He knelt on the floor, his fingers playing with the curls between her thighs. His broad shoulders were bare, indicating he'd shed his robe. Their eyes met, and her pulse jumped at his intense expression.

"Spread your legs for me, Allie."

Her gaze locked with his, she obeyed, splaying her thighs wide, her heart pounding in anticipation. He slipped his hands beneath her, cupping her buttocks, then slowly slid her toward him, lifting her.

The first intimate sweep of his tongue over her female flesh brought a cry to her throat she could not contain. Her arms collapsed beneath her, and she lay back, caught in a maelstrom of intense sensation as he worshipped her with his mouth and tongue, licking, kissing, teasing her, building the pressure until a long, raw moan ripped from her throat. Looking for an anchor, she fisted her hands into the counterpane as wave after wave of release rushed through her.

It seemed her shattering, deep, inner contractions had barely subsided, when, in a limp daze, she felt him move, lifting her body to settle her on the center of the mattress. Before she could so much as draw a breath, he slid into her in one breathtaking stroke.

"Look at me," he whispered.

She somehow managed to pry open her heavy lids. His expression was harsh with need, his eyes appearing nearly black with arousal.

"Allie," he whispered. And then he kissed her, deeply, his tongue mating with hers. The scent and taste of her own female musk, mingled with his unique masculine flavor, inundated her senses, and the magic started all over again. Wrapping her legs around his waist, gripping his shoulders, she met his increasingly urgent thrusts. His lips slid away from hers, and he buried his face in her neck.

"Now," he whispered, the word ending on a groan. "Come with me. Now."

Her orgasm pulsed through her, wringing a cry of pleasure from her. He thrust into her one final time, clasping her tightly against his damp chest as he found his own release. Then, before her heart had even started to slow down, he rolled them onto their sides. Still intimately joined, she snuggled her heated face against his chest, reveling in the sound and feel of his frantic heartbeat tapping against her cheek.

When her breathing finally regulated, she whooshed out a long sigh of utter contentment, then leaned back to look at him. He'd been so still, she'd thought he'd perhaps dozed off. But she found herself looking into dark blue eyes. Very serious dark blue eyes. Much too serious eyes.

She instantly sensed the need to lighten the mood, for feelings and emotions she was not prepared to cope with were unmistakable in his gaze. But before she could utter a word, he cupped her cheek in his hand and said the words she feared most. The words that would end their relationship.

"I love you, Allie."

Chapter 19

Robert looked into her wide golden-brown eyes and repeated the words that his heart could no longer contain.

"I love you," he whispered. A simultaneous sense of calm and elation rushed through him at finally telling her the words that would start them on their future together. Brushing back a tangled chestnut curl clinging to her soft cheek, he watched her, waiting for her response, waiting to hear her repeat the same sentiment to him.

Instead, all the color blanched from her cheeks, all traces of warmth vanished from her eyes, leaving her with a bleak stare, and her body went stiff and unresponsive in his arms.

She squirmed in his grasp, and even though he wanted nothing more than to keep her in his arms, he let her go. With jerky steps, she crossed to the wardrobe, pulling out a plain, off-white, cotton wrapper. She did not turn to face him until she'd secured the sash around her waist. He took the few seconds to don his own discarded robe, then sit on the edge of the mattress. When she did finally face him, he stilled at her expression.

She was smiling. But not the sort of happy smile he'd hoped for. This was an *indulgent* sort of smile . . . the sort he gave Emily or James when they pulled on his hands to lead him into a game.

"I thank you. However, everyone knows one mustn't take seriously any words said in the throes of passion."

Stunned, he simply stared at her for several seconds. Then, when he could trust his voice, he rose and erased the distance between them in three long strides. Grasping her by the shoulders, he opened his mouth to speak, but she laid her fingers across his lips.

"Don't say it again. Please."

He shifted his head to dislodge her fingers while fighting to hold off the unease and impatience pressing in on him. "Why the devil not?"

"Because such words are . . . awkward between two people who are merely lovers."

Her words stabbed him like a knife between his ribs. Before he could recover, she continued, "Indeed, it would be most unwise for you to think you love me. Given our situation, you really must put the idea out of your head."

His fingers tightened on her shoulders. "I do not *think* I love you. I know it. Absolutely."

She lifted her chin and raised her brows. "How can you possibly? You barely know me."

He could not decide if he was more stunned or more furious. He studied her eyes. Was that a flicker of fear he saw? Was she afraid of his feelings? Or was it her own that frightened her? Forcing himself to speak in a calm voice, he said, "Given the way we've spent our time in this bedchamber, I believe I know you extremely well."

Color stained her cheeks. "You are confusing love with lust."

There it was again, that flash of fear in her eyes. Some of the tension drained from his shoulders. She was merely afraid, no doubt because their relationship had progressed so rapidly. She simply needed reassurance. Completely understandable.

With his gaze steady on hers so she could read the sincerity of his words, he said, "Allie. I cannot deny I feel lust for you.

Passion. But I am not confusing that with love. Perhaps I was precipitous in telling you how I feel, but I could not hide it any longer." He brushed his fingertips over her soft cheeks. "I assure you that 'I love you' are not words I say lightly or frivolously. Indeed, except for my mother and sister, I've never said them to any woman."

"It takes longer than a week to fall in love, Robert."

"I disagree. There are women I've known for months, years, who, in spite of knowing them all that time, they have never inspired even a fraction of what I felt for you from the first time we met."

An almost desperate look came over her features. "Robert, believe me. You . . . you don't know anything about love."

"I beg to differ. I know everything about it. I've lived with it, experienced it, every day of my life. Look at my family— you cannot possibly have spent so much as an hour in their company and think that I do not know about love. It seems that the question is, do *you* know what love is?"

Her eyes went blank. "Yes. I had it once. That was enough."

He shook his head. "That wasn't love. That was one-sided hero-worship of someone who tricked you in the most despicable of ways. That was lies and deceit. Love is sharing. It's happiness and laughter."

"No, love is heartbreak. And I do not want any part of it ever again." Her bottom lip trembled, and her expression turned beseeching. "Robert . . . please. I do not want to hurt you."

"Then accept my love. Love me in return." He framed her pale face in his hands. "Marry me."

Allie stared at him in mute dismay, his words echoing through her brain like a death knell. *Marry me. Marry me.*

Dear God, how had she allowed things to progress to this point? He was looking at her, his eyes dark and serious, and frighteningly expectant. Terrifyingly hopeful. She tried to step away from him, from his compelling, unrelenting gaze, but his hands had slipped to her shoulders and he held her fast.

Anger seeped into her veins. Damnation, she was tired of

men believing they were in control of *any* facet of her. Her movements, or her future.

She lifted her chin. "I told you before we embarked upon our liaison that I had no desire to ever marry again. I wanted a lover, nothing more. I am not looking for forever. Why can we not simply enjoy each other for the time I'm here?"

"We can. But I *am* looking for forever. And I want it with you. Can you look me in the eye and tell me you do not have feelings for me?"

The bottom seemed to drop out of her stomach. She wanted to deny it. Desperately. But could she? God help her, no. Somehow, against her own better judgment and warnings, she'd come to care for him. A great deal. A humorless laugh rose in her throat, nearly choking her. How foolish could she be? How could she have believed she could take this man into her bed, into her body, and not involve her heart?

But she could not, would not risk herself again. Dear God, this was the same, *the very same,* mistake she'd made with David—allowing her heart to rule her head with a man she barely knew. A man with secrets he'd conveniently neglected to mention. How many more times would she need to make *the very same* mistake before she learned? Two? Three? Five? A dozen?

Zero. She would not make the same mistake again. No matter what her heart wanted. Her heart, as she'd learned the hard way, was entirely unreliable.

"Obviously I cannot deny I find you attractive—" she began.

"That is not what I asked." The look in his eyes was half fierce, half confused, and it tugged at her heart in a way she'd never before experienced. "Can you honestly tell me you don't feel it? This magic between us? How is that possible, when I feel it with every breath? Every heartbeat?"

"I . . . I care for you," she said. "You are a generous, exciting lover. But that is all I want. All I can give in return."

He shook his head, as if trying to align his thoughts into order. "Jesus. I thought—no, I *knew*—that once we'd made love, you would see . . . would realize . . ." He released her shoulders and dragged his hands down his face. Closing his eyes, he tipped back his head and looked at the ceiling. When he lowered his gaze back to hers, anger burned bright in his eyes.

"How long, Allie? How long are you going to allow that bastard to rule your life?"

She stiffened. "If you mean David—"

"*If* I mean David?" A harsh, humorless laugh escaped him. "Of course I mean David. He's ruled every facet of your life from the grave for the past three years, from your actions to the clothes you wear. He might as well be sitting in this bloody room with us. The way I see it, you've paid your debt. You've paid *his* debts. Exactly how many more years are you planning to give him? How much more of your happiness are you going to let him steal?"

Her hands fisted at her sides. "You don't understand—"

"You're right. I don't understand." He advanced a step toward her, and she involuntarily retreated a step. "Make me understand, Allie. Make me understand why you're not willing to put the past behind you and live again. Why you're willing to let one past mistake with a man who is *dead* ruin what we could have together."

"It is my past mistake I am determined not to repeat."

"What does that mean?"

"We barely know each other."

He drew a deep breath. "I know you, Allie. You've lived in my mind, in my heart, my entire adult life—all I had to do was find you. It is not necessary for us to know every single thing about each other to fall in love. As for me, I know everything I need to know about you. I know you are kind. Loyal. Honorable. You make me laugh. You make me happy. Those are the important things. We have a lifetime ahead of us to learn everything else."

"Clearly I was not specific enough. I should have said *I* do not know *you* well enough."

"That is easily remedied. What would you like to know?"

"What would you like to tell me?"

Her question and harsh tone stilled him, filling his eyes with a sudden unease. "I'd be happy to listen to any questions you wish to ask."

A very evasive, David-like reply, she noted. "Very well. I want to know about the fire."

His eyes went blank and a muscle ticked in his jaw. A deafening silence stretched between them, broken when he finally asked, "May I inquire who told you?"

"I cannot see that it makes any difference. What matters is that *you* did not tell me."

"I'd planned to."

"Indeed? When?"

"Eventually."

But she could see the true answer on his face, the guilt in his eyes. He clearly hadn't planned to tell her until after she'd married him—when it would be too late for her to reject him.

"It happened a long time ago, Allie."

"*What* happened?"

"What specifically do you want to know?"

"You could start by explaining your involvement."

He stared at her for several heartbeats, then said, "It is not something I like to talk about."

Hurt and anger waged a war in her. He wasn't going to tell her. Well, damn it, she was not going to accept that. "I only want to know one thing, and I want the truth. Did you cause this fire?"

He said nothing for a space of time that seemed to stretch into an eternity. It was obvious from his troubled expression that he was deeply conflicted. Finally, he said, "Yes, I did."

"Was it an accident?"

"No." The single, harsh word seemed ripped from his chest. "I was responsible for starting a fire in a nearby village. A building was lost. A man lost his life."

She actually felt the blood drain from her face. "You were not imprisoned?"

"No. My family wields a great deal of influence." He seemed about to say something more, but instead he pressed his lips together. Unreadable emotions flickered in his eyes, and his hands fisted at his sides. "That is all I am able to tell you."

Her heart felt crushed. It was obvious there was more to this incident—aspects he was unwilling to share with her. Dear God, how was it possible to feel so numb yet hurt so much at the same time? And why did she feel this ridiculous tug of pity for him? Was it the tortured look in his eyes? The way he seemed to be silently beseeching her for something she did not understand?

Well, she would not feel sorry for him. By his own admission he'd *committed a crime*. One he'd clearly had no intention of telling her about. It was as if she were reliving her worst nightmare. He was, indeed, just like David. *Just like David . . . just like David.*

Pulling her gaze away from the sorrow in his eyes, she looked pointedly toward the door. "I think it would be best if you left my bedchamber now. And did not return."

He grasped her shoulders, bringing her gaze back to his. There was no mistaking the pain her words brought him. "You want to end our affair?"

"I cannot share such . . . intimacies with you any longer."

"Because of one mistake in my past."

"Because of the nature of the mistake. And because you didn't tell me. You asked me to spend the rest of my life with you, yet you deliberately withheld information you had to know I would find pertinent—especially given my own past."

He moved one step closer to her and cupped her face between his hands, his own face taut with emotion. "Allie. Please. Let us both put the past behind us, where it belongs. I love you. So much, it hurts." His anxious eyes searched her face. "Do you love me?" The question seemed to erupt from him. "If you do, if you feel the same way I do, if you trust me, then we can conquer anything together. If you don't . . ." His words trailed off and he swallowed, his throat working. "Do you love me?"

Did she? God help her, she didn't know. So many conflicting

feelings were pushing at her, pulling at her, until it felt as if her head were about to explode. She'd been so determined not to love him, not to feel *anything* for him, but he'd somehow sneaked around her defenses. She needed to think, and she could not do so with him here, confusing her further. The only two things she was certain of was that she did not *want* to love him, and she would not allow herself to be hurt again.

His hands slid slowly from her face. "I guess I have my answer."

"Robert." She pressed her hands to her stomach, feeling the need to say something, but completely ignorant of what to say, not even certain why, in spite of everything, she felt this inexplicable need to comfort him. To make him understand. "You just don't know what it's like. To have your heart completely, utterly broken."

He appeared to look right through her. In a flat tone, he said, "You are completely, utterly wrong." He leaned forward, until his lips almost touched her ear. "You see, I just found out," he whispered, his warm breath a stark contrast to his chilling words. Then he turned and walked swiftly across the carpet. Without a backward glance, he quit the room. The door closed behind him with a soft click that seemed to reverberate with a funereal finality.

He was gone, and she knew he'd just departed more than her bedchamber, closed the door on more than a sensual interlude. He was literally gone. From her life. There would be no more passion-filled nights, no more laughter-filled days.

An ache such as she'd never known crushed her, stealing her breath. Nothing, ever, had hurt this way. Not even David's betrayal. Her entire body started to shake, and she staggered toward the bed. She climbed beneath the covers like a wounded animal, shivering, feeling more lost and alone than she ever had.

Yet she'd done the right thing. For both of them. She'd vowed never to marry again, to never give her heart to someone who could trample it into the ground. A man who would keep things from her. Who was capable of committing a crime.

And even if she was insane enough to push aside all the reasons he was the wrong man for her and consider his proposal, she could not ignore the fact that she was the wrong woman for him. An image of him, cavorting with his niece and nephew, flashed through her mind, leaving a poignant ache in its wake. Whatever Robert's faults, there was no denying he was wonderful with children. No skirting the obvious fact that he was a man who would someday want, and need, children of his own.

And no ignoring the fact that she could never be the woman who gave them to him.

The area around her heart went hollow, then filled with throbbing grief. The memory of him bouncing children on his knees, children who gazed at him with love-filled, excited eyes, should not hurt her so. She'd known her relationship with Robert would never lead to marriage, knew children were not in her future. But clearly they would be in his. And that filled her with a misery and longing too painful to contemplate.

Yes, she might possibly satisfy him for a short period of time, but he would eventually want children. And she could not give them to him.

He'd clearly put his past behind him, moved on with his life. She recalled his words about the fire. *It is not something I talk about.* It was as if he'd placed the entire incident in a box marked "In The Past—Do Not Discuss," then shoved the entire affair into a corner of the wardrobe, never to be seen again.

It did not matter. Their whirlwind affair was over. It had simply ended a bit sooner than anticipated.

Yes, she'd done the right thing. For both of them. Her mind absolutely knew it.

Now, if she could only convince her heart.

Robert entered his bedchamber and made a beeline for the decanters. Tossing back a hefty swallow of brandy, he immediately poured another. As he lifted the snifter to his lips, he caught sight of himself in the cheval glass. From the neck down, he looked like a man who had just emerged from his lover's bed—rumpled and disheveled. From the neck up, he looked like a man who'd just lost everything he held dear—empty, hollow-eyed, and drawn.

Inclining his head at his reflection, he raised his brandy in mock salute. "Well, *that* did not go particularly well, did it?"

He tossed back the potent drink, relishing the internal burn, which at least served to prove that he wasn't completely numb. Perhaps after a few more drinks he might start to feel better. A few dozen drinks might conceivably be necessary.

"Bloody hell, there's not enough brandy in the entire empire to make me feel better," he muttered. Of course, enough brandy might render him unable to feel anything which at this point would be a blessing indeed. Sloshing two more fingerfuls into the crystal snifter, he made his way to the wing chair flanking the fireplace and sank down. Leaning forward, with his elbows resting on his splayed knees, he stared into the low-burning flames, as if they held the answers to all his questions. And God knew he had plenty of questions. Problem was, he didn't like the damn answers. In truth, he'd only received a positive answer to one question: She did indeed taste like honeysuckle everywhere.

An image of them together, naked, his lips caressing her, flashed through his mind, bringing with it a wave of agony that stole his breath. He could still taste her on his tongue. Feel the imprint of her satiny skin . . . skin he would never touch again.

No! The word reverberated through his mind with pounding intensity. Things couldn't be over between them. They'd barely begun. . . .

But what choice did he have? Through his own stupidity he'd lost her. She'd made her feelings unmistakably clear. She did not want him. She did not love him.

He rubbed his palm over the center of his chest. Damn it, the fact that she had turned down his proposal hurt. But the fact that she didn't love him . . . God, that sliced like a rusty blade. She might as well have cut out his heart and tossed it on the floor. Stomped on it while she was at it.

Yet he had no one but himself to blame. He should have told her. He'd obviously been a fool to believe she wouldn't find out, but it had happened so long ago. Had Elizabeth told her? Possibly, but he doubted it. He supposed he could ask her, but the answer made little difference now. More than likely she'd overheard some servant gossip. Or perhaps Lady Gaddlestone had mentioned it during their ocean crossing.

In truth, it didn't matter how she'd found out. In her eyes, he was guilty. Not only of a crime but for not telling her. He recalled the look in her eyes. She'd looked at him as if he were a . . . criminal. Accusation had shone clearly in her gaze, all but screaming at him, *You're just like David.*

God, that hurt. But he could not blame her—not when he'd said nothing to disabuse her of the notion. He'd wanted to tell her the whole truth, so badly his skin had ached, but he was bound by promises he could not break. He'd never told anyone. And he'd given his word not to. Unfortunately, there was more involved here than just his wants and desires.

Damn it, he was not a criminal. *But he had committed a crime. . . .*

Yes, he'd done what he'd had to do, but damn it, he'd never considered that those actions would cost him the woman he loved four years later.

If he'd known, would he have made the same choices that night? He took a long swallow of brandy, then squeezed his eyes shut. *I don't know. God help me, I don't know.*

Of course, in the entire scheme of things, his past didn't really matter a jot anyway. It was simply the final nail in the coffin. He could have been a vaulted saint, and she still would have refused him. She did not love him. Did not want him. Did not want to marry ever again. By spouting out his feelings like a faulty fountain, he'd accomplished nothing but making an ass out of himself. He'd known she'd be reluctant to accept a proposal. His fatal mistake had been underestimating the depth of her reluctance.

He polished off his brandy, then set the empty snifter on the hearth. A long groan escaped him, and he buried his face in his hands. Damn it, it was over. He had to accept it. He'd offered her everything he had—his love, his heart, his name— and she'd turned him down. Why the devil could he not have simply fallen in love with an amenable English girl with no bloody former husband or problems or madmen after them or aversions to marriage? Someone willing to allow past mistakes to remain in the past? Someone who, when he asked her to marry him, would know that the correct answer was: *Oh, yes, Robert. I'd love to be your wife. I love you, Robert.* Not *I've no desire to ever marry again. I want a lover, nothing more. I am not looking for forever.*

An expletive he rarely used whispered past his lips. He briefly considered leaving Bradford Hall, escaping back to London—or anywhere—for the duration of her stay here, but he discarded the idea. With Elizabeth's warning of danger bouncing through his head, he refused to leave Allie alone, whether she wanted him to or not. And he needed to remain here to await Michael's arrival from Ireland. No, he would simply have to put his feelings aside and carry on as if nothing had occurred. As if his dreams of a wife and family hadn't been shattered. As if his heart hadn't broken.

Just how the hell he was going to do that, however, he did not know.

Lester Redfern slogged through the darkness, cursing the mud that sucked at his boots, making his feet feel as if they each weighed twenty stone. Bloody hell, a man of his caliber should not have to suffer being this cold, wet, miserable, and filthy.

Gusts of wind shook the surrounding trees, and his gaze darted from left to right, nerves jittering, heart pounding. Devil take it, he hated the woods. 'Specially at night, wot with all the spooky sounds and shadows, when a body didn't know where he was. Give him London any day of any week.

But as much as he hated the woods, it didn't come close to the way he hated horses—one horse in particular. That sway-backed nag wot had dumped him in the mud, after she'd bit his hand. He flexed his bruised fingers, and muttered a string of curses. And all that when he'd unhitched the beast after the mud had sucked up his gig's wheels.

By the devil, this was madness. He'd catch his death out here in the rain and cold. Wetness oozed through the soles of his boots, and he ground his teeth. With the rain all but washin' out the roads, he'd be lucky to get to Bradford Hall—assuming he'd ever find the bloody place—by next month. It had taken him the entire day to get the distance he could have traveled in an hour's time if this rain hadn't started.

Well, he weren't about to walk to Bradford Hall, that were for damn certain. The earl would just have to wait until travelin' conditions improved, to get his precious note.

"And he's goin' to have to pay up some extra blunt for all my efforts," Redfern grumbled. "He's goin' to replace my boots, and get me a fine greatcoat as well."

A loud squeak caught his attention. Squinting through the darkness, he spied what looked like the glow of a lantern ahead. With a flicker of hope ignited in his cold, wet, miserable, muddy self, he surged ahead. Rounding a corner, he almost fell to his knees with relief. Blowing in the gusty wind, its hinges squeaking loudly, was a sign—The Boar's Lair. An inn, or at the very least a pub, where he could get himself a meal, warm himself in front of a fire, and pray for this bloody rain to stop. And when it did cease, which it surely had to soon, he would continue to Bradford Hall. And to Mrs. Brown.

Chapter 20

Robert sat in the darkened billiards room watching the last of the glowing embers in the grate die out, counting the mantel clock chimes strike midnight. The windows rattled with gusts of wind, but at least the relentless rain had finally stopped. He'd wryly wondered if perhaps he and Austin and Miles should organize an effort to build an ark. For the past four days, sheets of water had fallen from the gray sky a sky that perfectly matched his mood.

Four days. Four days since that last encounter with Allie in her bedchamber. Four days of trying his damnedest to avoid her in a tremendous house that suddenly seemed no bigger than a crofter's cottage. Four endless, sleepless nights, lying in his bed, trying without success to think of something, anything, other than her.

The rest of the household had retired more than an hour ago, as had he, but he'd finally left his bedchamber, unable to face another sleepless night in his empty bed. Alone. He gazed at the brandy snifter cupped in his hand. Besides, he'd emptied the decanter in his bedchamber.

He and Allie had managed to avoid each other during the days, although he wasn't certain if that was more a case of him avoiding her or her avoiding him. He'd spent most of his time in Austin's private study, helping his brother with the estate accounts, throwing himself into the task with an enthusiasm that clearly baffled Austin. But he wanted, needed, to keep his mind and hands occupied so he wouldn't think of her. Wouldn't search her out and find some excuse to touch her.

When he wasn't helping Austin with the accounts, he kept to himself, reading in the library, playing billiards with Austin and Miles, spending time with James and Emily in the nursery, although it was pure torture to even look at the sofa in that room. He knew from Caroline that Allie had spent most of the last four days with Caroline and his mother, talking, doing needlework, playing card games. And according to Austin, she also visited with Elizabeth each afternoon.

He'd longed to escape from the house, where he kept catching elusive whiffs of her fragrance in the corridors, and take a long, bruising ride. The rain, however, prevented such outdoor activities.

Yet it was not as if he'd bumped into her around every corner. Indeed, the only times he'd seen her at all the past four days had been during dinner when the entire family had gathered in the formal dining room. And those four occasions had been nothing short of hell.

She'd sat across from him, wearing her damn black gowns, looking increasingly pale and drawn each night, partaking in conversation, but her efforts were clearly forced. And while his eyes were drawn to her again and again, she never looked at him—except for that one instant when their gazes had met, clearly accidentally on her part, this evening.

The effect of connecting with her golden-brown gaze had been like a blow to the heart. Everything faded away except her. For a breathless moment, he'd waited, hoping, praying, to see a spark in her eyes, some indication that she missed him. Wanted him. Loved him.

Instead, she'd lowered her lashes, hiding her eyes, and had

applied her attention to her dinner, her utter rejection simply another blow to his already battered heart.

With each passing day it grew increasingly more impossible for him to pretend that everything was all right. Not when everything was so very wrong. He'd spent a good deal of the last four years managing to put on a happy, smiling front when inside he was torn up with guilt, but now, laughter felt simply beyond him. For his family's sake, he tried, but he knew everyone was aware something was amiss, knew his family was concerned. He could see it in their eyes, hear it in Mother's and Caroline's voices when they'd hesitantly asked him if he was all right. He'd tried his best to reassure them, but he suspected he'd failed. Just as he'd failed at everything that mattered lately.

A noise near the doorway caught his attention, and he turned his head.

"May I join you?" came Austin's voice from the darkness.

Robert swallowed a sigh. He did not want company. Did not want to make conversation. Unfortunately, thanks to his freedom with the brandy, he also felt most disinclined to rise from his chair.

"Of course," he said, hoping Austin was not in a talking mood.

"Would you care for a brandy?"

Robert tossed back the swallow remaining in his snifter. "Absolutely. Bring the decanter."

He heard Austin cross the room. The clink of crystal, followed by the quiet splash of brandy pouring into the sniffer. Then Austin joined him by the fire, refilling his glass with a generous hand. He settled himself in the wing chair opposite Robert.

Robert nodded his thanks and swallowed a hefty gulp, relishing the fiery burn in his throat. The embers glowing in the grate were starting to merge together in his vision. Good. Maybe soon he'd find the oblivion he sought.

"Do you want to talk about it?" Austin asked quietly.

He didn't pretend to misunderstand. "Not particularly."

Nearly a minute of blessed silence passed. Then Austin asked, "Would you care to hear my observations?"

"Do I have a choice?"

"Only if you leave the room. And judging by your slouched posture and slurred speech, that isn't likely to happen."

Robert waved his hand in a rolling motion. "By all means. Observe away."

"All right. Both you and Mrs. Brown are utterly, abysmally miserable. Your comments?"

"I cannot speak for her. But in my case, you are correct. I am utterly, abysmally miserable. And not nearly drunk enough to forget it." He poured another swallow of brandy down his throat.

"And you are miserable because . . . ?"

A long sigh escaped Robert, and he let his head fall back against the back of the chair, and closed his eyes. "Did I not, at some point in this bloody conversation, say that I did not want to talk about it?"

"You might have mentioned it. However, as you're incapable of rising from that chair, and I'm not leaving until you answer me, you might as well tell me."

"Bloody hell. All right. If you must know, she turned down my proposal."

"What, precisely, did you propose?"

Robert turned his head to glare at him, and instantly regretted the decision. Three Austins swam before him. Slamming his eyes shut again, he muttered, "Marriage."

"And she refused you?"

"I must say, Austin, that note of confused disbelief in your voice is very kind and indeed a balm to my shattered ego. Yes, she refused me. Completely, irrevocably, and really, most emphatically. In fact, the lady wants nothing more to do with me in any fashion at all."

"Did she give you a reason?"

A humorless laugh tumbled from his lips. "*A* reason? No,

she did not offer *a* reason. She gave me closer to a half-dozen."

"Perhaps given time—"

"No. She made it quite clear that she wants no part of marriage again. To anyone. But most particularly not to me." He tipped the snifter to his lips and drained it. "She's already been married to one criminal, thank you very much."

"You are not a criminal."

"I do not like to think so. However, it has come to my attention, albeit a bit too late, that committing a crime does indeed make one a criminal. Even if it happened years ago and reparations have been made. Quite the slap on the arse, that realization, I assure you."

He felt Austin's hand grasp his shoulder. Prying his eyes open, he saw Austin leaning forward in his chair, his face unmistakably serious in the shadows.

"I'm sorry, Robert. I know how much it hurts when you believe the woman you love does not return your feelings."

"I appreciate the sentiment, brother. But you have no bloody idea. Elizabeth adores you."

"I did not always know that."

"That is because you are slow-witted."

"Then it clearly is a family trait, because you suffer from it as well. Indeed, you are more severely afflicted than I."

Robert shot him the most frigid glare he could manage. "No need to look so bloody happy about it. And what does that mean anyway?"

"It means that Mrs. Brown is obviously miserable and distraught. If she did not harbor feelings for you—*strong* feelings—then why would she be so upset? If she felt nothing for you, she would have refused you, then simply put the matter out of her head."

"I never said she felt nothing for me. Unfortunately her feelings run the gamut from disappointment to disgust." He leaned toward Austin and nearly toppled from the chair. "Bitter letdown, as I'd been hoping for love and devotion."

Austin shook Robert's shoulder with a vehemence that

rattled his teeth and set up an unholy pounding in his temples. "Listen to me, you daft sot," Austin said. "I'm telling you that I believe there's a chance she might care for you. As you care for her. It is the only logical explanation for her distress."

"She is distressed because I was not truthful with her. She is distressed by my criminal past."

"Because she cares for you."

"Because I remind her of her dead husband." He frowned. "Before he was dead, of course. And that, I'm afraid, is a very, *very* bad thing. And not going to vanish like *that*." He tried to snap his fingers and failed.

"Well, for your sake, I hope you're wrong."

"As do I. But you know how I am always right. Always rather enjoyed that, up 'til now."

Austin stood and held out his hands. "Come on. I'll help you up the stairs."

Grumbling, Robert allowed himself to be pulled to his feet, then flung one arm around Austin's shoulders as the floor shifted. "Bloody hell, who's moving the house?"

Austin wrapped an arm tightly around his waist. Bloody good thing, as his knees felt decidedly wobbly. "You're going to have one hell of a head tomorrow, Robbie my boy."

Robert winced. "Stop yelling."

"I didn't yell." They made their way slowly across the room. "You're most likely not going to remember any of this conversation in the morning."

" 'Course I'll remember. My mind is like a . . ."

"Sieve?" Austin suggested.

"Exactly!"

"Yes. Well, that being the case, I've two things to tell you."

"Whassat?"

"You're a bloody pain in the arse."

"Why, thank you."

"And I love you."

Robert tried to grin, but his lips seemed to have fallen off. But in the tiny part of his heart that remained intact, for beating purposes only, Austin's words warmed him as nothing else in the past four miserable days had.

Michael walked quickly up the gangplank of the merchant brig docked in Dublin, and ran through his litany of calming mantras, bludgeoning back the panic clawing at him. It didn't matter that it was one A.M. and both the sea and the sky would be black. It didn't matter that the brisk wind would bring rough water. It would also bring greater speed. That was all that mattered. Because time was of the essence. He had to reach England as quickly as possible. Then make his way from Liverpool to Bradford Hall—a fifteen-hour journey on horseback, if he was lucky. But he had to get the information he'd learned to Robert. And Mrs. Brown.

He could only pray he wouldn't be too late.

Not bothering to cover her night rail with her robe, Allie shuffled across the carpet in her bedchamber toward the window. Pulling back the thick green velvet drapery, she blinked her gritty eyes against the unexpected morning sunlight. Finally the rain had stopped. Finally she would be able to escape this house. Breathe some fresh air that did not contain lingering whiffs of his woodsy scent.

The days following her confrontation with Robert had been the most empty and miserable of her life. And indeed, the most difficult. More so than when David had died and she'd discovered his betrayal. For at least then she had not had to pretend to be happy.

She'd spent the long hours visiting with Caroline and the dowager duchess—time that she simultaneously enjoyed, yet which filled her with a poignant ache for her own mother and sister. Caroline, with her playful, teasing manner and tendency toward creative card-playing, very much reminded her of Katherine. And while the regal dowager was very different from Mama, they both adored their children, and Allie appreciated how the older woman treated her as kindly as she did Caroline and Elizabeth.

As the days wore on, however, she couldn't help but feel the weight of Caroline's and the dowager's speculative gazes, and Elizabeth's as well during their afternoon visits. She'd avoided talking about Robert with Elizabeth, changing the subject or answering noncommittally the two times Elizabeth had brought up his name, but she realized she couldn't continue to do so indefinitely. Given Elizabeth's "feelings," she most likely knew what was going on, but she was obviously waiting for Allie to bring up the matter.

But truly, one would not need any special powers of perception to sense the tension between her and Robert during dinner. To Allie, it seemed as if the very air between them at the table were thick enough to slice. Thank God she'd so far only had to face him at dinner. It was near torture, having him sit directly across from her. His presence lodged a lump in her throat, making it nearly impossible to eat. She couldn't look at him, didn't want to see him. For she sensed that to do so would . . . would what?

Make her want him more? Hardly seemed possible, as she already wanted him with an intensity that made her skin ache. Crumble her resolve to avoid him? Yes, that was a distinct possibility, and one she did not wish to contemplate. Make her reconsider his proposal? No, she couldn't possibly. Nothing had changed between them; they were still wrong for each other.

Force her to accept the fact that she loved him?

Leaning forward, she rested her forehead against the cool glass and closed her eyes, unable to shut out the truth any longer. She loved him. Completely.

How, *how* had this happened? A half-laugh, half-sob rose in her tight throat. Surely there was no woman alive more foolish than she. She could understand making a mistake—she was human and therefore prone to error. But to make the same mistake *twice*—and such a huge mistake as falling in love with the absolute *wrong* man—well, clearly she'd taken leave of her senses. If she was to continue making mistakes, why, oh why could she not make a *different* mistake? Something more along the lines of using the wrong fork. Or paying a shopkeeper an incorrect amount.

But no, she seemed destined to fall impetuously in love with handsome, charming men who did not feel obligated to be truthful with her. Men whose dashing exteriors concealed dubious, criminal pasts. Perhaps she should consider a visit to the closest jail. Surely that would save her time in choosing the next wrong man to give her heart to.

Yet even as the sarcastic thought entered her mind, she realized with a sense of finality that there would never be another man after Robert. She'd thought she'd loved David with all her heart, but what she felt for Robert made her feelings for David fade to near insignificance. *You thought you'd suffered a broken heart before?* her inner voice scoffed. *Ha!* Now *you know what it feels like.*

Yes, she did. And she could not bear to feel like this anymore. It was time to face her situation straight on and make a decision. She had three choices. She could change her mind and accept Robert's proposal—a choice she discarded for all the same reasons she'd turned him down in the first place. She simply could not give her heart to another David. Robert might *own* her heart, but she did not have to *give* it to him.

She could keep to her original plan and remain here for the next five weeks with Elizabeth. A pang of regret raced through her, for she knew she had to discard that choice as well. She loved Elizabeth, loved being with her, but she could not possibly stay here for another month.

That left only one choice, and as much as it pained her, it was the most logical option. She needed to leave here as soon as possible. She would return to London, then sail back to America on the first available ship. Before she made another mistake. Before she gave in to temptation and allowed her unreliable heart to overrule her head.

.   .   .

Lester Redfern approached the horse with a narrow-eyed stare. "If you bite me again, I'll shoot you where you stand, you useless nag."

The mare shook her head and bared yellow teeth. Grumbling, Redfern slipped his boot into the stirrup, then vaulted awkwardly into the saddle as the beast sidestepped away from him. Bloody hell, maybe he'd shoot the beast anyway. But after. After he'd gotten the note and finished off Mrs. Brown.

He squinted up into the bright sunshine. Between the sun and the rising temperature, the road would be passable. A grin eased across his face and he applied his heels to the mare's flanks.

By this time tomorrow, he would be a rich man.

Get ready, Mrs. Brown. Here I come.

Bent low over the gelding's saddle, Michael raced along the dirt road. Teeth clenched, he forced himself to concentrate on each pounding step that brought him closer to Bradford Hall. Forced himself not to think about the incredible, shocking story his mum had told him. Forced himself to push away the ramifications of that tale until later. Right now there was only one thing to focus on: getting to Bradford Hall and Mrs. Brown.

Before Geoffrey Hadmore did.

Geoffrey Hadmore slowed his mount to a walk, chafing at the delay caused by the numerous muddy ruts in the road. He took the opportunity to slip his handkerchief from his waistcoat and mop his overheated brow. In spite of the still less than perfect traveling conditions, the road was drying very nicely. By early afternoon, he would be able to move along at a quicker pace. Which was good. After all, he had a baby gift to deliver.

And at least one murder to commit.

Chapter 21

Allie hesitated in the corridor outside the nursery. She knew from Fenton that Elizabeth was in the room. She could only pray Robert was not present as well. Drawing a bracing breath, she stepped into the open doorway.

Her eyes were instantly drawn to the settee. Images of her and Robert, limbs entwined, flashed through her mind, leaving sadness and pain in their wake. Forcing her gaze away, she focused her attention on Elizabeth.

Her friend and James sat before a low, wooden table. Elizabeth's tall frame was folded into a child-sized chair, her rose muslin gown floating onto the rug around her. James sat in an identical chair. Both leaned over sketchpads, diligently drawing with charcoals. Such a lovely image . . . a mother and son together, heads almost touching, sunshine pouring through the windowpanes. Elizabeth raised her head, murmured something to James, making him giggle. He leaned forward and placed a noisy kiss on Elizabeth's cheek, to which Elizabeth laughingly responded in kind.

A lump of longing tightened Allie's throat, and hot tears pushed behind her eyes. She would never have this . . . a son who gazed at her with innocent adoration. A child to give her love to. A husband and family of her own. She'd wanted it so badly, and for a long time, she'd managed to forget how much. But so many feelings and wants that she'd successfully buried were now once again exposed, like open wounds, every nerve raw and bleeding.

"Allie, how nice to see you. Come in, please."

Elizabeth's voice jerked her back, reminding her why she'd sought out her friend. She tried to offer a smile, but clearly her effort fell flat as Elizabeth's own smile faded into a look of concern. "Did you need to speak with me?"

Not trusting her voice, Allie merely nodded.

Elizabeth immediately rose, crossed to the door, then pulled a bell cord in the corner. She dampened a square of cloth in a ceramic bowl of water set near the hearth, then returned to James. "Mrs. Weston is on her way, darling," she said, cleaning his small hands of the charcoal streaks.

Just then a plump, middle-aged woman with twinkling eyes appeared in the doorway. As soon as James saw her, he grinned. "Biscuits!" he said.

Elizabeth laughed. "Yes, Mrs. Weston will bring you to fetch some biscuits." She enfolded him in a quick hug. "Will you save one for me?"

He held out three not-quite-clean fingers. "Save you two!"

Scampering over to the waiting governess, he slipped his small hand into hers, then they left the room, closing the door behind them.

"I did not mean to interrupt your time with James."

Elizabeth pressed her hand to the small of her back and stretched. "Don't be silly. You're not an interruption. I was quite ready to rise from that tiny chair, and you can see how heartbroken James was at the prospect of eating biscuits."

"How are you feeling today?"

"Very well." Her gaze swept over Allie's face. " 'Tis plain you cannot say the same."

"No, I cannot."

"Would you like to sit down?"

God help her, she couldn't even bear to look at the settee.

She shook her head. "I prefer to stand." Then, before her courage and resolve deserted her, she said, "I cannot tell you how much I've enjoyed being here with you, Elizabeth. Seeing you again, meeting and getting to know your wonderful family . . . it has meant more to me than I can say."

"I feel the same."

Forcing herself to meet Elizabeth's gaze, she said, "But I must leave here. As soon as possible. I'm sorry . . ." Her voice trailed off as emotion clogged her throat.

"This has to do with Robert." It was a statement, rather than a question.

Allie pressed her lips together to keep them from trembling. The best she could offer was an affirmative nod. Then, to her mortification, a tear dripped down her cheek.

Elizabeth immediately crossed the room. "Oh, Allie." Wrapping her arms around her, she led her to the settee, then gently urged her to sit. Giving up, Allie sank onto the cushion.

"I've been waiting for you to tell me what happened," Elizabeth said, her eyes deeply troubled.

In spite of a voice that shook, and tears silently dampening her cheeks, Allie told her about her last conversation with Robert and their parting of the ways. Elizabeth listened without comment, her eyes filled with understanding and sympathy.

When Allie finished her tale, she looked down at her tightly clasped hands resting in her lap. "As much as I wish it were otherwise, I cannot stay here any longer, Elizabeth."

"Because you love him."

She raised her chin and looked into Elizabeth's kind but troubled eyes and simply could not lie to her. "Yes."

"Yet you think he'll hurt you. The way David did." There was no censure in the softly spoken statement.

"I . . . I don't *know* if he would, but I cannot rule out the possibility. They are similar in so many ways."

"But different in many more."

Allie shook her head. "It does not matter. I cannot risk myself, my heart, again."

"The fire happened a long time ago."

"I know. But it still happened. And he did not tell me about it."

"He did not lie when you asked him about it."

"But he would not have told me then had I not asked! Don't you see that is part of the problem? What little he did tell me was with great reluctance. And it is obvious that there is more to the tale than he is willing to tell me."

"I'm not saying this to defend him, but he *never* discusses it. No one in the family does. What he told you was most likely more than he's ever told anyone."

"Perhaps. But it does not change anything between us." She blew out a long breath. "Elizabeth. Try to understand. Pretend your husband drank to excess, gambled the family into debt, then died. Would you not be extremely reluctant to involve yourself in any way with another man—especially one who drank to excess?"

Elizabeth frowned, then nodded slowly. "Yes. I see your point. But I know Robert is a good, decent man."

"I believe he is, too. But he is not the man for me. And although he believes otherwise, I am not the right woman for him. It is better for both of us if I leave. I've no desire to hurt either of us any further."

"Your leaving will hurt him."

"My staying will only hurt him more. I cannot give him what he wants." Fatigue, both physical and emotional, swamped her, and her shoulders slumped. "And now, if you'll excuse me, I think I'd like to rest for a while. I haven't slept well the past few nights, I'm afraid."

"When do you plan to leave for London?"

"I would like to leave tomorrow, if that can be arranged," Allie whispered. *Tomorrow.* It seemed like a lifetime away. It seemed like only seconds away.

"I will see to it that you have a carriage at your disposal. But I will pray that you change your mind."

"I won't." Leaning forward, she kissed Elizabeth's cheek. "Thank you for everything. Most especially for the precious gift of your friendship." She then rose and quit the room, closing the door with a quiet click.

Elizabeth remained seated, staring down at her hands. Hands that looked normal in every way, but that so many times had enabled her to see too much. See things she wasn't meant to see. Leaving her with the moral dilemma of what to do with the information.

She sat for several more minutes, weighing her decision. Then she rose and quickly made her way to her private sitting room. Crossing to her escritoire, she withdrew a piece of ivory vellum from the drawer and dipped her pen into the inkwell.

And prayed she was doing the right thing.

Drained after her talk with Elizabeth, Allie was about to enter her bedchamber, when Caroline turned down the corridor.

"Allie, you are just the person I was looking for."

The concern evident in Caroline's eyes prompted Allie to ask, "Is something amiss?"

"No. But I was hoping to interest you in a walk outside so we could talk. The weather has cleared, and I'm anxious to go outdoors after so many days inside because of the rain."

Allie hesitated. Based on Caroline's expression, Allie suspected her invitation might well involve a desire to discuss Robert. As much as she'd prefer to avoid the subject, she did need to tell Caroline of her decision to leave. And the opportunity to escape the confines of the house for a short period was tempting indeed.

"Come with me," Caroline urged. "It would do you good to get some fresh air."

Again she hesitated, as Elizabeth's warning not to wander off alone flashed in her mind, but she shrugged off the admonition. She would not be alone.

"I'd love to walk with you, thank you."

Chapter 22

A very proper butler swung open the door for Michael. The servant sniffed with obvious distaste at his bedraggled appearance, but Michael didn't give a good damn. He'd suffered worse looks from uppity servants before.

"May I help you . . . *sir?*"

"I need to see Lord Robert. Immediately."

The butler raised his brows. "If you'll give me your card, I'll see if—"

The haughty words were cut off when Michael picked up the man by his perfectly pressed lapels, then stalked into the foyer with him. Kicking the door shut with his boot, he brought the wide-eyed man nose to nose with him.

"I don't have a bloody card," he said in a deadly soft voice. "My name's Michael Evers. He is expecting me, and let me assure you, it will be *your* head that he'll have if you don't get him for me *now*. Do you understand?"

The man jerked his head in a nod. As Michael lowered him to his feet, he asked, "Where is Mrs. Brown? Is she safe?"

The man swallowed, his eyes filled with a combination of fear and confusion. "Safe? Yes. Mrs. Brown is upstairs with the duchess, in the nursery."

"You're positive?"

The servant took several hasty steps backward the instant his feet hit the polished marble floor. "Yes. I directed her there myself."

A breath of relief escaped him. "Excellent. Now go get—"

"Michael?"

He turned toward Robert's questioning voice coming from the corridor. Before he could say a word, the butler blurted out, "Lord Robert, this . . . *person* who claims to know you *burst* in the doorway, and—"

"It's all right, Fenton," Robert said, waving aside the words. "I've been expecting him." His gaze locked on Michael's. "You have news?"

"I do. We need to talk. Now. Privately."

"Follow me," Robert said, and started swiftly down the corridor.

Michael pinned a glare on the butler, and said in a low voice, "Make certain Mrs. Brown remains in the house. The others as well. Don't allow anyone out. Or anyone else in. Do you understand?"

The man nodded.

Satisfied, Michael strode down the hall after Robert.

Fenton watched the stranger's broad back disappear around the corner. Removing his handkerchief, he mopped his brow, while indignation filled him. Uncouth, unkempt ruffian! Fenton looked down at his clothing and gasped. Good heavens, his jacket was wrinkled, his shirt askew . . . why, he was completely undone. He did not know who this Michael Evers was, but he was clearly not proper company to be entertained at Bradford Hall. Who on earth did that brute think he was, pushing his way into the foyer, manhandling him, then giving him orders?

An elegant sniff escaped Fenton. He would not take orders from that man. Certainly not. He took his orders from the duke! Due to this Evers person, Fenton now needed to retire to his room to repair his appearance. He could not oversee the

staff in his present disheveled state, nor allow the duke to see
him as such.

He summoned a footman to man the foyer, and managed to
ignore the young man's stunned expression at his appearance.
Heavens, he must look worse than he'd suspected. After explaining the proper procedure for opening the door, Fenton
headed for his rooms. This was *most* irregular. The moment
he'd put himself back to rights, he would certainly locate His
Grace and inform him about that abominable Evers person.

Robert closed the library door behind Michael, who was
clearly in a very agitated state. "What did you learn? Was your
mother able to translate the note?"

Michael plunged his hands through his already untidy hair.
"Aye. You're bloody not going to believe it. I barely do myself." He looked at Robert with an expression that appeared
bewildered and bitter at the same time. "I've raced like the
devil himself pursued me to get here, and now I'm not even
certain where to begin."

"Tell me about the note. Did it have something to do with
Allie's husband?"

"Only indirectly." His dark eyes bored into Robert's.
"When I showed the letter to my mum, she got pale as a sheet
and damn near swooned."

Confusion washed over Robert. "Why?"

A humorless laugh escaped him. "The bloody thing was
written *to her*."

"*What?* By whom?"

"By the priest who married her to my father." Michael began pacing in front of the hearth, and Robert forced himself
not to fire a barrage of questions at him, to let him gather himself.

"When Mum saw the note, she went all to pieces, crying
and asking me to forgive her. I had no bloody idea what she
was talking about. When she finally calmed down, she told me
this story . . . this story that was documented in the note." He

paused in his pacing and briefly squeezed his eyes shut. "Christ, I still can't believe it."

Alarmed by his normally unflappable friend's distress, Robert crossed to him and laid a supporting hand on his shoulder. "Michael. Tell me."

Michael looked at him through tired eyes. "I've no memory of my father," he said, his voice gruff. "He died when I was a baby . . . or so I'd always thought. Until this visit with my mum. She confessed that the man she'd married wasn't named Evers. It was just a random name she chose."

A frown pulled down Robert's brows. "Then who the hell did she marry?"

Michael's dark eyes met his. "That's the part you're not going to believe."

Allie breathed in the rose-scented air, and tipped her face up to the sun in order to capture more of the bright, warming rays.

"You're going to freckle," Caroline warned with a smile.

"I don't care. It just feels so wonderful to be outdoors."

"I agree. Four solid days in the house was about to drive me mad."

They strolled along for several minutes, the silence broken only by the chirping birds. Allie savored every second, committing to memory the beautiful gardens, the pastoral setting, and Caroline—a woman she genuinely liked and would miss. As she would miss so many things about this lovely place.

They paused at a fork in the pathway, and Caroline pointed to the right, toward the woods. "This path leads to the ruins of a centuries-old stone fortress. It was a favorite childhood place for all of us. Would you like to see it? The walk through the forest is lovely."

Allie glanced over her shoulder and noted that they were well within sight of the house. "Is it far?"

"No. Just a few minutes ahead."

"All right."

The instant they entered the forest, the temperature

dropped, cooled by the shade from the soaring elms and oaks. Allie continued along the path in silence, waiting for Caroline to broach the subject she sensed uppermost in the woman's mind.

Several more minutes passed before Caroline finally said softly, "Allie, a blind person could see that you and Robert care for each other deeply. And that you're both miserable. I do not want to pry—" A tiny laugh broke off her words. "Actually I want nothing more than to pry, but I promised Miles I would not. So I shall simply ask you. . . . Is there anything I can do to help? I thought . . . perhaps if I arranged a picnic for the two of you for tomorrow, you could talk to each other privately and solve whatever has come between you?"

A wave of desolation washed over Allie. By this time tomorrow, Bradford Hall and all its occupants would be no more than a memory. It was time to inform Caroline of her decision to leave. And to disabuse her of any notions that she and Robert could resolve their differences. "I'm afraid I won't be—"

Her words chopped off as she and Caroline rounded a sharp turn in the path. Both women halted as if they'd walked into a wall.

Less than ten feet in front of them, a man lay prostrate on the ground, another man crouching over him. A brown gelding stood to the side of the path, nervously pawing the dirt. Someone gasped—Allie wasn't certain if it was herself or Caroline—perhaps both of them. The crouching man jumped to his feet and swiveled to face them.

Allie's eyes widened in surprise, but before she could say a word, Caroline exclaimed, "Lord Shelbourne! What on earth has happened?"

His dark eyes shifted between them for several seconds, then he said in a breathless voice, "I . . . I don't know. I was on my way to Bradford Hall to extend my congratulations to the duke and duchess on the birth of their daughter, when just a moment ago I happened upon this man lying in the path. I heard a crashing in the underbrush, and I saw a man dashing that way through the trees." He pointed in the direction leading away from the house. "No doubt the scoundrel attempted to rob this poor man. I had just dismounted and was checking his injuries when you arrived."

"Is he alive?" Caroline asked, her eyes huge.

"Yes. But he needs help. He's bleeding, and it looks as if he sustained quite a bump on the head." Again his gaze darted between them. "Lady Eddington, would you be so kind as to go for assistance? And Mrs. Brown, would you assist me in administering aid while she returns to the house for bandages and help?"

Caroline hesitated. "I don't want to leave Allie alone—"

"She won't be alone," Lord Shelbourne broke in, looking affronted. "She'll be with me. Now be off, we must hurry."

"Of course," Caroline said, crimson rushing into her cheeks. "I'll return as quickly as possible." She turned and raced around the corner toward the house.

Allie dashed to the fallen man, lowering herself to her knees beside him. His face was turned away from her, and she gently turned his head toward her. "Sir? Can you hear me?"

Warm stickiness oozed over her fingers, and his head turned limply toward her. She froze and stared at the man's face in stunned disbelief.

"Good heavens, I know this man," she said. "His name is Mr. Redfern. He sailed with me on board the *Seaward Lady* from America." Questions bounced frantically through her mind. What on earth was Mr. Redfern doing here? And how serious were his injuries? Reaching out, she pressed her fingertips to his neck.

Geoffrey looked down at her, bending over Redfern's prone form, and fought to regain his composure. Damn her cursed timing! Because of her arrival, his plans were now in a shambles. He could only thank God she and Lady Eddington had not arrived upon the scene even one minute earlier, as they would have seen him thrusting his knife into Redfern's back.

He glanced downward. The hilt of his knife, just visible over the top of his boot, was stained with blood. He hastily rubbed his hand over it, only to notice the dark red streaks marring his fawn jacket sleeve and white cuffs. His heart slapped painfully against his ribs. Had Lady Eddington noticed? No, clearly she had not. And even if she had, she'd obviously assumed he'd ruined his attire attempting to help the bleeding man.

His gaze shifted to Redfern, and he recalled the man's reaction to coming upon him in the woods. Redfern's face had been the personification of stunned amazement. Geoffrey had generously given him an opportunity to produce the note, but alas, poor Redfern had not yet retrieved it. It was the last mistake he would ever make.

But now he needed to work quickly, before Lady Eddington returned with half a dozen people in tow. He needed to find out where the note was, then escape from here. And unfortunately for Alberta, she would have to accompany him.

"Alberta. There was a note in the ring box. Did you see it?"

Crouching over Mr. Redfern's body, frantically trying to find a pulse, Allie did not bother to even turn at Lord Shelbourne's question. *Where was the pulse? There had to be a pulse.* "Note? Um, yes. Yes, I saw it."

"Where is it?"

"It's—" Her hands suddenly stilled, and she frowned. Clearly Lord Shelbourne *had* known about the note. Yet he had not made any mention of it when she'd returned the empty ring box to him at his town house—but she recalled his odd behavior at dinner that evening.

"Tell me where the note is, Alberta. Now."

The urgency and menace in his command slowly sank into her brain. Something was not right. As if in a daze, she gently settled her palm over Mr. Redfern's chest, then slowly withdrew it, a sense of horror washing over her.

"He's dead," she whispered. She rose on shaky knees, then turned around to face Lord Shelbourne. "He's . . ." Her voice trailed off as her gaze riveted on his bloodstained sleeve, then rose to his face. The look of pure desperation blazing from his eyes shivered a chill of fear down her spine.

"Dead. Yes, I know." He erased the short distance between

them in three quick strides. Reaching out, he grasped her upper arms in a viselike grip. He lowered his face to within inches of hers, and she involuntarily recoiled. "Where is the note, Alberta?"

She stared into his ebony eyes that suddenly reminded her of a serpent's. Everything inside her stilled, then shifted as realization clicked into place. Redfern . . . the accidents on the ship . . . the abduction and robberies in London . . . the note . . . Lord Shelbourne . . . they were all connected. And while she did not know all the details, instinct told her she was now facing the danger that Elizabeth had warned her against. And based on Mr. Redfern's condition and the desperate look in Lord Shelbourne's eyes, the danger was deadly.

She tried to break free of his grip, but his fingers tightened painfully on her arms. She considered screaming, but realized they were too far away from the house for anyone to hear her. Perhaps Caroline would hear her cries, but that would only bring her running back—without help—and place her in danger as well. Besides, screaming might only anger him, give him cause to knock her out or stuff a rag in her mouth. Tie her up. Best to keep him as calm as possible.

And stall for time. Until Caroline returned with help. Swallowing to wet her dry throat, she said, "I know where the note is."

"Where?"

She debated the wisdom of claiming she'd burned it, but decided a story would take longer to tell him. And she needed time. "I gave it to someone."

His hands tightened, and she gasped against the pain shooting up into her shoulders. "Who, damn it?"

"A . . . gentleman in London. A language translator. The letter was written in a foreign language I could not read."

Clear surprise washed over his taut features. "Foreign language? What nonsense is this?"

"It's true. I think the language might have been Gaelic."

He frowned, then nodded. "Gaelic. Yes, I suppose that is

possible." His eyes narrowed sharply. "When did you give it to him?"

"The day before I left London."

"His name?"

"Smythe. Edward Smythe."

"His direction?"

"I'm not certain."

He shook her and her teeth rattled. "I don't know," she insisted. "I'd asked the butler to recommend a translator and he gave me Mr. Smythe's name. I simply wrote a letter of introduction, enclosed the note, then gave the entire affair to a servant to be delivered. I do not know where it went."

Dark eyes bored into hers for several seconds. Then a growl of pure frustration burst from him. "I have more questions, but they'll have to wait. We must get away from here."

She lifted her chin. "I am not going anywhere with you."

In a blink, he released one of her arms and withdrew a small pistol from inside his jacket. He pressed the metal under her chin, his expression fierce. "You're going to leave here with me, and you're going to do so quietly. If you scream, I swear it will be the last sound you ever utter."

She swallowed painfully. "You would have a difficult time explaining away two dead bodies."

"Not at all. I shall claim the same ruffian who attacked poor Redfern returned and we were forced to flee. He grabbed you, and although I tried to save you, he absconded with you—to God only knows where. I'll wipe a bit of mud on my face, adopt a horrified countenance, and say, 'Indeed, I barely escaped the scoundrel myself.' " He shoved her in front of him toward the horse. Mounting swiftly, he nearly pulled her bruised arm from the socket yanking her up and settling her in front of him. She noted he tucked his pistol back in his jacket. If only she could get it away from him . . .

One strong, muscular arm encircled her waist, nearly cutting off her air, and he applied his heels to the horse's flanks.

.   .   .

Robert sat on the settee, his forearms resting on his knees, and watched Michael pace before the fireplace.

"The man my mum married was named Nigel Hadmore. He was the second son of the earl of Shelbourne."

Stunned, Robert simply stared at him.

Michael continued, "This Nigel bloke came to Ireland as part of his Grand Tour, and he and Mum fell passionately in love. Of course, Mum wasn't a fancy lady, just the daughter of a tavern keep. Nigel decided to remain in Ireland with her, but, according to Mum, his father, a very controlling man, ordered him home. Nigel refused, and his father cut off his fancy allowance until he came to his senses and returned to England." He paused, staring into the flames.

"Did he return?" Robert asked.

"No. He'd apparently saved a decent sum and therefore wasn't worried about being cut off. Mum said that for the first time, he felt free of his father's suffocating control, and he joyously embraced life. He asked her to marry him, and she accepted. They married in Ireland without informing his family."

He turned toward Robert, his dark eyes stormy. "After the wedding—that's when the bastard showed what sort of man he truly was. Oh, at first he was happy in Ireland with his bride, even happier when Mum told him a baby was on the way. But after several months, his savings ran out. He quickly wearied of working in the tavern, and started to miss the life of luxury he'd left behind. By the time his son was six months old, poor Nigel couldn't stand it any longer."

Michael's upper lip curled with obvious disgust. "Where he'd once felt free, he now felt shackled. He couldn't understand how Mum was perfectly content with their tiny house out in the middle of nowhere, working day in and day out to earn only a pittance. Couldn't fathom why Mum didn't want more for herself or their son. He claimed to still love Mum and his child, but he just wasn't cut out to be a working man and live in such rustic conditions." Michael's tone turned more scathing. "He missed his clubs and glittering social gatherings. His fine clothes. Gourmet meals. Servants. He decided he would have to somehow make peace with his father and get his generous allowance reinstated."

"Was he able to do so?" Robert asked.

A look akin to hatred flared in Michael's eyes. "As it turned out, when he contacted his father, his father summoned him home. Seems Nigel's older brother had died, and Nigel was now the heir to the earldom. When Nigel arrived back in England, his father informed him that just before his brother's death, a marriage had been arranged between his brother and the daughter of a wealthy duke. The Hadmore family was facing financial ruin and desperately needed the duke's daughter's huge dowry. Nigel's father demanded that Nigel, as the new heir, honor the agreement and marry the duke's daughter in order to save the family name and the estate."

"Well, he couldn't very well do that," Robert mused. "He was already married."

Michael shot him an undecipherable look. "Yes, most men would be quite stymied by that, but not Nigel. No, he decided that he did indeed have an option. He realized that this marriage with the duke's daughter would have to take place quickly—before her father entertained other offers for her. There would be no time to arrange an annulment of his marriage to Brianne, and even if there was time, he had no grounds. And of course, divorce was out of the question. But . . ." Michael paused, his expression harsh. "No one in England knew he was already married."

They stared at each other in utter silence for several seconds. Robert shook his head. "You cannot mean—no, it's impossible."

"If only it were, my friend."

Geoffrey forced himself to take deep, calming breaths to stem the panic threatening to overwhelm him. Blinding pain thumped behind his eyes, and it took every ounce of his will to concentrate on guiding the horse through the woods.

Her words beat through his mind. *I gave the note to a lan-*

guage translator. Relief surged through him. If the note was indeed written in a foreign language, the chances of other people being able to read it were lessened. But was Alberta telling the truth? Or just attempting to save herself? His jaw clenched. He'd find out soon enough.

They moved swiftly, deeper into the woods, farther away from the house. After a quarter hour, he spied a clearing surrounding a small lake. An outcropping of large rocks surrounded the area. Perfect. Just the sort of place he could claim the same ruffian who'd killed Redfern had set upon them in their attempt to escape the scoundrel. Far enough from the house to do what he had to do. Drawing the horse to a halt, he slid from the saddle.

"Get down," he said.

She silently complied, and the gelding immediately moved toward the water to drink. Alberta faced him squarely. "What do you intend to do now?" she asked.

He considered for a moment. How to best determine if she'd lied? How to get what he wanted from her? An idea popped into his mind and he inwardly smiled. Ah, yes . . . appeal to her feminine sympathies.

Feigning a sheepish expression, he said, "Actually, I want to apologize for brandishing a firearm in your presence. It was imperative we departed, and I sensed I would not have had your quick cooperation without . . . incentive. However, I want to assure you I have no wish to harm you. All I want is the note from the ring box. It belongs to me."

Wariness crossed her features. He could almost see her brain working inside her pretty head, trying to figure out how to escape him. Grudging admiration filled him. There was no doubt she was brave. And clever. Indeed, under other circumstances, Alberta and her quick mind and luscious form could have appealed to him very much.

"I've told you, I do not have it."

"Tell me, Alberta, what sort of man is your father?"

A mixture of surprise and suspicion filled her eyes at the abrupt question. "A very fine man. Kind. Hardworking."

"Do you have siblings?"

"Two brothers and a sister."

He nodded. "I grew up an only child. Many people ask me if my lack of siblings proved lonely, but I always enjoyed not having to share my possessions, or my father's affection, with anyone. I worshipped my father as a boy. Of course, I did not see him often. Mother and I lived on the Cornwall estate, while Father spent most of his time in London. Those precious few weeks every summer when he visited were the highlights of my childhood."

A flicker of what might have been pity flashed in her eyes, filling him with unexpected warmth. Perhaps he really could make her understand. What his life had been like . . . until that day. He quickly continued, "As the heir to the earldom, my life, my existence, my identity was defined from the day of my birth. Every lesson, every thought, was focused on preparing me for my future role, which I would step into upon my father's death. It was a role for which I was well prepared. It was his death that I could not accept."

He paused to draw a breath, and hatred, hot and fierce, rippled through him, for the man he'd worshipped. The man who'd betrayed him in the most unforgivable of ways.

"Actually, it was more his deathbed confession that I could not accept," he said in a voice he could not quite keep steady. Reaching out, he grasped her hands, his gaze intent upon hers, willing her to see the depth of his pain. The magnitude of his need for that note. "Do you know what my father told me on his deathbed, Alberta?"

"How could I possibly know such a thing?"

"So you haven't read the note?"

"No. I told you, it was written in a foreign language." She tried to pull away from him, but his grip tightened. "Please let go of my hands. You're hurting me."

He ignored her plea. "He confessed to me that he had another son. An *older* son. By another woman. Another *wife*." A bitter laugh escaped him. "My noble, proper father had *married* some trollop he'd met in Ireland on his Grand Tour. He was a *bigamist*, which meant, of course, that I was not legally his heir. Then, to add insult to this grievous injury, Father had the gall, the temerity, to request that I *find* this missing half brother and make certain he was financially taken care of." A bark of outraged incredulity pushed past his lips. "I could not fathom that my father would ask such a thing. I'd worshipped him my entire life, believing him to be the epitome of strength, but he was nothing but a weak fool. And if there is one thing I cannot abide, it is a fool."

He looked deep into her eyes. "Do you understand what this man's existence means? If word of this got out, he could legally lay claim to everything that is *mine*. Take everything away from me. My home. My title. My birthright. My very existence. According to my father, the note contains proof that this other marriage took place—and that a son was born from the union. Do you not see that I must have that note, Alberta? I *must*. My very life depends upon it."

She licked her lips. "I understand. And given the circumstances you've described, I would gladly give it to you if I had it. But as I already told you, it is not in my possession. I swear it."

He studied her. It appeared that she was telling the truth. A roar of frustration boiled up inside him, and he clenched his jaw to keep it contained. Damn it, now he was going to have to find this bloody Edward Smythe person. And kill him, too. Would this nightmare never end?

"That man, Mr. Redfern," she said. "He caused the accidents on board the *Seaward Lady*. He was the person who abducted me and robbed the Bradford town house. All to get that note and ring . . . for you."

"It was the note that was most important, but I wanted my father's ring as well. As a physical reminder to never become the weak fool he was. Unfortunately, circumstances continually thwarted Redfern, who sadly did not prove as clever as I'd hoped. Certainly he was not as clever as your husband, whose intelligence and lack of morals I sadly underestimated." He made a *tsk*ing noise. "You just cannot trust anyone anymore."

"So that is how David had the ring. I was certain he'd stolen it. That was why I came to England—to return the ring to its rightful owner."

"He stole it from the Irish whore my father married. I hired David to find her and her son. Unfortunately, when he located her, the son did not live with her. Still, being the clever crook, David took it upon himself to relieve her of several pieces of jewelry, one of which was my father's coat-of-arms ring. David found the note hidden in the box's false bottom. He demanded an outrageous sum in exchange for the ring, the note, and his silence. I agreed to his terms, but he did not keep his end of the bargain. He escaped with the money *and* the ring." A muscle ticked in his jaw.

"After years of searching," he continued, "I finally learned David had escaped to America. I hired Redfern—whom I believed smart enough to do the job, but not clever enough to cross me as David had—and sent him to America to retrieve the ring. By the time Redfern found out where David lived, your husband was dead, and all his belongings gone. Redfern discovered that David had left a wife, but she'd moved away." He shook his head. "Such inconveniences. It took Redfern almost two years to find you, Alberta, and when he did, you were about to sail for England."

"So he sailed on the same ship," she whispered.

"Yes. And that brings us to where we are now, which, I'm sad to say, is quite an unhappy place." He released her, and she stumbled back several steps. Reaching into his jacket, he slipped out his pistol and pointed it at her chest.

Chapter 23

Michael dragged his hands down his haggard-looking face, and Robert curbed his impatience at the pause.

After blowing out a long breath, Michael continued, his eyes fierce. "That bastard returned to Ireland and told my mum his sad tale of woe about how his father would withhold all the money if he ever learned of their marriage. And that even though he loved her and their son, he loathed the thought of returning to a life of what was, to him, abject poverty." Disgust filled Michael's voice. "And how, now that his brother was dead, he had to assume his role as the heir, so that the estate that had been in his family for centuries did not fall into ruin."

"I hope your mother beat him with a skillet."

"I wish she had. No, Mum said she recognized that Nigel was no longer the carefree, happy young man she'd married. He was miserable living in Ireland, and she had no wish to cause him more misery, or to keep him from the life he so desperately wanted. She knew if she didn't let him go, he'd end up hating her, and, for reasons that I will never understand, she loved the bastard enough to let him go."

Robert raised his brows. "She couldn't possibly annul the marriage. She had *you*."

"Exactly." He spread his hands in a gesture of disbelief. "They simply agreed to live separately. Mum promised to move away and never mention their marriage—to prevent his father or anyone else from finding out about it—and Nigel vowed to financially provide for her and . . . me. With the help of the priest who married them, Mum used the money Nigel gave her to settle into a new life in another town. She took the last name Evers and claimed she was a widow. The only item she kept from her life with Nigel was a coat-of-arms ring he gave her, which she kept in a small ring box with a false bottom. In the false bottom she concealed a note written to her from the priest who married her and Nigel, which offered indisputable proof that the marriage took place and is still valid, a precaution she said she took to safeguard my future should the need ever arise. Just in case Nigel ever changed his mind and wished to acknowledge the union to his family, she told him about the note and where she'd hidden it.

"Unfortunately, the ring, along with the box and its secret contents, were stolen from her several years ago. You can imagine her surprise when I turned up on her doorstep bearing the note." Michael's gaze hardened. "But that was nothing compared to her shock when I informed her that not only had Nigel inherited his father's title but he'd married another woman and fathered another son."

The full impact of Michael's story hit Robert like a blow to the head. He stared up at Michael in complete shock. "Good God, Michael. Geoffrey Hadmore is not really the earl of Shelbourne. *You* are."

Michael's lips flattened into a thin line. "So it would bloody well seem." Reaching into his jacket pocket, he withdrew two yellowed documents and handed them to Robert. "Before leaving Ireland, my mum brought me to the church where she and Nigel were married and I was baptized. These are the official certificates of proof of the marriage and my baptismal record."

Robert stared at the documents, his mind whirling. "Hadmore must not know you could lay claim to his title. If he did—"

"Robert. I've had time to digest this, thinking about it all on my way here. I don't think he knows *I* am the man who could claim his title, but I'm positive he knows such a threat exists."

Michael's words sunk in, tightening Robert's gut with dread. He rose, then handed the papers back to Michael. "Jesus. All those 'accidents' that have befallen Allie . . . Hadmore must know the proof was in the note. And that Allie had the note. He's responsible."

"I agree."

He started across the room at a near run. "We must tell her. Warn her."

Michael caught up and grabbed his arm. "She's safe, Robert. She's in the nursery with your sister-in-law. The butler told me so."

Relief raced through him. "Thank God. But she must be told. Immediately." He quit the room, Michael following. They'd just entered the foyer, intending to climb the stairs to the nursery, when Caroline burst into the entryway from the opposite direction. Robert stared at her disheveled hair and gown, her panicked expression, and his heart nearly stuttered to a halt.

"Robert, thank God," she said, her chest heaving, her voice breathless. "You must come quickly. Miles and Austin, too. We need bandages. . . . There's been a terrible accident."

He grabbed her by the upper arms, his heart pounding with dread. "Is it Allie?"

She shook her head, and he squeezed his eyes closed in relief. "But a man's been hurt. I don't know how badly. We found him lying, unconscious, on the path leading toward the ruins."

His eyes snapped open. "We?"

"Allie and I. She's with him now—"

"Allie is *alone* in the woods with this man?" He barely resisted the urge to shake her, as icy fear gripped him. "Who is he?"

She pulled out of his grasp and glared at him. "I don't know

who he is. But no, she is not alone with him. Lord Shelbourne
is with her."

Robert actually felt the blood drain from his face. His eyes
met Michael's over Caroline's head. "Austin is in his study,
Caroline. Get him." He nudged her toward the corridor, and
she needed no further urging, taking off at a very un-
countesslike run.

Robert's hands curled into fists. "You know both Austin and
Miles. Wait for them, then tell them about Hadmore. They
know the way toward the ruins. Make certain you're armed.
There's not a moment to lose."

He left the foyer at a dead run, thankful his knife was already secured in his boot, for there was no time to retrieve his
pistol from his bedchamber. Exiting the house through the
rear, he did the only two things he could—run as fast as possible, and pray for all he was worth.

Ten minutes later, heart pounding, sweat trickling down his
back, knife in hand, he rounded the corner in the path and
came upon the man lying on the ground. Robert didn't recognize him, but one close look was enough to determine that he
was dead. And very much alone.

Damn it! Where was she? If that bastard Shelbourne hurt
her—

He viciously thrust the thought aside, and forced himself to
remain calm, think clearly. He scanned the area, focusing on
the soft ground. The imprint of horse hooves was clearly visible, leading farther into the forest. Without further hesitation,
he raced forward.

Allie stared at the pistol and fought the panic threatening to
overwhelm her. Surely her life would not end like this . . . at
the hands of this madman. Her gaze darted about, but there
was nowhere to escape. Because they stood in this small clearing, even if she attempted to run, he'd shoot her before she
made it to the closest tree.

A wave of anger rolled through her, pushing aside some of

her fear. No. She could not allow this to happen. Would not allow another man to control her, to steal something else from her—this time her *life*. Help was coming. All she needed was a little more time.

One look at her captor's face, however, withered any hope of him gifting her with that time. He appeared perfectly composed, the hand holding the pistol steady, his eyes intent. Still, she had to try to stall.

"Geoffrey—" Her voice cracked and she cleared her throat. "Think about what you are doing. If you kill me, you will *hang*. You will be caught, and it will all be for naught."

"But I will not be caught, my dear. I already told you my plan, my explanation for when I am questioned. No one will dare gainsay the word of the earl of Shelbourne." He inclined his head, and what looked like genuine regret passed over his features. "I wish I did not have to kill you, Alberta. You're a very beautiful woman. Under different circumstances, we might have enjoyed each other immensely." His gaze flicked down her body.

Her breath caught as a combination of revulsion and hope slammed into her. Commanding herself to concentrate on hope, she bit back her disgust, and forced a tiny smile to her stiff lips. *Say anything, do anything, to gain yourself a few more minutes. . . .*

"We still could enjoy each other," she said in what she prayed was a suggestive tone. "Your secret would be safe with me, Geoffrey. I would never tell anyone."

He raised his brows, and for several seconds mulled over her words. But then he shook his head. "A tempting offer, my dear. But I'm afraid this is the only way. Good-bye, Alberta." He raised the pistol several inches. Her brain shouted at her to run, but her feet seemed nailed to the ground.

"Stop!" The sharp, hoarse command came from her left and her knees nearly gave way with relief. Robert emerged from the trees, a knife gripped in his hand. Geoffrey's attention turned to Robert, and he swiveled the pistol in his direction. "Stay where you are, Jamison."

Her relief immediately turned to dread. Robert was alone. Her heart stuttered to a near stop. And now the weapon was pointed at *him*.

Robert's gaze raked over her, and she jerked her head in a nod to let him know she was unharmed. Then, with his gaze fixed on Geoffrey, he moved slowly toward her.

"Halt, Jamison, or I shall shoot you."

"Go ahead," Robert invited in a deadly voice, continuing closer toward her. "That's the only way you'll stop me."

Fear iced her blood. She wanted to scream at him to stop, but before she could utter a sound, he dashed forward the last several feet separating them and shoved her behind him, making himself a shield between her and Geoffrey.

"There are two of us here, Shelbourne," Robert said, "with more on the way. You will not have time to reload after your shot. It's over. Throw down your weapon."

"This does not concern you, Jamison." His eyes burned with hatred. "You have no right to interfere in matters you know nothing about."

"I know all about it," Robert said, his voice dripping ice. "All about the contents of the letter in the ring box. All about the dead man on the path back there, and the numerous attempts you've made on Allie's life. I know that you are not in fact the earl of Shelbourne."

Geoffrey's face contorted with crimson rage. "The only proof is that note. When I get it—"

"You're wrong. There's also a marriage certificate documenting the union between your father and his Irish wife. And the recording of their son's baptism. I've seen both documents."

Every drop of color drained from Geoffrey's face. "Impossible. You're lying. How could you have seen such documents?"

"Your half brother, the true earl, showed them to me when he arrived at Bradford Hall less than an hour ago. He retrieved them from the church in Ireland where his mother married Nigel Hadmore. It's over. Toss down your weapon."

Surely Geoffrey would realize the hopelessness of his situation and listen to Robert. But when Allie looked at Geoffrey from around Robert's broad shoulder, all hope died at the desperation and hatred contorting Geoffrey's features. Dear God, one tiny movement of that madman's finger would mean the end of Robert's life.

"Who is he?" Geoffrey asked, his voice a near-croak.

Robert's shoulders tensed. "I'll not say this again. Put down your weapon."

"Tell me who he is," Geoffrey screamed.

"There's really no need to, as you'll be meeting him face-to-face momentarily. But as long as you insist, it is Michael Evers, the pugilist. I know you're already acquainted with him, as I've seen you at his boxing emporium."

An eerie stillness fell over the group, and for a few seconds, the only sounds Allie could hear were the beating of her own heart and Geoffrey's ragged breathing.

"It's not possible," came Geoffrey's strangled words. "He's nothing . . . he's as common as street trash."

"On the contrary, he's the foremost pugilist in the country. And he is the earl of Shelbourne."

Hatred such as Allie had never seen blazed in Geoffrey's eyes. "You mock me with your falsehoods, you bastard. I may not win the day, but I can at least make certain that your lying mouth is silenced."

Before the full horror of his intention could truly dawn in Allie's mind, Geoffrey raised the pistol and squeezed the trigger.

Robert surged forward, and then crumpled into a heap at her feet.

Chapter 24

The sharp report of a pistol rent the air, followed almost immediately by a woman's sharp call for help.

Mrs. Brown. Without breaking his run, Austin veered swiftly toward the sound. "The lake," he shouted to Michael and Miles, who followed hard on his heels. His heart slammed against his ribs, and he forced himself not to imagine what he'd find.

Less than a minute later, they burst into a small clearing, and his worst fears were realized. Robert lay on the ground. Mrs. Brown knelt next to him, her face chalk-white, pressing her petticoat to his shoulder. A short distance away, Shelbourne lay in the dirt, his breathing labored, his features contorted with pain, the hilt of a knife protruding from his gut.

"See to Shelbourne," he said to Michael, then ran directly to Robert, with Miles following him.

"Thank God you're here," Mrs. Brown said, her gaze flicking over him and Miles for only a second before returning to Robert.

"Is he alive?" Austin asked, dropping to his knees. His stomach turned over at the ashen pallor of Robert's skin and the dark stain spreading on his jacket.

"Yes. But he's . . . he's bleeding badly. I don't know how serious the wound is." Her voice shook, but her hands were steady as she applied pressure to stem the blood. Austin watched the white petticoat turn a frightening red. "I . . . I couldn't rip my petticoat, so I just removed it. We need bandages. A doctor." She looked at Austin through frightened eyes. "He saved my life. Threw his knife as Geoffrey shot him and—"

"I know." Forcing his own fear aside, he looked at Miles. "We need a physician. As quickly as possible."

With a terse nod, Miles dashed off in the direction of the stables.

Austin then instructed tersely, "All right. Let's apply more pressure to slow this bleeding. Then we can examine the wound." He placed his hands over hers and pressed downward. And prayed for his brother's life.

Michael crouched down next to Geoffrey Hadmore. Pain glazed his dark eyes, and his chest heaved with shallow, panting breaths. His hands spasmed over his stomach, where crimson blood spread in an ever-widening stain against his white shirt. One look at the wound left no doubt it was fatal. Hadmore was clearly in agony, and God knew a knife to the gut was a miserable way to die. Yet it was difficult to dredge up sympathy for the man. Still, Michael removed his jacket, bunched it into a makeshift pillow, then slipped it beneath Hadmore's head.

Hadmore's pain-filled gaze focused on him. "You," he whispered. "You bastard."

Michael raised his brows. "Actually, it appears that *you* are the bastard, Hadmore." A humorless, disgusted sound pushed between his lips. "These past few years you've been coming to my boxing emporium . . . who would have guessed we'd have more in common than a love of sport?"

Geoffrey's eyes narrowed to hate-filled slits. "We have nothing in common."

"I would have to agree. The man who fathered both of us was indeed nothing." His gaze flicked down to the protruding knife hilt, then he asked with a sense of detached curiosity, "Why? Was this title truly worth your *life*?"

Geoffrey grimaced. "It *was* my life," he gasped. "Everything I was . . . from the day I was born." His eyes cleared briefly and burned with loathing. "You're nothing but trash. You'll never live up to the title. You'll be . . . laughed out of Society." His eyes slid closed, his breathing growing more labored.

Michael leaned closer to him and whispered, "At least I'll be around to hear the laughter, which is more than you can say."

"I hope . . . you rot . . . in hell."

Michael shrugged. "I may—someday. But you'll rot there first."

A trickle of blood oozed from between Geoffrey's lips. A final breath rattled in his lungs, then his head slumped to the side and he was still.

Michael stared at him for several seconds. *You died for something that means* nothing *to me. Something I don't want. Something I never would have taken from you.*

Now all he could do was pray that Robert didn't lose his life as well.

Allie stood in front of the fire in the drawing room, staring at the dancing flames. How much longer? She glanced at the mantel clock. Three hours. Three endless hours that felt like an eternity. An eternity during which they'd stemmed the bleeding from Robert's wound enough for the duke and Mr. Evers—or rather, the new Lord Shelbourne—to carry Robert back to the house. An eternity since she'd assisted Elizabeth and the physician in treating his injury. The gunshot had only resulted in a flesh wound—a deep one, but it could have been so much worse. Still, there was a risk of infection. And he'd lost so much blood. . . .

But most frightening was the fact that he had not yet regained consciousness. At first she'd been almost grateful, for at least he was oblivious to the pain and the number of stitches taken to close the wound. But as she'd wiped his face with a damp cloth, brushing back his hair from his temples, she'd discovered the lump on his head. Clearly he'd hit his head when he'd fallen to the ground.

Three endless hours. And he still had not awoken. A sob bubbled up in her throat, and she bit her lips to contain it. Surely God would not allow him to survive a gunshot only to die from the fall to the ground?

Robert had saved her life. She squeezed her eyes closed, reliving the image of him striding into that clearing, looking like an avenging angel, making himself a human shield between her and a madman. A madman he'd killed in order to protect her.

An image of his handsome face, so ashen and frighteningly still, flashed in her mind. Her stomach turned over, and she pushed the thought away. But she was instantly bombarded with other pictures of him: his blue eyes alight with mischief, his lips stretched in a teasing smile. Standing in the park with pigeons poised on his hat. Pounding out an off-key song on the pianoforte. Laughing with his niece and nephew. Desire and love burning in his eyes as he loomed over her, joining his body intimately with hers.

Dear God, she loved him.

Loved his kindness and strength. His compassion and bravery. He'd risked everything for her. He'd told her he loved her, but even if he'd never said the words, she would have known. His feelings were evident in his every action. He was nothing like David, and shame filled her at the great disservice she'd done Robert by ever believing they were alike. He'd given her everything a man could give a woman, and instead of embracing his love, thanking God for it, and giving him the love he deserved in return, she'd pushed him away. She'd thought she'd made mistakes before? A humorless laugh escaped her.

Refusing Robert's love, and refusing to acknowledge her own love for him, was the biggest mistake she'd ever made.

And it was one she intended to rectify.

She just prayed he would survive so she'd have the chance to do so.

She'd paced in the crowded corridor outside his bedchamber, praying along with the rest of the family for him to regain consciousness. Finally, however, she could not stand the cramped area another second. She needed air, space to move, quiet to think, so she'd escaped to the drawing room. But now it, too, felt like a prison.

"Allie." At the sound of Elizabeth's voice behind her, she turned swiftly. Her gaze raked over Elizabeth's face, noting the dark circles under her eyes.

"How is he?" she asked, barely pushing the words past the lump in her throat.

Elizabeth crossed the room, then reached out and clasped her hands. "He's awake."

Relief so intense it rendered her light-headed, rushed through her. *He's awake*. A half-sob, half-laugh bubbled up inside her. There might have been two more wonderful words spoken at some point in the history of mankind, but God help her, she could not imagine what they could have been.

Robert sat propped up in his bed, two fluffy pillows stuffed behind his back. His head, wrapped in a bandage, pounded as if a battalion of devils battered his skull with hammers. His arm and shoulder, secured in a sling, alternately ached and throbbed with an intensity that made him long to clench his jaw—except he'd quickly learned that the jaw clenching made his head hurt worse.

His entire family had filed into his bedchamber, surrounding his bed like a flock of cooing pigeons. Caroline had held his right hand, his mother clasped his left, while Austin, Miles, Elizabeth, and Dr. Sattler hovered near his feet. Thank God Michael had volunteered to arrange for the transportation of the bodies, otherwise he would no doubt have hovered and gawked as well. The only person missing was Allie, and as much as he loved his family and appreciated their concern, she was the one he now wanted, needed, to see. To assure himself that she was all right as everyone claimed.

Elizabeth had gone to fetch her, and one by one his family had left his bedchamber. The last to leave were his mother and Caroline, who both looked down at him with deep worry and concern.

Hoping to reassure them, he grinned. "Egad, if only I'd known that a flesh wound and a bump on the head would garner such slavish feminine devotion, I'd have thought of it sooner. If ever I'm feeling neglected, I might just cosh myself with a rock."

Their worried expressions relaxed a bit. Leaning down, his mother pressed a gentle kiss on his cheek. "Darling. If you *ever* frighten me like this again, I shall be forced to take V.D.A." She favored him the fiercest look he'd ever seen on her normally serene face. "Very Drastic Action."

"Why, Mother, I had no idea you were such a tigress. What, pray tell, would you do?"

"Remain by your side at all times, prepared to fight off all the bad men. Beat them senseless with my reticule if necessary."

He chuckled, forcing himself not to grimace when pain shot through his skull and shoulder. "I wouldn't dream of making you do anything so undignified. As for remaining by my side at *all* times . . ." He pursed his lips. "Hmmm. That could prove awkward."

She cocked a single brow. "Indeed it could. Therefore, you'd best not make me do it. As it is, I'll leave you with Caroline for now. But I shall return to check on you later."

"Is that a threat or a promise?"

She smiled at him. "Both." She left the room, closing the door softly behind her.

He turned his attention to Caroline. Looking into her

guiltstricken eyes, he squeezed her hand. "Stop staring at me like that," he said. "I'm fine."

A fat tear dribbled down her cheek. "But you might have been killed."

"But I wasn't."

"Allie could have been killed."

"But she wasn't."

"This is entirely my fault. If I had not left her alone with him—"

"I refuse to listen to such rot. You did not know, Caroline. None of us did. It is over, and Allie and I are safe. Let us be grateful for that and not feel guilty over things we could not control and cannot change." He offered her what he hoped was a reassuring smile. "I'm afraid that you're quite stuck with me for at least the next several decades."

She raised his hand and pressed her cheek to his palm. "Thank God."

"If you want to feel sorry for someone, lavish your pity on Michael. I know him well. Being the earl of Shelbourne is not a role he will embrace or relish or conform to without a fight."

A knock sounded at the door. Caroline dropped a quick kiss on his cheek. "That will be Allie." She gave him a searching look. "I hope all goes . . . well."

He did not offer a reply. After all, how *well* could things go? Although the threat to Allie's safety was now over, nothing had changed between *them*.

Crossing the room, Caroline opened the door. "Come in," she said with a smile.

Allie's anxious gaze instantly found his, and his heart thumped at the sight of her. She looked pale and worried. She nodded at Caroline, then quickly crossed the room, halting next to his bed. He couldn't shift his gaze away from her, but he heard the quiet click of the door as Caroline left them alone.

Allie gently clasped his hand, and warmth spread up his arm when their palms met. "How are you feeling?" she asked.

"I'm fine." At her frown, he qualified, "My head is pounding, and my shoulder hurts like the devil, but otherwise I'm perfectly fit. The doctor assured me that after a few days' rest, I'll be good as new. Of course, I don't intend to tell Austin that until I've convinced him to spot me several hundred points in billiards." He faked a feeble cough. "My horribly weakened condition, you know."

As he'd hoped, her worried features relaxed a bit. "Robert, I . . ." She swallowed audibly, then cleared her throat. "You saved my life. And nearly lost your own in the process. How do I thank you for that? I do not know what to say, how to adequately express my gratitude."

He indeed saw the gratitude shining in her eyes, and forced himself not to foolishly hope for more, reminding himself that she did not share his feelings. Offering her a half-smile, he said, "You say, 'Thank you, Robert.' "

A tender, warm look entered her eyes. "Thank you, Robert."

"And, well, if you were so inclined, you might also say, 'You are wonderfully brave, Robert.' "

Her lips twitched. "You are wonderfully brave, Robert."

"And strong and manly." He cleared his throat modestly. "And quite handsome."

"And strong and manly," she repeated in a soft, intimate tone that had him staring at her. "And *extraordinarily* handsome. Indeed, I think you are a *beautiful* man, if you would not object to the word."

He went perfectly still. "Um, no. No objection."

"But not just beautiful on the outside," she said, her eyes steady on his. "Beautiful on the inside. Kind, generous, and tender. Indeed, the most wonderful man I've ever met."

His heart slapped hard against his ribs, pumping with sudden hope. "I must say, you've gotten quite good at this repeating game."

She did not smile. Indeed, he'd never seen her more serious. "I told you I was afraid of duplicating my mistakes, and I am. And the biggest mistake I ever made was pushing you away, believing that I could live my life without you." She raised his hand to her lips and pressed a warm kiss against his skin. "I almost lost you today, and that is a mistake I will never make again. I love you, Robert." The words breathed across his skin. "W.A.M.H." Squeezing his hand, she whispered, "With All My Heart."

"Allie." It was the only word he could manage. He tugged on her hand, and she leaned down. He slipped his hand into her soft hair, pulling her lower until their lips met. *At last.*

He attempted to raise his other arm to hold her, and pain sizzled through his shoulder, forcing a sharp grunt from his throat.

She pulled back, looking down at him with stricken eyes. "I hurt you."

"On the contrary, you've made me extremely happy." He brushed his fingers over her smooth cheek. "Um, just to make certain I'm correct with all the details, given my head injury and all that, you did just tell me you love me—correct?"

A slow, beautiful smile lit her face. "Correct." She placed her palm against his cheek, and he breathed in the delicious scent of honeysuckle.

"God knows I don't want to say anything to jeopardize this reunion, but there is a point we need to settle. Now. So it can be laid to rest." He searched her eyes. "What about my past, Allie? I cannot change it. And as much as I do not want secrets between us, there are things about that night I cannot share with you."

Her smile faded, her eyes again growing serious. "I do not want secrets, either. But I can accept that you have reasons that are obviously compelling to you. I believe in your integrity. And I trust you. Completely."

His heart performed a slow roll. He clearly sensed that she wanted to know the details about the fire, and he would have given almost anything to oblige her, but, incredibly, she loved him enough not to press him. "Thank you," he said.

A frown creased her brow. "There is something else, Robert. Can you accept the fact that I cannot have children?"

"I know you are convinced that you are barren, yet I am not

as sure," he said. "But should that turn out to be a fact, then, yes, I can accept it."

She lowered her gaze. "You would make a wonderful father—"

"Allie." He lifted her chin until she looked at him. "If we cannot make a child together, we will lavish our attention on our nieces and nephews together. You'll note that the important word in that sentence is 'together.' And as long as we are, there is nothing we cannot do."

A smile lifted one corner of her lips. "That is one of the things I love most about you. Your optimism."

"*One* of the things you love about me? I could be convinced to listen to more."

"I'd be happy to comply, but I'm afraid it would take me a very long time to tell you all of them."

"Indeed? How long?"

"Forty years."

They stared at each other for several heartbeats, and all the love he ever could have hoped for, glowed in her golden-brown eyes. He pressed a kiss into her palm. "As luck would have it," he said, "I happen to be free for the next forty years."

Chapter 25

The next morning, with bright sunshine pouring through her bedchamber window, Allie adjusted the cream fichu Elizabeth had given her, then examined her reflection in the cheval glass. She wished she owned a gown in a color other than black to wear on this happy occasion, but as she did not, at least the ivory-colored lace at her throat somewhat relieved her unrelenting somber attire. There was her beautiful gold gown, of course, but it was not a garment suited for the daytime. Soon . . . soon she would have pastel gowns to wear, and she would pack away these morbid clothes with the rest of her past and embrace her bright future.

Leaving her bedchamber, she had to force herself not to skip down the corridor and giggle. Last night she and Robert had agreed to announce their engagement to the entire family during breakfast this morning. Amazement filled her that a mere twenty-four hours ago her future had seemed so bleak, and now she was near to bursting with happiness and anticipation of starting her life again. Here. With Robert. And once the announcement was made, she planned to write a long, newsy letter to her family, inviting them to visit. To see Mama and

Papa, Katherine and the boys again . . . yes, the future looked very bright indeed.

She'd just started down the wide staircase when she saw Fenton, on his way up. "Mrs. Brown," he said when they met halfway. "I was just on my way to deliver you a message. There is a Mrs. Morehouse here to see you. She awaits you in the drawing room."

Allie frowned. "I do not know anyone by that name."

"She lives in the village. Her husband worked in the Bradford Hall stables before his death."

"Why does she wish to see me?"

"She did not say. She only indicated that it was important she see you right away."

Puzzled and curious, Allie followed Fenton to the drawing room. Opening the door, he announced, "Mrs. Brown," then withdrew, closing the door behind him.

Allie walked into the room, offering a smile to the woman standing near the French windows. She was small and plump, with gray hair tucked beneath a dark green bonnet, which matched her pelisse. She clutched her reticule and appeared nervous.

After licking her lips, she inclined her head. "Good mornin', Mrs. Brown. My name is Sara Morehouse."

"How do you do, Mrs. Morehouse. Fenton said you wished to see me." She studied the woman's face, but felt no flash of recognition. "Have we met?"

"No, ma'am. But I need to speak to you, just the same."

"Of course," Allie agreed, totally at sea. "Would you like to sit down?"

Mrs. Morehouse nodded. After they settled themselves on the brocade settee, she said, " 'Tis about Lord Robert. You're makin' a terrible mistake."

Allie's brows shot upward. "What do you mean?"

"Yesterday I received a letter from the duchess. Lovely, kind lady the duchess is, always takin' time to correspond with me, tellin' me about the family. In this letter she mentioned that Lord Robert had fallen in love and asked for your hand, but you'd refused him. Because of the crime he'd committed. Because of the fire." Mrs. Morehouse worried the strings of her reticule. "He won't tell you the truth about that night 'cause he's honorable and bound by his word. He made a promise to my husband, and he's kept it all these years to protect us, but I cannot allow it to deprive him of a wife and marriage and the family he deserves." She drew herself up and lifted her chin. "You need to know, and *I* am not bound by any such vow."

"Mrs. Morehouse." Allie reached out and touched the agitated woman's hand. "I appreciate this, but I assure you, it is not necessary for you to tell me anything. I accepted Lord Robert's proposal last evening. I love him deeply, and his past does not matter."

The older woman nodded slowly. "I'm glad to hear you say it, Mrs. Brown. And I'm very happy for you and Lord Robert. You sayin' that I don't need to tell you just proves I'm right to trust you with the truth. Lord Robert and the duchess both love you, and that's proof enough that you're honorable." Her voice took on a brisk edge. "I know how secrets can eat away at a soul, and I don't want any secrets between Lord Robert and his wife. He risked everything for my family. It's about time I gave him something in return. I only ask that you not tell anyone else. For the sake of my daughter and her family."

"All right."

Mrs. Morehouse's fingers tightened around her reticule, turning her knuckles white. "Mrs. Brown, Lord Robert did not start the fire in the smithy that night. My husband Nate did."

Confusion filled Allie and she frowned. "But . . . how is that possible? Robert told me he caused the fire. He said he was responsible, that a building was lost. That a man lost his life."

"Lord Robert took the blame for startin' that fire to save my husband and my family, but it was my Nate who struck the match and set the smithy ablaze."

Allie's head swam with questions. She managed to push one word past her suddenly dry lips. "Why?"

"Four years ago, Cyril Owens, the village blacksmith, forced himself on my daughter Hannah. Nate and I, we didn't know what was wrong with Hannah, and we were so worried about her. She was sixteen at the time, and almost overnight she changed from smilin' and laughin' into withdrawn and morose."

Pity filled Allie, and she once again laid her hand over Mrs. Morehouse's. "I'm so sorry. What a terrible ordeal for anyone to suffer."

Mrs. Morehouse nodded, and her eyes dampened with unshed tears. "Lord Robert discovered the truth one night when he overheard Cyril braggin' in a London pub. He came directly to Nate and told him, promisin' to go with Nate the next day to talk to the duke so the duke could dispense justice. But Nate . . . he didn't wait. He was a good man, a law-abidin' man, but after hearin' what Cyril had done to Hannah, it were like somethin' inside him snapped. He went to the smithy. He let the horses out, then doused the place with lantern oil and set it ablaze."

"Dear God," Allie whispered.

"The mornin' after the fire, Cyril went to the duke, wantin' Nate charged with arson. Wanted to see him hang. Said he saw Nate lettin' the horses go, then settin' his business on fire. So there we were, Nate bedridden, fightin' for every breath 'cause his lungs were so damaged from breathin' in the smoke, both of us expectin' him to be hauled off in chains to be deported or hung for arson. Much as we wanted to accuse Cyril of rapin' Hannah, we knew it would be her word against his, and no matter the outcome, Hannah's reputation would be ruined.

"Then next thing I know, Lord Robert came to our cottage. Told us everything was fixed, not to worry. Cyril was gone— moved to another village, somewhere in Northumberland, and that he'd been fully reimbursed for the loss of his personal items. And that the smithy would be rebuilt at no cost to us."

She fixed a stare on Allie. "Do you know how that happened, Mrs. Brown?" Before Allie could answer, she continued, "Lord Robert had gone to his brother, the duke, and told not only the duke but his entire family and Cyril and all the village that he himself had started the fire. The poor boy—I should say man—he was so guilt stricken. Told me and Nate he felt responsible—as responsible as if he'd struck the match himself. If he hadn't told Nate about Cyril hurtin' Hannah, then none of it would have happened."

Mrs. Morehouse's bottom lip trembled. "We knew it wasn't Lord Robert's fault, but there was no consolin' him or talkin' him out of it. He said if people believed Nate started the fire, our life in the village, and Hannah's future, would be ruined. He knew the talk about himself would eventually die down because of his family's influence, and not have such adverse effects on *his* future."

She pulled a handkerchief from her reticule, then dabbed at her eyes. "The gossip spread quickly. 'The duke's brother started the fire!' they said. 'He's an arsonist! A criminal!' Things would have gone easier on him, silenced the worst of the gossip, if he'd claimed the fire was an accident, but he didn't. His honor ran too deep to diminish what he considered his responsibility. He just said he was responsible for the fire and that was all. I don't know for certain, but I'd guess that Lord Robert's family suspected there were more to the story, but they decided to trust him.

"As for me and Nate, we were completely torn. We didn't want Lord Robert takin' the blame, but there was Hannah to consider. Her future. A girl who's been raped, whose pa is a criminal—she has no future.

"But then things got worse, because two weeks after the fire, Nate died." A tear rolled unchecked down her cheek. "Lord Robert blamed himself for his death, and no words from me would change his mind. In his mind, he was responsible for a crime bein' committed and for Nate's death. Just before Nate died, Lord Robert promised him he'd never tell about Nate's role in the fire, allowin' my Nate to go to his death in peace, knowin' his actions wouldn't ruin Hannah's future. Lord Robert, who was liable to his brother for the destruction of the smithy, saw to the financial reparations. Once the smithy was rebuilt and the villagers saw Lord Robert was as good as his word, the talk died down, folks callin' the incident a youthful indiscretion gone bad, most of them even feelin' sorry for Lord Robert as his father had died only a few months earlier. And truth be told, no one in the village was sorry to see Cyril gone. Heard he died of lung disease a couple years back, and no one here mourned his passing."

Another fat tear rolled down her cheek. "Even though Lord Robert insisted he didn't want it, I made monthly payments to him—not much, you understand—but at least it was a little something toward repaying him. But do you know what he did with the money? He set up a trust with it, and last year, when my Hannah married—a fine young man, too, who loves her— he gave the money to her and Edward as a weddin' gift. And to this day Lord Robert has seen to it that I'm provided for." She paused and blew her nose with noisy gusto. "You could not ask for a finer man than Lord Robert."

Allie couldn't speak, could barely nod. Emotion tightened her throat, and hot tears pushed behind her eyes. Dear God, what he'd done for this family. Risking his own reputation to save a man from prison—or worse—and his wife and daughter from ruination. A sob rose in her throat. How could she ever have been foolish enough to compare such a man to David?

Swallowing, she pressed Mrs. Morehouse's hands between her own. "Mrs. Morehouse, I want you to know how much I appreciate you telling me all this, and I wish to assure you again that I will not ever betray your confidence."

Mrs. Morehouse nodded, then smiled. "Thank you, Mrs. Brown. My Hannah and her husband are expectin' their first child soon. And it's all possible because of Lord Robert. I couldn't let anything deny him the happiness he allowed my daughter to find." She stood. "I'll not keep you any longer. May God smile upon both of you."

Allie escorted her to the foyer, where she shook the woman's hand warmly, then bid her good-bye. No sooner had Fenton closed the door after her than Robert strolled into the

foyer. The snowy bandage encircling his head lent him a rak-
ish air, as did the sling supporting his arm. His warm smile
heated Allie down to her toes.

"Did we have company already this morning?" he asked.

"I had a visitor," she said, watching him closely. "Mrs.
Morehouse from the village."

He went still. Without looking away from her, he said,
"Will you please excuse us for a moment, Fenton?"

"Yes, sir." The butler walked down the corridor, turning out
of sight.

"What did Mrs. Morehouse want?" he asked.

Instead of answering immediately, Allie walked to him.
When she stood directly in front of him, she took his face between her hands and looked into his eyes. Such beautiful eyes.
Such a beautiful man. And how incredibly beautiful that he
loved her.

"She told me about the fire, Robert," she whispered. "Told
me everything. About Nate, and her daughter . . . what you did
for them."

He appeared momentarily stunned, then pain flashed in his
eyes. "I didn't do anything for them, Allie. I was responsible
for that fire."

She laid her fingers over his lips. "No. Not any more than I
was responsible for what David did. We cannot control other
people's actions."

"Why . . . how did she know to come here? To ask for
you?"

"Elizabeth wrote to her, telling her you'd asked me to
marry you and that I'd refused you because of your past."

"Elizabeth?" he echoed, frowning. "Why would she do
such a thing? She doesn't know the truth about the fire. . . ."
His voice trailed off, and they shared a long look. Finally he
said, "Yes, well, as we both know, it is not always necessary to
tell Elizabeth something in order for her to know it."

"Robert . . . what you did for that family . . . I do not know
the words to express my admiration." A tiny smile pulled at
her lips. "Actually, I believe I do. I can say, 'I hold you in the

deepest admiration, Robert. You are the most decent, honorable man I've ever known. And I love you. Passionately.' "

His eyes darkened, and he grabbed her hand. Raising it to his lips, he pressed a warm kiss into her palm. "How passionately?"

Heat shot through her veins, tempered by the laugh brought on by his exaggerated leer.

"Extremely passionately. But the foyer is hardly the place to prove it."

"I hope you don't want a long engagement."

A loud *ahem* sounded from the staircase. They turned and saw Elizabeth coming down the stairs. Her gaze bounced between them, her expression reflecting a combination of trepidation and hope. When she joined them, she said, "Good morning."

Robert inclined his head. "Good morning, Elizabeth. Allie and I were just discussing Mrs. Morehouse's visit this morning."

Relief and unease flashed across Elizabeth's features. "I see."

"You know the truth about the fire," he said.

She hesitated, then nodded. "Yes."

"You never mentioned it."

"Because it was none of my business. And it still isn't. But when I realized the truth would keep you and Allie apart, knew that your promise to Nate bound you to secrecy, I wrote to Mrs. Morehouse and mentioned your unfortunate romantic situation, hoping she would come here. *She* could tell Allie without breaking her word." Her gaze shifted between them. "I hope you will forgive my interference."

Robert drew a slow, deep breath, then looked at Allie and cocked a brow. "I don't know. Should we forgive her?"

Allie huffed out a dramatic sigh, then shrugged. "We might as well. If we claim we don't, she'll only need to touch us to know we're fibbing."

He turned to Elizabeth. "Very well. My bride-to-be says we should forgive you. Therefore, we do."

A slow grin eased over Elizabeth's face. "Bride-to-be?"

"Yes. In fact, the lady accepted my proposal last evening—even before talking with Mrs. Morehouse."

Unmistakable relief filled Elizabeth's eyes, and she opened her arms to Allie. They shared a tight hug, and Allie whispered into her ear, "Thank you. For everything."

Beaming, Elizabeth drew Robert into their circle and the three of them shared an embrace. As they pulled back, a small frown pinched between Elizabeth's brows.

"Give me your hand," she said to Robert. After he'd complied, she turned to Allie. "Give me one of yours." Allie slipped her hand into Elizabeth's. Elizabeth closed her eyes, and for several seconds silence reigned. Then she opened her eyes.

"Is something amiss?" Robert asked, looking worried.

"No. But I would strongly suggest a whirlwind engagement."

"We were thinking the same thing—but why do you say that?"

She leaned closer to them, smiled, then whispered, "Because your whirlwind affair has resulted in . . ." Her gaze settled on Allie's midsection in a meaningful way. "A baby."

Robert stared at her. "Are you certain?"

"Oh, yes." She turned to Allie. "And if you thought Austin was a mass of father-to-be nerves . . ." She shook her head and chuckled. "The Axminster rug is in for a *terrible* time with Robert." She patted them both on the cheek. "Now wipe those stunned looks off your faces, and I'll see you in the breakfast room. And I promise to act *very* surprised when you make your betrothal announcement." With that, she headed down the corridor.

Allie stared after her, stunned into silence. Finally she turned to Robert, whose gaze was alternating between her face and abdomen with an expression akin to awe.

"Did she say 'baby'?" Allie asked when she could find her voice.

"She did." He cleared his throat. "I hate to say I told you so, but . . ." A huge grin spread over his face.

Allie pressed her palms to her midsection. Tears pushed at her eyes, and unable to be contained, they spilled over onto her cheeks. Robert's gaze immediately turned stricken, and he gently grasped her shoulder. "Sweetheart, don't cry—"

"I'm not crying."

"Well, you're doing a fine imitation of it." He cupped her face in his broad palm and stroked the dampness from her cheeks with his thumbs.

She looked into his eyes, overwhelmed. "I never thought . . ." A sound of pure joy escaped her. "I'd buried the desire to be a mother years ago. Along with so many other dreams. And now they're all coming true."

Robert looked into her eyes brimming with happiness and love. Here was his girl from the sketch. The woman he'd waited a lifetime for. "My darling Allie. Of course they are. Did I not tell you that I always play to win?"

He drew her close and captured her lips in a deep, tender kiss. That "certain something," that indefinable magic he'd felt from the very first time he'd touched her, rushed through his veins, and utter contentment filled him.

At last.

About the Author

Award-winning author Jacquie D'Alessandro grew up on Long Island and fell in love with romance at an early age. She dreamed of being swept away by a dashing rogue riding a spirited stallion. When her hero finally showed up, he was dressed in jeans and driving a Volkswagen, but she recognized him anyway. They married after they both graduated from Hofstra University, and are now living their happily-ever-afters in Atlanta, Georgia, along with their very bright and active son, who is a dashing rogue in the making. Jacquie is currently working on her next historical romance for Dell, and she would love to hear from readers. Email her through her website at www.JacquieD.com